A Roomful of
PARADOX

A Roomful of
PARADOX

STANLEY L. ALPERT

ALPERT'S BOOKERY, INC.

Published by
Alpert's Bookery, Inc.
POB 215
Nanuet, NY 10954

Library of Congress Catalog Card Number: 98-93482

ISBN 1-892666-01-4

This book is printed on acid-free paper. ∞

Manufactured in the United States of America
October 1998

In loving memory of Benjamin Alpert

ACKNOWLEDGMENTS

I express indebtedness to all those who assisted and guided me
through the nativity and achievement of a dream.

Thanks to Beverly Bierman and Leslie Crowley-Srajek
for their technical assistance and recommendations.

Special accolades to Linda Bland—a great writer, editor, and friend.

And to Susan and Sharon for everything else.

the golden swan

A ROOMFUL OF PARADOX

O N E

Randomly positioned around the room were fourteen bodies. Each lay motionless on the plush carpeting. Of the eight men only one was shabbily attired, while every woman wore formal accouterments.

The room was immense. Decorated with many lavish pieces of furniture, it was perfectly proportioned. Meretricious molding, ornate wall covering, and priceless artwork enhanced the ambiance. Though lacking exterior windows, there was no sensation of encumbrance or restriction. Overhead, huge crystal chandeliers brilliantly illuminated every inch.

Unlike conventional design, the room was neither rectangular nor square. Instead, its multifaceted walls created many nooks. Four doors were present, none abutting another.

Classical orchestrations filled the air. Every selection mingled with the refinement of the room.

A large mahogany wall clock chimed loudly. While its tolls reverberated throughout the room, all those present were oblivious. No one stirred.

Situated along the shortest wall was a gigantic bookcase. On each shelf sat volumes of novels. The printed page was sufficiently represented by these tomes as well as magazines placed on the many tables.

A small kitchen was positioned in one of many corners of the room. An oven, refrigerator, water cooler, and freezer were present. Color-coordinated overhead cabinets brightly complemented the appliances. Abundant provisions filled the cupboards and a neighboring pantry. Cooking and eating utensils were neatly stacked on a shelf.

The room's only toilet sat fully exposed along the lengthiest wall. Beautifully embellished with an ornate design, it only enriched the overall decor.

Nearby, an oversized vanity with brass fixtures and a porcelain bowl contained an extensive reserve of personal grooming supplies.

T W O

Time seemed everlasting, possessing no significance. The fourteen bodies remained void of animation and spirit while the wall clock methodically tolled its rhythmic chiming.

The flickering of an eyelid suddenly infringed upon the funereal atmosphere that shrouded the room. Moments later, the oldest man lifted his head and sought to recollect his thoughts. Though still stupefied, he endeavored to gather his senses and identify his surroundings. As he surveyed the room, he became aware of the unfamiliar setting. Mustering enough strength, he stretched his stiffened body and then stood. He walked to the nearest body and knelt at her side.

Noting that she was alive, he gently touched her hand and attempted to illicit a response. Her eyes opened and stared in disbelief.

"Just lie still," he said as he rubbed her arm.

"What happened?" she questioned.

Helping her to a sitting position, he said, "I'm not really sure." Resting on an oversized sofa, the woman stated, "My name is Sandra Golden."

"I'm Father Donald McShane."

"Father, what's this all about? Who are those other people? Are they dead?"

"I don't know. How are you feeling?"

"Exhausted, though I feel as if I've been sleeping for years."

"That's exactly how I felt, but I do feel a little better now."

"How did I get here and where are we?" she inquired.

"I'm afraid I don't have any answers." Anxious to continue his investigation, he added, "You stay here; I want to check the others."

"No," she said, standing quickly. "I'll go with you."

They walked to a nearby body and examined it closely. "He's alive," announced the elder man.

"Are you sure, Father?" she asked.

"Positive. I can feel a slight pulse."

They checked each body and discovered all were alive, but comatose.

Looking around the room, Sandra stated, "It sure is beautiful."

The reverend took a deep breath. "It sure is."

A loud moan from across the room caused both to jump to their feet and hurry toward the source. The huge man was sprawled across the carpeting wailing loudly. Father McShane and Sandra each grasped a gigantic arm and attempted to awaken the slumbering giant. He opened his eyes, focused on them, and then awkwardly sat upward.

With a deep, husky voice, he spoke. "Who are you? Where am I?"

"I am Sandra Golden and this is Father Donald McShane."

The priest added, "As to where, your guess is as good as ours."

The mammoth of a man scanned the room. Pointing to the other bodies, he inquired, "What about them?"

"All are alive," answered the priest. "They're just unconscious."

Sandra cautiously added, "Just like we were."

Father McShane inquired, "You look very familiar. Do I know you from somewhere?"

"My name is Todd Warren."

"The professional football player?"

"Yes, Father. I'm a professional football player with the…"

"What is it?" asked Sandra when he did not complete his sentence.

"Nothing." He remained unusually silent for several minutes. "I'd like to look around," Todd finally said. Neither replied, but followed as the massive individual lumbered around the perimeter of the room. He said little, but examined every section with the greatest of interest and concern.

They sat in the kitchen area. "Have either of you tried the food or water?" asked Todd.

"No, the Father and I woke about the same time," explained Sandra.

Todd filled a small cup with water and sampled its contents. Smiling broadly, he said, "It's very good."

"Now what shall we do?" asked the priest.

"I suggest we wait until the others awaken and then we can decide as a group," suggested Sandra.

"I agree with Sandra. There's strength in numbers. The more heads we have, the better our chances of getting some answers," Todd concurred.

Father McShane nodded in agreement. "I see your point."

The sound of footsteps caused them to stop talking. A short, portly man was soon standing at their side. The Father was the first to speak. "Welcome, my friend, to—"

"To where? How did I get here?" the new person interrupted rudely.

"We all have the same questions, but unfortunately no answers," Sandra said.

"I am Dr. James Harrison."

"A doctor?" inquired Todd.

"Yes. I am a board certified orthopedic surgeon."

"Where are you from?" questioned the priest.

"I come from…" Stopping momentarily, the doctor tried another tack, "I live in…."

"I'm sure it will come back," Father McShane said reassuringly. "It's been quite a shock for all of us."

"Yes," agreed Sandra. "I'm sure we'll all recall our past with a little more rest."

The doctor reached into his pocket and withdrew a watch. He looked at it and then wound its stem. "Damn! My watch does not seem to be working."

"No sweat, Doc, there's a clock on the wall." As if on cue three rings filled the room. "See what I mean, Doc?" said Todd.

Without changing expression, the doctor responded, "Yes, I see what you mean."

The foursome decided to eat. Upon completion of the meal, Sandra cleaned the dishes while the others chatted. Finally, they moved to a more comfortable section of the room and waited.

THREE

Tara Smith and Phyllis Taylor awoke simultaneously. Though at opposite sides of the large room, each sat upright for several minutes, then walked over to join the others. Once the introduction of names was completed, the group examined the eight remaining bodies.

Bending over a raggedly attired male, Father McShane said, "I'm afraid he's not doing too well. His breathing is rather erratic and shallow."

Tara Smith interjected, "What do you think, James?"

As if surprised by the question, the stout physician retorted, "I am an orthopedic surgeon, my dear, not an internist."

"Aren't you a doctor?" asked Todd.

"Yes I am, however, my specialty is bones. Certainly not comatose derelicts!"

"Could you at least look at him?" the Father requested.

"I will not! I don't believe my malpractice insurance would cover me under these circumstances."

"Wouldn't you be covered under the Good Samaritan Act?" reminded Phyllis Taylor. "All my doctor friends at the club are."

"I will not take any chances; I am a bone specialist!" the doctor insisted.

Father McShane readjusted the male's tattered clothing and then joined the others. To avoid controversy over medical ethics, he changed the subject. "I believe we should make a sincere effort to inspect this room. There must be a way out."

"That makes a lot of sense," added Phyllis. "The faster I return home, the better I will feel."

"Suppose there's no way out?" questioned Tara.

"There is always a way out; we just have to find it."

"I agree with you, Father," Todd said. "Let's start with the doors. If worst comes to worst, we'll break them down. They're just made from wood."

Sandra retorted, "I don't think that's such a good idea."

"Why not?" asked the gigantic man.

"Things are not always best solved by destruction. Besides, how do we know we are actually being held against our will?"

"That makes no sense at all!" bellowed Todd. "Why are the doors locked?"

"Maybe they're locked for our protection," suggested Sandra.

"A most interesting point," Father McShane concurred. "After all, we do not know where we really are."

"That's a bunch of rubbish," Todd insisted.

"Perhaps you are correct, Todd, but how can you be so sure?" inquired the priest.

"What are we to do?" questioned Phyllis. "We can't stay here forever. I have to go home."

"So what are we going to do?" Todd asked as he directed his stare at Sandra's diminutive figure.

"I suggest we stay right where we are until we have gathered more information."

Tara agreed. "We can't go anywhere until we know where we are starting from."

"I still don't like the whole thing. None of this makes any

sense," Todd said.

"I agree with you, Todd," Father McShane said. "But, until we can find a few answers, I think Sandra is correct."

"What do you think we should do, James?" asked Sandra.

Pacing, he answered, "I'm not sure."

"Why don't you and Todd check the doors?" Father McShane suggested.

"I think that's a good idea, Father." Turning to the larger man, James asked, "Are you coming?" Rather than argue the issue any further, Todd headed toward the nearest door.

F O U R

"What do you think, Doc?" Todd asked.

Sitting down on the soft carpeting so he could study at eye level, the physician eyed the locking mechanism. He attempted to turn the handle several times; each time, however, it remained secure.

"Well Doc?"

"Todd, have a little patience." The doctor reached into his pocket, withdrew a penknife, and tried inserting its blade into the tiny opening. With no success, he cursed silently to himself and turned to his companion. "There's no way this lock can be picked."

"Then let me try my way." The huge man hurled himself against the door several times, but it did not budge. The structure remained intact. While he stopped to catch his breath, James scratched the blade of his knife on the door's surface.

"Forget force; the door's made of metal not wood." Examining it closer, he stated, "Probably steel!"

Rubbing his shoulder, Todd slammed his fist against the entrance. "Damn!" he shouted, "There must be a way out!" They inspected the remaining doors and discovered each was as solid as the first.

As they joined the others, Phyllis Taylor asked, "Well? Any luck?"

James looked at Todd and replied coldly, "No."

To boost the others' spirits, Father McShane suggested, "I propose we inventory the food."

"That sounds like a great idea." seconded Tara.

"I agree," added Sandra. "I think we should consider rationing whatever we find."

"Why?" countered Todd. Looking around, he said, "It looked like plenty to me."

"Because we should be extremely careful. God only knows how long we'll actually be here," said Sandra.

"I don't know about you, but I don't plan on staying," Todd replied in an irritated tone.

Noting friction developing between the two, Father McShane interjected, "I suggest we wait until the others awaken before inventorying anything."

"Suppose they don't wake up," questioned Phyllis.

"Then we'll have more for ourselves," jested Todd.

"Some sense of humor!" Sandra admonished.

Todd leered at the middle-aged woman and walked toward the other end of the room. Without another word, each member departed the group and sought refuge elsewhere in the room. The quiet was interrupted by four blaring rings from the great wall clock.

FIVE

Tara lay on a velvety, oversized sofa and closed her eyes. Bewilderment compelled the young woman to reflect upon what had occurred since her awakening. The entire situation was bizarre, unforeseen, and totally unexplainable. Muffled conversations among the others stifled her relaxation and added to her nervousness. To make herself more comfortable, she removed her shoes, placed her dainty feet on the fluffy cushions, and contemplated her next move. Her rest was violated by a soft whispering. "Are you awake?"

Opening her eyes quickly, she discovered Phyllis sitting at her side. Moaning slightly, she responded, "Yes, I was just taking a short rest."

"May I speak to you?"

"Certainly."

Phyllis took a deep breath and continued, "I'm troubled by this entire experience. Nothing makes any sense and I do not trust the men."

"Father McShane seems all right," said Tara.

"It's the others I am worried about. They give me the willies," explained Phyllis.

"I'm afraid I don't understand."

"My dear, you are too young to understand what I am suggesting." Lowering her voice, Phyllis whispered, "I am worried about them making a sexual advance toward one of us."

"They certainly look harmless enough," Tara remarked.

Laughing, Phyllis said, "No man is harmless; take it from an expert. I've had my share of men and they all make utter fools of themselves." Taking the young woman's hand, she said, "We must be careful."

"Have you spoken to Sandra about this?" asked Tara.

"No. She is sitting with Father McShane, but I will speak to her when the time is more appropriate."

Noticing Phyllis' genuine concern, Tara said, "I'll be very careful; I promise."

"We girls have to stick together. There's strength in numbers."

Noticing Sandra had moved away from the priest, Phyllis excused herself. Tara watched and then stared at James and Todd. Chuckling, she disregarded her newfound friend's suspicions. *They look so harmless*, she thought. *Especially Baby Bimbo.*

Looking upward to the ceiling, she became enthralled by the large, crystal chandeliers. The lights seemed to play overhead and dance among the shiny pieces of glass. For the longest time, she observed the visual promenade.

After listening to Phyllis' fears, Sandra tried to comfort the woman's apprehension. Though not totally appeased, Phyllis agreed to suspend her suspicions and concentrate on other pressing issues. At that point, Sandra joined Tara.

"What do you think of Phyllis' theory?"

Smiling, she said, "Not too much. I can't believe she actually worries about such things."

"It's not totally far-fetched; stranger things have been known to happen," replied Sandra.

"I'm not sure I understand what you are getting at," Tara probed.

Sandra replied, "Under exceptional situations, such conjecturing has proven accurate."

"Are you telling me you're worried too?"

"No. However, if we are here for an extended time, we'd better consider it as a distinct possibility."

Tara glanced at the men across the room and then to Sandra. "I guess I'd better start taking life a little more seriously."

"I didn't mean to alarm you; I was just speaking in a hypothetical sense." Touching the younger woman's hand, she continued, "I'm not really worried about it."

Tara said, "Maybe we should even include Father McShane."

Sandra laughed. "Be serious!"

"I am. No one is beyond reproach. Not even a priest."

"It sounds as if you are speaking from experience."

"If I am, I can't recall why," said Tara.

Sandra asked, "How old are you?"

"I can't seem to remember, everything is still a blank."

"I have the same problem. No matter how hard I try, I simply cannot remember a thing."

"Maybe we all have amnesia?"

"Group hysteria is a possibility; however, we do not seem to conform to its other symptoms."

"How do you know so much about these things?"

Sandra leaned back against the soft sofa and attempted to answer Tara's question. "I can't seem to recall...I just know it's true."

"No big deal. When it comes back, just let me know."

Patting Tara's knee, Sandra responded, "I will."

Looking at the remaining bodies, Tara asked, "Why did we wake up and they didn't?"

"I have no idea. Perhaps we're lucky."

"You call this luck?" Tara said sarcastically.

"I am not sure what to call it, but at least we're alive."

"I wonder if we can get any clues from the furniture."

"I already looked. There are no labels or tags on any of the furnishings."

"What about the drawers?" Tara asked.

"All empty," answered Sandra.

"Not a trace of anything?"

"Zero." With a stern facial expression, Sandra continued, "I even checked the labels on the food packages."

"Nothing?"

"You've got it. There is no physical evidence as to where we are."

Growing more concerned, Tara asked, "What can we do? We can't stay here forever."

"Right now, we have no choice. The doors are locked and there is no other way to exit."

Tara said, "Just great!"

"It could be a lot worse; at least we have the bare essentials."

"Maybe one of *us* is behind this confinement?" conjectured Tara.

"Anything is possible, we will just have to sit tight and see how the cards fall."

"I'm beginning to get frightened," Tara said.

Touching Tara's hand, Sandra responded, "I'm already there." She stood and walked to the kitchen.

SIX

"Don't you find it funny some of us remember more than the others about our past?" Dr. Harrison asked the priest.

Thinking momentarily, Father McShane responded, "I guess that's true, but it really doesn't give us any facts."

"That may or may not be true. How do we know someone here is not behind the whole thing? Maybe that person or persons know and remember everything and are behind the entire plot."

"I see what you're saying, but how can we tell?"

"We can't right now, but eventually they'll slip," predicted the doctor.

"And that's when we'll get them."

"Exactly," said Harrison repeating himself, "Exactly."

"Tell me, Doctor, where is your practice?" asked McShane.

"I was the head of orthopedic surgery at St...." Clutching his hands tightly, the paunchy professional tried desperately to recall any more details of his past, however, no additional facts could be extracted from his brain. "Damn!" he uttered. "It's so god-damn frustrating."

The priest comforted the physician. "It'll come back in time."

16

"That's not the point. I've always prided myself on my rapid recall. That was my trademark for years and now look."

"I have an odd premonition it will come back to all of us," said Father McShane.

"I certainly hope you are right, Father," the doctor mumbled.

"How did you get that scar on your hand?" asked McShane.

The physician instantly responded, "I cut myself with a scalpel."

"See what I mean? Things will come back."

They were interrupted by the approach of Todd. "What's wrong, Todd?"

"I'm having a hard time coping with this situation," Todd admitted.

"We're all in the same boat," responded Father McShane.

"I know that, but well, it's different," Todd replied.

"In what way?" asked the physician.

"I can't be stuck in one place too long. It just kills me."

"You're claustrophobic?" Doctor Harrison said. "That's not so unusual, I've had many a patient with the same diagnosis. In fact, many medications are given to remedy the condition."

"That's just great, but it doesn't help me right now."

"That's very true. Just try to relax and keep yourself as calm as possible," recommended the doctor.

"Thanks, Doc, for that marvelous advice." Todd said sarcastically.

"Listen, young man, I usually do not give free advice to anyone; consider yourself lucky." Without responding to the statement, the gigantic man stormed away. "Perhaps, you'd better take it a little easier with him," suggested the priest. "He is noted for being exceedingly strong and ill-tempered."

"I've handled that type of patient many times in the past," Harrison said confidently. Looking the priest straight in the eye, he said, "The kind of person who rules with their muscle can always be controlled by the mind."

"I still think you should not push him too hard," cautioned Father McShane.

"Father, I'm a professional; I know how to handle people."

The priest chose to redirect their conversation. "Do you have any professional opinion on the other bodies?"

"Off the record, it appears they're in some sort of suspended animation," replied Harrison.

"Like a deep freeze?"

"Precisely, but without the freeze."

"Will they wake up?" inquired the priest.

"It's hard to tell. The vagrant looks as if he'll probably die, but the rest are breathing shallow, but steadily."

"Can you do anything to save the vagrant?"

"As I told you before, I will not jeopardize my future for some worthless riffraff of society. Besides, I do not have any instruments with me."

"Is there anything I can do?"

Looking the elder man, he uttered caustically, "Pray."

S E V E N

Phyllis Taylor did not feel appeased after speaking to Sandra or Tara. Both seemed to dismiss her concerns as ludicrous. To maintain her sanity, she busied herself by examining the collection of artwork that lined the walls. She would study a particular piece in great detail. While scrutinizing a large canvas, her thoughts were interrupted by James Harrison.

"It's a beautiful piece of work," he stated.

She responded weakly, "Yes, it is."

"It's one of Bouguereau's better pieces."

Shocked, she asked, "You like art?"

"Absolutely." Gazing upward at the huge canvas, he said, "It ignites my soul."

"Do you enjoy Gauguin?"

"Yes, but my favorite period was Impressionism."

"Seurat?"

"His *Sunday Afternoon on the Island of La Grande Jatte* is my pet. I would sit and look at it for hours."

"He was a pointillist."

"His method is best described as divisionism."

She looked at him and then at the canvas. "I am particularly partial to this piece."

"*Nymphs and Satyr.*"

"Yes, but how did you know?"

Looking impatiently at her, he stated, "Madam, I am a connoisseur of all the arts."

"Do you like classical music?"

Without changing expression, the pontifical physician responded, "Yes."

"Do you like the selections we are hearing?"

"I told you, Madam, I am a refined and cultured individual. My waiting room and home display only the finest of artwork, and only classical sounds fill these ears."

"I also relish the works of Jackson Pollock. My husband and I own several of his…"

"Your husband?"

"Yes. I believe I have a husband." Whispering softly, she said, "I just cannot seem to recall…"

"Have you ever seen Lucifer?"

"Lucifer?"

"Yes, Madam, Pollock's most famous work!"

"Why, yes," she added. "I have seen it many times."

Beginning to lose patience with her slow recollection, the physician simply walked away. She returned to the observation of art.

EIGHT

"Father?" Sandra asked.

"Yes, Sandra. What is it?" McShane replied.

"I'd like to suggest we move the bodies to one section of the room."

"Any specific reason?"

"I find then disturbing."

"I see your point." Looking at the others, he suggested, "Let me ask Todd to help, he's the strongest."

"Since you have the best rapport with him, I believe that is a sensational idea. I simply cannot tolerate his animalistic tendencies."

"One must learn to deal with all kinds of people," McShane reminded. "Patience is a virtue."

Responding quickly, she quipped, "Few women possess."

The priest asked Todd for assistance. "No sweat, Father. I lift more weights than these bodies together." They dragged and pushed the remaining bodies to the farthest section of the room. After the eighth one was in place, Father McShane knelt on the ground to silently pray.

"What are you praying for? For them?" Todd interrupted.

Looking upward, McShane responded, "Yes."

"But they're just about gone…"

"I'm praying for their recovery," the priest said.

"Who needs them? We've got enough food and room for the six of us. Why share with more?"

"Suppose you were one of them?" Father McShane suggested.

"But I'm not and that's all that counts."

"Don't you think that's awfully selfish?"

"Why not? If I don't look out for me, who will?"

"But you were a team player."

"A team player! I took care of myself; that's what today's sports are all about. It's called covering your own ass!"

Not sure how to respond to the athlete's remarks, the priest thanked him for his assistance and resumed praying. A barely audible moan caused him to open his eyes and survey the nearly lifeless forms. He studied each very carefully, but nothing moved. After a while, he left for the kitchen.

"Thank you very much," Sandra said referring to the response to her request.

"Feel better?"

"Yes. It was so depressing walking by those bodies all day."

"Especially when we are eating," added the priest.

"Precisely. You could lose your appetite with them lying so close."

"That won't happen again."

"What did Big Todd have to say for himself?" asked Sandra.

"Not a thing," the Father said. "He helped me move the bodies and then went about his business."

"That's surprising, he usually has a rude comment about everything."

"Sandra."

"Yes, Father."

"At least try to limit your criticism."

"Why?" inquired the woman.

"Because we really don't know how he might react to some of them," said the priest in a concerned tone.

"Do not worry, Father. I can handle the likes of him anyday."

"I'm not so sure of that. Remember, professional athletes are not like us. They live in a world of competition and violence," said the priest.

The great clock chimed loudly seven times. Everyone listened, then returned to their activities. "Father, I'd like to inventory our supplies, even though no one has yet woken up. I am very concerned about running out," Sandra said.

"Do you think that's a possibility in the near future?"

"I will let you know when I am finished."

The priest departed while Sandra began the arduous task of counting each and every edible item within the room.

NINE

During their next meal, Sandra announced, "I have something important to say." Everyone stopped talking and listened. "I have tallied the precise amount of food we have. Though it appears sufficient for the present, there will come a time when our supply will become exhausted."

"How did you calculate?" inquired the Father.

"It's simple. I totaled the number of items and divided them by fourteen."

"Why fourteen?" asked Phyllis. "There are only six of us here."

"I included the ones still sleeping."

"That's utterly stupid," said James Harrison. "They're not eating now and may not survive."

"Suppose they do. Isn't better to be prepared for such a possibility?"

"I agree with the Doc," said Todd. "You shouldn't have counted the ones still in a coma."

Standing her ground, Sandra asked, "And why not?"

"Because I do not feel they will survive," answered the physician.

"How would you know? You've haven't examined any of them," countered Sandra.

Trying to control his defensive rage, James said, "Examination is not necessary; any fool can see they'll probably die."

"Yeah!" screamed Todd. "Why should we share anything with them. It belongs to us!"

"Besides, the supply will last longer that way," explained James.

"It appears we have a conflict," Father McShane intervened. "I think we should vote on it."

"Great!" Todd said. "Anyone stupid enough to vote for the idea will get what they deserve."

"And what is that?" inquired Phyllis.

"An empty stomach!" Todd answered.

"I want a secret ballot," Tara said.

"Why?" asked the priest.

"I don't want anyone to see how I vote. It's nobody's business."

"I think that's the best way," Phyllis agreed.

"Why?" demanded James.

"I just think it is," Phyllis meekly repeated.

"It's dumb. The whole damn thing is foolish. They're not even conscious!" Todd said angrily.

After much discussion, the group held a secret vote. Once the ballots were collected and tallied, Father McShane announced the verdict. "The vote was four to two—in favor of saving food for the others."

"You're all idiots!" yelled Todd. Pointing to Sandra, he screamed, "Why listen to her? She don't know nothing. She ain't a doctor."

"I will abide by the decision," laughed James. "For it really does not mean a thing. We'll still get their portions once they're dead."

"Yeah," added Todd. "It's already ours."

"Unless anyone has any objection, Sandra and I will divvy up the supplies," Father McShane proposed hoping to end the conflict.

"How do we know everything will be divided the same?" asked Todd suspiciously.

"Everyone can and will have the right to inspect the supplies whenever they want," suggested Sandra.

"And I will keep a close eye on the proceedings," grinned Todd demonically. "We wouldn't want anyone to cheat…"

By the time the clock's ringing filled the room, everyone had a designated drawer filled with food. Satisfied, they dispersed into smaller groups.

T E N

Tara Smith was beginning to feel more at ease with her surroundings. She kept to herself and socialized with only Father
McShane and Sandra Golden. Though she did not fear Todd
Warren or Dr. James Harrison, she avoided them and spoke little to
either man.

The young woman spent a tremendous amount of time reading
the many novels that filled the library. She consumed volumes of fic-
tion and then began reading the Bible. Father McShane was
extremely pleased with her current selection and offered additional
insight as she absorbed the book's many pages. "How did you find
the last section?" he asked her.

"Quite interesting, Father."

"When you have finished the Old Testament, I suggest you read
the New one."

"I will do that," she replied. "I'm sorry I didn't get a chance to
read it before."

"Were you brought up with any specific religion?" inquired the
priest.

"I don't think I ever knew my parents or their religion."

Attempting to recall her past, Tara stated, "I just can't remember any details."

Touching his collar, the priest said, "It's never too late to start finding God."

Instead of responding to his words, she inquired, "How are the others holding up?"

"I'm a little concerned about Todd. He's getting more cantankerous and irritable as time passes," the priest reported.

"That's why I stay away from that guy. He's one strong looking dude."

"I wouldn't worry too much, but I understand your reasoning."

"I passed by some of the bodies after our last meal and I think some of them are breathing more regularly," Tara said.

"I'd like to ask Dr. Harrison to examine each one, but he's still worried about a lawsuit."

"Isn't that just like a doctor!" said the young woman.

"I'm not sure. His approach is all new to me," Father McShane said.

"I guess you've lived in a dream world, Father. All physicians are like that in the real world. All they ever care about is money." Tara responded.

"Don't you think you're being a little harsh?" asked Father McShane.

"Perhaps, but I instinctively don't like any of them."

"I'll go check on the bodies. I certainly hope you are correct about their improvement."

The priest strode to the back portion of the room and examined each body with great tenderness. As he touched each face, a sensation of life could be discerned. The derelict, however, remained motionless. *It's lucky we divided the food the way we did*, he thought, *I'd hate to see Todd or James when they're all awake.*

ELEVEN

Sandra's shout caused everyone to run to her. "What is it?" asked Father McShane. "Are you all right?"

"Yes," she responded, "but look!"

"What are we supposed to see?" Tara inquired.

Growing somewhat impatient, Sandra stated, "Look at the food."

"For God's sake, woman! Tell us what you see," growled James.

Picking up a can of beans, she held it up for all to see. "Look."

Father McShane said calmly, "Please explain what you are so excited about."

"After our last meal, I took all the empty containers and placed them in the pantry," Sandra explained.

"So what's the big deal?" Todd remarked. "You do it all the time."

"Yes, but look." She held up a few cans for their inspection. "They're all filled with food."

"What do you mean?" asked Phyllis. "I am afraid I do not understand any of this."

"Our cans have been refilled—by some method," Sandra said at last.

"Are you sure?" asked the priest.

"Positive," Sandra said. "I marked the cans myself."

Everyone examined the filled cans one by one. "Does this mean what I think it does?" James Harrison asked no one in particular.

"I believe it does," said Sandra. "It marks the end of our worry about food."

"Does that mean our rationing days are over?" Tara inquired.

"Yes, Tara. It could very well be." Sandra added, "If it occurs again, I feel that challenge to our survival could be over."

"What about the shares we've saved for the sleeping ones?" asked Phyllis.

"If my theory turns out correct, then we can eat their supplies also. There will still be plenty for all of us even when they awaken."

"I told you saving the stuff was stupid," Todd said harshly.

Sandra turned to the large man, "Hindsight is much better than foresight."

"When can we begin to eat more?" inquired Tara. "I'm still hungry when I walk away from the table."

"You!" joked Todd. "Imagine how I feel when I'm done."

Everyone dispersed except for Sandra and the priest. "Do you have any idea what this is all about? It makes no sense to me," McShane said.

"Maybe someone wants us to stay alive…" pondered Sandra.

"Who would or could do such a sick thing, confining us like this endlessly."

"Father, I wish I had the answer. Maybe it was a holy spirit?"

"I don't find that's very funny."

"If you can come up with a better answer, just let me know."

"At least we won't go hungry when the others awaken," Father McShane said.

"If they do."

"Sandra, I will almost bet some of them are going to make it."

"Time will tell, Father," Sandra said leaving the kitchen.

T W E L V E

Sandra's prognostication was accurate. After each meal, members of the group would place their empty food containers in the pantry and shortly thereafter every can and box would be refilled. A thorough inspection of the pantry revealed no feasible explanation for the event. It was quickly discovered that the exchange would only take place behind a closed door.

"Do you have any new ideas?" asked Tara.

"None!" said Sandra. "I am as confused as before."

"Father McShane is calling it a miracle. Do you agree?"

"No." Sandra assumed a rigid posture and spoke, "I was never a strong supporter of organized religion. I doubt if I would alter my position. Everything in life can be explained, we just have to get more information to solve this mystery."

"You sound very skeptical," Tara ventured.

"I am." Thinking momentarily, Sandra said, "I was trained to be objective in my reasoning process. Why should I change now?"

"Believe what you want. It's still a free country," Tara replied.

"Things always have a way of working out for the very best," Sandra said conclusively.

"Somehow, I just don't believe that's always the case," Tara countered.

The six were surprised to find that their grooming and personal articles were also replenished. More mysteriously, every item, whether food or grooming supplies, was a particular person's favorite.

"How can anyone know so many things about us?" asked Tara. "I haven't used another toothpaste in years."

Father McShane offered little explanation other than his miracle theory. Others had different opinions.

"I believe we are all being held ransom," stated Phyllis. "But don't worry, my husband will buy our freedom."

"Who is your husband?" inquired Tara.

"Ronald." Hesitating to continue, she said, "I only know he is very successful and rich."

"That makes no sense to me," Todd said. "We're being held captive by some group."

"Who?" countered Sandra.

"How the hell do I know?"

The priest turned to the physician. "What do you think?"

"I do not know, but whoever they are, they have gone to a tremendous expense and effort in creating this scenario."

"Agreed," added Sandra.

"The paintings are all original and worth millions," stated James. "And I might add, probably stolen."

Father McShane asked, "How do you know that?"

"Many of these paintings are owned by the larger museums. If they're here, they must have been either purchased or stolen." Looking at the nearest rendering, he concluded, "I believe they are stolen."

"Goodness!" Phyllis cried. "That is terrible. Who would do such a thing?"

"We are back to square one," Sandra said. "Too many variables and not enough facts."

"Those are my sentiments exactly," added James. "Too many details are missing from this puzzle."

Todd stood and stretched. "This whole discussion is making me hungry." He left the group and headed to the kitchen.

"How did that man ever make it in football?" Sandra asked. "He is so thick."

"He may not be a rocket scientist, but he was the best linebacker who ever played professional football," reminded Father McShane.

"That may be true, Father, but he is still a liability here," Sandra argued.

"I believe he's in the Hall of Fame," McShane defended.

"Just what we need, another egomaniac."

"Perhaps we should try to get along better with one another while we're here," suggested the priest.

"No sermons please, Father. The man is just a total waste of flesh."

"Sandra, for my sake and the others, could you at least attempt to subdue your feelings for the time being?"

Nodding her head slowly in accord, she said, "I will do it for you, but just keep that jerk away from me."

"I will try."

THIRTEEN

"Dr. Harrison?"

Looking up from his reading, the paunchy physician responded, "Yes, Phyllis. What is it?"

"I know this may sound rather absurd, but something has been bothering me."

"Have a seat and tell old Dr. Harrison what is bothering you," he said.

In a somber tone, she continued, "I am serious: Something is wrong with one of the pictures."

"I'm not sure I understand what you are talking about."

Pointing to a large mural on the nearest wall, she explained, "The last time I examined that picture, the young man in it had blue eyes." Gasping slightly, she said, "Now the eyes are brown."

"Are you sure?"

"Certainly I am sure. I studied art history in undergraduate school and I know that picture very well. The youth had blue eyes."

They walked to the picture and closely studied the youngster's face. James Harrison touched the texture of the painting and said,

"The canvas is one hundred percent dry."

"I do not care. Those eyes were blue."

He studied the entire picture closely, "They're brown now."

Raising her voice slightly, she responded, "You told me you have an appreciation for art. Any idiot knows his eyes are supposed to be blue."

"There isn't any need to get upset; I am sure there is a logical explanation."

"Please do not humor me. I know my art. His eyes were blue the last time I looked."

"I'm not trying to humor you, my dear Phyllis. I'm only reporting what I can actually see."

She began to weep. "But they were blue…"

"Why don't you just relax and we'll discuss it later." He led her to an adjacent sofa and helped her lie down on the plush cushions. Afterward, he moved to where Father McShane was sitting and explained what had just occurred.

"Do you think something is seriously wrong?" asked the priest.

"I'm not sure; maybe it's just her nerves."

"Like a hysteria?"

"Father, I'm not a psychiatrist. I was trained as a surgeon."

"Can't you even venture a guess?"

"No. I deal with exactness. I let my fellow professionals handle this type of patient."

"How do we care for her?"

"I suggest we let her rest and then try to support her until she begins to act more coherently." Glancing at Phyllis, James said, "I'll tell her the eyes were blue and that will keep her happy."

"But that's a lie," countered the priest.

"Who cares, Father?" responded the physician. "I used to lie all the time to my patients. It was for their own good." Laughing, he added, "They believed anything I'd tell them; they were so gullible and stupid."

"And poor Phyllis?"

"The same. It's just a matter of pacifying her until we get out of here."

"*If* we get out…" McShane reminded him.

"We'll get out and then her husband can deal with her."

"In the meantime, what can we do to prevent the others from experiencing similar problems?" asked the priest.

"I believe we should keep them busy with some sort of project. The busier they are, the less chance we have for another occurrence."

"What shall we do?"

"Father, I leave that sort of stuff to you. I really don't give a damn." Continuing his smug attitude, he said, "They're not my responsibility and I refuse to be anyone's babysitter. My main concern is to leave this goddamn room and get back to my normal life."

Though offended, the priest redirected his conversation. "Do you remember any more about your past?"

"Yes. I made a lot of money and put up with mindless individuals like Phyllis throughout most of my professional career."

"I guess that goes with our chosen professions…"

"Don't give me that bull; I went into medicine for the money and I might add, I made quite a lot of it over the years."

"What about saving lives and helping your fellow humans?"

Realizing he was about to lose his temper, the stout physician left for the kitchen. There he tried to calm himself and collect his thoughts. "Dumb, naive fool! Does he think everyone wants to spend their lives poor and without material things?"

F O U R T E E N

During their next communal meal, the six discussed many topics. Though hostility was growing among certain members, everyone tried to be civil and avoid conflict. All eyes turned to Sandra as she requested the floor. "I would like to raise an important issue."

"What now?" muttered Todd under his breath.

Ignoring the football player's comment, she continued, "I do not feel we women should be washing the dishes after every meal."

"And why not?" inquired James.

"Because you men eat too!" Sandra replied.

"I'm afraid I don't see your point," responded Father McShane.

"You've done them before without any hesitation," the doctor pointed out.

"The real question is why. Why are we doing them after every meal and not you men?"

"Because that's your job," declared James.

"Where is it written?" countered Sandra.

"Sandra, you're just being argumentative and idiotic." The physician maintained his attack. "A woman's place is in the home!"

"Barefoot and pregnant? Come on, Doc, that thinking went out decades ago."

"I agree with Sandra," added Phyllis. "I never do dishes in my house."

"Who did them?" asked Todd. "The maid?"

"Yes."

"Regardless," countered James. "We have no maid here and therefore it's a woman's job while we're here."

"Who made you God?" said Sandra emphatically.

"I did." Glaring at Sandra, James continued. "I am an orthopedic surgeon. Do you think I do such menial or trivial tasks?"

"Who did your dishes then?" asked Tara.

"Who else? My wife!"

"My girlfriend did mine," Todd chimed in. "She also washed my clothes."

Sandra commented snidely, "She must have been a real clever girl."

"Please!" pleaded Father McShane. "No fighting."

"I agree, Father. This discussion is not worth anyone's time," the doctor said. "Sandra, you're just being obstinate and pigheaded."

Standing her ground, Sandra said, "What makes you such a genius? You're just a professional technician."

The physician's face turned scarlet as he said, "At least I did something besides taking care of drooling infants and changing diapers. Don't talk to *me* about helping your fellow man!"

"You pompous ass! I do not even have children. I am a college professor!"

"What did you teach?" taunted Todd, "Sandbox 303?"

"I happen to be a full professor at Harvard."

"Harvard University?" asked Tara.

"Yes. I was the head of their philosophy department."

Everyone remained silent until the priest remarked, "It appears some of our memories at returning. Hopefully, we will all remember everything about our past in the near future."

"Getting back to the topic. I have a way to solve the problem," Tara offered.

"What is it, Tara?" questioned the priest.

"Each person should do their own dishes." Everyone concurred with the decision. Although the two men did so begrudgingly, they couldn't argue with the logic of such an equivocal plan.

"Excellent," Sandra said.

"What about me?" asked Phyllis, who had no idea how to wash dishes.

"You have to do your own also," James stated. "There can be no exceptions."

"But I've never done them before..."

"Relax, Phyllis," joked Todd, "I'll give you a few private lessons."

Noticing Phyllis was becoming agitated by Todd's last statement, Tara comforted her friend. "Just relax; he didn't mean it seriously."

Todd continued to needle Phyllis, taking advantage of her discomfort. "What will the girls at your club say about your dishpan hands?" he teased.

Phyllis broke down and cried. Tara lashed out at Todd. "You big dope! Where are your brains?"

"I was just teasing her," Todd tried to sound innocent.

"Don't let it happen again," said Tara.

"Or else what, little girl?"

Tara held Phyllis' hand, ignoring Todd's remark.

Sandra turned to James. "Now that that issue is settled, I'd like to excuse myself."

"Certainly, Sandra," he replied.

"I wasn't asking your permission. And from now on, please call me Dr. Sandra Golden."

FIFTEEN

To keep in shape, Todd exercised regularly. Besides calisthenics, he performed a series of aerobic conditioning drills. Everyone, including Sandra, was amazed by his overall strength and endurance. "Tell me, Todd," inquired Father McShane. "Have you always exercised this vigorously?"

Gasping for breath, the huge man responded, "This is nothing. You should see what it's like in camp."

"Camp?"

Laughing loudly, he said, "Training camp. It's a real ball buster. Most guys drop the first day."

"Why do they work you so hard?"

"We've got to be in shape. Football ain't for kids. It's a real man's sport."

"I played a little in high school myself," McShane admitted shyly.

"No kidding, Father. What position?"

"Fullback."

"You're pulling my joint!"

"No. I was the starting fullback for three years."

"What about college?"

"I didn't play in college. The competition was too tough and I was too small."

"Were you any good?"

The priest said with a smile, "Not really. Our school was small and not that many guys actually played sports."

Tightening his forearm and fist, Todd said, "I was great."

"I saw you on television a few times. You seemed pretty good."

"Thanks, Father."

"Are all the pros really that good?" asked the priest.

"Compared to the college boys, we're great, but not many are as good as me. Why do you think I made the pro bowl so many times?"

"I'm afraid I haven't followed sports too much lately."

"Anything you want to know, just ask. I know all the dirt."

"Why are you working so hard now?"

"I gotta be in shape for camp." Admiring his own huge biceps he continued, "Too many young guys trying to get my spot on the team."

"Isn't your job safe?"

"Nobody's job is safe in football."

"Are you really worried, my son?"

"Father, there ain't a player alive who'll take my place, but in case someone tries, I'll be ready to kick his ass."

"What are you going to do after football?"

"Haven't given it much thought."

"What about TV?"

"Maybe." Shrugging his shoulders, Todd said, "We'll see. Sorry, Father, but I gotta get back to work."

The priest joined James. "What's he doing? Trying to set new Olympic records?" asked James.

"No. He trying to keep in shape for football."

"Give me a break," the physician said. "He's a has-been."

"I wouldn't tell him that to his face," advised McShane.

"What do you take me for, an idiot! The guy is a typical

Neanderthal."

"Perhaps we should all try to do some exercising?" the priest gently admonished.

"I get all the exercise I need. Beyond that, it's too much for me to handle."

"Isn't exercise important for one's overall health?"

"Father, you're so naive! Take it from an old practicing physician, those studies are all bull. They're usually sponsored by some exercise or fitness corporation. That's why the results always favor that type of activity."

"Do you know that for sure?" asked the priest skeptically.

"I've made thousands from those studies and other grants. It funds us physicians and all we have to do is to fudge the results in their favor."

"The whole deception sounds frightening to me," McShane mused.

"It's best you don't hear the truth about these things; otherwise, you'll lose your faith in modern medicine."

Thinking momentarily, the priest said, "I believe I did a lot of work in St. Joseph's."

"The one in Suffern?" asked the doctor.

Concentrating, he said, "Yes, that's the one."

"An excellent hospital. The orthopedic department is headed by a Doctor Jerome Resel. We were classmates in medical school."

"I think..." Father McShane stopped mid-sentence as a piercing scream filled the room. Everyone turned in the direction of the eight reclining bodies. Another screech caused all six occupants to seek the source.

"Which one was it?" asked Phyllis.

Looking at the reclining bodies, the priest responded, "I haven't a clue."

They waited a long time, but the shouting did not recur. Finally, they resumed their previous activities.

SIXTEEN

Phyllis and Tara quickly developed a close relationship and spent most of their time together. "I am beginning to recall much of my earlier life," stated Phyllis.

Frowning slightly, Tara said, "I still can't remember anything. No matter how hard I try, nothing comes back."

"I am sure it will in time," comforted her friend.

"What do you remember?" asked Tara.

The older woman continued. "My husband's name is Ronald Gerald Taylor and we live in a suburb of New Orleans. Ronald is chairman of the board of Louisiana Manufacturing."

"I'm afraid I've never heard of it," Tara said meekly.

"It doesn't matter, my dear. He's one of the most influential and powerful men in the entire state. In fact, we are personal friends of the governor and his wife."

"The Governor of Louisiana?"

"Old Loose Zipper himself!" Whispering, Phyllis continued, "That SOB has screwed more women than you can ever imagine."

"That's terrible."

"All men are the same and they will lie like hell about it. The last

43

time we got together, the governor tried screwing me in the bathroom with my husband and his wife downstairs."

"Did you scream? What did your husband say?"

"Of course I didn't scream. I let him feel me up for a few minutes and then I left the room."

Shaking her head in disbelief, Tara said, "A governor?"

"As for my husband, I never tell him of such things."

"He'd probably be mad."

"You must be kidding; he does the same thing to other women. I caught him several times in our bedroom with the maid."

"Why didn't you divorce him?"

"Economics! He's filthy rich!"

"It must be very hard on you."

"Not at all, I have an occasional affair myself. What's good for the gander is good for the goose."

"Do you have any children?"

"No. Ronald is sterile."

"Do you work?"

"No. I either go to our club or spend time doing charitable work."

"That's nice of you."

"I only do it to appease my husband. It is great public relations for his company."

"It sounds as if your life is kind of messed up…" ventured Tara.

"Not at all. I am very content. It is simply a mutual relationship of convenience."

"I don't think I could ever live like that with my husband…if I do have one."

"As I said before, one must sometimes resort to extraordinary means to survive." Smiling, Phyllis said, "Ronald and I are stuck with one another forever."

"I feel so badly for you."

"Why? I have everything I want and companionship is only a phone call away. I would not change a thing."

"It just seems so unnatural," Tara remarked.

"That's because you're still very innocent. When you get to be my age, then we will see how you feel about such matters."

"Perhaps you're correct and it's unfair for me to judge you the way I did." Changing the subject, Tara asked, "What do you think our chances are of getting out of here?"

"We better get out soon; I want to get home as soon as possible. I do not trust Ronald with our maid."

"Though I want to leave, I still get a feeling of safety and warmth."

"This room does nothing for me. I am tired of the artwork and sick of the furniture."

"At least we're alive," Tara pointed out.

"If you can call this living," retorted Phyllis.

A look of concern came over the younger woman's face. "Are you still worried about the men?" asked Tara.

"Of course I am, my dear, I do not trust any of them."

"What can we do?"

"Not a darn thing. Just wait and see what happens."

SEVENTEEN

Another earsplitting scream filled the room. "What the hell is going on?" asked Harrison. By the time everyone had assembled by the bodies, two new individuals were sitting and staring at the group.

Father McShane was the first to speak to them. "Just remain calm and we'll brief you later."

"What is this?" inquired the recently arisen young man. "Is this for real or am I on a bad trip?"

"I'm afraid this is for real," answered Sandra.

"You've got to be kidding. Who are you guys?"

"As I said before, we'll explain what we can later on," the priest answered.

They assisted the two in standing and walking to the kitchen. They ate eagerly until filled. Pulling the priest aside, Sandra whispered, "Aren't you glad we divided the food into more portions like I suggested?"

"I guess you were correct," the priest replied.

Directing his question to the young man, James asked, "What is your name?"

"Mike Schwanz."

"And yours?" James inquired of the young woman.

"Iris Lansing."

"Can either of you recall anything of your past?"

Mike answered first. "Sorry, Father, my mind remembers zip."

Iris also responded, "I can't seem to remember anything."

"Iris, I notice you have a foreign accent." Sandra continued, "It sounds Russian to me."

"I'm afraid I can't be of any help. Everything is still unclear."

"Russian!" said Todd. "Are you a communist?"

Iris stammered, "I'm not sure."

"Leave her alone," stated Sandra. "What difference does it make what she is? We are all stuck in here together."

"Yes," added Father McShane. "Let's try to be civil."

James explained, "Under these conditions, we have established certain rules. And we try very hard to abide by them."

Michael inquired, "So what are they?"

"We attempt to respect each other as much as possible," said Sandra.

"Yeah," Todd joked. "When someone's using the john, you look away."

"You mean the toilet is in the open?" asked Iris, aghast.

"Yes," Tara said. "Everyone will give you privacy."

"What else?" inquired Michael.

"Each person has a drawer full of food. Eat only what is in your own section," James said. "Eat as much and as often as you want, there is always enough food."

Tara turned to Iris, "When you want to wash your clothes, just use the sink and let them dry on the rack."

"Some system!" uttered Michael.

"It's the best we could arrange given the circumstances," Father McShane said. "It has been difficult for all of us."

Sandra stated, "Some of us are less open-minded, but the rest

47

have learned to accept and adjust to their limitations." Todd ignored her.

Pointing to the bodies, Iris asked, "Who are they?"

"People like us," Sandra said. "Hopefully, they will awaken and help us solve our problem."

"Each of us has adopted a particular location," Father McShane said. "Feel free to look around and settle into a comfortable spot."

Iris surveyed her surroundings. "I can't believe this is happening; it's like a strange dream."

"I'm afraid it's for real," stated Sandra flatly. "Try to do the best you can to adjust."

Michael shrugged his shoulders, looked at the ornate surroundings, and then at the others. After shaking his head, he walked toward the nearest sofa.

"Father, he's on your sofa," Todd pointed out.

"Let him be; I'm sure he's still in a state of shock." Sitting on a kitchen chair, McShane stated, "I'll find another spot, let him have that one."

EIGHTEEN

"What do you think about the new people?" asked Phyllis.

"It's hard for me to make any judgment," Tara said. "After all, they've only been awake a short time."

"Iris is a rather strange one," Phyllis remarked.

"Are you saying that because of her accent?" Tara accused.

"No! I have a southern accent." Looking across the room at the youngish woman, she said, "There is something very odd about her."

"I don't see it."

"That's because you're still gullible. Remember, it's a cold, cruel world out there."

"Michael seems nice," mused Tara.

"Perhaps," Phyllis said.

"Phyllis, why are you so negative all the time?" Tara asked bluntly.

"Experience has hardened me to the ways of the world. Michael is a man and all men are the same."

"That's unfair."

"Have you ever met a honest man?" questioned Phyllis.

Shaking her head, the younger woman responded, "I still can't remember anything. Why does everyone else recall things of their past and I don't?"

"It will come in time; just try to relax," comforted Phyllis.

Todd finished his workout and joined Michael sitting near the bookcase. "Hi." Looking up at the athlete, he replied, "Hi yourself."

"How's it going?"

"Just great, man, just great."

"Mind if I join you?" asked Todd.

"I don't know...is this a free country?"

After sitting down, Todd asked. "Do you know who I am?"

"Am I playing Twenty Questions? You said your name was Todd...something."

"Todd Warren. Don't you recognize my name?"

"Can't say I do..."

"Don't you watch football on television?"

"Nah. That stuff is boring," Mike answered.

Todd slammed a nearby book to the floor. "Boring, my ass! It's the greatest."

"That's a matter of opinion. I personally find the game silly and overrated."

"What do you do for excitement? Jerk off?"

"Sometimes," Michael responded. "But if I'm lucky, I'll get someone to do it for me."

"I can't believe you're for real!"

"Why? Because I don't like football?"

"What are you gay or something?"

"As a matter of fact I do practice certain unorthodox sex."

Standing quickly, Todd lashed out, "You're a goddamn homo!"

"Hey, big guy, why don't you leave me alone?"

"A gay pig! Just what we need!"

"I think you'd better do a few more push-ups and burn up some of that hot air," Mike advised.

Before Todd could respond, Michael stood up and walked over to Sandra, leaving the huge athlete steaming. "What happened to him?" Sandra inquired.

"I just pulled his chain a little," replied Michael. He explained the previous conversation and watched her laugh.

"I'm surprised he didn't slug you!"

"I move too fast."

"Are you really gay?"

"Hell no, I just wanted to see his reaction."

"What do you do for a living?"

"I'm a musician."

"Which orchestra?"

"Try rock and roll."

"Oh. I know nothing about it," admitted Sandra.

"Too bad. It's really good stuff." Looking at the ceiling, he asked, "Speaking of music, how do we change the crap that's playing now."

"You can't. The controls are nowhere in the room."

"Are you sure?"

"We have looked over the entire area. It continues to play all the time."

"Just great."

"It is really not that bad once you learn to appreciate it."

"Forget it. My life is rock and roll."

"Did you play in a band?" asked Sandra.

"Yeah. It was called God and the Angels."

"God and the Angels!"

"Yeah." Smiling, he continued, "And you're sitting next to God himself. I was the lead guitarist and singer."

"Were you good?"

"Sandra, I was the best. That's why they named me God." Not knowing what to say, Sandra offered the young man an apple. "Where did you get that?"

"I found it with my food. Do you want it?"

"No. I wonder if I can get some cigarettes anywhere?"

"I doubt it."

"No smokes or booze? What a joint!"

"I guess you'll have to wait until we get out of here."

"I'll have a stroke first." Whispering, he asked, "Anyone got any grass or crack?"

Shocked, Sandra managed to control herself. "I am afraid I haven't seen any of those items either."

"If you do, just let me know."

After he left, she looked around at the others and shook her head. *I certainly miss my classes!*

NINETEEN

The great wall clock chimed seven rings. James again examined several of the doors. He picked, pushed, and pulled against each of the stationary structures.

"How's it going?" asked Iris.

Startled, he answered, "I can't seem to get it unlocked."

Looking at the latch mechanism, she asked, "May I try?"

"Why not? I'm not having any luck."

She attempted to turn the handle once and then studied it more closely. "It is very unusual."

"I could have told you that; I've been trying to unlock it since I woke up."

She sat on the floor, reached into her pocket, and withdrew a single bobby pin. After placing it into the tiny hole, she turned it several times. A clicking sound caused both people to freeze. "What do you think?" asked the doctor.

"I'm not sure, Doc." She moved the pin again slightly and waited. Again, another sound was heard.

"Keep going!" James shouted. "You're doing great!"

Others came running as the young woman turned the knob and

slowly opened the door. The overhead lights filled a dark hallway. Phyllis screamed, "I'm going home!"

"Thank God," uttered Father McShane as he peered into the darkness. "I miss my church."

"Maybe it's dangerous..." suggested Iris.

"Let's go!" Todd said boldly as he pushed past everyone. "I'm gonna see what's there."

Leading the way along the passage, the huge athlete stopped several times to allow the others to catch up. Ahead, a light drew them closer. Everyone rushed toward its source. Panting, Todd shouted, "We're home! We're home!"

As they followed the light, they found themselves in another large room. Unlike their previous chamber, this one was stockpiled floor to ceiling, with boxes of food and other supplies. Everyone stood in awe at the tremendous quantity. James and Michael surveyed the perimeter, but discovered no exits.

Extremely disappointed, everyone simply stared. Todd turned to Sandra and sneered. "It looks like your rationing crap was all wet. There's enough food here to last us forever!"

Sandra ignored his statement, and said, "I suggest we inventory these boxes."

"You're mad!" Todd shouted. "I want to see if Iris can get the other doors from the main room open."

"Maybe one of them will get me home," uttered Phyllis.

Tara took her friend's hand, "Come, Phyllis, we'll see."

Iris was soon working on a second lock. Each member urged her on as a series of clicks could be heard. Grasping the handle tightly, she said, "Here goes." The door slowly opened revealing a small shower room.

Everyone was again disappointed. Phyllis dropped to her knees and wept loudly. Tara touched her friend's shoulder as everyone else stood silently. "I want to go home," Phyllis sobbed. "It's not fair; I just want to go home."

"Let's try another door," James suggested. "One of them has to get us out of here."

"I agree," said Sandra. "The odds are gaining in our favor."

"It's better than sitting and crying about it," Todd said.

"Please, Todd," Father McShane admonished. "Please try to have a little patience. We're not all as strong as you."

"Yeah, man, cool it!" Michael chimed in.

Todd glared at Michael and then at the others, "You're all a bunch of wimps."

"Nothing can be solved by fighting. Please, let's try to get out of here," Father McShane entreated.

"I concur with Father McShane," Sandra added. "We'll all be better off at home."

They walked to the third door. For the longest time, Iris twisted her pin, but despite her attempts, nothing budged. Frustrated, she looked up at the others and asked, "Now what?"

"Let's try the last one," James suggested. All agreed. Within minutes, Iris was able to turn the handle. As the door swung open, everyone held their breath in anticipation. Instead of an exit, however, they discovered a small storage room filled with boxes.

James walked inside to examine the contents. "Jesus Christ!" he shouted. "Sweet Mother of God!"

"What is it? Are you okay?" asked Sandra.

"Stay right there, I'll be right out." Moments later, he exited holding a large container. After placing it on the floor, he pointed to the top. "My name is printed on this one; all the others have names on them—your names."

Todd, James, and Michael carefully removed the other thirteen boxes from the room and set them on the floor. Looking at the neatly printed names on each, Phyllis said. "I wonder what is in mine?"

"Probably a big diamond," said Todd.

"I think we should take this matter a little more seriously," Father McShane warned.

"I agree with you, Father," James said. "We have no idea what to expect."

"Maybe they're bombs..." said Michael.

Iris examined the box with her name inscribed. "There is nothing unusual about the writing; looks like plain old script."

"Does anyone see any other markings on their boxes?" inquired James.

None could be found. "I'm for opening the boxes," Todd said. "I love surprises."

"What about the others?" Sandra inquired. "We have no right to theirs."

"I think you're right," Iris concurred. "After all, Michael and I didn't wake up until later on; maybe they'll do the same."

Father McShane read the names of the sleeping persons aloud: "Hugo Winters, Jeffery Graff, Alice Serrano, Franklyn Vincent, Joanne Hauser, and J.C. Smith."

"Do any of them sound familiar?" asked Sandra.

"Joanne Hauser is the name of a famous actress," Tara answered.

"Anyone else?" Sandra asked again.

"I'm tired of all this bull, I want to open my box!" Todd bellowed.

"I want to open mine in private," Sandra said. "It is my business alone what is in there."

"I agree with you," Phyllis said.

"Won't you share the diamonds?" Todd jested.

The decision was made that all parties would open their boxes in private. After they restacked the other people's boxes in the room, everyone carried their own box to a secluded portion of the room.

TWENTY

Father McShane placed his box on the floor and stared at the writing. Taking a deep breath, he opened the top and began to withdraw the contents. *The Holy Bible* was the first item to be recovered. He smiled as he felt its texture, then put it safely at his side. Next he removed a small bottle marked holy water, garments of the priesthood, a rosary, several books of religious history, and finally a bottle of Irish whiskey.

Holding the bottle for closer inspection, he stated, "My favorite!" Observing no one was looking in his direction, he stealthily opened the bottle and brought it to his lips. The biting fluid entered his body, causing him to grin. "God, how I missed that!" He then returned each object back to the box and placed it safely at his side. Smiling, the priest licked his lips and savored the residue of his present.

James Harrison cautiously removed one object at a time. A stethoscope, blood pressure cuff, and several other medical instruments were the first items to be discovered. Next came a prescription pad bearing his name, address, and other professional information. James studied it in great detail and was shocked that everything was correct, including his license number and tax I.D. Placing them aside, he removed the final object. His hands trembled as he gazed upon the periodical. After making sure no one could see, he leafed through the pages. A familiar flush and tingling to his loin occurred as he gazed upon the many pictures. Finally, James replaced the pornographic magazine back into his box, covering it with the other objects. The detailed, lascivious pictures caused him to smirk as he relished past experiences.

Sandra Golden slowly untied the wrappings, lifted the lid, and peered inside her box. A huge grin formed as she extracted the first of many books.

Title after title revealed her favorite philosophers: Aristotle, Descartes, Spinoza, and Kant. A heavy volume covered subjects such as humanism, existentialism, pantheism. The last book caused her tremendous excitement: *The Modern Day Atheist*. She said to herself, *I'll be able to work on my next book; all the reference material I need is right here.* Clutching her own book to her chest, Sandra began to outline her ensuing manuscript.

Michael Schwanz's box was the largest. Tearing the top in sections, he reached inside and beamed. Using two hands, he removed a guitar and studied its workmanship. "Just like mine!" he stated as he caressed the glossy finish. Holding the instrument in position, he played a few chords. "Just beautiful!" he said. "What a feel!" After several minutes of strumming its strings, he cautiously lowered the guitar onto the soft carpeting. Next he reached in the box and withdrew several finger picks, two books of popular music, and a small harmonica. A tiny object caught his eye and he immediately grasped it within his hand. *Heaven, baby!* he whispered to himself. *God is back in business.* Hiding the bantam-sized plastic envelope of white powder in his shirt, he took a deep breath and then clutched his guitar to his chest. *This ain't so bad! After all, I got what I need right here.*

Phyllis Taylor's name was attractively engraved on her box's surface. Though small, the recipient was only too happy. After savoring the prospect for a long time, Phyllis slowly removed the wrappings. She experienced ecstasy as she recognized the contents: The fifty or so diamonds were perfectly cut, displayed a brilliant shine, and weighed at least five carats apiece. A necklace of emeralds and rubies was carefully packed among the countless other gems and golden coinage that filled the small box. At the bottom of the container was a stack of thousand-dollar bills. Not knowing what to do or how to protect her treasure, Phyllis repacked the contents and kept it hidden from the others. *There must be at least two million dollars worth of gems alone! Wait until the girls at the club see me now!*

Todd Warren joyfully removed a professional football, kicking tee, several play books, and a sports jersey with his name embossed on the back. Under the shirt, he discovered a stack of betting coupons. Closer examination revealed that each coupon had rather easy selections with considerable payoffs. Looking at the number listed on each piece of paper, he shook his head, *I never placed any bets with these guys. They must be new.* Realizing his current situation, he cursed, *How can I make a bet when I can't get to a goddamn phone?* Picking up the football, the huge man, put his legs up on a footrest, and tossed the ball high overhead.

Iris Lansing gazed at her box; apprehension prevented her from immediately opening the wrappings. Finally, she removed the items. First she withdrew a medium-sized crystal ball, which shone brightly and was secured on a worn wooden base. Tarot cards, tea leaves, and a palmist chart followed. At the bottom of the box lay several leaflets on metaphysical and magical deception. Holding the crystal ball in her hands, she focused on the clear glass sphere. The ball clouded then darkened. Grinning, Iris thought, *I haven't lost my touch. Maybe, I can make a few extra bucks while I'm here.* She looked in Phyllis' direction. *I bet she'll pay for advice and counseling. As P.T. Barnum once said, 'There's a sucker born every minute!'*

Tara Smith looked inside her box. Nothing made any sense—especially the erotic garments neatly folded among other sexually related material. *Why can't I remember like the others?* she pondered as she touched the silky cloth of an exceedingly low-cut blouse. *This stuff is just awful! Why me?* Instead of examining the objects in any greater detail, the young woman rewrapped the box and placed it under her sofa. *I hope the others do better than me! Somebody's got some sense of humor!*

During the next meal, Todd was the only one to discuss the contents of his box. "Man, you should see the football I got."

Turning to the men, he asked, "Anyone want to play catch?"

Michael egged him on, "Sure, big guy, I'll play with your ball anytime."

Todd leered at the younger man, "I'm talking catch with a football, you jerk!"

"Maybe I'll toss it around with you later on," Father McShane said.

"Good," Todd said. "I'm glad there's at least one other man in this room."

While the others retreated to their private locations after eating, Todd and Father McShane tossed the football to one another. "You're pretty good, Father."

"Thanks, Todd." Laughing, McShane asked, "Good enough to make the pros?"

"Let's just say you have good potential for an old man," Todd teased.

"Are you trying to tell me something?"

"I think you'd better stay with your church," Todd suggested good-naturedly.

TWENTY-ONE

Only the tolling of the wall clock offered any clue to the passage of time. Without any functioning watches, no one could accurately calculate a second, minute, or even an hour. With no windows, no external signs could be obtained. Intermittently, the overhead lights would automatically shut off; during this time, most of the group slept or rested.

"Have you noticed anything unusual?" inquired Sandra.

"*Everything* here seems unusual," Tara responded.

"I am speaking about the clock."

Looking more closely at the great timepiece, the young woman answered, "I don't see anything extraordinary about it."

Sandra pointed and spoke. "There are no hands or numbers on the face."

"I've seen many clocks like that," Tara said.

"The pendulum does not move and yet, it chimes out the time."

"Maybe it works by a battery…" Tara mused.

"Possibly, but there's something about it that does not seems right." After a slight pause, she continued, "I cannot put my finger on it, but I know I am correct."

The clock rang seven times. "It's working," chuckled Tara. "Time waits for no one."

"Even in this room," Sandra added. "Perhaps my imagination is getting the best of me."

"I think we're all a bit edgy. After all, look at our situation; it isn't exactly a bed of roses."

"For a young kid you have pretty good insight."

"Thanks, Doc." Laughing, Tara said, "If I take your course, will you guarantee me an 'A'?"

"No, but I do guarantee you will learn a lot about philosophy."

"I wish I could learn about my past…"

Holding her friend's hand, Sandra said, "You will in time."

"It seems all we have is time. Depressing, isn't it?"

"Not really. Do something constructive."

"Such as?" Tara asked. "Shall I write a book?"

"Why not? You have paper and pencil readily available."

"Maybe I'll write about my past experiences!" Tara said in a sarcastic tone.

"Try keeping a daily journal and see what develops."

"We'll see. In the meantime, what shall we do about your clock?" questioned Tara.

"What *can* we do?" Sandra answered, "but keep an eye on it."

"What am I looking for?"

"Probably nothing. You are most likely correct. Just forget I said anything at all."

"I'll keep a close eye on the clock and at the same time, I'll write an autobiography," Tara said.

"Sometimes you amaze me." Touching Tara's arm, Sandra continued, "You appear well educated and extremely rational. You will recall your past very soon. I can tell."

"I hope you're right because it's a terrible feeling not knowing anything about yourself."

Sandra excused herself and walked to the great clock's location. Looking upward, she said to herself, *I do not care what anybody thinks, I can tell when something is not correct.* Pointing at the clock's face, she boldly whispered, "And you, my friend, are not as perfect as you appear."

As she walked away, the clock rang one deafening ring. Without turning back, Sandra commented, "Ahhh! We both know I am right!"

TWENTY-TWO

Following a darkened period, one of the previously unconscious bodies suddenly arose and walked to where Iris was resting. The lanky male poked at her arm and with a stern voice ordered her awake. "Get up, lady, and let me have your seat."

Startled, Iris said. "What?"

He repeated himself. "I said get up and let me have your seat."

"Who are you?" asked Iris.

"My name is Jeffery Graff."

"Jeffery Graff!" blurted Iris remembering his name on an unclaimed box.

Speaking more earnestly he asked, "Why are you still sitting? I asked for your seat." Moving aside, she watched as he sat down. "What is this place?" he asked.

"I think everyone should explain it to you."

"There are others?"

"Yes," she replied. "You stay here and I'll get them."

Soon everyone was excitedly standing by the sofa. "Welcome," James Harrison said.

"Welcome yourself. Who's in charge here?" Jeffery asked in a thick French accent. Everyone looked at one another, but no one responded to the question. "Are you all deaf? I asked to speak to your leader."

"I'm afraid no such animal exists," Sandra began.

"Every group has a leader. That's the law of the jungle," Graff said.

"I'm very sorry, but this group is an exception to the rule," Father McShane said.

James then added, "We have a democracy."

"That's lovely. Just the type of government of which I approve."

"Do you remember anything about your past?" inquired James.

"Of course. Do I look stupid?"

"It's just that it took many of us a great deal of time before we could recall anything," the stout physician added in a professional tone.

"I can't say I have that problem," Jeffery replied.

"Where are you from?" asked Father McShane.

"Paris," Jeffery responded.

"France?" Phyllis said, shocked.

"No, Paris, North Pole!"

"You don't have to be sarcastic," Sandra countered.

"We're just trying to learn more about you," Father McShane appeased.

"Perhaps I prefer my privacy," said the newcomer.

"If that's your choice, then we will respect your decision," Father McShane said. "We are all trying to hold together under some very trying conditions."

"I apologize for my behavior," Jeffery said. "This whole thing is such a shock."

"Why did you demand that I get up from this sofa?" questioned Iris.

"For some reason, I felt attached to it…. Again, I apologize for my earlier actions."

"You are forgiven."

"I live in Paris, France," Jeffery stated.

"What do you do for a living?" James asked.

"I am the Minister of Defense."

"For the whole nation?" Todd inquired.

"Yes."

"Wow!" said Todd. "A real politician."

Phyllis quickly asserted, "I know a great many politicians in the United States. My husband Ronald is very close friends with the governor of Louisiana. Do you know him?"

Shaking his head, the man politely responded, "I'm afraid I do not know either one."

"What about the Secretary of Transportation?" Todd asked. "I met him at one of our football games. He's a real nice guy." Jeffery shook his head no.

James extended his hand, "I'm Doctor James Harrison, head of orthopedic surgery."

"It is a pleasure meeting you, Doctor."

"Please call me James; I allow everyone to call me that while we're here."

"I'm Todd Warren. I'm a professional football player in the big league and I made the All-Pro Team every year."

"That's very nice, but I know nothing of football. We prefer soccer in France."

"Hey, man," Michael said. "Are the girls really good looking over there?"

"If you are referring just to France, then I will say yes."

"Are you hungry?" inquired Sandra.

"I could eat something," Jeffery replied.

"Why don't we take Jeffery to our kitchen and while he is eating, we can explain our rules and regulations," said Sandra.

"That would be nice; I'd like to hear everything."

"We'll fill you in on what we've found," Father McShane added.

"And I'll even let you have this sofa," Iris said generously.

"Thank you; there is something drawing me to this spot."

"After we eat, I'll collect my box and find someplace else."

"Your box?" Jeffery asked.

"Yes, my box," Iris answered. "I must take it with me."

"Don't worry, Jeff," Todd quickly said. "You'll get one too."

"I am afraid I do not understand any of this…" said Jeffery.

"While you're eating, we'll brief you on what we know."

"Thank you, Father. I would appreciate it greatly."

TWENTY-THREE

After everyone left him alone, Jeffery unwrapped his box and removed the first item. His eyes sparkled as he observed a newly printed *Robert's Rules of Order*. Leafing through, he was pleased with many of the newer modifications

"Wait till I use these!" he mumbled. "I'll show them a thing or two." Next, he removed another book: *Who's Who In International Politics*. Listed among presidents, dictators, heads of state, and other government officials was his name. He reread his own short biography several times, placed the book at his side, and withdrew a wallet from the box. Inside he discovered several francs totaling a great deal of money, a small safety deposit box key, and a driver's license. He read the name and smiled. *Jacques DeCart!* Looking at the wallet, he wondered *How did it get in here?* DeCart was Jeffery's arch political opponent and bitter enemy for years. The disclosure of DeCart's personal billfold only added to the sweetness of the moment. Tearing up the license, he dropped the fragments into the box, and placed the wallet into his pocket. *Too bad, Jacques my friend. I guess you're out some money.* The last object removed from the box was a bank passbook. Upon opening the cover, he was shocked to read the deposited amount: *Fifteen million Swiss Francs.* Since there was no name on the book and its identification number matched that of the safe deposit key, he realized he could claim the amount without any difficulty. *No more blackmailing corporations,* he promised himself. *I can retire and live like a king.* Securely replacing everything back in the box, Jeffery watched the others. *Peons! How did I ever get stuck here!*

TWENTY-FOUR

With the disclosure of the large storage area, everyone enjoyed the copious food selection. Community meals became more commonplace with the task of cooking shared mostly by Tara and Iris.

"This is great," bellowed Todd. "What's it called?"

"It's an old family recipe," responded Iris.

"It tastes like a dish one of our maids used to cook. She was of English descent," Phyllis said.

"How do you make it?" inquired Sandra.

"It's a secret," Iris stated.

"When we get out of here, I'll send you the recipe."

"You mean *if* we get out of here," Jeffery reminded.

"We'll get out!" Father McShane said quickly. "It's just a matter of time."

"Yes," Phyllis added. "We'll get out soon."

Trying to change the subject, Sandra inquired, "Has anyone actually counted the different kinds of foods in the big room?"

"Are you trying to ration again?" Todd asked.

Refusing to become defensive, Sandra stated, "Not at all, I was just curious."

Iris spoke, "There are at least one hundred different things in the room."

"Yes, I agree," Tara said. "We are constantly finding new things each time we're in there."

"Find any French food for Jeffery?" Phyllis asked.

"There are some packages written in another language; I'll get them the next time we go in for food," Iris said.

"Thank you, my dear, that's very thoughtful of you," Jeffery said. "Perhaps I'll cook you a native meal from my country."

"That would be great," James said. "I used to eat in the greatest French restaurant years ago."

"Me too!" Phyllis added. "Ronald and I always loved French food."

"Can you make French crullers?" Todd asked.

"I'm afraid not," Jeffery responded. "I never heard of them."

"Are you sure you're really from France?" Todd joked.

"Positive. I was born in Paris."

"Everyone knows about French crullers. You can buy them at any donut shop in America."

Trying to keep the athlete from insulting Jeffery further, Father McShane suggested, "Why don't you tell us about your last Super Bowl?"

Responding in an excited tone, Todd said, "It was the best game of my life. I played great."

"I saw that game," the priest said. "You did an excellent job."

"Won myself the most valuable player award."

Jumping up from his seat, Michael shouted, "Do we always have to hear about his damn football?"

"Sit down, you faggot, and keep your mouth shut!" Todd screamed. "What shall we talk about? Kinky sex with homos?"

"Please, Todd," Father McShane said. "Let's stop fighting."

"Tell that jerk to keep quiet or I'll blast him," Todd fumed.

Michael countered, "Just try it, you big asshole."

Todd leaped forward and tackled the smaller man. He managed

to land two punches before the others dragged him away. Tara and Iris helped Michael to his feet and escorted him to his sofa while the others tried to assuage Todd's temper.

Pressing a cloth to Michael's bleeding cheek, Iris questioned, "Why do you always egg him on? You know he's got a terrible temper."

"Because I hate everything he stands for," replied Michael.

"Many of us hate a lot of things, but you must try to control yourself while we're in this room." Tara said. "There's no place to run; for your own safety, just keep your mouth shut."

Looking up at her concerned face, Michael said, "I'll try, but I really hate that guy."

Iris commented, "We all hate someone during our lifetime, but we learn to cope with those people."

Tara spoke, "It's all part of life. For my sake too, please try to stay away from him."

Touching her hands, he said, "Not only will I stay away from him, but I'll write a song in both of your honor."

"Sounds great!" Iris said.

"I don't think I ever had anyone do that before," Tara added wistfully.

"I'll record it and give you each a copy."

They continued to speak to Michael while the others worked on restraining the huge athlete. Finally, after a long time, Todd relented and walked back to his chair. There he picked up his football and played catch with himself.

"That was close," Father McShane said.

"You can say that again," James added.

"You almost had a patient," Jeffery remarked.

"Sorry, Jeffery, I don't take care of fighting fools. I'm an orthopedic surgeon."

"I don't get it," the politician said.

"Don't ask for an explanation," Sandra said. "It's too complicated—and absurd."

James refused to defend his position and instead walked away. "Did I offend him in any way?" Jeffery asked.

"Not at all," Sandra said. "He's just a strange duck."

Father McShane turned to Jeffery. "I can't wait to try your French food."

"I'll cook it for you one of these days," promised Jeffery.

Sandra added, "I am afraid days cannot be measured. You will have to take an educated guess as to when the time is right."

"What about the clock?" Jeffery inquired.

"*You* try to figure it out; I cannot. What about you, Father?" Sandra asked.

"Don't bother me with such things. I'll leave that stuff to you educated folk."

"It's beyond my scope, my specialty is philosophy," said Sandra.

Jeffery looked upward at the great clock and listened as it tolled three times. "What's the big deal? It's 3:00 p.m." Smiling, Sandra just walked away. "What's with her?" asked Jeffery.

"I believe it's her nerves," the priest said. "Being confined in this room seems to play tricks on some of us. She's a good girl, but too suspicious of everything."

"Really?" questioned Jeffery.

"Give a woman like that an education and that's what you get," Father McShane remarked.

"Trouble!" the Frenchman concurred.

"We'd all be better off if they'd stay in the kitchen," McShane remarked.

"I agree with you, Father. Thank God we have more control over such things in my country."

Shaking his head, McShane said, "Even in my own church, the nuns are demanding more rights. It's such a pity."

"Tradition is going to the dogs," Jeffery commiserated.

"You can say that again," added the priest.

"I found wine in the big room," Jeffery asked. "How about joining me for a sip?"

"No thank you, my son. I'm afraid I don't touch alcoholic beverages," the priest said piously.

"I'm sorry, Father. I forgot myself."

"It's okay." Touching the Frenchman's arm, he said, "You go ahead and take a drink. I've got some reading to do."

"You're one great priest, Father," Jeffery added. "I wish you were my priest. You are a good person."

TWENTY-FIVE

James watched as Phyllis strode hurriedly in his direction. The room offered him no sanctuary from her nearly constant pestering. Frantically, she pointed at a picture. "Her hair is a different color!" she cried.

"Didn't you tell me that before?"

"No. It was another one."

"Are you sure?" James questioned.

"Positive. Her hair was black; now it's blond."

Instead of disputing her claims, he tried to pacify and acknowledge her observations. Looking at the picture, he stated. "I believe you are correct. It was black."

Looking at him, she said, "Are you trying to appease me?"

"Not at all. I'm simply agreeing with your astute observation."

"Well," she stated.

"Well what?"

"What is causing it?"

"I have no idea. Perhaps you should keep a close eye on all the pictures." James quickly thought and added, "Why don't you keep a written log on the changes?"

"Why go to all that trouble?"

"So you'll have written evidence of the changes."

Still not fully comprehending his suggestion, she asked, "Why?"

"So you can provide precise data to the experts when we get out of here."

"Excellent!" Phyllis shouted gleefully. "A great idea. I will call Jeanette Bacherman at the Museum of Fine Arts about it."

"Remember, only written evidence will be accepted," James said, relieved to have distracted her so easily.

"I see your point," Phyllis said. "Just like medical research."

"Precisely. Document everything and leave nothing to chance."

With great anticipation, she borrowed a pencil and paper, and positioned herself strategically in front of several pictures. James watched her out of the corner of his eye and snickered. *You dumb old bitch! So goddamn stupid—just like my first two wives!*

TWENTY-SIX

Being a solitary person by nature, Michael tended to sit away from the others and play his guitar. Except for community dining, he had little interaction after his confrontation with Todd. A motion caught his attention. Placing his guitar safely on the ground, he walked to one of the unconscious women. Squatting, he stared at the body and waited. Suddenly, the mouth twitched, followed by the opening of two eyes. "Are you alive?" Michael asked. A slight nod and finger movement ensued. The young rocker waited for some time and then asked, "Do you want to sit up?" He assisted the woman to a sitting position and waited.

Finally after a long period she spoke, "Thank you, I feel much better."

Noticing the occurrence, Father McShane and Sandra came running. Michael retreated and left the others to assume control.

"Where am I?" she asked.

"We'll tell you everything in time, but how do you feel?" the priest inquired.

"Better. I'd like to stand."

Once up, the woman studied her surroundings. "Very charming. Who are you people?"

"Just have a little patience and we'll explain," Sandra said.

"What is your name?" Father McShane asked.

"Joanne Hauser."

"The actress?" questioned Sandra.

"Yes. I am rather thirsty; may I have something to drink?"

"Certainly," the priest said. "Let us help you to our kitchen."

Once she felt refreshed, the others congregated. Introductions were made and a detailed history of the events in the room was presented by Sandra. Shaking her head, Joanne looked at the small group. "And that's what happened?"

"Every detail," Father McShane stated.

The wall clock chimed ten blaring chimes. "What was that?" Joanne inquired.

"Just a clock," James said. "One gets use to the noise after awhile."

"I just love your movies," Phyllis said to Joanne.

"Why thank you, my dear. I'm always glad to meet a fan."

Todd carried over a medium-sized box and placed it at the actress' feet. "This is for you."

"That's awfully sweet of you."

"It ain't from me," Todd answered. "Everybody got one."

"From who?"

"That's one of the great mysteries of the room," McShane said. "They were just here."

"With my name on it?"

"Precisely," James responded. "Everyone here has one with their name on the box."

"That's very odd," Joanne said.

"It's more than that. It's frightening!"

"Don't be so melodramatic, Sandra. I'm sure there's a logical explanation for all of this," James countered.

Turning to the physician, Sandra stated coldly, "Well, Doctor, what is your diagnosis?"

Ignoring her question, James continued to speak to Joanne. "There's an extra sofa next to mine, should you want it."

"I also have one near me," Phyllis said.

"Please don't fight," Joanne urged. "While I'm here, I'll visit with each of you."

Noticing an empty sofa near Michael's place, she said. "I believe I'd like that one."

"But," Phyllis said. "It's so far from everybody."

"I think I could use some peace and quiet. My last movie was most strenuous."

The group escorted the star to her selected site and then walked away. She gazed at Michael, smiled once, and placed her head upon the soft cushion. Sleep quickly embraced her well-proportioned body.

TWENTY-SEVEN

"Can you believe it?" Phyllis said to Iris.

"Believe what?"

"Joanne Hauser."

"What about her?"

"I cannot believe she is actually here."

Iris countered, "I can't believe any of this is actually happening. It's like a dream."

"Well, I cannot wait until I get home; my friends at the Club will just go crazy."

"Crazy over what?" questioned Iris.

"Crazy because I met Joanne Hauser in real life."

"So what's the big deal?" Iris said, a bit annoyed.

"Please, my dear. Do not be so naive. She is the biggest draw in Hollywood."

Turning to see the sleeping woman, Iris said, "I didn't realize she was so famous."

"She has been number one for years."

"Gee…that's pretty good."

Phyllis whispered, "Maybe I can get her to sign an autograph for me." Laughing, she reiterated, "My friends will just go nuts."

"Over an autograph?"

"No, over hers. Joanne Hauser never signs anything. Her signature is quite valuable."

Shaking her head in disbelief, Iris said. "She seems so nice."

"Do not let that fool you. Everyone says she has a terrible temper and is difficult to work with on the set."

"Who told you that?"

"I read it in the gossip columns. They always write something about her. They call her Ms. Bitch!"

"I don't want any part of her if she's really that mean."

"Just learn to tolerate others and use them accordingly. That's my husband's favorite motto." Smiling, Phyllis added, "If I really get to know her, I wonder if she would join me for lunch someday at my club. God, I can just see everyone's face when we walk in together."

Iris didn't say a word as Phyllis stood. "I wonder what she is getting in her box?"

"What did you get?" Iris questioned.

"Nothing big. Just a few odds and ends." Phyllis said vaguely.

"Me too."

"I will, however, take my box home with me as a lasting memento of this experience." Walking to the kitchen, Phyllis chuckled to herself, *Some lasting memento!*

TWENTY-EIGHT

The actress was awakened by a distant sound. Lifting her head, she observed Todd Warren running along the distant wall. She closed her eyes and attempted to rest, but the erratic sound made relaxation impossible. Then, she remembered her box. She pulled it closer and opened the top. She removed a stack of glossy photographs taken during her first movie. "I can use these for autographs if these people ask." After studying each picture, she reached in and withdrew a small golden statue. Immediately, the actress recognized its shape and pulled it to her chest. *An Oscar! I wonder whose it is?* Examining it closer, she tenderly rubbed its smooth surface, *This must be the one I never received.* With mixed emotions, Joanne put the statue down and looked again inside the box. Her heart pounded as she recognized a small black address book. *How did this get here?* she wondered as she leafed through the pages. Chuckling, she thought, *"They're all here, my little darlings!"* Newspaper and magazine clippings on her past filled the remainder of the box.

"What a pleasant surprise!" she said as she rewrapped the contents and pushed her box under the sofa.

Her concentration was interrupted by Phyllis' presence. "Ms. Hauser, am I disturbing you?"

The actress said, "Not at all, I was just daydreaming."

"May I sit down?"

"Please do, it is always a pleasure to have company."

"I always wanted to meet you in person. My husband and I are great fans of yours."

"I am touched. Thank you for the compliment."

"There are so many things I always wanted to know about you." Fidgeting slightly, Phyllis attempted to maintain her composure. "I am just so nervous."

"Just relax. I am, after all, only human."

"Oh no, Ms. Hauser, you are the greatest actress ever."

In an attempt to calm the woman, Joanne asked, "Which is your favorite movie?"

"There are so many you have done... I really loved *An Affair in Hollywood*."

"That was many years ago, but I *also* consider it one of my best."

"I believe you were nominated for an Oscar for your part. Am I correct?" Phyllis inquired.

"Yes. I was nominated for three others also."

"I thought you deserved it for all of them."

"I agree, but you know Hollywood." Whispering, she added, "If you do not go to bed with the nominating committee, then you can forget the award."

"Really?" Phyllis responded, shocked.

"Without a doubt. That's why I never actually won an award. I have too high morals for that sort of riffraff. I am, above all, a woman of character."

"I'm glad there are still a few of us left."

"By the way, please call me Joanne."

"Really, Ms. Hauser, may I?" Iris said, honored by the request.

"Positively. After all, this is such a trying situation."

"It has been pure hell for me. I have had to associate with these lesser forms since the beginning. I am so glad there is someone else of my status."

"I understand what you are saying," Joanne continued. "The world is so full of these people; it is just nauseating and intolerable."

Phyllis continued, "I know how you feel. That is why we joined our club. That way we do not have to mingle with the masses."

"I can tell, you and I will get along admirably," remarked Joanne.

"Oh thank you, Ms. Hauser. I am so glad."

"My name is Joanne."

"I am sorry, Joanne. I am just so pleased."

"What did you say you did for a living?" Joanne asked.

"I assist my husband when necessary; he is a very important and wealthy man in our community."

"Oh, I see." The actress then asked, "What is his name?"

"Ronald Taylor."

"I am afraid I've never heard of him."

"Well, some day I will introduce you formally."

"I believe I would like that."

"Good." Phyllis then asked, "Joanne, would you do me one small favor?"

"Just ask."

"Would you give me your autograph?"

"It would be my pleasure." Joanne wrote a small inscription on one of her pictures and handed it to the woman. "I think this will do nicely."

"Oh thank you, Joanne. It means so very much to me."

The two spoke a while longer then Phyllis joined Tara. "See what I have?" Phyllis beamed as she showed the younger woman the autographed picture.

"It's very nice of her," Tara remarked.

"It certainly was. I will cherish it forever." Speaking softly, she said, "Maybe she will give you one also."

"I'll see. Right now, I just want to eat."

The group, except for Michael, ate their meal. Joanne did most of the talking as she gathered more information about the room and its influence upon their lives.

TWENTY-NINE

"Jeffery, may I have a word with you?" Father McShane inquired.

"Yes, Father."

"I'd like to ask your help in a small matter."

"You just name it and consider it done."

"Well," the priest stated, "I'm concerned about Todd and Michael. They haven't spoken in quite some time and Michael is slowly isolating himself from the rest of us."

"So, what's the problem?" Jeffery questioned.

"I think we should attempt to resolve their differences."

"Why? They each have their separate opinions and we must respect them both for that."

"But we're a small group and it's very uncomfortable," the priest insisted.

"Father, disagreements are a part of life itself. They are as old as humankind."

"That doesn't make it right," Father McShane asserted.

"Nor does it make it wrong," Jeffery countered. "It's just a matter of how one perceives the facts."

"Anyway, I thought you might mediate the problem."

"Me?" Jeffery answered in a surprised tone. "I've never mediated anything in my life."

"You *are* a government official, aren't you?"

"Yes."

"I thought government officials perform such duties."

"Yes and no; some do and some don't."

"Would you please try to help?"

"Father, I am a man of war. I am the Minister of Defense and I detest any talk of peace. I make my living through war; why would I want to prevent even the smallest of fighting?"

The priest excused himself and joined Sandra. He reviewed his talk with Jeffery and then asked for her assistance. "I am very sorry to reject your offer, Father; I could not care less if they speak or not. Todd Warren is a walking accumulation of muscle without a brain and Michael Schwanz is a crackhead. I really could not give a damn about either one of them." Father McShane tried each member of the group, but all voiced a negative response to his plea.

Finally without any assistance, he decided to undertake the challenge himself. Sitting at Michael's side, he spoke, "I must ask you to do me a favor."

"Sure, Father. What do you want?"

"I want you to join us at meals."

"No."

"I'm begging you. It's not good for the group's morale."

"I couldn't care less about the group's morale. As long as he's there, I'm not!" Thinking fast, the priest said, "Todd has apologized to me for his actions."

"You're kidding me."

Fidgeting slightly, the priest expanded his lie, "No. He is deeply troubled by what he did."

Questioning the validity of what he was hearing, Michael inquired, "Why didn't he apologize directly to me?"

"I believe he's a proud man and couldn't do it in person."

"You mean a stubborn ass."

"Please, Michael, I'm trying to be a peacemaker."

"Sorry, Father."

"Anyway, will you accept his indirect apology and rejoin us for meals?"

Pausing slightly, the rocker said, "I'll do it for you and the others, and only because he apologized."

"Good. That settles that."

"But don't expect me to be friendly toward the bastard. Words are meaningless, he tried to kill me."

"Just ignore his presence, but please don't aggravate him anymore."

Taking a deep breath, Michael said, "I promise. He's gonesville in my book."

Satisfied, the priest walked to Todd and was immediately questioned by the huge man. "What did the queer want?"

"He wanted me to apologize to you for his behavior."

"You're kidding me. That jackass apologized?"

"Yes," the priest lied.

"I guess he knew he was wrong all the time."

"He didn't go into any explanations; he simply asked me to apologize to you for his behavior."

"Good."

"Does this mean you'll be civil when he joins us for meals?" asked the Father.

"Well..." Todd hesitated.

"Won't you do it for me?"

"Okay, I'll be civil, but if he says the wrong thing, I'll kill him right there and then."

Knowing Todd meant it, Father McShane said, "Thank you for accepting his apology. I'll see you at the next meal."

Todd did not respond, but picked up his football and tossed it to the priest. "How about a game of catch?"

"I have to decline your offer, I'm very tired. But we'll play soon."

Father McShane hurried to his site, reached into his box, and withdrew the bottle. After making sure no one was looking, he drank several mouthfuls of the whiskey. After hiding the bottle, he placed his feet up on a nearby stool and shook his head. *They're like two nincompoops. I bet I could sell them the Brooklyn Bridge.*

THIRTY

"What's troubling you?" Iris asked Tara.

Tara nearly shouted, "I'll tell you what's wrong! Everyone remembers their past but me."

"Some do not recall everything," Iris said trying to console her.

"I still can't remember a damn thing. Not one little thing."

"It'll come back," Iris said. "Have patience!"

"Patience! Even the ones just waking up remember more than I do!"

Iris asked, "Have you ever asked yourself why?"

"Why?"

"Yes. I mean why."

"Stop double talking me," Tara said, frustrated.

"Don't you find it pecular that you're the only one not recalling anything. Maybe there's a reason…."

"Why me?"

"I don't think any of us are in a position to question anything at this point. After all, we're still in this room."

"So what can I do?"

"Nothing. Just sit and wait. In this world, there are reasons for everything."

"Then why are we still locked up in this room?"

Shrugging her shoulders, Iris responded, "Your guess is as good as mine, but I'm sure of one thing."

Tara couldn't resist asking, "What is it?"

"Our being in this room has a reason."

"Great. More for me to worry about and not know."

"Relax and enjoy. I'm sure we'll all find out soon enough."

THIRTY-ONE

A piercing scream caused everyone to turn in direction of the sleeping bodies. Father McShane and Todd were the first to arrive. By the time the rest of the group reached the area, everything was still again. "Does anyone see anything?" Tara asked.

"I don't see nothing," Todd answered. "They're still just lying there."

"Wait a minute," Sandra said. "Something has changed."

"What is it?" asked Iris eagerly. "I don't see anything different."

"It's John Doe."

"What about him?" Father McShane questioned.

"He's on his stomach!" Sandra stated.

"So?" Todd said.

Sandra continued, "We placed all the bodies on their backs. Why is he on his stomach?"

"Did anyone move anything here?" Jeffery asked.

"I don't even come to this end of the room," Phyllis said. "It gives me the creeps."

"How did he get turned over?" Sandra asked.

"Let's ask him," Todd joked. "Maybe he'll tell us the answer."

"Please be serious, Todd," Father McShane warned.

"Sorry, Father. I'll behave," he responded.

Michael and Sandra gently turned the lifeless body onto his back. "He's still breathing badly," Sandra observed.

"I agree with you," Michael said. "He don't look so good to me."

All eyes turned to James. He stepped backward and said boldly. "I told you before, I'm an orthopedist, not an internist."

"You are still a medical doctor," Jeffery reminded him.

"Yes, I am." Standing his ground, the physician said, "I'll see who I want to see when I want to see them."

"Won't you at least render your opinion? No one here is going to sue you," Sandra begged. "For God's sake, this man needs medical help."

James turned abruptly and walked away. "If you are so worried about the bum, take care of him yourself."

Iris checked his pulse and noted that his respiration was still shallow and irregular. "I'm no doctor, but he still seems really bad."

"Who made the noise?" asked Jeffery.

No one could venture a guess. Everything else appeared status quo.

"Now what?" Todd inquired.

"Just go back to our business and wait," Father McShane advised.

The clock rang four times. Looking at its position on the far wall, Sandra cursed loudly, "I hate that damn thing. When we get out of here, I'm going to tear it off the wall."

"I think I'll join you. It really gets my goat too," Todd agreed.

"Why, Todd," Sandra said, "don't tell me you and I agree about something."

"Don't let it go to your head, little lady. I just hate the clock."

"Me too!" added Iris. "It's really getting on my nerves."

"How about if I cook one of my French specialties?" Jeffery suggested.

"That sounds great," Father McShane concurred. "I hope it's as good as your last meal."

"Could you go a little easier on the spices?" Iris asked. "My stomach isn't used to that rich stuff."

"I love it spicy," Michael said. "Just like Mexican food."

"Suppose we compromise," Jeffery responded. "I'll make two dishes: One will be very spicy and the other bland."

"What shall we do about the scream?" Tara asked.

"Nothing," Todd said. "Let them sleep. The longer they're out of it, the more we'll have for ourselves."

To prevent an argument, Father McShane spoke quickly. "Why don't we all help you with the cooking?"

"Great idea," Jeffery said. "The more the merrier."

"I won't cook; it's a woman's job," Todd interjected. "Just make sure you call me when everything is ready. I'm starving!"

THIRTY-TWO

A previously sleeping body awakened, stood momentarily, and then walked toward the assemblage. Michael caught the first glimpse and nearly choked on his meal.

"What is it? Are you okay?" Tara asked as the young man began to choke. Pointing to the erect form, he responded, "There! Look over there!"

Everyone turned as a man approached. Upon reaching the kitchen, he asked, "May I please have something to eat; I'm ravenous."

For a few fleeting seconds, no one responded. Finally, Father McShane spoke, "Please have a seat, there is plenty of food left."

The newcomer quickly consumed whatever was put in front of him. Once satisfied, he belched loudly and then commented, "Thank you. That really hit the spot; I was starving."

"May I ask your name?" Sandra inquired.

"My name is Dr. Franklyn Vincent."

"Another doctor," Todd moaned.

"What is your area of specialization?" James asked, "Orthopedics?"

"I am not a medical doctor. I have a Ph.D."

"Oh," sighed James.

Eagerly, Sandra asked, "What is your degree in?"

"Applied physics."

Probing farther, Sandra queried, "Where do you teach?"

"I don't; I do research."

"What university?" Sandra asked.

"None. I work for the government and…"

Jeffery hastily interrupted, "Which one?"

"I'm afraid I can't say."

"Why not?" Jeffery asked.

"It's classified."

"Do you work with James Bond?" Todd joked.

Without expression, Franklyn responded, "My work is classified." Looking around the room, he questioned, "Where am I?"

"I'm glad you do research. Perhaps, you can answer that question for all of us."

"Could you be more explicit?"

"We don't have any idea where we are or how we got here," Iris informed him.

Looking at each member, Franklyn said, "You're kidding me, aren't you? This is some sort of joke!"

"I wish it was, but I'm afraid it's for real," the priest said.

Standing, the researcher studied his environment and hummed to himself. "What do you think?" Sandra inquired.

"Too soon to say. I'll have to study it in greater detail."

"Please," Phyllis cried, "Find a way out of here. I miss my Ronald."

"The doors?"

"No exits," Iris said. "There is no way out of here."

"We got in, didn't we?"

"It appears that way," Sandra commented.

"Then there must be an exit." Touching a nearby wall, Franklyn added, "It's just a matter of finding it."

"How can you be so sure?" Tara asked.

"Believe me. In all my years of research, I've been faced with many challenges. This is just another puzzle to solve."

"How will you start?" Father McShane asked.

"As all scientists do. I will gather facts. I would like each of you to now tell me exactly what you remember."

One by one, each outlined their experience. Franklyn did not comment or question, but merely listened, and took occasional notes. Upon completion of the task, the priest asked, "Did that help?"

"I now have a base from which to start." Turning to James, he asked, "What is your professional opinion about the bodies?"

"I have none."

"How are their vital signs and blood pressure?"

"I don't have any instruments here." Standing, he said, "Please excuse me, I have something important to do."

"Do not expect any assistance from him," Sandra stated. "He is most uncooperative."

"And the rest of you?"

Father McShane acted as a spokesperson and said, "You can count on us for any help you need."

THIRTY-THREE

Phyllis waited until Todd was relaxing before she approached him, "Hi, Phyllis, what brings you around?"

"I thought I would watch you with the football."

"You're kidding me." Smirking, he added, "What do you know about it?"

"I am afraid nothing; however, I was hoping you would teach me a few of the rules."

"Why?" Todd inquired.

"Well, it's kind of confidential."

"If you don't tell me, then I won't help you," he replied obstinately.

Trying to change the subject, she asked, "Where did you get the football?"

"In my box. What did you get?"

"Nothing important."

Probing farther, he asked, "What is nothing important?"

"It's kind of personal."

"So tell me what you got."

"Why are you being so pushy? I got nothing of any value."

"I'm curious. I just wanted to know what a filthy rich woman would get, that's all."

"Can we just drop the topic?"

"No sweat." Picking up the football, he started to walk away.

"Where are you going? I want to learn about football."

"Since you're not telling me what I want to know, why should I help you?

"That's not very friendly."

A look of disgust crossed her face before she finally relented, "Oh, all right. It's really no big deal."

Todd waited. "So what was in your box?"

"In my box were some magazines, perfume, a hairbrush, and a new dress."

"What color?"

"What color was what?" Phyllis asked.

"What color was the dress?" he demanded.

"Blue! It was blue."

"That's a good color. Maybe you'll wear it sometime."

Without responding to his suggestion she again inquired, "Could you now tell me a few of the rules?"

"One more question," Todd persisted.

Growing intolerant, she asked, "Now what?"

"I still want to know why you want to know about football? Are you planning to start a ladies team at your club?"

"No," she said. "My husband is considering buying a ..."

Sitting bolt upright, Todd looked at the woman more closely. "Your husband is going to buy a team?"

"Please don't say anything. I wasn't supposed to tell anyone." Scared, she said, "He'll kill me if it gets back to him."

Touching her arm, he said, "I won't tell; I promise."

"Oh thank you, Todd. Ronald has such a violent temper."

"By the way, was it going to be a new team?"

Looking around, she whispered, "I think so. He and some of his friends were approached by the league office. They want them to buy a franchise."

"Down south?" Todd became very animated. "That's great news!"

"Why?" Phyllis asked.

"Because I always wanted to play in the South. The weather is better and I'd last longer."

"The weather is very nice...."

"What are the chances of your husband doing it?"

"I think pretty good." Leaning forward, she said softly, "They have already made arrangements for the financing."

"How about putting in the good word for me?" Todd pleaded. "Why should I?"

"Because I'm good and could help the team."

"That does not mean anything to me."

"What do you want?" Todd asked.

"Perhaps we could make some sort of business arrangement?"

"Like what? I've already got an agent."

"We can discuss the details later on. Do we have a deal?"

"For a woman, you want a lot," Todd observed.

Phyllis countered, "You are right—and do not ever forget it. Do we have a deal?"

"Yeah," Todd grunted. "If you do it, I'll go along with what you want—as long as you leave something for me."

"I will only bleed you a little bit, my dear." Rubbing his arm, she said, "You will still have plenty left for yourself."

"Wow! I'm going to the South."

"Not a word to anyone or our deal is off."

"I promise."

"Good. Now teach me something about your silly game."

THIRTY-FOUR

"Sorry to bother you," Father McShane said.

"No problem, Father. I was just trying to catch up on my reading." Franklyn responded.

"I have a surprise for you."

"A surprise!" Chuckling, he said, "I don't know if I can stand any more surprises."

"I'm afraid you're getting one more." The priest motioned with his hand as Todd carried a fairly large box over to where they stood. Placing it on the floor, Todd walked away.

"Is this some kind of joke?"

"I'm afraid not! We have all received a gift box from some anonymous person and we voted that each person should open theirs in total privacy."

Franklyn responded, "You can stay, Father, I'm sure there's nothing secretive about my gift."

"No. I'll respect your privacy. If you want to show me what you received later on, then you can do so."

"You've got yourself a deal…unless it's an amoral or evil present sent by the Greek Gods." Franklyn studied the wrapping and then carefully opened the box.

His eyes gleamed as he withdrew the new microscope. *Someone really knows their stuff!* he thought as he examined the costly instrument. *This must have cost a bundle.*

He cautiously placed it aside and removed other scientific implements, including a thermometer, magnet, prism, portable laser, and a multitude of vials containing assorted chemicals and substances.

At the bottom of the box were pages of handwritten letters and notes. Franklyn shook his head in disbelief. *Incredible!* was all he could utter. *Absolutely incredible!* When finished, Franklyn repacked everything very carefully and stared at the box. *This is the greatest gift I've ever received. I can't believe it!*

THIRTY-FIVE

As the lights relit after an extended darkness, Sandra shouted for everyone's attention.

"What is it?" asked Iris.

"Look!" Sandra said as she pointed to the kitchen table.

"Where the heck did it come from?" Tara inquired.

"Don't look at me, I was sleeping," Todd stated.

"How about you, Jeffery? Is this another one of your gourmet surprises," Father McShane inquired.

"I'm afraid I can't take the credit, Father. It would take days to prepare such a feast."

Looking more concerned, Sandra pleaded, "Whoever did it, please let us know." Everyone remained mute, staring at the food-laden table. "Let's eat before it gets cold," Todd suggested.

"Yeah, I'm starving," Michael added. "This stuff looks pretty good."

Noticing a change on Father McShane's face, Tara asked, "What's wrong, Father? Are you okay?"

"Yes. I'd like to say a prayer over our gift."

"Give me a break!" Michael said.

"Keep quiet!" Joanne said. "Let Father McShane say grace."

Most stood and bowed their heads as the priest began his prayer. "Thank you, dear God, for the food which we are about to eat. Thank you for guiding us through our uncertainty and may you continue to bless and keep us in good health, and secure from harm. In the name of the Father, the Son, and the Holy Spirit."

Noticing the priest had stopped speaking, Michael interjected, "Can we eat now? I'm starving."

Lifting his head, the Father responded, "Yes, my son. Eat to your heart's content."

After consuming his portion, Michael said irreverantly, "Dear God, could you give us a few more meals like this one? It was dynamite." Instead of being angered, everyone laughed.

THIRTY-SIX

James studied the painting. With a careful eye, he inspected every detail and stroke the artist had created. Shaking his head, the physician stood abruptly and searched for Phyllis. Noting where she and Iris were talking, he walked over. With total disregard for their privacy, James interrupted. "Phyllis, come with me."

"I am busy with Iris right now; I will join you shortly."

"Come right now, it's important."

"What's so important in this room?" Iris asked, annoyed.

"Please, Phyllis, I need your opinion on something."

"That's a switch," Iris laughed. "The great Dr. James Harrison needs something from someone else."

"All right, James, I'll come with you, but it better be for a good reason," Phyllis said.

"Yeah," Iris added. "We were discussing important things."

Ignoring their comments, James took Phyllis' hand and led her to the picture.

"So?" Phyllis asked impatiently. "What do you want?"

"Look at the picture," James demanded.

"It was painted by Pablo Picasso and it's called 'Three

105

Musicians.'"

Growing aggravated, he stammered, "I know that; I'm not stupid." Pointing, he demanded, "Look at the picture carefully."

"James, stop wasting my time. Just tell me what you want me to see."

"The guitar is red!" he shouted loudly. "It's red!"

"So it's red."

"But it is supposed to be yellow."

"It was yellow when I first arrived, then it was blue, pink, green, and now red."

"How can that be?" he questioned.

"If you recall my previous conversations with you concerning this matter, you'll remember you rudely dismissed my observations and cast me aside like an old shoe."

"But—" he began.

"But nothing." Sweeping her arm past several of the other pictures, she explained, "They all change on a regular basis."

"But how?"

"I'm just a plain old housewife, Dr. Harrison. What would I know?" she said mockingly.

Shaking his head, he uttered, "Pictures can't change; it's impossible. There must be a logical explanation."

"I do have a suggestion for you, Dr. Harrison."

"Yes, Phyllis. What is it?"

"I suggest you document everything on paper. That way the investigators will have objective data from a reliable source."

"But—" the doctor said, recognizing his own words.

"Now if you will excuse me, Doctor, I must get back to Iris. We were discussing more relevant topics."

THIRTY-SEVEN

"Tell me, Todd. How do you live on a football player's salary?" Joanne asked.

"You've got to be kidding. I do pretty damn good."

"I thought only the man throwing the ball earns a decent living?"

"Who told you that?"

"A male friend of mine."

"He don't know nothing about football."

"I believe he used to play."

"What's his name? I want to see if I ever heard of him."

"Harold Gordon."

Thinking for a moment, Todd grunted, "Never heard of him..."

"Maybe he played before you did."

"If he was any good, I'd know his name."

"Regardless, I don't think he'd lie to me."

"Why not?"

"Let's just say he's a very good friend."

"That don't mean crap!" Todd said. "He still don't know what he's talking about."

"That's his word against yours," Joanne surmised.

"Listen, I ain't a quarterback, but I still make a bundle."

"What do you consider a bundle?"

"I do good for a linebacker," Todd said defensively.

Pushing him harder for an answer, she inquired, "How much do you make?"

"My salary is $440,000 a year plus bonuses."

"That's not too bad."

"What do you mean by that?" Todd asked. "It ain't exactly chicken feed."

"Well," Joanne said. "We tend to do better."

"We?"

"The stars of Hollywood."

Looking at the woman, Todd asked, "What do you make a year?"

"Including royalties, I earn over $6 million."

"You're pulling my leg..."

She looked at him, "I expect to make more this year."

"Damn. That's good for a woman."

"It is good for anyone. Do any of you football players make that much?"

Shaking his head, he said meekly, "I don't think so."

"You bet your sweet ass. You guys are just stupid."

"Hey!"

"Don't hey me! You break your butts and get peanuts." Continuing, she added, "And your careers are over fast."

"That's true I guess."

"Of course it's true. My friend tells me all the time about the exploitation you guys suffer. My friend was very smart, however; he invested in real estate."

"I got me a house."

"What about a pension or other investments?"

"My agent handles that stuff."

"Don't you ever question him about them?"

"No."

"So how do you know how they're doing? Maybe he lost all your money...."

Todd thought for a few moments and then said, "I'd better call him when we get out of here."

"Are you a professional corporation?"

"No. I'm a New York Spartan!"

The actress burst into laughter, "God, are you thick. I can't believe your stupidity."

The huge man clenched his fist and rose from his seat. "Who are you to call me stupid?"

"Someone who knows more about finances than you do." She calmly motioned him to sit. "The truth sometimes hurts. When we get out of here, I'll give you my friend's number."

"Do you think he would help me?"

"Absolutely. He's a great guy." Joanne lowered her voice, "He'll make sure you're set for life."

"Great!" Todd responded. "I don't know how to thank you. Do you want any season tickets to our games?"

Smiling she answered, "No thank you. Football is not my favorite pastime. We'll think of something else once you're financially set."

The great clock rang eight times. "I'd better take a shower before we eat. Thanks again," Todd said.

After he left, she smiled, *Oh, Joanne, you have such a wonderful gift of gab and a knack for making money.*

THIRTY-EIGHT

Michael was resting with his eyes closed as Franklyn Vincent approached. "Are you awake?" the scientist whispered.

"Yeah. I was just thinking."

"Just thinking about what?"

"Just thinking." Looking at the decorative guitar sitting on the floor, the scientist asked, "Is it yours?"

"Yeah."

"It's a real beauty. May I hold it?"

"Sure."

Franklyn picked up the instrument and strummed several chords. "Nicely tuned," he said.

Michael watched closely as the man played several songs. "You play pretty good," he remarked.

"Thanks. I used to play in a band."

"No kidding!"

"We were called Oppenheimer and the Four Atoms."

Laughing loudly, Michael said, "Wild name!"

"We thought so too. That's why we selected it."

"What kind of stuff did you play?"

"Mainly popular music." Strumming several bars, he added, "Lots of rock and roll, and jazz."

"No shit!"

"Honestly. You're looking at one cool dude with a guitar."

"Ever cut a record?" Michael questioned.

"Sure! Lots."

"Wow! We are supposed to cut one soon."

"Great! What company is recording it?"

"Tetraplex."

"Good group. I used to be a studio musician for them."

"No shit. My friend does it once in awhile."

"It paid good money and I had lots of fun."

"Do a lot of live stuff?" Michael asked.

"Not like you guys! We did small clubs and bars."

"We done that route already. We just got a contract for a session and if they like us, maybe even an album and tour."

"Have you had this guitar long? It's a real beauty."

"No. Just got it in my box."

"Some gift. I bet it cost a lot of money."

Michael concurred, "A bundle! Only the big shots have them. I can't wait to show it to my group."

"I'm really happy for you."

"What did you get?"

"Some really topnotch research instruments."

"That sounds exciting…" Michael said in a sarcastic tone.

"It actually is! It's stuff I needed for my home lab."

"I'm glad for you." Whispering softly, the rocker asked, "Hey, man, you want a drag?"

Standing, Franklyn answered, "No thanks, my car is too slow."

Michael watched the man walk away and then chuckled. *That guy is all right.*

THIRTY-NINE

"Sandra, have you noticed anything odd about the music?"

"What am I listening for? It's typically classical."

Father McShane continued, "I've been keeping track of the selections since we first arrived and they seem to follow a pattern."

"In what way?" the woman asked.

"I'm not exactly sure, but I'm positive I'm correct."

He showed her his master list and she studied it. "I see what you mean. There is some type of pattern here."

"For instance, just before the lights go dark, a Beethoven concerto or symphony is played."

"Come to think of it, I believe you are correct."

"And when the lights go on, Bach is played."

"Please go on."

"Before every meal, Mozart is played."

"And after we eat?"

"Hayden."

"Maybe it's a tape?" Sandra suggested.

"That's probably true or some other kind of recording device. The pattern is too predictable."

Looking at his list, she agreed, "Yes, you're right, but what does it all mean, Father?"

"Someone must be watching—or somehow knowing—what we are doing at all times."

"Why do you say that? Maybe the music just plays by itself in a prearranged pattern?" Sandra said.

"How do they know when we're going to eat or when we're done? We eat at different times." Pointing to his list, he continued, "Look, we ate at three, twelve, five, and then six clock rings. No set times at all."

"An interesting point. If we are being watched, by whom and why?" Sandra said.

"I don't know…"

"Have you told anyone else of this discovery?"

" No," the priest stated. "I wanted to talk to you first."

"Good. Let's keep this under wraps until we find out more facts. I do not want anyone alarmed."

"Don't you feel we owe it to them?"

"Yes, but not now. Let's strengthen our case."

"The thought of someone actually spying on us scares me to death," the priest stated.

"It is frightening, but let's make sure before we offer any information." Father McShane studied his list once more and then showed Sandra another interesting factor. "The music played between meals and when the lights go out is played in alphabetical order."

"Really? That is most interesting."

Folding the paper and placing into his jacket pocket, he admitted, "The music is beginning to get on my nerves."

"Try not to concentrate on it too much. Perhaps, if you devoid your mind for a while, you will calm yourself."

"I'll try."

"Good. In the meantime, I will try to listen more intently."

"Sandra?"

"Yes, Father."

"I hope I'm wrong about being watched."

"I agree. That would be a terrifying thought."

He touched her arm tenderly. "I'll pray for all of us."

"You pray and I'll observe. Hopefully, one of us will get an answer."

FORTY

While sitting for their next meal, Franklyn Vincent asked, "What is our purpose?"

"Could you be more specific?" Sandra wondered.

"What are we going to do?" replied Franklyn.

"Go home," Phyllis said. "We want to go home."

"If that's the case, why are we sitting around wasting valuable time?"

"What can we do?" Todd said. "We already tried the doors."

"Yes," James added. "We have searched and re-searched this room many different times."

"Fine. Again I ask, what is our purpose? Don't you think we should develop a definite set of goals."

"You sound so formal, like a scientist!" joked Joanne.

"I am one and that's what's troubling me. We have no direction or goal."

"I agree," Sandra said. "We have been floundering for quite a while. Maybe we'd better consolidate our efforts."

"What efforts?" Michael questioned.

"Yeah. We've done nothing but sit on our asses," Todd

observed. "I'm getting out of shape."

"I really would like to see my Ronald. I miss him so!" Phyllis chimed in.

"How do we begin?" Father McShane inquired.

"It's very simple. We identify a common goal and work toward it with a united effort," explained Franklyn.

"What is our goal?" Iris asked.

"To get out of here!" Phyllis shouted. "I cannot stand being in here for another minute."

"I agree with *her*," James said. "The faster I leave, the faster I can get back to my practice."

Everyone concurred and Franklyn assumed command of the project. He assigned each person a specific area of the room. "Touch, feel, probe, and push. Leave nothing to chance." Excitement sparked as each person walked to their assigned section. The great clock tolled several times while the group labored. Books were removed from the bookcase, furniture repositioned, artwork taken from the walls, and the shelves and counters detached. Nothing was found. Dejected, everyone sat silently while Iris served them their food.

"There has to be an answer!" Franklyn stated.

"Yeah? What is it?" Todd replied. "We just wasted a lot of time."

"No. We did not waste any time at all; we've simply eliminated one element."

"Come on, Franklyn, stop it," Jeffery said. "There's no way out of here."

"What about the remaining locked door or the large inventory room? We haven't checked them yet."

Sandra agreed. "We must continue our search, otherwise, we are totally wasting our time."

"Wasting time?" Michael objected. "I already wrote three songs."

"And I read four books," Iris added. "I never had time before."

"Time! That's the problem," Jeffery said. "That's all we have is time."

"I suggest we explore the inventory later. Why don't we take some time off, and then we'll hit the room."

Sandra seconded the motion. "Everyone is fatigued from all the work." Looking at the great clock, she added, "When the clock rings three times, we explore the room."

After everyone meandered off, Sandra stayed with Franklyn. "Thanks for your support," he said.

"No problem. We intellectuals must stick together."

"What do you think are our chances of escaping the room?"

Looking at his face, she responded, "Truthfully, I think we have no chance at all. I believe we are being held here by someone and only when they're ready will we be freed."

"Why us? We have nothing in common," Franklyn said.

"That is what's so damn intriguing. If I can solve that problem, then I will know why we are here."

The group completely tore apart the huge storage room, but nothing was found. Disgusted and dismayed, they stared at Franklyn. "Now what, Dr. Vincent?" James questioned.

"I'm not sure."

"Just great. Some scientist!" Todd remarked.

"It was not his fault!" Sandra objected. "He was only trying to help."

"We wasted a lot of time!" Phyllis shouted. "My hands are filthy."

"Let's try to compose ourselves," Father McShane then said. "I think Franklyn's idea was a good one because it forced us to think and act as a group."

Turning to Todd, Michael laughed, "We didn't fight once."

"See what I mean?" the priest said. "It was really good."

"I will continue to search for an answer," Franklyn said. "There must be an answer."

"When you find it, let me know!" Joanne responded in a seri-

117

ous tone.

"I'll let you all know. None of us wants to be here."

Tara drew Joanne to a secluded spot. "What's the matter?" the actress asked.

"I'm still very upset. I'm the only one who can't remember anything of my past." Trying to lift the young woman's spirits, she said, "You will in time."

FORTY-ONE

Jeffery stared upward and shook his head. His thoughts were disturbed by Michael's abrupt appearance beside him. "Anything up there worth looking at?" asked the musician.

"Could you tell me what color the trim is along the room?"

"Sure, man, it's blue. Dark blue."

"That's what I thought." Pointing upward, Jeffery said, "Look again."

Michael gazed upward. "Hey, man, what happened?"

"I don't know, but somehow this section is green and yellow."

"I don't get it. I don't remember those colors before."

Jeffery agreed, "Nor do I."

The rocker jested, "Does anyone have a paint can here?"

"I'm afraid I can't find it funny. How can it change?"

"Ask Doctor Brains. I'm sure he'll know."

"You mean James?" Jeffery inquired.

"Not him! Ask the smart one: Franklyn."

"Good idea."

Looking again at the trim, Michael stated, "I really like these colors better than the blue."

"Aren't you curious or concerned over it?" Jeffery asked.

"Nope. All I'm concerned about is how to get out of this place."

"We all have the same wish, but until then, you'd better take these changes more seriously."

"Why should I?" Michael then stated, "Life's nothing but one big trip anyhow."

"Things are surely different in France."

"Like hell they are! Young people are the same all over. It's you old geezers who ruined society."

"I refuse to discuss it any further. You obviously have no idea what you are talking about."

Michael continued his provocation, "I know enough to realize a politician is a politician regardless of where they live!"

Jeffery was becoming agitated. "You're nothing but a waste to humanity. You talk, but do little to help."

"What about you guys? It's your kind that created the mess in the first place."

"How can you make such generalizations? You are not privy to the inner circles of government."

"It's a good thing I'm not; I certainly would do things a lot differently."

"Talk is cheap!"

"And so are politicians!"

"I can't believe you are speaking like this to me."

"Why not! I speak for the masses." Turning red in the face, Michael continued his tirade. "You speak for special interest groups and big business."

"That's bull! Try getting your facts straight."

"I know all I need to know."

Shaking his head, Jeffery said, "Of all my luck!"

"Yours? Give me a break!"

"To avert a further disagreement, I will excuse myself."

"Not a bad idea!" Michael said. Looking first at the ceiling and then at the rocker, Jeffery started to walk away.

"Hey man, I got a question for you."

"What is it?"

"How are politicians and bananas the same?"

Not knowing what to expect, Jeffery shrugged his shoulders and responded, "I have no idea."

Michael said, "They're all yellow, they hang around in bunches, and there's not a straight one among them." Jeffery turned without another word and quickly walked to the other side of the room.

FORTY-TWO

"Are you married?" Iris inquired.

"Never!" Sandra responded. "I would never be dependent upon anyone—especially a man!"

"Oh."

"What does that mean?" Sandra responded.

"I was just wondering, that's all."

Sandra asked, "What about you?"

"I was married once, but we got divorced."

"I'm sorry."

"Don't be sorry. I'm the one who wanted it."

"Sometimes things just do not work out. Incompatibility is a strange beast."

"He was everything a woman could want," Iris said. "I just decided one day to leave and try to find myself."

"Many women have experienced a similar situation."

"So I hear."

Sandra continued, "How did he take it?"

"Not so good. After he gave up trying to find me, he took the kids and moved to another state."

"Kids?"

"I had four young children at the time."

"And you left them also?"

"Yes."

"That took a lot of courage," Sandra stated.

"Not really. I just packed my bags and left."

"Have you heard from them at all?"

"No," Iris said coldly. "I heard he remarried and is making a lot of money."

"What about your children?"

"I know nothing at all about any of them. His new wife adopted them and that's all I know." Iris then asked Sandra, "Any kids?"

"Me?" Sandra answered, shocked.

"No, I'm speaking to God."

"I hate children; I would never have one!"

Iris laughed, "I agree. They really messed up my life."

"Any regrets?"

"No way. I do what I want and answer to no one."

"That is the only way to go. I am totally independent and can more than adequately care for myself."

"I'll drink to that."

"What do you do for a living?" Sandra asked.

"I'm a psychic."

"Really?"

"I really am. I also do fortune-telling and faith healing."

"Does it work?"

"You'd better believe it. I'll tell yours sometime."

"Do it to someone else. I do not believe in it."

"Many are skeptical at first, but they change."

"Are you really a faith healer?"

"Yes."

Pointing to the remaining bodies at the far end of the room, Sandra said, "Try healing them."

"I thought about it, but figured James and the others would

ridicule me."

"The heck with them. Do it anyhow."

"Maybe I'll do it when no one is looking…"

"I would like to join you."

"No sweat. I like people looking, it psyches my juices."

"When you are ready, please let me know."

"I promise."

"Do you require fancy equipment?"

"Nothing at all." Touching her chest, Iris added, "Just little old me."

"Did you ever see a ghost?"

"Many."

"Were you frightened?"

"Nothing supernatural frightens me at all," Iris said with self-assuredness.

"I am a pragmatic individual. Before I can believe in anything such as ghosts, hard facts must be presented and proven."

"They exist; that's all I can tell you. I have both felt and seen many of them."

Changing the subject, Sandra asked, "Would you be willing to come to my university and discuss your beliefs?"

"It depends."

"It depends on what?"

"If I am given a fair chance to present my experiences, then I would do it." Looking Sandra in the eye, Iris stated, "If I'm going to be subjected to mockery, then I will not come."

"I guarantee you will be treated fairly."

"Then I'll do it."

"I will call the Dean and make the proper arrangements when we get out of here." Touching her friend's arm, Sandra added, "You can stay with me when you come, and afterward we can paint the town."

"I look forward to both."

FORTY-THREE

Father McShane looked at Joanne. "I've never really met anyone famous before."

"Father, I never got intimate with a priest before either," Joanne jested.

Laughing, the Father asked, "What's Hollywood really like?"

"You really don't want to know."

"But I do!"

She paused slightly, "It's both terrible and marvelous; it's a contradiction of people."

"I'm afraid I don't understand," stated the priest.

"Let's try to keep it nice and simple. People will do anything to succeed. They will abandon every inch of morality and human decency to gain success and fame."

"I can't believe it's really that bad. I hear so many nice things about the people."

"All made up by their publicity agents."

"What about someone like the singer Sharon Leah? I always see her on the television raising money for the poor."

"All a bunch of bull! I've worked with her many times. Pardon my French, Father, but she's a bitch!"

Shaking his head, he said, "I can't believe everyone is bad."

"There are no exceptions. People will cut their neighbors' or friends' throats to get ahead."

"A regular Sodom and Gomorrah!"

"I'm afraid I don't understand your comment."

"That's okay. I was just speaking to myself." Looking at Joanne, Father McShane asked, "But you? You seem so nice."

"Father, no one in Hollywood is nice, including me. I've had to scratch and fight all the way up. It's one dirty business."

"I'm glad I'm not living there."

"If you were, you'd probably be unaware of these things. You'd be in your own little church, isolated from the real world."

"Perhaps I've lived in a dream world all my life."

"Why do you say that?" Joanne asked.

"My entire priesthood has been spent away from the real world. I was isolated by the various bishops and cardinals during their tenure. Usually I performed secretarial and other non-public tasks."

"I think you are better off in the long run."

"I'm not sure, Joanne." Shrugging his shoulders, the priest sighed, "I'm really not sure."

"If I had a drink, Father, I'd offer you one."

Quickly responding, he said, "Thanks for the kindness, but as a man of the cloth, I really don't drink alcoholic beverages."

"I'm sorry, I forgot."

"That's okay. We all forget things once in awhile."

"Yeah, but that's a big one. I should've known by your collar and suit."

Trying to reliever her, Father McShane asked, "Do you have any big movies coming soon?"

"I just finished one with Steve Kennedy. It'll be out in the summer."

"I'm sure it'll be a hit."

"I hope so, Father. I could use the money."

"But I thought actresses make a lot of money?"

"We do!" Whispering, she added, "I happen to be going through a rather difficult time and am somewhat short of funds."

"Can I help in any way?"

"Not unless you have several million laying around."

Coughing, he said, "I really don't think that number fits within my budget."

"That's okay, Father. I've got something brewing that will get me out of the jam."

"I wish I could help in some small way."

"Perhaps a little prayer might help." Sighing, she added, "I think you'd better make it a big one. I need all the help I can get."

FORTY-FOUR

"James, don't you think it's a little odd that Tara doesn't remember her past?" Iris asked.

"Is this a professional consultation?"

"For God's sake, Dr. Harrison, get off your high horse. I was just interested, that's all."

"One can never be too careful." Looking around, he whispered, "I really do not think she is odd in any way. She appears coherent and cognizant of her surroundings. Her vital signs seem within the normal ranges and she displays no bizarre behavior."

"It just bothers me."

"Why?"

"Intuition."

"I don't believe in that stuff. If it's not a hard fact then I don't believe it exists."

Iris remarked, "That's rather cold and callous."

"It might be, but I can't put false hope or faith in just anything."

"What about God?"

"God?"

"You can't see or feel Him and yet, He's there."

"Who said so?"

"Don't tell me you don't believe in God?"

"Without causing any arguments, let's just say I'm skeptical."

"What about your patients and their healing?"

"I do that, not God." Looking sternly at the woman, he stated coolly, "I am their God. I am responsible for their recovery and health."

"But what—"

"No buts about it. Modern medicine is saving lives, nothing else."

"But I have healed many people," Iris stated.

"Do you have a medical degree?" asked the surprised physician.

"No." Holding up her hands, she responded, "I have these."

"Just great! Another Christ!"

Getting defensive, Iris countered, "I can help people just like you can."

Smugly James commented, "I'm sure you can, my dear, I'm sure you can."

Iris started to stammer, "I'll show you! You ain't God!"

"No, but I'm the closest thing to it in this room."

"Try helping them," she said as she pointed to the sleeping bodies.

"I happen to be a gifted and celebrated physician, and therefore can pick and choose my patients. Those comatosed persons will remain in that condition until I decide—and nobody else—when they will get better. If you don't like my attitude, heal them yourself!"

"I will, damn it. I will!"

As she walked briskly away, he uttered, "Stupid fool! Try healing yourself!"

FORTY-FIVE

"Great!" Michael shouted as he lifted the plastic cover off his food. "I haven't eaten chili dogs in years."

"I wonder how it's done?" Jeffery asked.

"It don't matter; the dogs are great." Looking at the fully garnished table, Michael said, "Hey, see what you got."

Jeffery moved the cover and smiled. "Crepes!"

"They look like pancakes." Sampling a taste, Jeffery grinned, "Simply delicious."

"Can I try some?" Michael inquired.

"Sure," he said, "it's about time you found out what real food tasted like."

Michael lifted the filled fork to his mouth, tasted a small amount, and quickly gagged. "That's terrible. How can you eat it?"

"What are you talking about? It's great."

Sandra watched with curiosity and asked, "May I try some?"

After sampling the food, she also gagged. "I agree with Michael. The food is spoiled."

Jeffery tasted his crepes and argued, "You're both crazy! These are the best I've ever had."

No matter who sampled Jeffery's meal, each immediately retched. Turning to Sandra, Jeffery asked to taste her roasted chicken. He instantly experienced a similar sensation. During the next few minutes, each person tried another's food; all had the same response.

"What do you think, Franklyn?" Sandra asked.

Shaking his head, the scientist said, "I have no idea. Apparently, we can eat our own food, but not someone else's."

"That means nobody here can have any of mine," Todd stated as he pulled the fried ribs closer to his chest.

"This is all new," Sandra remarked. "We never had this problem before."

"Yes," Father McShane stated. "We often shared food."

"Let's see what happens during our next meal," Sandra suggested.

"I'd like to test the food after we eat. Will everyone save me a few scraps?" Franklyn asked.

"What will you be testing for?" James inquired.

"I'd like to see if there is anything similar among the dishes."

Once the meal was completed, Franklyn set up his microscope and studied the various samples. "Anything unique?" James asked.

"Nothing. Everything looks normal."

"May I look?" James queried.

"Certainly. I'd like another opinion."

James peered into the instrument and then changed slides. After inspecting several, he stated, "You're correct. Everything is normal."

"You handle the microscope pretty well."

"I did a lot of work as an intern in the lab."

"It shows."

"Thanks, but it didn't help us find an answer."

"Perhaps our instrumentation is inadequate."

"True," James agreed. "But I'm still not sure it's physical."

"What are you suggesting?"

"Mass hysteria. With all the pressure, anything is possible."

"Highly possible," Franklyn stated. "That might be a plausible explanation."

"Can you come up with anything better?"

"Not at this time."

"Fine. Then that's my diagnosis."

"Then what's the cure, doctor?"

Laughing, he said, "Everyone only eat their own food!"

FORTY-SIX

The great wall clock chimed six loud rings. Todd looked up at the timepiece and shouted, "Can't you keep the noise down?"

Trying to mend their relationship, Sandra walked to his side and chimed in, "Please! Not so loud!"

The huge man studied her tiny features and asked, "What do you want?"

"I have come with an offering of peace."

"What?" questioned Todd.

Holding her breath, she again stated. "I have come to bury the hatchet."

At last realizing he might not fully comprehend her statement, she said, "I have come to apologize for my rudeness and lack of tolerance."

Standing, he asked, "Are you serious or just pulling my joint?"

"I am very serious."

"Why?"

"Because we are all in this room together; I want it to be bearable for all of us."

"So you finally admit you're wrong?"

Biting her tongue, she softly said, "Yes. I think there should be peace for all our sakes."

"You didn't admit you were wrong."

Trying to control her temper, Sandra stated, "Fighting will get us nowhere; we must have harmony to survive."

"Fine. Where is your apology?"

Looking the huge man straight in the eye, she mumbled, "I apologize."

"I didn't hear you."

Speaking louder, she said, "I apologize."

"Good. I knew you were wrong all the time. You women are all the same. Burn the bras and down with men."

Sandra simply walked away and joined Father McShane. Through clenched teeth she said, "The man is a walking jerk."

"But you patched things up?"

"Yes, Father, are you happy?"

"Very much. A divided wall can't hold up a house."

"Extremely philosophical, but not practical. He serves no useful benefit to any of us."

"We'll see. There's strength in numbers."

"Just keep him away from me. I cannot tolerate his face."

"I will and thank you again."

Sandra walked to her sofa and thought about her dealings with Todd. It angered her greatly, but she decided appeasing the priest was also important. She hated Todd's oral demeaning of her character, but quickly dismissed his attacks as moronic. She swore to herself, *Just keep him away from me, Father, or I swear I will kill him somehow.*

Across the room, Todd spoke to Phyllis. "Your friend is an ass."

"Who?"

"Sandra."

"Why? She is an intelligent woman as well as extremely gifted and cultured."

"Is that so?"

"Yes, she is."

"I hate to break your bubble, but she's nothing but a big dummy."

Realizing she might need the huge man in the future, she asked, "How can you say that?"

"Just believe me. She's got no backbone."

"I understand she is one great fighter."

"Then why did she apologize to me?"

Shocked, Phyllis questioned, "She what?"

"She apologized to me. I told you she was wrong."

Phyllis looked at Sandra and then back to Todd. "Is it true?"

"I swear to God."

"Why?"

"Because she's wrong!" Todd shouted. "She's nothing."

Instead of discussing the subject further, Phyllis asked, "Do you really think you could help my husband's team?"

"No question about it. He needs me a whole lot."

Placing his hand on her thigh, he gently squeezed and added, "Maybe I can help you too?"

Smacking his hand and abruptly standing, she said, "Let's keep this a business relationship, Mr. Warren." Staring directly into his face, she said emphatically, "Do I make myself perfectly clear?"

"Yes, Mrs. Taylor. I understand perfectly."

"Good." Turning she said, "I'll speak to you later; I want to have a long talk with Sandra and see what's going on."

FORTY-SEVEN

At their next meal, everyone was apprehensive about their food. Father McShane turned to James and asked, "That chicken piccata looks delicious. May I try some?"

"Are you sure?" James inquired.

"Yes. We've got to find out one way or the other."

Everyone watched as the priest placed the portion into his mouth and chewed. His smile brought cheers from the entire group. "It's as good as it looks."

Sandra boldly asked, "Would anyone like to try some of my mashed potatoes?"

"I would," Tara said. Every person tasted the various foods throughout the remainder of the meal.

Upon cleaning his plate, Jeffery asked, "Why is the food okay again?"

"Maybe only the last meal was bad," James responded. "After all, it was the only time it happened."

"I agree," Franklyn stated. "Probably just a fluke."

"Why *that* time?" Sandra probed.

"I don't think we'll ever have an answer. I couldn't detect anything unusual," Franklyn said.

"Nothing?" Sandra again questioned.

"Not a single thing! Everything appeared normal. I suggest we use some caution, but it appears we can safely interchange meals with one another."

"Great!" the huge man shouted. "I really like variety."

"It certainly shows," Joanne commented.

"What do you mean by that?" Todd demanded.

"Nothing bad. I just mean you like to eat."

"Good food is important to a football player. Like fuel to an engine, I have to eat a lot."

No one even commented on Todd's statement. Instead Iris asked, "Does anyone have any idea how long we've actually been locked in this room?"

"Days? Weeks? Months? There is no way to even guess," Sandra stated.

"I can give you a rough answer," Michael said.

"How?" Franklyn inquired.

"I shave once a day. So far I've shaved fifty-three times in this room."

"How do you know for sure?" Jeffery asked.

"I save the blades."

"Not very scientific, but perhaps the only answer we have at this time," Franklyn said.

"We shall designate our time as Michael Standard Time," Sandra jested.

Everyone laughed until Phyllis stated, "I can't believe it, we've been in here for fifty-three days." Everyone was visibly shaken.

"That's one long time," Todd agreed.

"What is my husband doing without me?" Phyllis wondered. "That's almost two full months. Why haven't they found us yet?" She started to sob. "Two months. God! We'll never get out of here."

Tara calmed her companion while James asked, "Why *haven't* we been found as yet?"

"Yeah!" Todd said. "Where are my damn teammates?"

"Why haven't the police found us?" Phyllis cried.

"Maybe nobody's looking," Michael said.

"That's bull! The team can't do without me!" Todd screamed. he pounded his fist. "Where are they?"

"Fifty-three days!" Sandra uttered. "It makes no sense at all."

"So *long* in this room," Tara mumbled.

"What about my medical practice?" James uttered. "I could go bankrupt. Who's covering my office or performing my surgeries?"

Father McShane stated, "My church! Who's doing my masses?"

Franklyn spoke, "I was supposed to report on an important project. I think it's over by now...all that work!"

"I was booked for several clubs," Michael said. "No one is going to hire me now."

"You!" Joanne shouted. "That's nothing. I was to start a movie. I'll probably lose my part."

Sandra pointed to the bodies and said, "How can they stay alive for so long without food or water?"

"Beats me!" James said. "I've never heard of anyone lasting that long."

"Me neither," Franklyn concurred. "It's physically impossible for the human body to sustain life that long without sustenance."

"So *how?*" Father McShane asked.

"No idea," Franklyn stated. "But they're all still alive. I just checked on them before we ate."

"None of this makes any sense," Sandra said.

"I guess we won't get any answers until we get out of here," Iris stated.

"You mean *if* we get out of here," Tara added. "Nothing looks positive at this point."

Phyllis was shaking, "My husband is missing me." Turning to Todd, she sobbed, "Please help me get home."

The huge man looked sadly at Phyllis and gently touched her cheek. "I'll try. I will really try."

"Any ideas?" Father McShane asked. No one could offer any suggestions. Instead all listened as the great wall clock chimed three loud rings. As the sound echoed throughout the room, each person silently walked to their own secluded area.

FORTY-EIGHT

James and Franklyn surveyed the room. "James, what if Michael's calculations are incorrect?"

"That's possible. After all, look at who's supplying the information," the physician stated sarcastically.

"Not the most reliable reporter."

"You can say that again," James answered in a mocking tone.

"But suppose he's correct?"

James looked at the scientist and stated, "Then we're in deep trouble."

"Do you shave every day?" Franklyn asked.

"Certainly."

"Do you have any idea how many times you've shaved since waking up?"

"None," James laughed. "Who keeps track of such things?"

"Evidently Michael did." James looked serious for a moment. "Suppose he made the whole thing up."

"That would be an extremely cruel joke," Franklyn stated. "Suppose he did count, but his beard didn't grow exactly the same?"

"I'm not sure what you are getting at..." James said.

"I think my beard is growing at a slower rate. Of course, that's only a subjective statement. I'm only judging it by intuition."

"If that's the case, Michael's might be doing the same."

"Precisely," Franklyn said. "And that means only one thing."

James thought for a moment, "He may be underestimating the time totally."

Franklyn nodded in agreement. "We have no way of knowing."

"*More* than fifty-three days in this room!"

"God only knows how long it's been."

James coldly stated, "I wish God would at least tell us the answer."

"Or give us a clue."

"Shall we speak to the others about it?" the physician asked.

"Why?"

"I believe in being totally honest with my patients. I like to tell it as it really is."

"That might be good elsewhere, but you saw their reactions to the news. Everyone took it hard."

"Including us."

Franklyn agreed. "Including us…That's why we can't alarm the others. We could have a riot or overreaction to the news."

"I see your point. They are all emotionally frail."

"I'm glad we have *our* full senses," the scientist stated. "Can you imagine if we lost our cool? The entire situation would become chaotic."

"It's a good thing they have us."

Franklyn nodded his head. "You're so right."

They agreed to keep their discussion secret. "Tell me, Franklyn, what kind of work do you do?"

"Classified."

"Can you at least give me a hint?"

"Classified."

"For God's sake, man! I'm not going to tell anyone."

"If I could I would, but walls always seem to have ears."

"Look around here. There are no ears anywhere."

"Can you be so sure of that?" Franklyn questioned.

"Just give me a little hint."

"No. My work is classified by the government. I could go to jail for disclosing anything about the project."

"Fine," James stated. "I was just trying to make conversation."

"Let's change the subject," Franklyn suggested.

"Good idea."

"What kind of work do you specialize in?"

Turning to the scientist, James frigidly stated, "It's classified."

"You don't have to be snippety about it."

"Who's snippety?" James countered. Looking around, he added, "I've got to be very careful what I say. I believe we've spoken enough about the topic." He said good-bye to the priest and left.

Once Father McShane was sure no one was looking, he reached into his box and removed the bottle of whiskey. Licking his lips he anticipated the taste of his favorite beverage. Tilting the bottle upward, he stared at the liquid's level.

"Sweet Mary," he uttered. "It refilled by itself." Quickly, he sifted through the box to see if there was another bottle. Finding none, he gazed lovingly at the filled container. *I don't know how it's done, but please keep it coming.* Drinking quickly he concealed the bottle and then read from his Bible.

His thoughts were interrupted by Tara's abrupt appearance. "Sorry if I startled you, Father."

"That's all right, my child. I was just catching up on my reading."

Looking at the elderly man, she stated, "I smell liquor of some type."

Becoming defensive, the priest said, "I had a cough and took some medication. That's probably what you smell."

"I wasn't trying to suggest anything, Father. We all know how you feel about drinking." Touching his hand, she continued, "I'm very sorry if I offended you in any way."

"You didn't, my child. Your deduction was logical and understandable."

"Oh thank you, Father. I'm so embarrassed."

"Don't think twice about it. Can I help you in some way?"

"Yes. I'm upset."

"What's troubling you?" he said in a concerned tone.

"It's bad enough I can't remember my past, but I'm now starting to—" Unable to complete her sentence, she began to weep.

Father McShane probed further, "Tell me what's wrong."

Sniffling she said, "Father, I'm starting to hear voices."

"Voices?"

"Yes."

"What kind of voices?"

"I'm not sure; everything is muffled."

"Are you sure you're not actually hearing some of us?"

"Positive. Whenever it happens, nobody is around."

Trying to show genuine concern, he asked, "What do they say?"

"I'm not exactly sure; everything sounds so far away."

Shaking his head, he inquired, "Has anyone else heard them?"

"No one has said anything to me about them."

"Nor to me either."

She cried, "What am I supposed to do?"

"At this point, there is nothing you can do. Just listen and try to get some facts."

"Such as?"

"Who is speaking and what are they saying."

"Then what?" she asked.

"Then provide me with the information. Once I have real facts, I can come to a logical conclusion."

"Father, I am really frightened. This whole thing is like a nightmare for me."

"For all of us. Just try to cope with the situation as best you can."

"I'll try, Father." Kissing his hand, she said, "Thank you for your support and advice."

Watching her walk away, the priest commented silently to himself, *I thought only drunkards heard voices. Maybe she got the same gift I did in her box.* Picking up his Bible he reread the Holy Scriptures. Chuckling, he tried to regain his composure. *No wonder she can't recall anything; the bottle probably ruined her life. Thank God I can control my drinking.*

FORTY-NINE

Walking close to the three sleeping bodies, James peered over his shoulder to make sure he wasn't being observed. Most of the others were either napping or resting, and none seemed to be looking in his direction. Stooping by the first body, he placed his stethoscope by the woman's chest and listened. After performing a quick examination, he moved to the next person. As before, he checked the male's signs and general condition. Upon completion of the task, he spoke softly to the body. "It looks like the two of you have a good chance." Shaking his head, he continued, "I don't know how, but you'll probably live."

Though repulsed, he knelt by the comatose derelict. He refused to use either his instruments or his hands, but observed the untidy body. *Poor color, faint and erratic respiration, probably malnutrition, filthy, alcohol.* Whispering softly, he said, "One less bum and one less burden to the world and our welfare system."

Standing he surmised, *Two out of three. That isn't a bad percentage.* His thoughts were interrupted by Tara's approach.

"I thought you wanted nothing to do with the bodies," she challenged.

"I don't" he said, "I was just looking for my wallet."

"Around here?"

"Yes and every place else."

"What do you think?" she questioned.

"The two bodies are—" he stopped. "I mean it's got to be around here somewhere."

"Maybe one of them took it?" she stated.

"Don't be so damn stupid. They're in no condition to do anything."

"How do you know for sure? Have you examined them?"

"No," he clearly stated. "Any fool can tell the bum is probably going to die."

"What about the other two?"

"Their chances are good because—" he stopped and then said, "they appear to be in better shape."

"Professional opinion?"

"Not at all. Simply a layman's observation."

"I see."

"Don't get so sarcastic, young lady. I don't have to take any of your crap."

"I apologize. It wasn't meant to be sarcastic; I was just curious."

"I'm afraid I can't add anything to either increase or decrease your current knowledge." Gazing at the huge clock, he said, "I've got to be going. See you at the next meal."

Kneeling at the derelict's side, Tara gently wiped some dirt from his cheek, smoothed his clothing as best she could, and felt for a pulse. *Fight, damn it! Fight and show him you've got a chance.* Nothing stirred as she maintained a short vigil near the three bodies. Though the other two seemed more stable, she concentrated on the vagrant. Finally she stood up among the bodies.

"Any luck?" Jeffery asked.

"Luck?" responded Tara.

"Did you have any luck speaking to them?"

"No. They're still sleeping."

"Why do you insist on trying to help them so much?" he asked.

"Wouldn't you want someone to help *you* if you were still sleeping?" she countered.

"Do you really think you can help?"

"I can at least try."

"With no background in medicine?" he said.

"I can only try! That's more than anyone else is doing."

Nodding, Jeffery commented, "I agree. Some of those best qualified don't do a thing."

"I wonder why all of us are here," Tara mused.

"A damn good question, but unfortunately no answer."

"I know. I've tried to find one but nothing makes any sense."

Jeffery nodded in agreement. "We have nothing in common and yet, we're all in the same locked room. There is no common denominator."

"Why did *we* wake up and not them?" Tara asked.

"Another question and no answer," the politician continued.

"Too many questions!" she pleaded, "What can we do? It's so frustrating!"

Jeffery answered in a gloomy tone, "Nothing, but wait and see what happens."

Touching a lock of the derelict's hair, she said, "He looks so helpless and pathetic."

"Him? I'd say he looks pitiful and worthless."

Gazing at the other two bodies, he said, "It's *them* I worry about. Even if he does awaken, what good could he do?"

"I don't know," Tara said. "I just don't know."

"If you're going to continue your regular talks with their bodies, I suggest you spend your time on the other two."

Tara excused herself and walked to the huge supply room. There she selected her next meal. Jeffery gazed at the derelict and shook his head, *How did you ever get to this room? You're nothing but cheap, black trash!*

FIFTY

James called for attention and asked, "Does anyone play chess?"

"I play chest!" Todd volunteered. Looking at Iris, he added, "I'd like to play some right now."

"Please be polite," Father McShane requested.

"I found a chess set on the shelf and want to have a game with somebody."

"I'll play you." All eyes turned to Joanne.

"*You* want to play *me*?" James inquired.

"Yes. What's wrong with that?"

Stammering, he said, "I never expected you to..."

"To what?" she demanded.

"Nothing," he responded.

"I only thought—"

"Do you want to play me or not?"

"Play her!" Todd shouted. "Show them what we can do."

"Yes, play her," Sandra added. "I would like to see it myself."

"Me, too!" Phyllis stated. "It might prove interesting."

"Now just wait a minute!" James shouted. "No one can force me into anything."

"Are you chicken?" Phyllis asked.

"Doc ain't afraid of anything," Todd stated. "Just ask him!"

"All right. I'll play you one game."

"Right on!" Iris responded enthusiastically.

"I'll play her as long as no one else is there."

"That is not fair!" Sandra said. "I want to see the game."

"That's my rule. Take it or leave it."

Joanne answered calmly, "You're on."

"Does anyone else play?" James asked. Getting no response, he inquired, "Does anyone want to learn the game?"

"Boring!" Michael immediately replied.

"Too slow," Todd said. "Anyone want to play football?"

James and Joanne moved to an isolated corner of the room. The egotistic physician opened the game board and stated, "Which hand?"

Joanne and said, "The right."

Opening his hand, he disclosed a white pawn. Each set up their individual pieces. James examined the board and then impatiently stated, "Your bishop and knight are incorrect. Move them so we can get started."

"Sorry," Joanne said. "I haven't played in quite some time."

"Are you sure you ever played at all?" James added.

"Yes. I used to play every night with my father."

"That's nice." Satisfied the board was correctly set up, he requested that she start the game.

Joanne moved her king's pawn two squares ahead. James quickly countered. The game progressed rapidly, and within the hour Joanne easily checkmated the physician's king. "Damn!" he cursed. "I demand a rematch!"

"No problem."

The second game terminated in less time with Joanne once again victorious. James angrily pushed the pieces aside and stared at the actress. "Where did you *ever* learn to play like that?"

"I told you I used to play with my father."

"Your father must have been a good player," he stated.

"I'd say better than good; he was excellent."

"How can you say that?" James said. "There are many good players out there."

"He was a grandmaster."

"I've played for years. I don't ever recall a grandmaster named Hauser."

Joanne explained, "Hauser is my stage name; Mogell is my maiden name."

"Bruce Mogell was your father?"

"Yes."

"He was the greatest chess player of all time."

"I told you he was excellent."

James meekly inquired, "Why didn't you tell me?"

"You didn't ask."

"I can't believe it. Bruce Mogell's daughter."

Joanne said, "I'd better join the others."

"Certainly." Still somewhat dazed, he said weakly, "Thank you for the game."

"No problem. Practice a little more and then maybe we can play again."

Joanne walked to Sandra's side. "So how did it go?"

"Just as planned."

"How did he take it?"

Chuckling, Joanne responded, "Just as we expected."

"Did you purposely mix up your pieces?"

"Yes."

"What did he do?"

"Got extremely impatient."

"And then?" Sandra asked.

"I destroyed him."

"I can't believe it," Sandra continued, "That'll teach the pompous ass a thing or two."

Smiling Joanne added, "There's more!"

"What else?"

"I told him my father was Bruce Mogell."

"Who is that?"

"A famous grandmaster chess player."

Sandra looked at the woman. "Was he really your father?"

"Of course not. I just made it up."

"How did you ever hear the name?" Sandra inquired.

"My second husband loved the game and told me all about him."

"Who taught you to play so well?"

Joanne answered, "Several people taught me. Over the years, I just got better."

"You must be pretty good to beat James."

"I won by my skill and some help."

"What kind of help?" Sandra asked.

"I moved pieces when he wasn't looking."

"And he never caught on?"

"Nope. I just let him talk; he never noticed a single switch."

"Why did you do it?"

"I didn't want to lose. He's such a loudmouth; he'd never let me live it down."

"So you cheated yourself to a victory?"

"I'd rather refer to it as a strategic decision."

"I don't think I'd ever play you in cards for money."

"A good conclusion; I know plenty of good ways of cheating and fixing the deck."

"Where did you learn that stuff?" Sandra asked, amused yet curious.

"Experience and skill." Giggling, Joanne added, "I also play a mean game of strip poker."

"You're incorrigible!"

"No I'm not; I'm thirsty. How about some tea?"

The two walked slowly to the kitchen area. There they were met by Iris. Within minutes, Joanne was retelling the chess story to the younger woman. "I'm sorry you did that to him," Iris said.

"Why?"

Giggling, Iris conceded, "Because I wish I had thought of it first." Staring at him across the room, she added, "He really deserves everything he got."

Joanne smiled as James practiced the game by himself. "Go to it, Doc, practice makes perfect!"

FIFTY-ONE

Franklyn scraped a small sample of wallpaper from the wall and examined it closely under his microscope. Collecting his data, he moved to another section of wall and repeated his analysis. His thoughts were broken by Father McShane's presence. "Find anything?" the priest asked.

"Nothing abnormal. The internal structure of everything I've tested has exhibited normal characteristics. I'm attempting to uncover a clue; anything that would help us solve this mystery."

"Perhaps you won't find anything at all."

"Father, there's always an answer, it's just a matter of locating it."

"Sounds very optimistic."

"Optimism has nothing to do with it. I am a scientist and work solely with scientific methodology. This room contains the answers I seek, I just have to untangle the mystery."

"What if you can't?"

"That's my role as a scientist; I will resolve our dilemma."

"What about the doors?"

"Nothing unnatural," Franklyn continued. "The frames and

doors are composed of steel."

"Can they be forcefully opened?"

"Not unless you have a cannon! They're at least several inches thick and solidly constructed."

"What about the walls themselves?" inquired the priest.

"Equally as solid."

Scanning the room, Father McShane commented, "It doesn't look too good for us?"

"Think positive, Father, and don't lose faith. I've faced many difficult situations in the past."

"But have you always solved them?"

"Absolutely. There's nothing I can't solve once I've uncovered the facts."

"I hope you're right. This place is starting to get on my nerves."

"I can understand your feelings. Just have a little patience and I'll get us out of here eventually."

"Is that a promise?" asked the priest.

"You have my word on it."

Their conversation was interrupted by Sandra's approach. "So how's it going?" she inquired.

"No luck so far," Franklyn responded.

Father McShane excused himself as Sandra asked, "I was wondering about the air ventilation system."

"So was I! There isn't any."

"How can that be?" she inquired.

"Your guess is as good as mine. I've looked everywhere for a vent or outlet; nothing exists."

"Where does the fresh air come from?"

Franklyn said, "There must be an exchange of air; otherwise, we would have all died from carbon dioxide poisoning."

"What about the walls or ceiling?"

"I've examined the walls and found they're completely solid. I can't get up to the ceiling, but so far I haven't seen anything that looks like a vent or air exchanger."

"Any guess as to how it's done?"

"I do not guess at anything; I use facts to discover the truth."

"Very objective, scientific, and unbiased."

"Exactly!" Franklyn agreed. "That's how science works."

"Go, wondrous creature! Mount where science guides—" Sandra began.

Grinning, Franklyn asked, "Who said that? Shakespeare?"

"Pope." Sandra answered and then added, "Go, teach Eternal Wisdom now to rule—Then drop into thyself, and be a fool!"

"I'm very impressed, Dr. Golden, but it still doesn't help us out of here."

Turning serious, she asked, "What do you really think about this room?"

"I'm not sure, but for some reason, we're being kept alive. That's all I know."

"Why and by whom?"

Shrugging his shoulders, Franklyn picked up his instruments and headed toward the supply room. "I'm going to check out some of the food. Care to join me?"

"No thanks, I'd rather do some deductive thinking. Perhaps I can discover the real answer."

"Philosophers, you're all the same," he said in a snickering tone.

"At least we're not myopic in our thinking."

"Back to the Dark Ages!" he chided. "Welcome to the age of irrational logic!" Before she could defend her rationalizations, he exited the room.

Mumbling to herself, Sandra said, "Typical scientific imbecile! Some day, he will learn the meaning of logical thinking."

FIFTY-TWO

Todd watched Jeffery as he exited the shower. "What took you so goddamn long? I'm tired of waiting."

"I must take my time," Jeffery stated in a defensive tone.

"Why? Are you really dirty?" Todd jeered.

"No. I take longer than most."

"Why?"

"Personal reasons."

Pushing harder for an answer, Todd questioned, "Personal reasons? Do you jerk off in there?"

"I find that remark in rather poor taste."

"So what's the big secret?"

"If you must know, I have an artificial leg and have to be extremely careful with my stump."

"Are you a tree or something? Where is the stump?"

"I don't find your jokes the least amusing." Walking away, Jeffery mumbled several obscenities under his breath.

"Artificial leg! What next?" Todd took a quick shower and joined the others for their next meal.

Noticing Jeffery was unusually quiet, Michael inquired, "Are you okay?"

Without looking, he responded with a thick accent, "I am fine!"

"That doesn't sound very convincing to me," Father McShane said. "Are you ill?"

"Please leave me alone. I'm well."

Todd shouted from across the table, "Tell them about your stump!"

Jeffery stared at his food. Father McShane touched the Frenchman's arm gently and asked, "I'm worried. Are you okay?"

He responded meekly, "I am fine. Please, Father, I just want to—"

Once more Todd yelled, "Show us your leg!"

"What's he screaming about?" Phyllis asked.

Jeffery stood, grabbed a knife, and glared at the huge man. "Shut your goddamn mouth, you big jackass!"

Todd merely grinned and continued his verbal onslaught. "Come on, show us your leg!"

Jeffery lost his temper and slammed the knife into the wooden surface. Instead of verbally returning Todd's assault, he walked away from the table.

Franklyn was the first to speak. "What was *that* all about?"

Todd answered, "I was just having some fun."

"I don't get it," Father McShane said.

"Why was Jeffery so upset?"

Todd laughed, "He's got a wooden leg."

"The poor dear!" Phyllis said.

"I don't see *any* humor in it," Sandra said.

"I think, in fact, it was a rather sick joke, Todd."

"Me too!" Iris commented.

Looking at Todd, Tara spoke, "I think you should apologize to Jeffery."

"I agree," Father McShane said. "Your remarks were extremely insensitive."

"I ain't apologizing! It was just a joke."

"Somehow none of us finds it funny," Joanne said.

James added, "Handicapped persons are not to be laughed at, but revered for their bravery."

Getting more angry, Todd stood. "I said before, it was nothing but a joke."

"Some joke!" Michael said.

Turning to the musician, Todd sneered, "Up yours!" The football player walked toward his sofa. "I ain't apologizing to anyone; especially a crippled Frenchie!"

"Someone better check on Jeffery," Tara said.

Sandra spoke first, "I'll do it."

"I'd like to join you," the priest added.

"Glad to have you. I think I will need all the help I can get."

They joined Jeffery as he sat quietly on his sofa. "Are you okay?" Father McShane asked.

Sandra touched his arm. "Please, Jeffery, do not let him get to you."

"He was just teasing; don't play into his hands," Father McShane advised.

Jeffery took a deep breath, "I'm sorry I lost my temper."

"I can certainly understand your reaction. I would have reacted in the same fashion," Sandra said.

"I also would have done the same," Father McShane added. "Your actions were entirely justified considering the circumstances."

"That's not the point, I must learn to control my temper."

"Please don't be so hard on yourself," Father McShane said. "It could be a lot worse."

Jeffery countered, "Oh yeah? You try living with a piece of wood and plastic; it ain't a picnic."

"I can well imagine," Sandra said sympathetically.

"It must be very trying at times," Father McShane added.

"Especially when an imbecile makes it even more difficult."

"What can we say to ease your pain?" the priest asked.

"Nothing," Jeffery said. "I'll be just fine as long as you keep that idiot away from me."

"We can try, but the room's limited."

"Father, I don't care how it's done, just keep him away from me."

Father McShane rose to leave, "I want to speak to Todd."

Once she and Jeffery were alone, Sandra stated, "Todd's a total ass! Just tolerate his outburst until we get out of here. It will be better for everyone without the added friction."

Looking at Sandra's face, Jeffery replied, "I will try for your sake, but keep him away from me or else I may forget my agreement."

"Thank you." Sandra then inquired, "May I ask you a personal question?"

"Certainly."

"Did you lose your leg in a war?"

Chuckling, Jeffery responded, "I'm afraid to burst your bubble."

"You need not tell me anything."

"As long as you promise to keep it a secret, I'll tell."

"You have my word on it."

"My leg was cut off by a surgeon."

"Was it diseased?"

"Neither. He did it intentionally."

"Intentionally! Did they hang him for doing it?"

"No."

"How could that be?" Sandra questioned.

"It's a long, complex story, but in essence, he did it out of revenge."

"Revenge?"

"Yes, he believed I was having an affair with his wife."

"That's horrendous! Did you sue him?"

"No. I just waited until my hospitalization was over and then moved to another city."

"I am afraid I do not understand."

"It's quite simple: I was his patient and he sent me to the hospital under false pretenses. There, under the medical veil, he arranged to have my leg amputated."

"I can't believe it."

"It's all true and to make matters worse, his wife wasn't worth the cost."

"You mean—"

"Yes, she was my lover."

Shaking her head, Sandra replied, "I cannot believe it."

"It's the truth. It was the only time I managed to get caught." Patting his wooden leg, he said, "And there were many, many others."

"I think I should get back to Tara." Slightly upset over his story, Sandra added, "Please try to forget this Todd incident."

"I will as long as he stays away from me, or else I'll kill him."

FIFTY-THREE

"Have you noticed anything different about my hair?" Phyllis asked.

"Not really," Tara answered. "Do you want me to cut it again?"

"No." Slightly aggravated, the older woman pushed for an answer. "Look closer this time."

"I don't see a thing."

"It's my hair. It's changing colors."

Laughing, Tara tactfully answered, "We all get a little gray after a while."

"It's not the gray I'm talking about. My hair is turning red."

Tara examined the hair. "You're right! It's got a red tint to it."

"That's what I'm talking about. My hair is turning red."

"Did you use coloring of some type?"

"No. It's happening by itself."

"Maybe your shampoo has a coloring agent in it."

"I checked twice. Nothing in there resembles a coloring of any type."

"Does red hair run in your family?" Tara inquired.

"No."

161

Looking closer, the younger woman said, "It's definitely turning red."

"Oh no, my husband hates redheads!"

"Maybe it's the lights…."

"Then why isn't everyone else having the same problem?"

"I see your point. So what's the answer?"

"I don't have the faintest idea, do you?"

"None."

"What should I do?"

"Just let it grow naturally and I'll color your hair once we get out."

Phyllis added, "Before my husband sees me?"

"Certainly," Tara promised.

"God," Phyllis cursed. "Of all colors, red! I hate it the most!"

"It could have been a lot worse," Tara stated.

"You're right. I could be back home with red hair." Phyllis shook her head, "I'm certainly blessed with lots of luck!"

FIFTY-FOUR

Michael approached Sandra. "Can I talk to you?"

"Have a seat," she said.

"Thanks. I've got to ask you something."

"It's not going to get me upset or mad, is it?"

"No way!" the musician assured her. "I want to write a book and need some advice."

"Why me?"

"Because I heard you did some writing."

"That's true. What is the topic of your proposed book?" she inquired.

"I want to write about my life and music."

"An autobiography?"

Confused, he responded, "No. I want to write about me."

Instead of making the correction, she asked, "Why?"

"Why what?"

"Why would a publisher want to buy your book? What makes it special?"

"Because I lead a cool life."

"So do many others," she responded gently.

163

Getting angry, he asked, "Are you busting my chops or what?"

"No," Sandra stated. "I was just curious. Publishers do not want to print anything that will not produce revenue."

"My book will make money for them."

"How can you be so sure?"

"Just trust me. It'll be good."

"Good is not enough; it must have popular appeal for the masses."

"It will!" Michael said in a positive tone.

Changing the subject, she asked, "What can I do for you?"

"I told you already; I need some advice."

"What kind?"

"Give me the name of your publisher or someone who'll publish my book."

"My publisher handles only college texts."

"Give me his name; I want to speak to him."

"It's a her! And she probably will not speak to you. She's very busy."

"I'll tell her you sent me." Chuckling, he said, "I bet she'll talk to me then."

"I prefer my name is not used."

"Why not? Are you afraid she'll like my book better?"

Sandra was about to argue, but elected to play along with Michael's request. "I'll give you her name and number when we get out of here."

"No way! Give it to me right now! Once we're out of here, you won't give me a second thought."

Taking a piece of paper, she wrote out a name and phone number and handed it to him.

"Sharon Louis," Michael said.

"That is her name, and I changed my mind; go ahead and mention me as an intro."

"I will, and thanks." As he walked away, she laughed to herself,

Jerk! Wait till you call that number. Sharon Louis! How did I ever come up with such a stupid name?

FIFTY-FIVE

Everyone stopped talking when Franklyn made his announcement. "I think I might have located a possible exit."

"Thank God!" Father McShane cried loudly.

Once the pandemonium subsided, Franklyn continued, "I've been doing a careful analysis of the walls and after a meticulous examination I've discovered a section that—"

"For God's sake!" Todd demanded. "Cut the crap and tell us where it is!"

"Please," pleaded Phyllis. "Get me out of here!"

"Franklyn," Father McShane said. "Please show us the section."

Leading the small group through the maze of furniture, Franklyn stopped in front of a large picture. "Here."

"Where?" Michael shouted. "What part of the wall?"

"Come on, you dumb ass!" Todd screamed. "Show me!"

Franklyn placed his hand on a section of wall that stood four feet off the floor. "If you tap this part, you'll notice a distinct difference in texture and sound."

Todd pounded in several areas. "He's right! This part *is* different."

"Please hurry!" Phyllis cried out. "My husband is waiting!"

"How do we know it's the way out?" Sandra asked.

"You're always a pessimist!" Joanne said. "Try to think positively for once in your life."

"Yeah!" Michael added. "I can feel it! We're going home!"

"What do we do now?" Father McShane inquired.

"I don't know about you, but I'm going to get it open somehow," Todd said. "Nothing is going to stop me now!"

Franklyn did not say a word, but watched as Todd, Michael, and James attempted to create an opening in the wall. The physician picked with his knife, while the other two tried to shatter the obstruction with nearby furniture.

"Stop a minute!" James eagerly shouted. "I think I see something." Straining, he peeked through a small hole created by their effort.

"What do you see?" Michael asked.

"Come on!" Todd asked. "Do you see the outside?"

"I see darkness," James said. "It seems to be a tunnel."

"A tunnel?" Phyllis asked. "What about a way out?"

"Everything is too dark."

The two men continued their assault on the wall. After a long time, a three-foot portal was created. Again, James peered into the darkness. "It seems we've found a tunnel."

"Can you see a way out?" Father McShane asked.

"It's too dark to see anything. I think someone should go in there and find out where it leads," James suggested.

"Who?" Father McShane asked.

"Since the opening is so small, I think one of the women should go," Jeffrey stated.

"I'm not going anywhere until I know it's safe," Phyllis said adamantly.

"We have no idea what's in there. For all we know it might be some sort of trap," Sandra commented.

"Please, Sandra. Let's not get melodramatic," James said. "It appears safe enough."

"What do *you* know about safety, Doctor?" Joanne commented.

"Don't be so sarcastic," Father McShane said.

"Let's all try to keep level-headed until we're definitely out of here!" Iris pleaded. "Bickering will not get us anywhere."

"I'd go," Todd offered, "But I'd never fit."

No one spoke for a long time. Finally Tara said, "I guess it'll have to be me, I'm the smallest." The young woman walked to the wall. Todd lifted her easily until she secured herself in the opening.

"Keep talking to us so we can monitor your position," Franklyn suggested.

"I will," she assured them as she crawled into the darkness.

"Are you okay?" Father McShane shouted.

"Yes, but it's really eerie in here."

"Did you find anything yet?" James inquired.

"No."

"Please, God," Phyllis whispered, "let her find a way out."

"Are you okay, Tara?" Getting no response, Franklyn yelled, "Are you okay?"

"Yes. I'm..." a faint voice called back.

"Tara!" Sandra shouted.

Moments later, Tara answered, "I can't go any farther."

"Did you find a way out?" Phyllis screamed desperately.

"Please, Phyllis," Father McShane said. "Let her talk."

"Tara! Is there an exit?" Franklyn shouted.

No response could be heard. Again Franklyn shouted his question, but as before, the young woman did not answer. "Maybe she's dead!" Phyllis cried.

"For God's sake, keep her quiet!" Franklyn said. "I'm trying to listen."

Before anyone could react to his request, Tara stuck her head out of the opening. "Are you okay?" the priest asked.

"Yes."

"Did you locate an exit?" Joanne inquired.

Shaking her head, Tara answered dejectedly, "There's nothing at all. Only a tunnel."

"Leading nowhere?" Franklyn asked.

"When I got to the end, everything was solid. There was no way out."

"Did you look carefully?" James questioned.

"I even tried the ceiling; nothing budged."

"Now what am I going to do?" Phyllis moaned.

Holding a small box, Tara announced, "I did find this at the end."

"Let me see it!" Franklyn demanded.

Once she was down on the floor, Tara handed the box to Franklyn. Immediately, he tore open the wrappings. All eyes stared as he removed the contents. "What the heck?" he said as he showed everyone the three keys."

"Maybe they'll open the last door," Sandra suggested.

"That's the way out; I can feel it!" Iris shouted.

The entire group rushed to the unopened door and watched as Franklyn inserted one key. Finding it did not work, he tried the other two. None opened the door. "Now what?" Father McShane moaned.

"The next time you get me excited, just make sure it's the real thing," Todd said angrily.

"Yeah, I hate this stuff. It psyches me up too much," Michael added.

Franklyn moved to the other doors and soon discovered each key unlocked them. Shaking his head, he spoke to Father McShane, "The key for the last door must be around here somewhere."

"But where?" Sandra asked.

"That's a good question; I'll try to locate it as soon as possible."

"Any ideas?" James inquired.

"Perhaps in another tunnel. I'll just keep searching until I find it."

Everyone dispersed as Franklyn resumed his inspection. Tara and Sandra spoke afterward. "What was it like in there?" asked Sandra.

"Just dark."

"Were you nervous?"

"Of course I was. I was scared to death."

"I am glad you made it back."

Touching her friend's hand, Tara replied, "Thank you for your concern."

FIFTY-SIX

The clock rang eleven times. Todd strolled up to Michael who asked, "What do *you* want?"

Without changing his expression, Todd spoke, "I got a question for you."

"Is it about my sex life?"

"Yes and no," Todd responded.

Instead of arguing, Michael merely stated, "Fire away; I'm all ears."

"I want to know if a rocker's life is really exciting?"

Instead of answering, Michael asked, "I hear a jock's life is great. How about telling me some dirt?"

Appeasing Michael, Todd sat on the floor, "It's better than great, it's terrific."

"Are cheerleaders as good as I hear?"

"They're the best! Most of them will do anything just to date a star."

"The same with groupies."

"That's what I heard; my friend is a rock star and the stories he tells me shock the pants right off my butt."

"Who's your friend? Maybe I know him."

"Tom Costerible."

"No crap! He's one of the best bass players in the business."

"He's my best friend. We go back many years."

"If you know Tom, then why are you asking me about a rocker's life?" Michael inquired.

"I just want to see if he's full of bull."

"Probably not. A star like that can get just about anyone he wants."

"That's what he said too!"

"I ain't as big, and I get more than enough."

"He's says girls follow him from show to show and beg for his body."

"It's the truth! I've got a few that follow me around too!"

Michael then asked, "What about you, stud?"

"Girls are around for us players too. In fact, the coaches arrange them during the season."

"What about the married players?"

Todd laughed. "They're the worst."

"And you?"

"I'll lay anything in a skirt."

"You sound like a horny old toad to me," commented Michael.

"I get my share and then some," the huge man boasted.

"It sounds as if we both get more than we can handle."

"I can handle anything they give."

"What about here?" Michael asked.

"It's none of your goddamn business."

"Getting any from Phyllis?"

"Up your ass. That old bag is a waste. I just need her for her husband. I'd puke before I'd sleep with her."

"If you could shack up with anyone here, who would you pick?"

"No contest! I'd take Joanne or Tara."

"Tara?" Michael inquired. "Why her?"

"I like those young innocent things."

"I see what you mean. She certainly acts like a virgin."

"Probably never touched a man." Laughing, he added, "Probably have a heart attack."

"That Joanne psyches me out. Her body is great."

"Forget her, she only beds with the big shots."

"But they're not here now...."

"That's true and the longer we're here, the better looking we'll get."

"Keep dreaming, rocker," Todd chuckled. "You'll never get into her pants."

Leaning back on his sofa, Michael said, "We'll just see about that."

Instead of arguing, Todd added, "If you do, I want seconds."

"For now, big guy, just take some cold showers."

"You too!"

"I already do," Michael responded. "They work beautifully on my urges."

"I didn't think you do such things."

Michael paused momentarily and then decided to toy with the larger man. "I could do much better if I had company."

"I don't think any of the girls would go with you."

Smiling, he continued to kid Todd, "I wasn't thinking of girls."

Todd stared at Michael, "I knew you where a fag; I just knew it!"

"I'd say I'm more bisexual."

"A goddamn queer." Leering at him, Todd continued, "Just stay away from me."

"I thought many football players were gay."

"Up your ass. We're real men, not pussies like you guys."

"Anyhow, if you change your mind, just let me know."

Todd ignored Michael's taunting, walking away in disgust.

The rocker silently laughed. *You dumb fool. I can't believe you're so gullible.*

FIFTY-SEVEN

Iris pulled Sandra aside. "I want to try my powers today."

Not wanting to discredit her friend, Sandra agreed, "I think it's a wonderful idea. Do you think you are prepared?"

"Yes. I'm always ready."

"Let's try not to alert the others."

The two women approached the unconscious bodies. Sandra checked frequently to be sure they were not being watched. Arriving at the far end of the room, Sandra inquired, "Which one are you going to work on?"

"I'm not sure; I never had three at once."

Looking at the bodies, Sandra asked, "How about her?"

"Why her? Any reason?" Iris questioned.

"Because she's a woman!"

Iris knelt beside the comatose body and gently placed her hands over the woman's head. Softly, she uttered several phases. Sandra, in the meantime, watched and waited. Minutes passed and still Iris continued her chant.

Sandra was quickly becoming impatient and squirmed slightly. Without looking upward, Iris urged her to remain silent. Moments later, the flickering of an eyelid caught their attention. Iris increased her cadence and velocity as her voice reverberated. Soon others joined to watch the proceedings.

Placing her hands on the woman's chest, Iris rocked slowly. Suddenly the woman's eyes opened and stared upward. "You did it!" Sandra shouted.

"Please be quiet and let me finish," Iris stated.

By the time everyone was present, Iris had the woman sitting. She asked, "Where am I and who are you?"

"It's rather involved," Father McShane said. "There's plenty of time to tell you."

"Yes," Michael added, "We've got all the time in the world."

"What is your name?" Sandra inquired.

"Alice Serrano."

"Where are you from?" James asked.

"Mexico City."

Tara whispered to Phyllis, "Everyone remembers but me."

"Mexico?" Todd questioned. "You don't look like a Mexican."

"I was born in Sweden. I've lived there for the past twenty-four years."

"Are you with an industry?" Jeffery asked.

"No. I'm a federal judge."

"A judge?" James asked. "But you're a woman!"

"I was the first female judge ever appointed in all of Mexico."

Alice looked closely at the group. "I don't mind the questions, but when will I get a chance to cross-examine you?"

"You are correct," Father McShane said. "We're being very rude. We'll talk later."

Alice joined Joanne and Tara while Iris and Sandra remained behind. "Are you going to try it again?" Sandra asked.

"Maybe later. Right now, I'm beat!"

"I apologize," Sandra began.

"For what?" Iris questioned.

"For doubting you."

"That's okay. I'm used to it."

"I just cannot get over it. The mind is certainly powerful."

"We're just learning to tap its true energy. Many of my colleagues are more gifted and talented."

"I'd love to see them work. It must be fascinating."

"Once we're out of here, we'll give them a call," Iris promised. "I'm sure they'd love to have you observe."

"I just can't get over it."

"Don't be too shocked yet. I still have some more surprises left."

FIFTY-EIGHT

Joanne whispered to Todd, "Do you notice anything different around here?"

"Yeah. There's another live one!"

"Please be serious."

"Nothing is ever different around here. It's always the same old crap. I really wish something *was* different."

"Are you sure you don't see anything different?"

Todd asked, "What are you driving at?"

Pointing to a nearby sofa, she said, "Look at it carefully."

The huge man stared, "What am I supposed to see?"

"For God's sake, don't you see?"

"I don't see anything different! Just tell me what it is."

"The legs are different."

"The legs?"

"Yes." Attempting to remain calm, Joanne took a deep breath and then added, "There have always been six legs on that sofa." Pointing, she continued, "Now there's only four."

Todd counted the legs and said, "There *are* four!"

"But it always had six legs!"

177

"I'll have to take your word on it; I really never paid any attention to those things."

"Where did they go?"

"Maybe someone took them."

"Why? Who would take two sofa legs?"

"Beats me."

"Where could they have gone?"

"Maybe there were only four, and your memory is going."

"My memory is perfect. I'm telling you two legs are missing."

"What am *I* supposed to do about it?"

"Find out where they are!" she demanded.

"I'm not wasting my time over two dumb wooden legs....I do know where *one* is for sure."

"Where?"

Laughing loudly, he said, "Jeffery has one."

"Can't you ever be serious? This is important."

"The only thing important to me is surviving this mess and getting back to my football."

"I can see it was a big mistake to tell you in the first place."

"Not really."

"And why not?" she asked.

"Who else would have been dumb enough to listen to your stupidity?"

Trying to control her temper, she stated, "I think I'd better be getting back to Sandra. At least I can carry on an intellectual conversation with her."

"Go to it, babe, and while you're at it, ask her about your missing wooden legs." Once she left, Todd stared at the sofa. *Six legs...what kind of jerk does she think I am?*

FIFTY-NINE

"How do you think she did it, Father?" James inquired.

"Probably just plain luck," the priest responded. "Iris was simply in the right place at the right time. What was Alice's exact status before waking up?"

"She appeared comatose," James responded.

"How can you be so sure? Did you personally examine her?"

"No. But her outward appearance seemed to support my theory."

"But you didn't personally examine her, did you?"

"No," James answered defensively. "You know how I feel about those things. Why is it so important to you?"

"I am a man of God. I have been trained to disclose anything contrary to God's laws."

"I see," James said. "What exactly are God's Laws?"

"Those detailed in the Bible and followed by my personal religion."

"Does that mean other religions are wrong?"

"In my eyes and that of God, the answer is yes."

"Don't you think that is rather narrow?"

"No. It's the only way."

"So Iris' accomplishment is a threat to you?"

"Exactly. She is a threat to every God-fearing Christian."

"So what are you going to do about her?"

"Right now, nothing, but before we leave this room, I'll have her back on course."

"*Your* course?" James asked.

"*God's* course!" Father McShane said loudly. "It is the only course to follow."

Smiling, James said, "Good luck, Father, I think you'll need all the luck you have. She's a tough old bird."

"I don't need any luck; God is on my side."

"What if she doesn't respond?"

"She will. No one can fight against the Almighty."

"How do you change someone who is so set in their ways?"

"James, I've been doing it for years. It's my role as a priest."

"To convert them to your side?"

"Precisely! My side is with God and is the only correct answer."

Shrugging his shoulders, James uttered, "I wish you success."

"I will succeed! She's no real challenge." The priest then asked, "By the way James, I was wondering something."

"What?"

"What religion are you?"

"I am a practicing atheist."

"Dear God. You're an atheist." Father McShane proceeded to cross himself. "How do you live like that?"

"I never thought anything about it. Actually, I live quite well."

"I guess I'll have to work on you also."

"Father, do us both a favor. Save your salvation crap for someone else. I'm perfectly happy the way I am."

Father McShane stated simply, "We can solve your problem later on, in the meantime however, Iris must be enlightened first."

"I agree, Father. We can't have any more of her voodoo around the masses. They may begin to believe."

"Yes. Iris must be converted quickly. I don't want anyone else contaminated by her superstitious thinking."

Smiling, James said, "If I can help, Father, just let me know."

Looking serious, Father McShane stated, "You need all the help you can get, my son. We must get you back on the proper course."

"Thank you, Father. I feel better already."

"You won't be so sarcastic when the truth is disclosed."

Walking away, James turned, "I'm perfectly content being an atheist. If you wish to continue our relationship, may I suggest you direct your energies to Iris and the others. They need your support, Father, but I don't."

"Everyone needs help, my son."

"I don't, Father. Remember, I am a physician!"

S I X T Y

Todd carried the oversized box and placed it at Alice's feet. "Here's your box."

"My what?" she asked.

"Your box," Father McShane said.

"Everyone gets one," Todd explained.

Alice looked at the box and started to unwrap its paper.

"Everyone opens their box in private," Father McShane said as he motioned to Todd to leave.

"That's certainly a stupid rule," she remarked.

"Regardless, that's the rule." The two men exited. Alice resumed opening the box. Reaching inside, she withdrew a gavel and walnut base. Smiling, she tested it several times and placed it at her side. "Wonderful!" she stated pulling something else out. "I can't believe it." Once the thirty journals were placed on the table, she began leafing through the pages. Shaking her head in disbelief, she read several of the shorter abstracts. Her thoughts were interrupted by Phyllis' appearance. "Have a seat, I was just looking through some journals."

"I'm not keeping you from anything important?"

"It can wait. I found these in my surprise box."

"That's nice. I hope you enjoy them."

"By the way, what did you get?"

Hesitating slightly, Phyllis stammered, "I got nothing very exciting."

"So what did you get? What's the big secret?"

"It's no secret and I'm certainly not defensive about it at all."

"So?"

"If you must know, I got several of my favorite books."

"That's lovely. I always enjoy reading."

"Me too!"

"What ones did you get?"

"There were quite a few; let me think for a moment." Pausing, Phyllis then said, "I got several novels by Stanley Alpert."

"I just love his works. Did you get *Gertrude and The Printed Page*?"

"I believe that was one of them."

"Good. I'd love to borrow it from you. I recently had an urge to read it again."

"I haven't got to it yet."

"No problem; I can wait. Besides, I've got plenty to read right here."

Phyllis stood. "I better get going."

"Did you want something?" Alice inquired.

"No. I just stopped by to be sociable."

"Why thank you and please come again."

"I will," Phyllis stated and quickly walked away. Instead of going to her sofa, she headed for the large bookcase and began examining the many titles.

"Looking for anything specific?" Sandra asked.

Startled, Phyllis responded, "Yes. I'm looking for *Gertrude and The Printed Page*."

"An excellent book. Read it several times myself."

"Is it here?"

"Yes and no."

"What does that mean?"

"Yes, it's in the room, but no, it's not available."

"Why?" Phyllis asked eagerly.

"Because someone is reading it right now."

"Dear God! Who?"

"Todd."

"Todd Warren?"

"Yes, I believe I saw it by his sofa a little while ago."

"Do we have any other books by Alpert?"

"None. That was the only one here."

"Damn."

"Can I suggest another one I feel is almost as good?"

"No!" Phyllis shouted. "I've got to have *that* one."

"Todd is one heck of a slow reader. It took Father McShane the longest time to get one back from him. I suggest you read another instead." Kidding, Sandra added, "You might die before he returns it."

"I've got to have that book right away."

"Then ask him for it. Maybe he will listen to you because he does not listen to anyone else."

"I think I will do it right now."

"I wish you luck."

Phyllis walked to Todd's section as the huge football player sprawled on the floor. Looking upward, he noticed her presence. "Hi, Phyllis, what brings you around?"

Sitting on a nearby chair, she whispered, "I want the book *Gertrude and The Printed Page.*"

"I'll give it to you when I'm done with it."

"I must have it right now."

"I'm halfway through it; I'll be done soon."

Almost pleading, Phyllis asked, "I must have it right now."

"I told you I'd bring it over when I'm done reading the damn thing."

"It's very important to me to have it now."

Sitting up, he said, "I'll give it to you when I'm done."

"I must have it right now. I'll do anything for it."

"Anything?"

Taking a deep breath, she responded resignedly, "Anything."

"Would you speak to your husband about adding me on his new team?"

"Yes. I'll speak to him as soon as we get out of here." Phyllis continued. "Can I now have the book?"

"I want a no-cut, long-term contract."

"I give you my word."

"With incentives."

"Yes, you'll get whatever you want in the contract."

"Good."

She reached forward, but he held the book out of reach. "There's one other small thing I want."

"For God's sake, what else?"

"Let's just say I could use a little relief."

"Relief from what?"

He said, "You can't be *that* stupid!"

She thought for a moment and then sneered at him. "Are you asking for sex?"

"Honey, I'm sick and tired of doing it myself."

"You're one sick cookie. I can't believe you would even ask such a thing."

"You're the one who wants the book so badly. I'm such a slow reader, it could take me forever to finish the damn thing."

Phyllis looked nervously at him, then across the room to Alice. "We can't have sex here; everyone will see what we're doing."

"Come over after the lights are out."

Taking a deep breath, she answered. "I'll be here, but can I take the book with me now?"

"Not until we're done."

"Why not?" she demanded.

"Insurance."

"I'll give you my word."

"Not good enough. When we're done, I'll give you the book."

"How do I know you'll give it to me then?"

"You'll just have to take your chances."

A few minutes after the lights dimmed, Phyllis crawled quietly to Todd's sofa.

"Let's get this over with," she stated.

Whispering, Todd said, "Glad you came."

"Me too," Phyllis stated. "I'm thrilled to death."

Todd managed to open her blouse and began to play roughly with her breasts. She froze initially, but soon her body started to override her mind. Primal instincts prevailed as he tore wildly at her panties. He muffled her moans by kissing her passionately. By the time his huge organ entered her body, she was matching him stroke for stroke. "God!" she uttered. "You're tearing me apart."

"Love it, don't you?"

Glassy eyed and near convulsions, she responded, "Yes, damn it! I love it!" Breathing heavily, she added, "I can't believe it's so big."

After they reached their climax, she rested in his arms. "Do you think anyone heard us?"

Todd answered softly, "I doubt it."

"You sure are one hell of a stud."

Smiling, he answered, "I've been told that before."

Kissing his chest, she whispered, "I can sure believe it. It was really great."

"You're not so bad either."

"You mean for an old lady?"

"Honey, you're as good as the best of them."

"Why, thank you for the compliment. Now do I get the book?"

"Sure. I would have given it to you before if you asked nicely."

"Then why did you want sex from me?"

"Two reasons. First because I was horny as hell and secondly, insurance."

"Insurance? I don't get it."

"This way I *know* you'll speak to your husband."

"Are you blackmailing me?"

"Let's just call it insurance."

"You don't need anything like that, honey. After tonight, I want your buns around me all the time."

"You mean we can do it again?" Todd asked incredulous.

"This old lady will give you more than we bargained for, my big stud. Let's see if you can do it once more before I go back to my sofa."

SIXTY-ONE

Franklyn waited for everyone's attention. "Please! Can I have a moment of silence?"

"What now?" Michael laughed, "Not another tunnel!"

"As a matter of fact, I did discover another possible exit."

"How many is that?" Todd jested. "Number five?"

"I don't think that's fair!" Tara shouted. "At least, Franklyn's trying to get us out of here. What are *you* doing to help?"

Michael smirked, "Are you going to crawl in another hole for him?"

"Yes, I will!" Tara retorted. "I'll do anything to get out of here."

"I agree with you," Sandra stated.

"Me too!" Iris responded.

"You don't have to get so hyped up over it. I was only joking." Michael quickly added.

Todd stared at Franklyn. "Okay, where is it this time?"

Franklyn led the group to another section of wall and again tapped against the wooden base. Excitedly he shouted, "It's hollow right *here!*"

"Let's get it over with, so I can get back to my music," Michael said sarcastically.

Father McShane touched Michael's arm and pleaded, "Have patience, my son; some day Franklyn will find an exit."

"Will you put it in writing?" Michael inquired.

"Please don't be so nasty," Tara admonished.

"For you, my little white dove, anything in the world," Michael responded.

Without countering, Tara entered the newly opened hole and crawled into the darkness. Each person stared at the portal with subdued anticipation. Minutes later the young woman returned. Phyllis was the first to speak. "Well?"

"Nothing." Sighing, she added, "Nothing at all."

"Are you positive?" Franklyn asked.

"It's a short tunnel and all the walls are very solid."

"I told you!" Todd shouted. "I'm sick and tired of all this crap. From now on, count me out."

"Me too!" Michael screamed. "I've got better things to do with my time."

Franklyn shook his head, "Why are there tunnels to nowhere throughout the room?"

"Perhaps they're a decoy?" Sandra conjectured.

"Could you explain that?" Tara inquired.

"Maybe the real exit is not through a tunnel or door, but elsewhere."

"But where?" Phyllis asked.

"Possibly anywhere. Maybe there's a secret exit under a rug?"

"That would be too logical," Franklyn stated.

"But so are tunnels. They're too easily discovered."

"So where does it leave us now?" Father McShane asked.

"Nowhere," Franklyn answered. "We still don't have a single objective clue."

"This is all a bunch of bull. I am going to play football," Todd muttered.

When he and Michael left, Franklyn, Tara, and Sandra

remained behind. "Did you see or feel anything?"

"Franklyn," Tara answered, "They're all the same."

"Sandra, maybe you're correct, the tunnels are not the answer."

"I'm afraid we'll still have to check them all out," Sandra countered. "Just suppose I'm wrong."

"This sounds very complicated to me," Tara added. "What are we going to do?"

"There's really no choice. We must check every new tunnel and also inspect the floor and all other structures," Franklyn concluded.

"You're right," Sandra stated. "We cannot leave any stone unturned."

Smiling, Tara said, "I'm always ready for another new tunnel adventure."

"You're hired," Franklyn assured her. "Meanwhile, Iris and I will lift some of the carpeting and check the floor."

They finalized their plans and departed to their individual sofas. Shortly thereafter, the great wall clock chimed eight rings and the lights suddenly darkened.

S I X T Y - T W O

Jeffery pulled Alice aside after their next meal. "I'd like to speak to you for a moment."

"Since I'm not going anywhere in particular at this point in time, fire away."

"It's rather personal." Looking around, he asked, "I hope you will honor my confidentiality."

"I'm not sitting on my bench, but I'll do my best."

Seeming apprehensive, he whispered, "How well do you know Felix Gomez?"

"I know several persons named Felix Gomez."

"I'm talking about the Minster of Agriculture."

"Oh," she stated. "*That* one. Yes, I know him."

"How well?" he asked.

"Quite well. We socialize frequently."

"Good."

Staring at Jeffery, she inquired, "Why are you asking me about Felix?"

"I've been trying to reach him for months. He's never available for my calls."

She replied, "That sounds like Felix. In fact, it sounds like the whole Mexican government."

"It's not so funny when we're talking about big money."

"Big money?"

"Yes. I'm speaking about billion-dollar contracts."

"Be more specific."

Jeffery surveyed their surroundings before continuing, "I have a particular friend who has been trying unsuccessfully to sell his products to the Mexican government for years. He approached me to act as his agent for the transaction."

"What kind of products?"

"Chemicals."

"What kind?"

"Those used in manufacturing and agriculture."

"I believe Felix does have the final word in those areas."

"That's why I've been trying to reach him."

"I see."

"Do you think you could help me in this matter?"

Looking him straight in the eye, she responded, "It all depends."

"It all depends on what?"

"It all depends on what it's worth to me."

Without blinking an eye, Jeffery answered, "Two percent of gross."

"Two percent! Is that all?"

"We're speaking of billions of dollars. This transaction alone will make you rich."

"My dear, I've been doing this type of thing for years, my usual percentage is four percent."

"But there are too many players already. At four percent, I won't have much left for myself."

"Take it or leave it. Those are my terms."

"Some choice."

"I'm afraid they're isn't any. By the way, did you include a five percent take for Felix."

"Yes. That I already expected."

"Felix and I have a Swiss bank account. We'd like our percentages wired directly over there."

"Of course. Everyone does business the same way."

"As soon as we get out of here, I'll make all the arrangements for the sale."

"But what about the introductions?"

"Not necessary. Consider the sale finalized."

"But don't the terms have to be worked out?" Jeffery inquired.

"Not at all. Just give me the details and everything will be enabled quickly."

"What about payment?" Jeffery continued.

"Upon delivery."

"I never heard of such a thing. How can you do it?"

"Just don't ask any questions. Your money will come directly from the Mexican government on the same day."

"Is this usual procedure?"

Laughing, Alice replied, "It's special for those who use our country's proper channels."

"Is this common for you to get involved?"

"I and others have been involved in such transactions in the past. We consider it a service to our country and to many outside vendors."

"It doesn't hurt your pocketbook either."

"Let's just say it helps compensate for the rather poor pay we receive as civil servants."

"Are you sure you can pull it off?"

"No doubt in my mind. Consider it done already."

"But how can you speak for Felix?"

"We're very close friends."

"Are you close enough?"

Smiling, Alice responded, "He's my husband."

"But then you're both taking a higher percentage together than

I make myself!"

"That's your problem, not ours."

Thinking a moment, Jeffery countered, "Suppose I go to someone else?"

"You can. Everyone in the government has their particular arrangement. Chemicals belong solely to Felix and me."

"I see."

"So, my dear Jeffery, those are my terms."

"I guess I have no other choice." Shaking her hand, he added, "Consider it a deal."

"I'll take care of everything when I return home."

"Good." Jeffery walked away to his oversized sofa. Grinning, he thought, *Dumb bitch! I would have given you much more. God, are these Mexicans stupid.* Mentally counting his portion, he considered, *Not a bad haul, Jeffery, not too bad at all.*

SIXTY-THREE

"I think we'd better do something about everyone's morale," Sandra observed.

"I agree, but what?"

"That's why I came to you, Father."

The priest quipped, "Since when am I an expert in such matters?"

"But you are a priest!"

"Sandra," Father McShane said, "I am only one man; what can I do?"

"I am not sure, but I know we had better come up with something fast."

"Why? What's the urgency?"

"Too much squabbling among the others. Just recently, Todd and Michael went at it again."

Shaking his head, Father McShane said, "I know, I saw the whole thing. It was terrible."

"That is exactly what I am getting at; we need a common objective to hold us together."

"I see what you mean. But what?"

"I thought you might come up with something."

"Why me?" The priest then added, "You are a college professor."

"My degree is in philosophy, not psychology."

"What about James? After all, he's a doctor."

"Too egotistical!"

Looking more concerned, Father McShane asked, "I understand the dilemma, but I can't come up with an answer."

"Just think and I am sure you will."

"What about asking Franklyn?"

"He is too involved in his research. Besides, everyone is still upset over his inability to locate an exit."

"What about—"

"Father, there is no one else but you."

Shaking his head, he relented, "I will think about it, but I can't give you any guarantees."

"Just try. Things are getting bad."

During their next communal meal, the priest asked for everyone's attention. "I have decided to hold a regular mass and invite everyone to attend."

"I ain't Catholic!" Todd objected.

"Me neither," Iris added.

"I think I used a poor choice of words," the priest said. "I'd like to hold an informal prayer meeting for those of you who desire to attend."

"What are we going to do?" Phyllis inquired.

"We shall pray for our release from this room."

"That'll do a lot of good," Todd said.

"It certainly can't hurt," Joanne asserted. "Nothing else seems to be working."

"It will be neutral, not slanted toward any one religion," the priest promised. "That way, everyone will feel comfortable."

"I don't want any part of that stuff," Michael said.

"Me neither!" Todd added.

"What about the rest of you?" the priest questioned.

"Let's try it," Jeffrey said.

"I agree," Tara chimed in. "Maybe it'll help."

Sandra watched as everyone voiced their opinion. In the end, the majority felt Father McShane's suggestion had merit.

Afterward, Sandra approached the priest. "An excellent idea."

"I hope it will work. Everyone seems so hostile."

"If anyone can do it, it will be you."

"What about those who elect not to attend?"

"There is nothing we can do about them."

"Maybe God will show them the light," the priest said hopefully.

Sandra laughed, "Please Father, remember we're doing this for psychological and sociological reasons."

"And for religious reasons also."

"Do not try to convert anyone, Father, or you will have more trouble than you can handle. Just be neutral and try to hold them together until we get out of here."

"Will you be attending?" the priest asked.

"What for?" Sandra laughed. "I do not need your verbal support; save that for the masses."

"But everyone could use a little religion now and then."

Getting angry, Sandra responded, "I am an atheist. I rely on nobody else."

"But—"

Sandra walked away. "Let's not ruin our relationship, Father, just concentrate on the others and leave me alone."

SIXTY-FOUR

Tara and Franklyn stood by the two remaining comatose bodies. "They're quite a contrast," Franklyn noted.

"In what way?"

"Just look at their appearance: One is magnificently attired while the other is dressed like a tramp."

The young girl looked at each and then said, "They *are* quite a contrast. I wonder why they are the last to awaken?"

"Perhaps luck?"

"Maybe," Tara stated.

"What are you getting at?"

"Nothing specific, but there are still too many unanswered questions." Kneeling at the vagrant's side, she said, "He's so out of place."

"I see your point," Franklyn concurred.

Touching the other man's meticulous suit, she said, "He must have a lot of money. These clothes cost a fortune."

As she touched his lapel, the man's eyes suddenly opened and he grasped her hand tightly. "What are you doing, young woman?"

Startled, Tara stammered, "I—"

The man took in his surroundings, "Where am I and who are you?"

Franklyn interjected, "Just calm down and we'll tell you all about it."

Struggling to his feet, the new man pointed to the sleeping vagrant and asked, "Who is that?"

"We don't know. Do you know him?"

"You've got to be kidding. Why would I know a bum?"

"This room is beautiful; where is it?"

Tara ran to summon the others while Franklyn assisted the newly awakened man. While walking to join the others, the man stated simply, "My name is Hugo S. Winters, III and this is one hell of a dream!"

SIXTY-FIVE

Hugo listened intently as Father McShane summarized the events leading up to their current status. His speech was only interrupted by three loud chimes from the great wall clock. Slowly shaking his head, Hugo absorbed every word as Sandra added further details to the Father's recollection of the past. Once everyone added their personal comments, the tall, stately man surmised, "It makes no sense at all."

"Agreed," James added. "But those are the facts."

"Tell us about yourself. Maybe it will add some insight to this room," Sandra said.

"I am the senior partner in Winters, Sayram, Parker, and Monroe."

"Sounds like one heck of a group," Michael commented in a mocking tone.

Without cracking a smile, Hugo responded, "We are the largest and most prestigious firm on the street."

"The street?" Father McShane asked. "What street?"

"Wall Street, of course!"

"Are you a stockbroker?" James inquired.

"No," Hugo said proudly, "My firm is the largest and best known advertising firm in the world."

"Advertising!" Tara commented.

"We handle most of the Fortune 500 companies and have offices throughout the world."

"Sounds very impressive," Father McShane said politely.

"We are, Father. We're the very best in the business."

"You're a senior partner?" Phyllis asked.

"That's correct. Peter Sayram and myself started the firm thirty-five years ago and now we're number one."

"Do you have an office in California?" Joanne inquired.

"Yes. We have one in San Francisco and another in Hollywood."

"Hollywood?" Joanne said excitedly.

"Yes. We handle most of the larger studios and performers."

"Like who?" Joanne asked.

"Carol Kennler and Ellen Brestam are two of our biggest stars under contract."

Joanne laughed, "You don't have me."

Hugo looked directly at her and said, "No, but we've spoken to your agent."

"You spoke to Billy?"

"Yes, Ms. Hauser, I personally have spoken to Mr. Costa on several occasions. He's actually a decent sort of chap."

"What about rock stars?" Michael asked eagerly.

"We only handle the larger and more stable ones."

Michael pushed, "Which ones?"

Thinking momentarily, Hugo responded, "I believe we handle The Walls, Roonie and Sloons, The Bleeding Wheels, and Crazy Jake."

"Man, they're the best," Michael said, awed.

"That's why they come to us because we're also the very best at what we do."

"How many employees do you have?" Franklyn asked.

"Tens of thousands. We have two hundred and fifty-eight senior partners alone."

"What about sports?" Todd inquired.

"What about them?" Hugo replied.

"Do you have any players?"

"We have a separate corporation that handles only athletes." Smiling, Hugo continued, "It is our fastest growing and most profitable division."

"It appears you're a very successful man," Father McShane stated.

"Yes I am and I'm very proud of my accomplishments." He looked around and added, "That's why I can't waste my time in this room, I've got to find a way out of here."

"We've been trying for the longest time, but so far we've had no luck," Sandra remarked.

Staring at the group, Hugo said, "I'll give ten thousand dollars to anyone getting me out of here."

"Cash?" Michael asked.

"However you want it, just get me out of here. I've got an important client waiting for me."

"I'll add another thousand," Phyllis said. "My husband will pay it."

"Let's not get too carried away," Father McShane said.

"Yes, I agree," Sandra added.

"We all want to get out of here and I do not think a financial reward is necessary."

"Don't speak for me," Michael objected. "I could use the bucks."

"Let's try to remain reasonable," Father McShane advised as the group became more boisterous.

Alice inquired, "Do you have an office in Mexico?"

"No, but I'd like to." Hugo asked, "Do you know anyone?"

"We can speak some other time."

"Tell us more about yourself," Sandra said.

Hugo spoke about his life and career. As he was about to speak about his family, the lights started to dim. Nervously, he asked, "What's happening?"

"No big deal, it's nap time," Todd said.

"Nap time?"

"Yes. We can talk later, but for now, find yourself a spot and get comfortable," Jeffery said.

"You'd better hurry; we don't have much time," Phyllis warned.

"There's an empty sofa by me, come and I'll show you," Phyllis offered.

Todd glared at Phyllis, but didn't say a word. As the lights finally darkened, everyone settled into their sites and waited for the next light period.

SIXTY-SIX

Hugo's thoughts were interrupted by the approach of Father McShane. "How did you sleep?"

"Like a log, Father. I haven't slept better in years."

"Everyone says the same thing; perhaps there's something about the air."

"Maybe," Hugo replied and then added, "What does one do for fun?"

"Whatever you want. There's an ample supply of books in the library and many different board games if you can find a suitable opponent."

"What about cards? Does anyone play bridge?"

The priest thought for a moment and then said, "Announce it during our next meal, I'm sure someone knows the game."

"I hope so," Hugo said.

"Do you play well?"

"I'm a Master."

"I suppose that's pretty good," Father McShane said.

"It's like being a Cardinal."

Looking at Hugo, the priest spoke. "I'm sorry, I forgot my reason for coming."

"I thought you came over to say hello."

"That also, but I have something for you."

"For me?" Hugo inquired.

"Yes. Everyone gets a box, including you."

"Why thank you, but from whom?"

"We don't know. We all got one."

Hugo followed the priest to retrieve his box. He examined it with great care then began opening the wrappings.

"I will be going."

"Wait and see what I get."

"Each of us opens our own gift in private."

"It doesn't matter; I've got nothing to hide."

Despite Hugo's insistence, Father McShane excused himself and joined Sandra. Hugo reached into the box and withdrew a pack of playing cards. He studied the wrapper carefully and grinned. "What am I going to do with a fixed deck of cards?" Placing them aside, he removed several bulky, sealed parcels. Sitting on the floor, he studied one carefully. Noting no markings, he slowly unfastened the seal and looked at the contents. "Holy shit!" he uttered as he examined each page carefully. Quickly, he inspected the other envelopes. Again, he discovered similar material. For the longest time, he tried to absorb the written literature. "This is worth millions!" he uttered as he gazed upon the pages. "How the heck did they get here?" He quickly repacked the contents and carried the box to his sofa. *I can't believe it. How did the post office screw this one up? All my competitors ideas and proposals! How were they sent here? Wait until my partners see this. Sweet Jesus, this is sensational!*

Father McShane interrupted his thoughts. "How did you enjoy your gift?"

"Very much so."

"Were you shocked?" questioned the priest.

"Yes."

"As we all were." Sitting at Hugo's side, Father McShane

added, "I found you someone to play with."

"I'm afraid I don't understand what you mean."

"Bridge! Iris, James, and Jeffery play bridge."

"Thank you, Father. I'm very grateful."

"It's the least I can do; after all, we've got to do something to kill time."

"I don't plan on staying here much longer."

"Do you know something I don't?"

"Only that I've got to get back to my business very soon."

"My son, we're all in a rush, but so far no exit has been found."

"Have faith, Father, Hugo is here."

"I will try, but in the meantime, the other three are ready to play bridge whenever you are."

"Thanks again, Father, but right now I'm really tired."

"By the way, if you want to join my discussion group, please feel free to sit in," the priest offered.

"Right now, I just want to be alone."

"I understand. Take all the time you want. God only knows it's hard to adjust to this situation."

SIXTY-SEVEN

Tara raised her hand and spoke. "Father, do you realize that this is our twenty-eighth session?"

Smiling, the priest responded, "Time flies when you're having fun."

"I've learned so much," Iris said.

"Me too!" Joanne added. "This group is the highlight of my day. In fact, it's the only thing so far that's been positive."

"Why thank you," Father McShane replied as he winked at Sandra. "I've enjoyed these meetings myself."

"What are we going to discuss today?" Tara asked.

"I thought I'd open the floor for suggestions instead of selecting the topic."

"But Father, you're so good at it," Iris said.

"I have one picked out for our next meeting; however, today's will be yours."

Everyone sat silently for several moments before Sandra inquired, "Father, what do you think of alcoholism?"

Hesitating he inquired, "Any particular reason you're asking?"

"I have several colleagues, who are Roman Catholic, and they consume a rather formidable amount of alcohol each day."

"Any person, regardless of their religion, should be extremely careful when dealing with alcohol. Like any other addictive substance, alcohol can and probably will have a grave, negative affect on their lives. I have witnessed this sad fate many, many times throughout my career as a priest."

"Are priests permitted to drink?" Iris asked.

"Mine drank like a fish," Joanne confided. "He was drunk during every sermon."

"One must remember priests are human beings and therefore subject to social pressures. Though I have heard such stories, I have never experienced such a problem with any of my peers."

"My priest ran AA meetings at our church," Iris added.

"As I have said, we priests are humans. I, however, am repelled by even the smell of liquor."

"You couldn't be a priest at my church," Joanne jested.

Father McShane thought for a moment and stated, "But if I were, I would fight like heck to correct the problem."

Phyllis clapped. "Hurray for you, Father. You're a champion among men and an example for us to follow."

"I'll say," Iris added. "We need more good people like you where I live too."

In an attempt to change the subject, Father McShane posed a question to the group. "What will each of you do if we get out of here?"

Joanne immediately stated, "You mean *when* we get out of here, don't you, Father?"

"Why yes," the priest responded. "I meant when."

"I'm going to take a long vacation with my husband," Phyllis stated. "And then I'm going on a very long shopping spree. God, am I sick of the same old clothes!"

"I'm going to call my agent and get into the next available movie," Joanne said. "I miss my work terribly."

Sandra answered next. "I going to enjoy my classes and then

write a bestseller about this experience."

Joanne laughed, "I hope it's a good one; I always relish free publicity."

Iris looked around and said, "I'll probably go back to my business."

"That fortune stuff?" Joanne inquired.

"Yes. I make a nice living from it and my clients are usually satisfied."

Father McShane turned to Tara and asked, "What about you, my child?"

"I'm not sure," she answered timidly.

"Not sure?" Phyllis stated critically. "That's dumb."

"Perhaps, but how can I plan for the future when I can't remember a single thing about my past?"

Father McShane attempted to console the young woman. "I'm sure you'll remember in time."

"What about you, Father?" Iris asked.

"Probably return to my parish and resume my holy work."

"Can I visit you and listen to one of your sermons?" Iris questioned.

"Certainly, I'd be honored to have you attend."

Turning to each person, he added, "I'd want every one of you to visit."

Tara lowered her voice and asked the group, "What if we don't get out of here? Then what?"

"Perish the thought!" Phyllis shouted.

Iris agreed. "What a terrible thought."

"Let's try to think positively. I'm sure many people are looking for us right now."

"I agree with you, Father," Sandra added, "when this many people disappear at once, it always draws a lot of attention."

Phyllis spoke with certainty. "My husband would spend any amount of money to get me back. He'll continue his search forever."

"I can feel their presence already," Iris said. "We'll be rescued shortly."

Tara hugged the fortune-teller and smiled. "I guess I'm just a little discouraged; I'm sure all of you are right."

"Never lose hope, my child," the priest said tenderly.

"Remember," Sandra interjected, "where there's life, there's hope!"

"And I still have a lot of living to do!" Phyllis said.

"I'm sure we all feel the same," Joanne said. "Iris knows. After all, she did wake up Alice."

"Father?"

"Yes, Sandra."

"I'd like to select a topic for our next meeting."

"I have no objections. Does anyone else?"

Sandra went on, "I'd like to discuss determinism and free will."

"What?" Phyllis asked.

Sandra repeated her topic. "It sounds like an interesting subject," Father McShane said. "But try not to make it too complex."

"I will, Father. I'll keep it on an elementary level."

"I hope I can understand what you're going to say. After all, I didn't go to college," Phyllis said.

"Me neither," Iris added. "Please make it simple."

"I'll make it both enjoyable and educational."

"I got all the education I need," Phyllis said abruptly. "Thanks anyhow."

To maintain harmony within the group, Father McShane intervened. "I look forward to our next meeting." Seven loud rings sounded through the room causing the priest to add, "Let's eat; I'm starving."

SIXTY-EIGHT

"What's the matter?" Jeffery inquired. "You look so sad."

Tara tried to disguise her emotions. "It's nothing."

"Was it today's meal?"

Smirking slightly, the young girl said, "No. Your dessert was delicious."

"Thank God, I thought my cooking career was over." Sitting at her side, he placed a hand on her knee and asked, "So what's wrong?"

"Everything." She began to weep. "Everything is all wrong." He rubbed her back while she cried, "There, there, everything will be all right."

"Nothing is right. Nothing..."

"What can I do to help you?"

"There's nothing anyone can do. We're stuck in this room and I'm scared to death."

"But everyone's afraid. You're not the only one."

Gazing into his face, she asked, "Are you?"

"Just because I don't show it, doesn't mean I'm not frightened. In reality, I'm probably more terrified than you."

"You don't look it."

"Neither does anyone else, but we're all afraid. It's only natural."

Sniffling, Tara pointed to the far end of the room and continued. "And I also feel sorry for him."

"Who?" Jeffery asked.

"The one who's still sleeping."

"Why him?"

"Because we were like him at one time."

"But we woke up!"

"Why didn't he?"

Moving his hand up her thigh, he gently caressed her leg. "Just try to relax and stop worrying about everything. Before you know it, someone will find us and free us from this room."

Tara hastily removed his hand and said, "It's not right that he is alone. Suppose he wakes up…"

"If he does, he joins us."

"But all of us woke up with someone nearby."

Re-placing his hand on her thigh, he asked, "Does it really matter?"

"To me, it certainly does. I'd hate to wake up in this room without somebody at my side."

"I think you're being a little dramatic. After all, he's just a bum."

Watching Jeffery's hand creep higher, she stated coldly, "Take your hand off me."

"I was just trying to console you, my dear."

"That kind of support I don't need. If you really want to assist, help me bring him over to my sofa."

"You mean bring the bum over here?"

"Yes. I want him to see someone when he wakes up."

"I don't want his kind by me or my things. Who knows what diseases he may be carrying."

"I can't believe you. Any of us could be diseased. How do you know for sure he's sick?"

"Just look at him; he looks disgusting."

"Will you help me?" Tara asked again.

"Absolutely not! Let him stay over there."

Tara excused herself and joined Father McShane. She expressed her desire to bring the sleeping man near her sofa. "I don't think that's a good idea, we know nothing about him. He may be a killer!" the priest responded.

"But we knew nothing about each other."

"That's true, but we all looked normal; he's dressed so poorly. God only knows what he did to get in that condition!"

"So you won't help me?"

"No. For the good of our group, I believe it's unsafe to have him so close. Besides, James doesn't think he stands a chance of living."

Raising her voice slightly, Tara replied, "What does James know anyway, he won't even check him out."

"He's a doctor of medicine and offered his professional opinion."

"He's nothing but a pompous jerk."

"Why are you so obsessed over this man?"

"Because I don't think it's right. I wouldn't want to be treated like this."

"Like what?" the priest asked.

"Neglected."

"He's probably close to death and isn't aware of us at all; judging from his appearance, it seems he's been neglected for quite some time."

"Father, will you help me?"

"No. I think he should be isolated from the group."

"Thank you."

She proceeded to ask each member for their assistance. None offered any help. Todd was the most vocal. "I don't want that bum near me. Bring him over here and I'll kill him myself."

"I can't believe any of you," Tara said at last.

"Maybe you should look at yourself first. Forget that bum and come over when the lights go out," Todd suggested with a leer. "I guarantee you'll forget him after that."

Tara walked to the far end of the room; there she knelt by the still figure. "Are you awake? Can you hear me?" she asked. She took a deep breath, and with difficulty dragged his body across the room. Everyone stared, but none helped. Once she had positioned him near her sofa, she rested. Tara whispered, "At least, you'll have someone if you wake up."

SIXTY-NINE

Sandra dropped to her knees and examined the edge of the carpeting. Leaving nothing to chance, she tugged, pulled, and poked along every inch of the rug.

This had been a daily ritual and one she expected to follow until the entire room's carpeting had been scrutinized. With Franklyn investigating the walls and Father McShane checking the storage room, Sandra was determined to locate an exit. Despite constant ridicule from Michael and Todd, she undauntedly performed the task.

Pushing aside a heavy table, her fingers suddenly touched an unfamiliar object.

Cautiously she traced its perimeter attempting to contain her excitement. As she reached the final section, Sandra shouted for Franklyn. Seconds later, he was at her side, gasping for air. "What is it?" he panted.

"Feel this."

After tracing the border with his hands, he smiled. "I think you found it."

"It certainly feels like a door. Doesn't it?" she asked with enthusiasm.

"Let's not get too optimistic just yet," he warned as he began cutting the rug, "Let's just see what you found."

Assisting him in removing several pieces, she beamed as several edges of the concealed trapdoor were exposed. "Look!" she shouted. "I was right."

"Just give me a few more..." With great effort, Franklyn pulled away the last vestige of carpeting.

"I told you! I told you! It's a door."

"But to where?"

Regaining her composure, Sandra calmly responded, "I hope to our freedom."

Hearing their commotion, Alice strolled to the area. "What's all the fuss?"

Trying to remain poised, Franklyn carefully responded, "We've exposed this trapdoor."

Alice asked, "Is it a way out?"

"We haven't opened it as yet; we just removed the carpeting," the scientist reported.

"Let's hurry! I can't wait to leave this damn room," responded Alice.

Sandra placed her hands on the closed door and said to the others, "Let's keep this development among ourselves for now."

"Why?" Franklyn inquired.

"I'm tired of everyone's ridicule."

"I agree with you," Alice added. "Those men are nothing but low-class pigs!"

Sandra attempted to lift the door upward, but quickly discovered it was fastened tightly shut. Franklyn and Alice each took a turn, but to no avail; the door remained unmovable.

"Now what?" Alice asked.

Franklyn suggested, "Let's break it open."

"Are you sure?" Sandra said. "After all, we really do not know what is on the other side."

"Can it be any worse than this room?" Franklyn pointed out.

"I agree with Franklyn, it may be our only hope," Alice concurred.

"Let's discuss it with the others," Sandra suggested.

"Why the change of heart? I thought you hated those men as much as I do," Alice asked.

"It is not that. I am just afraid."

"Of what?" Franklyn inquired.

"Of the unknown."

"This whole room is the unknown. In fact, this door is simply an extension of a mysterious picture."

"Franklyn is right; we must open it immediately."

"I'm still not sure," Sandra hesitated.

Turning to Franklyn, Alice spoke in an authoritarian manner. "I demand that we open this door right now! Why keep us locked up any longer than necessary. Our freedom could lie within inches of that door."

Sandra watched as Franklyn and Alice physically pried the security mechanism from the trapdoor. As the lock shattered, the door creaked slightly but remained stationary. The three looked at one another; finally, Alice grasped the edge of the wooden entrance and lifted it slowly upward. Peering downward, Franklyn asked, "Does anyone see anything?"

"Who can see anything? It's so damn dark!" Alice said as she peered into the blackness.

"I found a working flashlight in the storage room," Franklyn remembered. "I'll be right back."

Upon his return, they lifted the door again and stared inward. "Look," Sandra stated, "a ladder."

"I see it!" Alice said.

"Keep your voice down!" Sandra whispered.

"I'm sorry," Alice apologized. Straining, she asked, "I can't see anything else. How about you?"

"All I can see are the top rungs of a ladder."

"That's all I see," Sandra said. "The rest is totally black. We've got to see what's down there."

"Maybe we should get the others," Franklyn said.

"No way! It's our find," Sandra now objected.

"I agree with Sandra; once we get out of here, we'll send someone back to let them out."

Franklyn agreed to their terms. "Who goes first?" he asked.

Alice spoke, "I'll go."

Slowly they raised the door and assisted her downward into the darkness. "Be careful," Franklyn whispered.

Alice looked up at their faces, smiled nervously and then descended out of sight. They followed the light from her flashlight as it traveled downward and soon it eluded their vision. Neither spoke as they stared into the hole.

The great wall clock emitted one earsplitting ring that reverberated throughout the entire room. Reminded of the time Sandra then remarked, "She has been down there an awfully long time. I am beginning to get worried. What should we do?"

"Let's wait a little longer. Maybe she's found a way out."

"I wish I could be so optimistic. Perhaps she is hurt."

Franklyn looked around the room. "I wonder if anyone has seen us?"

"I doubt it, otherwise, they would have been here already." As Franklyn was about to speak, they heard a noise from the bottom of the hole. Sandra whispered, "Alice, is that you?"

Hearing no response, Franklyn tried, "Alice?"

Finally, they heard someone climbing the ladder. Shortly, Alice's face became visible. "Alice! Did you find a way out?" Sandra questioned. The woman exited the hole and collapsed on the floor. Her body was bathed in sweat while her clothing was torn and dirty. Sandra asked again, "Did you find a way out?"

Alice shook her head and weakly answered, "No."

Franklyn retrieved a glass of cold water and helped Alice drink. "Well!" Sandra said impatiently, "What did you find?"

"Nothing." Raising her voice in anger, Alice reiterated, "Not a goddamn thing; there's no way out down there."

"Are you sure?" Sandra questioned.

"Go down there yourself and look."

Franklyn interceded, "What did you find and what took you so long?"

Alice said softly, "The ladder leads downward to a small cave. I followed it to the end and found nothing."

"Are you sure?" Sandra inquired.

Alice stared at Sandra. "Yes, I'm very sure. I checked every inch of the place. There's nothing but stone."

Franklyn shook his head. "Now what shall we do?"

"We relock the door, cover it up, and say nothing to anyone about it."

"But why?" Alice asked.

"Why should we be the subject of their jokes?"

"Who cares?" Franklyn responded. "At least we try."

"I care!" Sandra stated boldly. "I refuse to be ridiculed by those illiterate peons."

They agreed to maintain their silence concerning the trapdoor and cave. "Why are you so sweaty?" Franklyn asked.

"Because the entire tunnel was like a blast furnace. All the walls were extremely hot and the air is humid."

"Do you think we're near a volcano?" Sandra wondered.

Franklyn shrugged his shoulders, "I hope not."

The three closed the door as best they could and then replaced the carpeting. To further camouflage their discovery, Franklyn dragged a heavy table to the site and placed it directly on top of the hidden opening.

"You go wash up; dinner will be served soon," Sandra commanded. Turning to Franklyn, she stated, "Go back to your work and remember, don't say a single thing."

"I promise."

"Sandra?"

"Yes, Alice. What is it?"

"I feel rather weak. Could you come into the shower and help me?"

Looking at Alice, Sandra smiled, "Sure, why not? In fact, maybe I will even take a shower myself. All this excitement has gotten me sweaty." Neither said another word, but headed for the small, singular shower stall.

SEVENTY

James scanned the nearby shelf for another book. Since awakening, he developed a voracious appetite for reading. Regardless of the subject, the physician sought to expand his intellect. Choosing his next selection, he returned to his site.

"Good book. Have you finished it yet?" Father McShane asked.

Without looking up, James responded, "I just picked it out."

"May I join you for a moment?"

Moving aside, James made room for Father McShane. "What brings you so far from home?"

"Just thought I'd take a trip to visit my neighbors."

"If I didn't fill my time with reading, I think I'd crack," remarked James.

"I know what you mean. Thank God I have my Bible."

Looking at the priest directly, James asked, "Aren't you troubled about this room?"

Shaking his head in agreement, Father McShane responded soberly, "Tremendously."

"So many questions and no logical answers."

"I know what you mean. It makes no sense at all."

221

"And us? Why us? Why are we here?"

The priest shrugged his shoulders, "I'm afraid I have no answer."

"If it's blackmail, who and why?" Scanning the room, James continued, "We have nothing in common: a priest, a football player, a fortune-teller, and whatever."

"And the boxes..."

"Precisely."

"So what can we do?" Father McShane asked.

"Nothing at all." James sighed. "We're at the mercy of our captors."

To change the subject, the priest inquired. "What about organizing a discussion group?"

"Who, me?"

"Yes."

"And discuss what? The weather?"

"The books!"

"Father, I appreciate your suggestion, but the answer is no!"

"Why not?"

"Because I cannot deal with morons!"

Coming to their defense, Father McShane countered, "Many are fascinating once you get to know them."

"Father, I prefer my books. The thought of dealing with such idiots turns my stomach. In the hospital where I worked I refused to have anything to do with these kind of people and I will not change now! I am a professional; I will not lower myself to their level."

Their conversation was interrupted by a high-pitched sound. "What was that?" the priest asked.

"The jerk found an amplifier for his guitar."

"Michael?"

"Who else? The wonder boy of strum himself."

"Where did he find it?"

"After the last dark period, he found it in the storage room by his food supply," James said.

"I don't recall seeing it in the past."

"Neither did he, but it was there."

Another chord reverberated throughout the room, causing Father McShane to gasp. "It's just awful!"

"I'm not exactly a fan of rock myself."

The entire room shook as Michael began to play. The priest shouted to James, "What can we do? It's so loud."

"I'd like to burn the goddamn thing; that's what I'd like to do!"

Michael continued playing; chandeliers and tables quivered as the pitch increased.

Finally, Father McShane walked to Michael's site. He stared as the musician labored over his work. "May I speak to you a moment?" the priest asked. Not hearing or acknowledging the Father, Michael continued his playing. Father McShane shouted, "Michael! I want to speak to you!"

Finally glancing upward, Michael turned down his newly discovered amplifier. "Hi, Father, how do you like it?"

Stuttering slightly, the priest asked, "May I speak to you for a moment?"

"Surely! Have a seat."

The Father looked at the complexity of equipment. "You just found it?"

"Yeah. This stuff is the best you can get; it's worth a fortune."

"I see. Whose is it and where did it come from?"

Michael responded easily, "Who cares! It's mine now!" He strummed a chord, causing the priest to cover his ears with his hands. "Wild sound! Ain't it?"

"I was wondering if I could speak to you about your playing?"

"Sure. Do you want me to play a special song?"

"That's not what I had in mind," Father McShane said.

Placing his guitar carefully on the floor, Michael asked, "What then?"

"Well," the priest began, "I was wondering if you could keep the volume down."

The musician looked at the priest in disbelief and tried to control his temper. "My volume!"

"The noise is disturbing to me and the others."

"Tough shit!"

Father McShane attempted another approach. "Don't get me wrong, we love the music, it's just very loud."

"Father, this baby is only at half volume. I could turn it up higher if you want."

"Please!" the priest pleaded. "It's high enough."

Picking up his guitar, Michael prepared himself for another selection. "Do you want to hear *Rose's Love*?"

"I'm afraid I've never heard of it." Pausing momentarily, Father McShane repeated, "Would you consider lowering the volume?"

"Father, all the time we've been here, I've had to listen to Todd's goddamn football, Franklyn's tearing the walls apart, and everybody else's noises; now, they can hear mine."

"But—"

Michael strummed a few dissonant bars and then grinned. "Father, I'll practice when I want and how loud I want. Get it?"

The priest nodded and rejoined James.

Eagerly, the physician asked, "What did he say?"

"He said he would practice loudly for awhile and then reduce the volume."

"Thank God; the noise is making my reading impossible."

"Just have a little patience; after all, he's just like a child with a new toy."

Tossing his book unto the floor, James shouted, "I hope you're right, Father, because that noise is already driving me crazy."

SEVENTY-ONE

Franklyn stretched his arms high overhead. His body adjusted nicely to the darkened periods and he instinctively arose as the lights reappeared. He scanned the room and suddenly became aware of the changes. As if in a trance, he walked through the room; bewilderment filled his mind.

Sandra appeared at his side and asked, "What happened?"

He looked at her and then to the wall. "I just don't know."

"Walls don't just repair themselves!"

"That's a logical deduction," he said. "But somehow these did."

"Maybe someone here did it." she mused.

"When?"

"During the dark period," she replied.

"Nearly impossible," he stated. "Where did they get the supplies and how did they work in the total darkness?"

"Good points," Sandra agreed.

"And lastly, the paint and paper are dry."

They walked to the closest repair and examined the wall. Sandra asked, "How long do you think it would take to do all this work?"

"Weeks of constant work."

"How long do you estimate a dark period is?"

Thinking momentarily, he guessed, "Probably no more than eight hours."

Running her hand along a seam, she sighed, "Notice how exact the coloring and print detail is; everything matches precisely." She studied the workmanship and observed, "Even the ornate moldings are exact."

"It's the same all over," Franklyn continued. "Every hole I made, including the smallest, have been redone."

Thinking for a second, Sandra inquired, "What about the trapdoor?"

"I didn't check."

"Maybe we should."

Together they walked to the spot. Noticing everyone was still asleep, they noiselessly pushed aside the furniture and examined the rug. Finding it not repaired, they pulled it back and lifted the trap door slightly. Darkness greeted their eyes. Upon replacing the protective covering, they returned to his couch.

Sandra questioned, "Why?"

"Maybe the mystery repairer doesn't do carpets."

"I do not find that funny," Sandra responded.

"Come up with a better answer," he said, gazing at the wall, "I can't."

Noticing several of the others were walking in their direction, Sandra inquired, "What shall we tell them?"

"Whatever you want. I'm at an absolute loss."

"Shall we tell them about the trapdoor?"

"Absolutely not!" he stated emphatically.

"What about Alice? What if she says something?"

"You go speak to her and I'll take care of the group."

After describing his observations, the scientist tried to answer their questions.

"Does this mean you're no longer going to look for a way out?" Phyllis inquired.

"To the contrary, I'll look even harder."

"Why do you think it was done?" Iris asked.

"Perhaps I was getting close to something and it is a way of delaying finding it."

"But which one had the exit?" Tara asked.

"I'm not sure, but I'll start opening the last tunnel first and then work backwards."

"Maybe you're right," Todd added. "I'll give you a hand."

"Me too!" Joanne stated. "I've had enough of this place."

Franklyn organized the groups and delegated responsibilities to the various members. They labored without rest as they uncovered three tunnels by darkness. None, however, offered an exit from their imprisonment. Upon awaking, they were shocked to observe that each tunnel was again repaired to its original condition. After three recurrences most members became greatly discouraged and refused to work any longer.

"What are you going to do now?" Sandra asked.

"Keep looking," Franklyn stated boldly.

"But you're fighting a losing battle."

"I'll never give up; there has to be a way out of here."

"I agree," she said. "But it's so damn frustrating."

"I know that, but I've got to continue. What other choice do we have?"

"I guess you're right." Sighing, she said, "Where do we work next?"

"The same spot I left off."

Sandra worked faithfully at his side for the next five light periods, only to get more frustrated with each setback. She finally excused herself and joined the others. Franklyn awoke at the next light period, ate rapidly, and started breaking through another section of wall.

SEVENTY-TWO

Iris and Phyllis relaxed after one of Jeffery's meals. "The roast was superb," Phyllis said.

"I agree, but I liked the sauce the best." Giggling, Iris jested, "There goes my girlish figure!"

"Where do you think he found those mushrooms?" Phyllis asked.

"I overheard he and the Father speaking; he found them in the storage room."

"It's amazing; that room has everything we'll ever need." Phyllis pointed out.

"James thinks we're in some sort of secret military base," remarked Iris.

"Military?" Phyllis questioned. "I have nothing to do with the military."

"Neither do I," Iris continued, "but he feels the large supply room and strict security must be related to the military."

"I guess it makes sense, but why us?"

"Maybe we're here by mistake and they're really after one of the others."

Phyllis whispered, "Like who?"

"Jeffery."

"Yes, he's involved with the government." Thinking momentarily, Phyllis added, "But it could be Franklyn."

"That's possible. He does secret work."

"So why are we involved?" wondered Phyllis.

"I'm afraid I don't know the answer," Iris said.

Phyllis looked at the woman and then inquired, "Why don't you use your fortune-telling for the answer?"

Iris squirmed in her seat and gazed at the floor. "It wouldn't work."

"Why not?"

"It just wouldn't."

Phyllis pushed harder. "I thought that sort of stuff worked with this type of case."

"Maybe it does for others, but it doesn't work for me."

"How can you be so sure, unless you try," Phyllis urged. "You told me of the great things you've done in the past."

Iris sighed, "I exaggerated about most of them."

"You mean you can't do any of that stuff?"

"Let's just say some of it is real and some is an act."

"An act!" Phyllis asked. "You mean you're a fraud?"

"No," Iris responded. "I provide a desired service to those who require my specialty. I council most and offer them hope."

"Based on what? Your tarot cards?"

"You don't have to be so sarcastic. I'm well respected among my peers."

"Other frauds."

"No," Iris said in a cold tone. "Other counselors."

"And the ball and cards? What are they?"

"Merely objects to assist my counseling; each is necessary to create an atmosphere or mood for my service."

Phyllis stared at the woman. "And to think my husband uses one of your kind to make business decisions. Wait until I tell him about this."

"Fortune-tellers are like other professional counselors; your husband receives advice and it's his sole decision whether to follow it or not."

"I can't believe you! Million dollar deals shouldn't depend on a fake crystal ball."

Iris drew herself up and stated, "I'm sorry you're taking this the wrong way because I do provide an essential service to my many clients. In fact, I have saved many lives just though my advice."

"Please don't come to help me if I'm in trouble."

"Who would you go to? A minister or a priest?"

Phyllis said, "Of course. They're qualified."

"They're no more qualified than I am. They have one set of mysterious objects and language and I have another."

"I can't believe you would even say such a thing," Phyllis said, appalled. "That's sacrilegious."

"It's just on what side of the fence you're sitting. In my eyes, formalized religion is no different than fortune-telling."

Phyllis stood. "I think I'd better get some fresh air. It's suddenly very sticky around here." Turning, she added, "I wouldn't tell Father McShane about this conversation; I think it would break his heart."

Iris watched as the woman walked away. Picking up her tarot cards, she began shuffling the deck. Placing a card on the table, she exposed the first card and instinctively withdrew. Quickly she replaced it within the deck and reshuffled. Once more, the same card appeared. After two more attempts with identical results, she picked up the death card and stared at its design. The skeleton holding a scythe seemed to glare back as her hands shook. After a few minutes, the fortune-teller gathered the cards and placed them at the bottom of her box. Clutching her hands to her face, Iris wept.

SEVENTY-THREE

"May I speak to you for a moment?" Hugo asked.

"Have a seat," Joanne answered.

He touched her hand gently and said, "Ms. Hauser, there's something I must ask."

"Please call me Joanne and ask away."

"It's rather personal and I would hope that you treat it with the respect and admiration I offer."

"I'm afraid I do not understand what you are saying."

Without any hesitation, Hugo continued, "I've always considered you an extremely beautiful woman; in fact, you're the most attractive woman in all of Hollywood. I would like the privilege to represent you through my agency."

"You mentioned you have spoken to my agent; what did he say?"

"Nothing. He didn't return any of my calls."

She admitted, "That's just like him."

"Quite truthfully, I believe the man is unqualified to be anyone's agent."

"I take offense to that statement; he's always looked out for my best interest," Joanne said flatly.

"Has he really?" Smiling, Hugo asked, "Are you positive?"

"Why yes!" she stated. "I've done very well over the years."

"Maybe you could have done better with a more professional, team approach."

"He's always—"

Cutting her short, Hugo inquired, "I'd like to know what percentage of gross he gets."

"That's between him and me."

"We're speaking as friends; I'd just like to get an idea of what he gets for his services. Sort of a friendly comparison."

Pausing slightly, Joanne then answered, "Fifteen percent."

"Fifteen percent! That's robbery. Someone as famous as you shouldn't have to pay that amount. Dear God, he's living off the fruits of *your* labor."

"But he's been with me through all these years."

"Do you have a written contract?"

"We shook hands many years ago—" Hugo grasped the actress' hand and squeezed gently. "My dear, you are being had."

"I don't think he would do that to me."

"How many other accounts does he have?"

"Several."

"Anyone famous?"

"I'm not sure."

Pushing harder, Hugo said, "One last question."

Slightly upset, Joanne replied, "Okay, but only one."

"Are you worth more than fifteen million dollars?"

"Gosh no! That's an awful lot of money."

Shaking his head, Hugo replied, "We have lesser known stars with much more money. You should have a net worth of at least twenty-five million dollars."

"Twenty-five million!"

"Yes, if you came over to my company, I'd personally guarantee that myself." He continued his sales pitch. "Within ten years, you'd probably be worth at least fifty million dollars."

"How can you do it?"

"We use the team approach and are a full-service organization.
We will negotiate your contracts, collect your fees, handle your
PR, arrange for additional means of income, and invest your assets
to ensure monetary growth."

Joanne was overwhelmed. "But I've used him for years..."

"I believe you have simply outgrown the man. Besides, you have
no written contract at all."

"He told me it was not necessary, he called it a mutual trust."

"Don't be so naive. Business is business and that's how the
world works. Our contracts are designed to protect both our agency
and our clients."

Joanne faltered. "But how can I switch after all this time?"

"Think about what's best for you. By the way, our fee is only
eight percent."

"Eight percent?"

"Yes. We do have other riders, but they are based on our per-
formance and incentives."

"How—"

"Just leave everything to good old Hugo. I'll take good care of
you from now on."

"Maybe I'd better think about it."

"Take all the time you want; after all, it's your money." Hugo
continued. "If you give me the go-ahead right now, I'll talk my partners into taking only five percent."

"Five percent!" Joanne said in an excited tone, "That's
unheard of!"

"That's my deal and it's only good right now. If you call me after
we're out of this room, I'll raise the fee to eight percent."

"That's not fair!" Joanne said. "It's such a big decision."

"Those are my terms. Keep your do-nothing agent and pay
more, or switch to my firm right now and retain more of your
profits."

"Wow! It certainly sounds enticing."

"Add this," Hugo said. "I'll throw in one chauffeured limousine every year we continue to do business together."

"How can I say no to that?"

Staring her straight in the eye, he asked, "Well?"

Without further thought, Joanne shook his hand. "You've got yourself a deal."

Grinning, Hugo said, "Welcome to our family. Our lawyers will handle everything from now on; all you have to do is enjoy life and spend your money."

"How can I ever thank you?"

Pausing, he whispered, "There is one small favor I might ask."

"What is that?"

"Let's just say a man gets awfully lonely when he's without a woman for any length of time."

"Are you suggesting something, Mr. Winters?"

"I'm only stating a fact. Friends and business associates often must turn to one another during the most trying of times."

Joanne asked, "And these are the most trying of times?"

"Extremely."

"Are you suggesting we go to bed with one another?"

Hugo commented, "I'm only stating a fact of life. Since we are going to work extremely closely in the future, why not officially inaugurate our relationship with something very special?"

Whispering in his ear, she said, "Like a good screwing."

"I believe I'd use another term. Screwing is too crude a word for a lady of your stature."

Joanne looked at his features and smiled. "I agree with you, Mr. Winters. Friends should assist one another in the hardest of times and this is certainly one of them."

He squeezed her hand. Looking around, he added, "We must be discreet."

"I couldn't agree with you more."

"I think—"

She cut him short by placing her hand on his mouth. She then whispered, "Expect me tonight when the lights go out."

"I can't wait." He raised his voice to a normal volume, "It was very good speaking to you, Joanne. Thank you for your time." Once he was out of range, Hugo muttered to himself. *Dumb bitch! First, I'll get your body and then your money.*

SEVENTY-FOUR

Jeffery watched as Franklyn feverishly broke through a new section of wall. He had long given up counting the tunnels the scientist had opened and witnessing the frustration he felt each morning. Noticing Franklyn was taking a short rest, Jeffery moved closer. "How's it going?" he asked.

Sweat pouring from his skin, Franklyn took a deep breath and slowly answered, "The same."

Sitting at his side, Jeffery inquired, "Any idea how or who is rebuilding the walls?"

"Not even a clue."

"I never saw anything like it."

"And you probably never will again," the scientist said. "It defies every rational and scientific theory and law I have ever studied."

"What about the materials?"

"An exact match. I've studied them under my microscope and can't distinguish between any of them."

"So what are you going to do?"

Franklyn's response was instantaneous. "Continue as is, there is simply no other choice."

"Do you agree with James' military base theory?"

"No."

"Why?"

"I've had plenty of experience with military bases and this doesn't conform to anything I've ever seen. There are no monitoring devices or military mechanisms anywhere within the entire area." Taking another deep breath, he continued, "Probably civilian."

"Civilian? But who?"

"Don't ask me."

"Maybe someone is after information."

Franklyn conjectured, "That covers *us,* but why Tara, Father McShane, and the others?" Shaking his head, he added, "That's an irrational assumption."

"Perhaps your approach is too logical," Jeffrey suggested.

Franklyn said, "I don't understand your thinking."

"I'm not sure myself, but perhaps we must think illogically and not within the scope of the expected."

Franklyn nodded slightly, "Like the chaos theories..."

"Precisely."

"That just threw me for a loop and will give me plenty to think about," said Franklyn.

Jeffery laughed. "Glad I could be of some help."

The scientist mumbled to himself, "Like chaos..."

"By the way, how is Project Kendra coming?"

Franklyn stared at Jeffery. "Project Kendra? I-I never heard of it."

Jeffery again asked him point blank. "I know all about Project Kendra. Don't play dumb; how is it going?"

"That's a highly classified government project!"

"I know all that. Were you able to finally synthesize the Goldenstoom?"

"I don't understand; how could you know about it?"

"Franklyn, diplomatic channels run both far and deep. When one government is working on such an important project, sooner or later, everyone will know about it."

"But how? Only a few of us had access to the information."

"How is not the issue; but rather, did you finally perform the synthesis?"

"I can't give you that information; I could be shot as a traitor."

"Don't be so naive; it's done all the time."

Franklyn started to pace. "I can't believe this is happening."

"Let me put it to you another way. Five years ago, you wrote an article on cold fusion that brought you worldwide acclaim as well as a Nobel Prize."

"That's true, but what does that have to do with my work?"

Jeffery said, "We both know you stole that data from a colleague."

"That's not true. I—"

"Dr. Arnold Swistzer originated that study and he confided in you for assistance. You, in turn, claimed the study as your own. The rest is history; he committed suicide and you reaped the rewards of his work."

Franklyn stammered, "That's an outright lie! You can't prove a thing."

"I can and will unless you agree to my terms."

Franklyn began to shake. "What do you want from me?"

Jeffery responded quickly. "Were you able to synthesize the Goldenstoom?"

The scientist looked meekly at the floor and whispered, "Yes."

"I didn't hear your answer."

Franklyn's voice quivered as he spoke louder. "Yes."

"Excellent. I expect to receive a copy of your formula once we get out of here."

"I can't do that; my God, that's illegal!"

Jeffery inched closer and stated coldly "You cannot afford *not* to cooperate with me! We wouldn't want everyone to know about your past."

"That's blackmail!" Franklyn said.

"Not really. You'll be paid handsomely for the information."

"I don't want any of your goddamn money."

"We'll see. I'm sure I can get you around two million dollars for the data."

"Who would pay that much?" Franklyn responded.

"That's none of your business. Just get me the information and the money will be deposited in a Swiss bank account in your name." Jeffery laid a hand on the scientist's shoulder. "You'll be contacted within ten days of our leaving this room. Make sure the information is accurate and don't try anything foolish."

"Or what?"

"You're career as a scientist will be over. I'll have you black-balled from every laboratory in the world. Besides, the police might be interested in a certain letter we have within our possession."

"Letter?" Franklyn asked, incredulous.

"A copy of a letter he wrote just before his tragic death."

"I never saw a letter."

"Trust me! It does exist and will be destroyed once you have completed your end of the deal."

The scientist nervously inquired, "How do I know I can trust you?"

"You have my word on it. All we want is the formula."

Franklyn slumped forward and moaned, "Dear God..."

"Don't be so melodramatic; this type of thing is done all the time." Jeffery continued, "Meanwhile, why don't you try to find a way out of here? These people and this place are beginning to get on my nerves."

SEVENTY-FIVE

Tara and Father McShane interrupted James during his usual after-meal nap. "Sorry to bother you, James, but I have a small favor to ask."

"Now what, Father?"

"Don't bother, Father, he won't want to do it," Tara concluded.

James immediately asked, "Do what?"

"Nothing" Tara pleaded. "Come, Father, let's go."

"You've already woken me up, you might as well ask."

Tara pulled on the priest's arm, "Forget it."

Father McShane pulled away from her grasp and asked, "We need your professional assistance. Doctor, will you help us?"

"I told you many times before, I'm an orthopedic surgeon, not an emergency room physician."

The priest continued, "It has nothing to do with the sleeping person. Tara requires your help."

James laughed loudly and stated, "I'm not a gynecologist."

Tara's anger intensified. "Please, Father, he won't help."

James stopped laughing and asked, "Okay, Father, what do you want?"

"Some time ago, during our previous conversations, you mentioned you had taken a few courses in hypnosis."

"That's true. I took them as a continuing education course at the hospital. We were going to try hypnosis prior to surgery."

"*That's* the story you told me." Pausing, Father McShane asked, "Would you try to hypnotize Tara?"

James looked at the two and said, "Are you serious? Why would you want me to do that?"

"To help her remember her past."

Tara squirmed, "Please, Father, let's go. I told you..."

"Hypnosis could possibly help her," James stated. "I remember Dr. Gails reporting several studies on the topic."

"Then you'll do it?" the priest asked in an optimistic tone.

Looking at the Father and then to the young woman, he stated, "Why not! I've got nothing else to do with my time."

"Thank you very much."

"Don't thank me yet, Father, I'm not sure I can help her. It's been a long time since I used that stuff."

"At least you're willing to help. That's all that counts. After all, the poor girl remembers nothing."

Turning to Tara, James asked sternly, "I want your word in front of a witness that you will not sue me or my estate if anything goes wrong."

"I promise," Tara said quickly. "I have no interest in that sort of thing; I just want to know who I am."

"You are a witness to her statement, Father."

"Yes, I am. Can we get started?"

"Right now?" James asked.

"I'd like to get this over with. I must find out some answers," Tara said.

James shrugged. "Why not? It's better than sleeping."

The physician instructed Tara to relax on his sofa. He then began to swing a small shiny object before her eyes. Father McShane watched silently as James began to speak in a deep voice.

"You are beginning to get very sleepy..." Within a short time, the young woman was in a deep trance.

The physician started his questioning. "What is your full name?"

The woman stirred slightly and answered in a shallow raspy tone, "Tara Anne Smith."

"Where were you born?"

Straining, she responded, "In a house."

"Where? What country?"

"America."

"What state?"

She moaned, "I can't recall."

"Think harder and try to remember." Changing his tactic, James inquired, "Did you come from a big family?"

"Yes," Tara recalled easily.

"How many children?"

"I'm not sure, but it was big."

"What was your mother's name?"

"Mary."

"What was your father's name?"

"Mathew."

"I'm sorry, I missed the name of your home town."

"San..."

"San what?"

"I can't remember."

"Did you live in California?"

"I can't remember."

"Did you have a happy childhood?"

Smiling, she said, "Oh yes. It was very good."

"Tell me why?"

"I just remember it was good."

James looked at the priest and then to his subject. "What religion are you?"

"Catholic."

"Are you sure?"

"Yes."

"What church do you attend?"

"St. Anne's."

"What town is it in?"

"I can't remember."

"How old are you?"

"Thirty-eight."

"Married?"

"I don't think so."

"Tell me about yourself."

"Like what?" she asked.

"Anything that comes to mind."

She remained silent for a moment and then smiled, "I recall having a dog."

"What kind and what was its name?"

Shaking her head, Tara seemed confused. "I can't..."

"Never mind, it's not important." James continued. "What do you do for a living?"

"My job is..." The woman stopped short and sobbed, "I can't recall."

"Do you remember anything else?"

"No."

Glancing at the Father, James whispered, "I think she's had enough."

"But we didn't learn too much."

"I'm going to bring her around. One can't be too careful; it could be dangerous."

Without waiting for approval, James said, "Tara Smith, can you hear me?"

"Yes."

"When I count to three, you're going to wake up. When you do, you'll feel like a new person. Your body will tingle and you'll remember everything we discussed. Do you understand?"

"Yes."

"One, two, three." James finished counting and waited.

Noticing the woman remained unchanged, he asked, "Tara, are you awake?"

"I..."

Father McShane studied her face and quickly inquired, "Is she okay?"

"Let me try again." The physician repeated his instructions and waited. As before, she remained stationary.

"Dear God," the priest stated. "What have we done?"

"I told you not to get me involved with anything medical."

Trying not to raise his voice, James mumbled, "Damn!" He shook her tiny frame slightly and ordered her to awake.

Father McShane asked, "Is she going to be all right?"

Turning to the priest, James sneered, "Shut your goddamn mouth; look at the trouble you got me into."

Out of desperation, he grasped her body and pushed it against the back of the sofa. She moaned slightly and opened her eyes. "I..."

"Thank God," the priest said loudly. "Praise be to God."

"God had nothing to do with it," James stated in an agitated tone.

Slapping Tara's face, he demanded, "Wake up."

She regained her senses and asked, "What happened?"

James remained silent as Father McShane summarized the events. "Is that all I said?"

"Yes, that's all I recall," the priest responded.

"Can we try it again? Maybe I'll do better."

The stout physician bounded to his feet and shouted, "Never again and don't get me involved in your problems! I've got enough of my own." Father McShane assisted Tara to her feet and walked her back to her sofa. James repeated his remarks, "No more! Go find yourself another sucker. I'm not risking my career on any scatterbrain ideas."

SEVENTY-SIX

Iris and Sandra listened as the wall clock struck ten rings. Laughing, the college professor said, "When we get out of here, I'm going to throw my shoe at that damn clock."

"I agree. It sounds like the old rooster I had as a child."

"A farm girl?" Sandra asked.

"Yea. I was born and raised on a big old farm. Straw in my hair, manure between my toes, and hayseed under my nails."

"It sounds awful!" Sandra said.

Iris sneered, "It was worse than awful. It was the pits."

"Thank goodness I grew up in the city."

"I totally agree." Iris grinned and said, "Guess what our Saturday night entertainment was on the farm?"

Sandra thought for a moment, "Milking the cows?"

"Even worse! My parents used to sit us around the kitchen table and force us to read the Bible. That's why I left at an early age and moved to the big city."

"To seek your fame and fortune?" Sandra said.

"You might say that, but nothing could be worse than living

with a houseful of religious fanatics."

"I know what you mean. My parents tried to force religion down my throat, but I rebelled when I went to college."

"What happened?"

"I got sick and tired of kosher food and going to temple every Friday night and Saturday morning."

"Wow! That could kill one's social life."

"It did, until I moved away from home." Grinning, she recalled, "But I made up for it real fast."

"How did your parents like the change?"

"When they eventually found out, they were really mad. In fact, my father still doesn't talk to me."

Iris asked, "Does it bother you?"

"Not really. It's his loss, not mine."

"I don't speak to my parents either. They're too ashamed of my profession and views."

"It appears our roads ran parallel."

Iris lowered her voice and said, "I have a rather personal question. Do you mind me asking it?"

"It depends on the subject."

"Several friends of mine are college professors. I always thought teachers don't make a lot of money, and yet they live like royalty. What's the story?"

Sandra looked at the woman. "Most college professors do not really make a lot of money from their job. The benefits are usually above average, but the gross salary itself is far from generous."

"So how can my friends do it?"

"What about inheritance?"

Iris stated, "Both sets of parents are lower middle class."

"It's not unusual for college professors to supplement their income by other means."

"Such as?"

Sandra continued, "Many write books and articles, others travel the lecture circuit, while some utilize their God-given talents to secure income from other methods."

"What about you?" Iris questioned. "Do you do anything to earn more income?"

"To live in the style to which I have become accustomed, I've managed to supplement my basic salary."

"How do you do it?"

Sandra looked slightly uncomfortable, but continued, "I've formed a service corporation with several of my colleagues."

"That sounds exciting, what do you do?"

"Provide sundry services to our students," Sandra stated vaguely.

Inquiring further, Iris asked, "Such as?"

"We assist students in tutoring and writing papers."

"You mean correcting their papers, don't you?"

Sandra said, "No. We actually write the papers for them. We've even done master's and doctoral theses."

"But that's not fair."

"If they are willing to pay our price—and it's a rather stiff amount—we'll provide them with a fully acceptable finished product."

Iris responded, "I can't believe things like that happen in our colleges."

"It does in most; in fact, we also ghostwrite books and articles for other professors."

"How do most of your students do on their tests?"

"Not one who has come to us for tutoring has ever failed their exam or course."

"That's an amazing record, how do you do it?"

Smiling, Sandra said, "It's actually quite easy, we get the exams ahead of time."

Shocked, Iris inquired, "How do you manage that?"

"Usually directly from their professors."

"Why would a professor do such a thing?"

"To supplement their income."

"That's some racket."

"Why thank you. I was the one responsible for setting it up on our campus."

"Doesn't the administration give you a hard time?"

Sandra answered, "If you grease the right palm or make the right party an officer in the company, things manage to go undisturbed."

"Now I see how my friends can live so nicely."

"You'd better believe it and most of the money is not recorded."

"Cash?"

"Precisely."

"And I thought I was the only one who enjoyed that luxury."

"Not at all. The underground cash society has evolved throughout many sectors of our community, including the academic environment."

"Do students ever give you a hard time?"

"Never. If they do, we have enough clout in the right places to make their lives intolerable."

"Sounds like a monopoly."

Sandra grinned. "It is. We purposely make the courses difficult so most of our students are forced to seek outside assistance."

"How do they find out about your company?"

"Word of mouth. Finding enough business is never a problem; getting enough material is."

"So what do you do?"

"Recycle our older merchandise."

"You rewrite old papers?"

"That's a waste of time. We just use them again."

"What do the professors say?"

"Nothing. They simple pass our students and agree to look the other way."

Iris looked at Sandra, "I can't believe a college professor would do such a thing."

"We recycled three doctoral theses last year alone and we are working on developing an exchange program with other companies throughout the entire academic community."

"It sounds very big."

"It's big—and profitable. That's why your friends and I can afford to live without any financial concerns."

"Wow!" Iris responded. "I'm glad I asked. Now I understand how they can do it."

"They probably made extra income by passing students in their classes. That's the most popular method for professors."

"You do that?"

"All the time. For a simple D, I get $1,000.00."

"$1,000.00 for a D!"

"Higher grades cost more." Sandra smiled and added, "That's how I get enough money to travel."

"Amazing."

"Iris, it's just a business!"

SEVENTY-SEVEN

James saw Father McShane approaching his area. He placed his book on a nearby table and waited. "I told you the last time, I'm not doing any more hypnosis."

The priest shook his head. "I'm here to apologize, not to ask for anything more."

"You certainly had some nerve."

"I did it for that poor child; she was so desperate."

"Father, wake up and smell the roses. The world is filled with girls like Tara. They are nothing but insignificant, worthless creatures."

"I'd rather not discuss Tara at this time."

"I ac cept your apology; please let me read."

Father McShane held out a package. "This is for you."

The physician accepted the gift. "But why?"

"I wanted to thank you for your time."

James laughed, "Unless this bag is filled with hundred dollar bills, you're far short of my usual fee."

"It's the best I can do under the circumstances."

Opening the package, James found an unopened bottle of Irish whiskey. Studying the label, he nodded with approval. "My favorite!"

"I was hoping it would heal any hard feeling that might have developed over the incident."

Placing the bottle on the table, he said, "Consider it forgotten."

The priest sat down on an adjacent chair and said, "Thank God. I'm greatly relieved."

"Where did you get the whiskey? I didn't see any other liquor around here."

Father stuttered, "I found it in the storage room."

"How did I miss this beauty before?" Opening the bottle's seal, he smelled the whiskey's strong aroma. "Just what the doctor ordered."

"I'm glad you enjoy the gift."

"Enjoy? I love it." After pouring whiskey into two glasses, he offered one to the Father.

"I'm not a drinker."

"Come on, Father. I shouldn't drink alone."

"Well, if you insist, I'll have just a tiny nip."

Within a short time, the two men had consumed half the bottle. Feeling no pain, James asked, "Why isn't Michael killing us with his music as much?"

Father McShane laughed, "I asked him to practice less."

James slurred his words. "Come on, Father, he doesn't listen to anyone."

"I told him my cousin was an agent and that if he did me the favor of playing less, I'd introduce the two of them when we get out of here."

"Good thinking on your part." The physician then inquired, "What label does he work for?"

"Who?"

"Your cousin."

The priest giggled and whispered, "I don't have a cousin in the record business."

"But you told Michael you did?"

"I had to think of something fast; the music was driving me up a wall."

"And the jerk fell for it."

"Wouldn't you if a priest told you something?" said Father McShane.

James nodded. "I see your point." Lifting a filled glass to his mouth, he slurred, "Have another, Father, it's getting cold."

"One more and then I'd better get going."

"Don't worry about the traffic, Father, I'll make sure you get home safely."

After several more drinks, the priest looked at the bottle and asked, "Jimmy, wasn't that bottle half-filled, four drinks ago?"

"I'm not sure," the physician said. "But who really cares; this stuff is the best I've ever had."

Slapping his fellow drinker on the back, Father slurred, "I know you're an atheist but what religion were you born into?"

"I was raised Methodist."

"That's a very nice religion," Father McShane added. "One of my golfing friends is a Methodist minister." Sighing, he said "He's really a great guy!"

"How's his golf game?"

Giggling almost uncontrollably, the priest took yet another mouthful and said, "He's terrible and he cheats like hell."

"He cheats?" James said laughing. "Why?"

"He is so bad he'll do just about anything to win so we just look the other way and pacify him once in awhile."

"Sounds like a real role model."

"He's okay for a minister," the Father continued, "but a real shitty golfer."

James took another mouthful of whiskey and relaxed on the floor. "Hey, Father, why did you ever become a priest?"

"I didn't want to work for a living. The church takes pretty good care of us when we get old."

"Don't you miss sex?"

"No." The Father then whispered, "I get all I need from some of the Sisters—but don't tell anyone."

"No big deal, Father. Besides, I get all I want from the nurses at my hospital."

"Speaking of hospital," the priest asked, "why won't you take care of that sleeping guy?"

"You want the truth?" the physician slurred softly.

"Why not? I'm a priest and won't tell anyone else."

"I don't do emergency work at all." Taking a deep breath, he added, "I never passed my residency in that area, I screwed around too much."

"But how did you become a doctor?"

"I dated the head of the department and she forged my papers." Giggling, he added, "She was one hot number."

"What about during your surgeries if some emergency happens?"

"I step back and call a code." James looked with bleary eyes at the priest, "I let the peons play God and I just collect the money."

"I'm glad I didn't use you for my surgery."

"Me too!" the physician joked. "I'd hate a lose a good guy like you."

Noticing the lights were starting to dim, Father McShane asked, "Do you mind if I sleep here tonight?" Sighing, he added, "I don't think I can make it back to my sofa."

"No sweat," James stated before he passed out.

Both men awoke midway through the next light period. Neither recalled anything discussed during their drinking spree. Looking at the bottle, Father McShane said, "I guess we didn't drink too much, the bottle is still three-quarters filled."

James just moaned, held his head, and muttered, "That one quarter was dynamite; I have one hell of a hangover."

SEVENTY-EIGHT

Todd continued to lift makeshift weights and jog daily. Passing Tara's site, he stopped and rested. "What's the matter?" he asked.

"Nothing," she responded weakly.

"You mean you normally sit and cry during the day?"

"I guess I'm just a little upset."

"Why don't you exercise? It's great for the body and mind."

"Maybe that's what I need to do." Looking up at the burly athlete, she inquired, "Would you show me what exercises are the best?"

"That's my specialty. I'll whip you into shape real fast."

"How do I start?"

Todd demonstrated several stretching exercises and watched as she repeated his actions. "Move slowly and don't jerk your leg."

"I never realized how tight I am," Tara stated as she continued to lean forward stretching her hamstring muscles.

After almost forty continuous minutes of exercising, the young woman collapsed on the floor. Todd briskly rubbed her lower back and offered her further encouragement. "You did a good job for the first time. If you want I'll work with you some more."

"I'd like that very much."

"Once we get you stretched out, we'll do some laps."

Tara responded quickly, "I can't run; I'm too old."

"You've got to change that line of thinking. Work with me and I promise you'll be running laps around this room."

"Will you put it in writing?"

"I don't have to," he said confidently. "I know it will happen."

Shrugging her shoulders, Tara added, "I've got nothing to lose; I'll run with you every day."

"In the mean time, spend some more time stretching."

Laughing, she said, "Yes, coach."

Tara decided to stick to her new plan. Early each light period, the young woman would stretch and exercise. She soon noticed a distinct change to her musculature and fitness. Todd offered her a great deal of encouragement as well as updating her program regularly. During the mid-afternoon period, they would run around the perimeter of the great room. Initially, Tara experienced difficulty maintaining an even pace, but soon she was matching Todd stride for stride. Others would observe, but no one commented on her progress.

After a grueling session, Tara and Todd rested near his sofa. Once she caught her breath, she questioned him about his past. "I'd like to ask you about college athletics."

"What do you want to know?"

"I've heard so many conflicting stories about college athletes. Do they get actually get paid for playing?"

"I thought you couldn't remember anything about the past."

She thought for another moment, "I'm not sure how I remembered that."

Noticing she was about to become despondent from her sudden but paltry recollection, he quickly answered her question. "The real truth is that the majority of college athletes do get money for playing."

"How much?"

"That depends on the school and the value of the player to their team."

"What about you?"

Todd recalled, "I had a great life while in college; I got a full scholarship plus loads of spending money."

"Aren't you a star player?"

"I was the best there ever was; All-American four years in a row. I even got a new car from the alumni every year."

"And you went to the pros after that?"

"Number one draft pick."

"I don't understand what it means exactly, but I'm sure it's good."

"It means a big contract and big bucks."

Smiling, Tara joked, "And to think I have such a celebrity as my coach."

"I agree, you certainly are privileged to have me." Todd stated in a half-serious tone. "By the way, I was wondering if I could ask something of you?"

"Surely, you've been so good to me. What is it?"

"How about giving me a little?"

"Giving you a little what?" she responded.

Without backing off, he said, "How about going to bed with me?"

Taken back by his boldness, she quickly answered, "No."

"Just no!"

"Just plain no."

"But why not? Most women would kill for the chance and I might add that I'm quite a stud." Stroking her thigh, he added, "I guarantee you won't regret your decision."

Pushing his hand away, she said, "I can't. It wouldn't be right."

"Why not?"

"I don't remember anything about my past. Maybe I'm married."

"So? That doesn't make any difference."

"Maybe not to you, but it does to me."

"Come on, Tara, get off your high horse and give me a little. Besides, you owe me."

"I owe you?"

"Yeah. Consider it payment for the lessons."

Enraged, Tara spoke deliberately, "I'd never go to bed with you even if you were the last man alive. I can't believe that you'd ask such a thing."

"It's your loss; don't come to me later on."

"I'd never—"

Cutting her off he added, "And our lessons are now officially ended. Train yourself!"

She ran back to her sofa. Cursing to herself, she muttered, "Damn that bastard! They're all the same!" Placing her head on a pillow, she began to cry.

S E V E N T Y - N I N E

Alice stared at the ceiling. Noticing her, Michael put down his guitar and asked, "What are you doing?"

"Nothing really."

"Why are you looking at the ceiling?"

"I was just looking, that's all! Is it a crime to look?"

"Chill baby! I was just curious."

Apologizing for her outburst, Alice said, "I'm sorry."

"So what's so interesting about the ceiling? Is it falling?"

Without changing her facial expression, she stated, "I'm counting light bulbs."

Michael laughed loudly. "Counting light bulbs? Why?"

"It's none of your business."

"Come on, Alice! No one goes around and counts light bulbs without a reason. What gives?"

Sitting on the nearest chair, Alice spoke softly, "There's definitely something wrong in this room."

"The whole thing is wrong to me, but why light bulbs?"

Clutching her hands she continued, "During the last few light periods, I noticed a difference in the intensity of the overhead lights." Pausing, she stated, "So I've been counting them daily."

"What did you find?"

Alice looked at the young rock star. In a wavering voice, she said, "They change every day."

"What do you mean *change*?"

"The number of bulbs changes on each chandelier after every dark period."

He asked, "Are you sure? Maybe your eyes are playing games with you?"

"I'm positive."

"Wow!" Michael gazed at the nearest fixture. "I count twenty-four bulbs."

"That's what I counted. Yesterday, there were thirty and the day before, eighteen."

"How can that be? Have you spoken to Franklyn about it?"

"You must be kidding! He'd think I'm crazy."

"But you counted..."

"It's only my word."

"And mine."

Touching his hand, she said, "But you have no proof either."

"Suppose we count the bulbs together for the next few days and then the two of us can go and speak to him."

"It's fine with me." Alice added, "There's strength in numbers."

Five dark periods passed and the two compared their numbers. "I don't get it," Alice stated. "Nothing has changed."

Michael seemed impatient when he said, "Maybe you made a mistake before."

"Are you calling me a liar?"

"No. I'm simply wondering."

Alice began to raise her voice, "I don't like your insinuation."

"I haven't made any; I've spoken only the truth. We've counted bulbs for the past five days and nothing has changed. Each day, we see twenty-four bulbs."

"Someone's playing a trick on me."

Michael snickered and responded, "Like who? The keeper of the lights?"

"It's not funny." Alice looked upward and recounted. "Twenty-two, twenty-three, twenty-four!"

"See what I mean, it's been the same right along."

The woman slumped in her chair and brought her hands over her head. "It can't be; it's a trick."

Michael said, "I'd better speak to Father."

"About what?" she asked.

"About you."

"What about me?"

"I just think he'd better speak to you about the bulbs."

Alice again raised her voice. "Just leave me alone."

"But you need help."

"You stupid jackass!" she cried. "I was only pulling your leg. Can't you tell!"

"You mean you weren't serious about the bulbs?"

"Of course not."

"Then why make me waste my time counting the bulbs?"

"To have some fun." Alice forced a smile and added, "The joke's on you, my dear."

Michael stormed away, leaving Alice alone. Sitting back, she began to recount the bulbs. "Twenty-two, twenty-three, twenty-four, and twenty-five." Gazing overhead, the woman stared in disbelief. Knowing she could not tell anyone about her discovery, she sighed deeply and pondered her next move.

E I G H T Y

Despite Father McShane's daily classes and other attempts by Sandra, the members of the group drifted further apart. Most kept to themselves and managed to fill their time with unproductive activities. Except during meals, the majority neither spoke nor mingled with one another. Each secretly hoped they would be rescued and the nightmare would be terminated. Meanwhile music filled the room while the great wall clock regularly alerted the group to the passage of time.

EIGHTY-ONE

Hugo finished eating his meal and whispered to Phyllis, "Do you think I might have a word or two in private with you?"

"In private? Is there anything in particular you'd like to talk about?"

"It's a rather personal matter."

Looking to the others, she nodded and responded, "Meet me later in the stock room."

Once the kitchen area was cleaned and everyone departed for their individual sites, Hugo strolled to the storage room. He waited until Phyllis sat on an adjacent carton before speaking. "I'm so glad you came."

Phyllis responded, "Why so private?"

"I have a rather personal matter to discuss."

"Oh," Phyllis said. "What is it?"

Without changing his facial expression, Hugo answered, "Phyllis, you are an extremely beautiful woman. In fact, you are the most mature, delightful woman in our group."

"Why thank you, Hugo. That's a very nice compliment."

"And well deserved."

"It's been a long time since I've heard such beautiful words, and God only knows every lady loves to hear them."

"I'll make a mental note of that for the future."

Phyllis blushed and added, "Thank you again and I'm very flattered, but why this private meeting?"

"I certainly couldn't say these things to you in public."

"I guess you're right."

"Besides," Hugo stated, "there's more I want to say."

"More?" Phyllis chuckled. "I don't know how much more I can take. Remember, I'm not a youngster anymore."

Without cracking a smile, Hugo said matter of factly, "I want to go to bed with you."

Phyllis stared in disbelief at the man, "I'm not sure if I heard you correctly."

"I said I want to go to bed with you."

"No one has ever spoken to me like that." She started to walk away until he grabbed her arm and forced her back onto the carton. She shouted, "How dare you! Who do you think you are?"

He raised his hand and glared downward at her seated body. "Shut your mouth and listen," he said.

"Don't ever—" He slapped her hard across the face and shouted, "You will have sex with me anytime I want! Understand?"

"You can't force me—"

"Phyllis, you are going to do it of your own free will. I guarantee it."

"You're mad. I'd never consent to such a thing. Have you forgotten I'm a married woman?"

Taking her hand, he squeezed it tightly, "What about Todd?"

"What *about* Todd?"

"Don't play dumb with me! I know what's going on between the two of you."

"I don't know what you're talking about," Phyllis said weakly. "We're just friends."

"Friends! He's screwing you just about every night. I've seen it myself."

"I—"

"Phyllis, all I want is a little for myself now and then. You can keep Todd on a nightly basis; I prefer daytime sex myself."

"What if I refuse?"

"You can't, my dear."

"And why not?"

"I don't think your husband would appreciate knowing all the details."

"Are you blackmailing me?"

"Let's just call it an incentive for your cooperation."

Realizing Hugo was serious, Phyllis pleaded, "Please, Hugo…"

Pulling her to his side, he kissed her roughly on the mouth. She held back until he slapped her again. "I'm not going to say it again! You'll do it when and as often as I want. You understand?" Frightened, she remained rigid as he began unbuttoning her blouse. Tears flowed down her cheeks as Hugo slipped the garment from her shoulders. Caressing her exposed skin, he whispered, "Now that's better, just lay back and enjoy it."

EIGHTY-TWO

Michael and Jeffery stood by the longest shelves of books. "Besides playing music, Michael, what hobbies do you pursue?"

"I don't have a lot of free time; I'm constantly on the road with my band."

"No matter how much business I have scheduled, I always set some time aside for my leisure activities."

"As I said, music and the band *is* my life."

"That's dedication! I must have free time once in awhile or I'd crack."

"What hobbies do you have?" Michael inquired.

"My favorite hobby is hunting."

The rocker laughed, "You don't look like a hunter to me!"

"What does a hunter look like?" Jeffery countered.

"To me, a hunter is someone like Todd."

"Like Todd? Why him?"

"Big, strong, and no brains."

"As a matter of fact, most hunters are people like me! Recent studies by the International Gun and Rifle Association profiled its membership. I'll send you a copy once we get out of here, I'm sure you'll find it most educational."

"No thanks, Jeff, I'll take your word on it."

"But it's no problem, I'm on the board of directors."

"Don't waste money on the postage, I won't read it."

"Okay, but remember what I told you; hunters are just normal people."

"And Todd Warren is a girl!"

"I do not find you funny. In fact, I find you outright rude and sarcastic."

"Jeffery," Michael calmly stated, "Cool it, I was just pulling your joint."

After taking a deep breath, Jeffery asked, "What do you do in the limited free time you do have?"

"I hunt!"

"I thought you stopped making jokes..."

"I did," Michael said, "I love to hunt."

"What do you hunt?"

"Anything. I just love to kill things."

Not knowing if the rocker was serious or not, Jeffery asked, "What kind of rifle do you have?"

"I have a pistol."

"Do you hunt anywhere special?"

"Nope."

"What kind of game do you like best?"

"I have no favorites; I just love to kill them all."

"I believe you're toying with me."

"No way, man!" Michael placed his hand on the man's shoulder and continued, "After a tough gig, the whole band usually goes hunting."

"The whole band goes?"

"We're a very close group."

"One of my greatest thrills was to kill an African elephant. It took me only one shot and he died instantly. Have you ever gone after any big game?"

"Sure. Killed a few elephants myself, but do you know what my favorite animal to kill is?"

"No. What is it?"

"I just love to kill young girls."

"Young girls!" Jeffery said. "I don't get it."

"Jeffery, I love to stalk and screw anything young."

"What does that have to do with hunting?"

Michael laughed loudly. "I hunt two-legged beasts and when I get them, I screw them to death."

"So, you don't hunt animals."

"Don't you get it? I don't waste my time killing animals. I'll leave that to you killers."

Jeffery lost his temper. "I find your sense of humor downright insulting."

"And I find you boring!"

"I believe I'll join Father for an intellectual conversation."

"Maybe you can get him to go hunting with you. I'm sure he loves to murder those sweet, innocent defenseless animals."

"It's obvious you do not know anything about nature and the conservation of the animal kingdom."

Michael instantly replied, "I do know about the senseless slaughter of harmless creatures and the extinction of many species."

"We help the balance of nature and support many worthwhile projects."

"You're nothing but a cold, calculated killer whose victims can't defend themselves against your weapons. That's not a sport; it's a one-sided massacre."

Jeffery shouted, "You're nothing but a stupid, animal-loving idiot!" He grabbed a book from the nearest shelf and stormed away.

Michael chuckled and said, "I can't wait to ride him about his receding hairline."

EIGHTY-THREE

Despite the fact that each wall and inspection site was rebuilt during the dark periods, Franklyn steadily worked his way around the room. Discovering no exit, he began again. Without their assistance, Franklyn generally stayed by himself. Despite pleas from Father McShane, he continued his self-imposed isolation. At the urging of the priest, Iris walked to the latest construction site and watched. "Find anything yet?"

Franklyn answered abruptly, "No."

"Didn't you check this area already?"

"Yes."

"Need any help?"

He studied the woman, "Why are you here? Did someone send you here to taunt me?"

"No. I came here to help you. I don't think it's fair that you're the only one trying to find a way out."

"I agree."

"I'll do anything to get out of here; what do you want me to do?"

"I'm trying to find a tunnel. I think it's around here."

"Is that the tunnel in which Tara skinned her knee?"

"Yes, you have a good memory," Franklyn said.

"Who could forget anything around here?"

Picking up an improvised hammer and chisel, the scientist began striking the wall. Iris knelt at his side and started to tear at the exposed wallboard. After hours of labor, they uncovered an opening. "I think we've found it," Franklyn stated in an excited tone.

"Do you think it's the same one?"

"I have no idea, but we better work quickly before the darkness sets in."

With their tools, they crawled into the darkness. Using his flashlight, the twosome made their way farther into the tunnel. Iris pressed on the walls and whispered, "They feel solid."

"Just like every other tunnel I've found so far."

"What kind of rock is this?"

"I'm not a geologist, but I believe they're composed of granite." Striking his chisel against a nearby stone, he stated, "See what I mean; that baby is really hard."

As the light from the room disappeared, Iris questioned, "How far does this tunnel actually go?"

"I'm not sure."

"Do you think it's safe to travel any farther?"

Shining the beam of the flashlight into her face, he asked, "You do want to find a way out of here, don't you?"

"Yes," she answered resolutely.

"Then what choice do we have?"

They traveled inward only to discover that the temperature of the enclosure was intensifying. As they rounded a bend, both stopped. Franklyn probed the exposed barrier and shrugged his shoulders. "Looks like we've reached a dead end."

"Are you positive?"

The scientist retested the rocky blockade with his tools and found them immovable, "Let's get back and we'll try another one."

The heat intensified causing their retreat to be arduous. As they observed the room's light just ahead, their surroundings suddenly began to vibrate. Iris grasped at his arm and shouted, "What's going on?"

"I don't—" His words were cut short by the dimming of the room's lights. "My God" he screamed. "We've got to get out of here! The darkness is coming."

Before they could reach the portal, a loud rumbling occurred. They were knocked down onto the heated ground as the entire tunnel abruptly blackened. Frantically they crawled forward until they reached the entrance. Iris touched a blockage that prevented their exit and cried, "What are we going to do?"

Franklyn slammed his hammer against the wall and immediately discovered it was immovable. After many attempts, he collapsed onto the ground and tried to catch his breath. Iris stared at the barrier and then back into the darkness. Again she cried, "What are we going to do? I don't want to die in here!"

The scientist tried to calm his companion, "Shouting and crying will do no good. Let's try to be rational."

"How can I be rational? We're stuck in here!"

Pulling her shaking body into his arms, he spoke. "They know we're in here and they'll try to get us out once the dark period has ended."

"How can you be so sure? Maybe they'll leave us here to die."

"Why would they do that?"

"They'll get our food and supplies."

"Father won't let that occur."

With only the light from their flashlight providing vision, Franklyn eased himself against a nearby rock and pulled her close. "Just relax and try to get some sleep."

Iris sighed, "How can I sleep here? I don't want to die in this tunnel."

"You won't," Franklyn said with certainty. "I promise. Somehow, we'll get out of here."

"Promise?"

He touched her arm gently, "I promise." The scientist turned off his flashlight and waited. After a long time, both fell asleep.

Hours later, they were awakened by a surge of heat and vibration. As they grabbed for one another, both were knocked violently. Moments later, calmness returned. "Look!" Franklyn shouted as he pointed to the tunnel's barrier. "It's sheet rock again!"

They scrambled to their feet and began striking the wall with their tools. Soon the light from the room was visible. Franklyn shouted through the newly created opening, "Help!"

"We can hear you. Are you okay?"

"Yes!" Iris screamed. "Get us out of here!"

Attacking the wall from both sides, they soon created an escape hole for the two explorers. Everyone listened intently to their story.

"Does that mean we can't get out of the room?" Phyllis asked.

Franklyn responded, "Not at all, it just means we've got to be more careful about working in the darkness. I will still continue to search for a way out of here." Turning to Iris, he asked, "And what about you?"

Taking a deep breath, she said, "I think I'll take a little rest from working. Maybe later on I'll help, but right now I'm too frightened to go into another tunnel."

Patting her hand gently, the scientist said, "I understand."

The next dark period, the wall was fully repaired. Franklyn arose, gathered his tools, and immediately went to another section of the room. There, unassisted, he picked up his hammer and chisel and began another quest for a possible exit.

EIGHTY-FOUR

After his latest discussion group, Father McShane joined Sandra for lunch. "Father, your views today were more liberal. Am I changing your perspective?"

The priest laughed loudly and boasted, "Not at all, my dear, I thought I'd toss you a small bone. Tomorrow, be prepared for another argument."

"I look forward to it. After all, it's the only intellectual stimulation I get since coming to this room."

"I couldn't agree with you more." Sighing, he added, "I miss my Sunday sermons and weekly religious groups."

"And I miss my classes and research."

Joking, the priest added, "At least we've got each other."

"Some combination! A Roman Catholic Priest and a devout atheist."

"Regardless, we're each helping the other."

Touching his hand, she said, "I agree, Father. Without this stimulation, I think I'd lose it from lack of intellectualism."

"And I would have no reason to prepare my lectures so carefully." The priest grinned, "You certainly keep me on my toes."

"Flattery will get you nowhere; however, if you weren't a priest, I might go for you myself."

Looking upward, he said, "Thank you, dear God, for saving my old body from this charming young woman."

Turning more serious, Sandra asked, "Father, how does a priest manage to live without any income?"

"God provides for our needs," he said.

"I'm serious, Father, how do priests survive without money?"

"We have our ways; it's hard, but we muddle through life with little difficulty."

Unsatisfied, Sandra continued to push for an answer. "College professors have our own methods of supplementing our meager income, but a priest gets nothing. How do you do it?"

"God provides."

"Why are you being so evasive? Why don't you just answer my question?"

Sighing, Father McShane responded, "If you must know, my congregation is extremely generous."

"You mean they give you money."

"Not directly."

"I've afraid you are confusing me. Could you be more specific?"

"I receive many gifts from the members of my church. For example: my car is repaired for free and I eat without cost at their homes. I never pay for shining my shoes, cleaning my clothes, movie or theater tickets, or golf balls."

"Golf balls! How do you manage that?"

Smiling, Father stated, "The club pro is a member of my parish. I get unlimited use of the course, tennis courts, and swimming pool, as well as use of their dining room."

"All for free?"

"All for free."

"What's the catch?"

"Once in awhile, I say a little prayer or provide them with an ecumenical smile."

"That's all they ask?"

"My dear," Father McShane laughed, "these simple spiritual gestures are enough to boost their egos and cleanse their souls. Most are willing to share any materialistic item for my holy presence."

"That's a little strong."

"But true! It's an easy way for them to buy their way to heaven. Cater to a priest and get a free ticket to the Pearly Gates."

"Sounds better all the time."

"Now you see why I can do so many things without having a lot of money."

"What do you do if you need cash?"

"God and my congregation provide me with more than enough."

"How does God provide you with money?"

Father McShane whispered, "Through the poor box and other collections. I usually take whatever I need from there."

"Isn't that money intended for the poor?" Sandra queried.

"It's intended to assist the running of the church and besides, who's poorer than a priest?"

"I guess we all have our methods."

"Every priest I know does the same thing. In fact, so do most rabbis and ministers. It's an occupational perk."

"Maybe I should throw in my books and become a nun."

"You can't if you have any bad habits."

Sandra giggled. "You're improving, Father."

"I try, my dear. I try very hard under these terrible conditions." Looking more serious, he said, "I just can't wait until they release us from this room. The confinement is beginning to get to me."

"I understand how you feel, but try to remain strong. You're the inspiration for many of us; if you buckle under, most will also crumple."

Looking at the locked door, he sighed, "That's a huge burden for any man to carry; I only hope I can live up to your expectations."

Sandra handed the priest a copy of the Holy Bible. "Try this book, Father, I highly recommend it for times like this. Many find courage, conviction, and inspiration within its pages and verses."

Holding the book, Father McShane looked at its cover and then turned to a particular page. After reading the scripture, he muttered, "Perhaps, this is what I seek." Sandra walked away. The priest attempted to quell his fears, but no relief could be found. Finally, he placed the book on the table and closed his eyes. *Please,* he moaned softly to himself. *Please help us find a way out of here fast.*

E I G H T Y - F I V E

Noticing the actress was relaxing after her daily calisthenics, Phyllis joined Joanne. "You certainly work very hard," she commented.

Joanne answered, "I've got no choice, I must stay in shape."

"I prefer other forms of exercise. Ones that do not require so much sweat and strain. My favorite is shopping."

"I would be utterly bored without my work."

"There are so many stores in this country for me to shop, I could never get bored."

"You have one major luxury I cannot enjoy."

Phyllis asked, "What is it?"

"You can go anywhere and not be recognized. The minute I walk into a store, I'm usually attacked by hordes of fans and autograph hounds."

"I guess that could be a problem, especially when the big holiday sales are on."

"I haven't shopped in a store in years."

"How do you purchase your clothes?"

Joanne looked at her clenched hands, "The studio uses a buying service that shops for all its stars."

"Do you pick them out?"

"No. Everything is delivered at my door whenever needed."

"Don't you ever buy birthday or Christmas gifts for your family and friends?"

"No."

"Don't tell me...the buying service?"

"Yes. I provide them with a list of sizes and items and they do the rest."

"Do you dine out?" Phyllis inquired.

"My agent and studio make all arrangements for those things. Of course, I am isolated from the masses and usually sit in a reserved, secluded spot in the restaurant."

"Ever go out for a pizza?"

"Never. I couldn't take the chance. The studio's hierarchy would have a heart attack if anything happened."

"I never thought your life could be so limited. It is always being portrayed so glamorously in the tabloids."

Joanne laughed. "That's what they want you to think. Actually, my life is really quite dull."

Phyllis sat for a moment, "May I ask you a rather personal question?"

"Certainly."

Squirming slightly in her seat, she asked, "It's about your husband."

"You mean my *former* husband?"

"Yes. I meant your former husband."

"You want to know if I really killed him, am I right?"

"Yes. There were so many terrible articles about it in the newspapers and on television that I was just curious."

"You and the rest of the world want to know; in fact, I'm haunted by the media on a daily basis and probably will be for the remainder of my life."

"Please forgive me; it wasn't right for me to ask."

Shrugging her shoulders, Joanne responded, "It really doesn't matter anymore; what's done is done."

Phyllis, in a matronly gesture, touched the actress' shoulder and whispered, "I'm so sorry, please forgive me."

"Perhaps it's better that I speak to someone about it other than a shrink. It's always better to speak to someone who can be more objective about such things."

"You don't—"

Joanne interrupted her, "Harold was my fourth husband. After three rather short and unsuccessful marriages, I swore my marriage to Harold would be my last. I did everything, and I mean everything, to try to make him happy. I bought him everything he requested plus anything else I thought he would enjoy. I guess it wasn't good enough. I came home unexpectedly one afternoon and found him in bed with another woman. I lost my temper and ended the problem."

"The papers said you shot both of them."

"That's exactly what I did. The bastards both deserved it. How would you like to come home and find your husband in your bed with another woman?" Before Phyllis could answer, Joanne spoke. "I ran to the bureau and found his pistol. After four shots, both were dead."

"You mean you actually killed them?"

"I stood there and slowly pulled that trigger. First, I shot them in their genitals and then after they suffered for a few minutes, I ended their misery with a bullet right between their eyes."

"You poor thing, I feel so sorry for you."

"Don't feel sorry for me. I'm just fine."

"But the papers said you were hospitalized."

"It was entirely fabricated by my agent and studio. With their help and enough money in the right places, we had the major charges dropped."

"The articles said you were on probation."

"One big joke. I call my probation officer once a month and let her know how I am doing."

"That's all?"

"You got it! They're both dead and I'm still around to tell the story. In fact, I've gotten more free press over the situation than I've ever gotten in my career."

"What about his children and their lawsuit?"

"Settled out of court."

"Amazing."

"Not amazing at all, my dear." Joanne smiled, "It's just a matter of knowing the right people and having enough money to pay them off."

"So I guess you don't have any regrets over it?"

"You must be kidding, it's one of the best things that could have happened to me," Joanne chuckled and added, "I may decide to get remarried one more time, just to see if it could happen again."

"You're not serious!"

"I'm dead serious except I'd use eight bullets this time."

"Thank God I don't have that problem. My husband and I have an absolutely wonderful relationship."

Looking at her friend, Joanne stated, "I'm very happy for you. Such relationships are unheard of in Hollywood. I had hoped to have one like yours some day."

"Yes," Phyllis said, "we are, indeed, very lucky."

EIGHTY-SIX

James looked at the sleeping form and laughed, "Why are you wasting your time? He's close to death."

Tara immediately countered, "How do *you* know? You haven't examined him."

Gazing at the form lying beside the young woman's sofa, the physician answered, "One doesn't have to be a rocket scientist to know he's too far gone to survive. His vital signs appear to be almost absent."

"His vital signs? What are they?"

Responding in a caustic tone, James said, "His respiration and circulatory functions!"

"Could you say it in simpler words?"

"His breathing looks shallow and irregular and his pulse is probably also faint."

"How do I find out?"

"Take his pulse."

"How?"

"You can check a pulse in several areas, but I'd suggest checking the one in his wrist."

Tara pressed her fingers until she felt a slight flutter. "I found it!" she shouted. "It's here."

"Does it feel strong and regular?"

After several moments, she answered, "It seems unsteady and hard to feel at times."

"Just like I told you, his vital signs are poor."

"Would you check to make sure I'm correct?"

"No. I told you a thousand times, I'm not going to ever help him. Why should I risk my professional career and license for some derelict? Do us all a favor and let him be."

Tara cleansed the sleeping man's face with a moist cloth.

The gesture seemed to inflame James as he quickly exited. Kneeling, Tara whispered, "Don't let him upset you. Just try to stay alive and wake up." As was her daily ritual, Tara proceeded to wet the man's lips and comb his long, black hair. As she was about to stand, a feeble moan emitted from the man's mouth. Though startled, she remained and listened. Again, a slight sound exited the man's lips. Not knowing exactly what to do, she shook him and shouted, "I hear you! I hear you!" Noticing the man remained immobile, Tara raced to locate James.

"Please," she pleaded. "He's alive. Help him!"

Harshly pushing her hand from his arm, the physician stated coldly, "Leave me alone! I'm not interested in helping anyone!"

"But he moaned!"

"I don't care if he sat up and sang *Happy Birthday*, he's not my problem."

Realizing the futility of any further pleading, the young woman sought Father McShane. "Come, Father, you've got to come!"

Frightened from a leisurely nap, the priest sat upright. Rubbing his eyes, he inquired, "What's the problem?"

"Come quickly, he's alive!"

"Who?"

"The last sleeping one!"

The priest asked, "Are you sure?"

"Yes. I heard him; he moaned twice!"

Together they walked quickly to her sofa and knelt by the motionless body. Tara pushed at the sleeping form and waited. After several more unsuccessful attempts, she turned to the priest, with tearful eyes, and sobbed, "He moaned. I heard him!"

Father McShane attempted to locate a pulse. "I'm afraid I wasn't trained in medicine; let me get James."

"He won't come!" Tara cried. "He refused!"

Shaking his head, Father McShane again shook the man's arm and waited. As before, nothing stirred. Finally, they sat on the sofa. "Are you positive it was him? Maybe it came from someone else in the room."

Tara answered assertively, "He made the sound! Nobody else! Are you questioning my word?"

"No," the priest stated, "It's just that he hasn't moved or spoken since."

"I know that, but he did before."

Trying to calm her down, Father McShane said, "I'm sure it happened. That's why I'm here."

Looking at the sleeping man, she questioned, "How can he still be alive? He hasn't eaten or drank."

"I don't know, but I don't think his chances are very good."

Sobbing, she clutched her hands, "But he moaned..."

"Perhaps it was just gas?"

"Gas?"

"Yes. Bodies sometimes expel a gas from their openings."

Realizing what the priest was attempting to say, Tara countered, "It wasn't gas, he moaned."

"I believe you heard something. If it was a moan, then more are sure to follow. Just let me know and I'll come over again."

Not sure how she should react to his last statement, the young woman nodded. "I'll do that, Father. Thanks for your help."

Once the priest had walked away, she dropped to her knees and continued to moisten the man's lips with a wet towel. *I know you're alive and I know you moaned. Please wake up; nobody believes what I'm saying.* Stroking his hair, she started to weep. *Please wake up and show them that I'm not going crazy! Please.*

EIGHTY-SEVEN

Iris placed the crystal ball on the low table and then checked the other contents of her box. Her concentration was broken by footsteps. She noticed Sandra walking in her direction. She quickly pushed the box under the sofa and waited for her friend to sit. "What's up?"

"Nothing really, I was just taking a walk."

"How's your writing coming along?"

"Pretty good. I've outlined my chapters and will probably start writing chapter one today."

"How long do you think it'll take?"

"I am not sure; probably a year or two."

"Wow! I can't believe it takes that long to write a book."

"That's a short time; many books take years to complete."

"I wish I was educated enough to do something like that."

Sandra replied. "All of us possess a special gift or talent, it is just a matter of acknowledging its presence and capitalizing on its potential." Looking at the crystal ball, she continued, "Like using that ball."

"Anyone can do that; it requires no special talent."

"That's not true. Show me how it works."

"I'd really rather not.."

"Come on, I've always been curious about this sort of thing," Sandra pleaded. "Just show me a little."

Iris leaned forward and clutched the small clear ball within her hands. "I'll try." Moments later, Iris started to emit bizarre sounds and strangely rock in place. Sandra remained silent and stared as Iris slipped deeper into a catatonic-like state. The wailing intensified as did the erratic patterns of motion. Suddenly, Iris sat erect, stared directly at the clear sphere and muttered, "I see a fuzzy brown puppy....one leg is broken.... and his eyes are missing."

Sandra listened and said, "It's my Freddie."

Unaware of Sandra's response, Iris continued, "I see a knife stuck in his chest and a young girl taunting the animal."

"I was just playing, that's all, just playing. It was an accident."

Iris rocked again and continued to gaze into the crystal ball. "I see a student sitting in class...I think it's a science class and she's putting something into a glass...she's pouring it onto another girl...my God, the other girl is in pain; the acid is eating at her skin."

"It was an accident!" Sandra cried, "It slipped out of my hands!"

Iris lurched forward and grasped the cloudy globe. Sweat poured from her face as she maintained a steady dialogue. "I see two people in a bedroom...he's much older...his wife is in the next room...the teenage girl is flirting with him...she's pushing him on the bed and pulling at his pants...."

"He did it to *me*," Sandra said frantically. "He started it. I didn't know he was married."

"I see a darkened room and someone breaking into a file cabinet...she's changing something on a paper...."

"I deserved that grade. He only gave me a B." Grabbing Iris by the shoulders, Sandra attempted to awaken the woman. "Wake up!" she shouted. "Stop it now!"

Iris stared into the ball and turned to Sandra. Soaked by her own perspiration, and as if possessed, she continued. "I see a man- uscript—"

"No!" Sandra yelled. "Not that!" In desperation, she tore the crystal ball from Iris' hands and threw it to the ground.

"I see...I see..." Iris became motionless.

Sandra composed herself and then touched Iris on the arm, "Are you okay?"

The woman groaned, "What happened?"

"The ball."

"I don't remember a thing," Iris added. "Tell me what hap- pened."

"You really don't remember anything?"

Shaking her head, she stated. "Nothing. Everything's a blank."

"Why don't you lie down. You'll feel better after a little rest."

"Thanks." Reclining on the sofa, Iris inquired, "Did anything happen?"

"Nothing at all. You looked into the ball and suddenly became very quiet. You never said one single word, but only stared into space. It took me a long time to awaken you."

"Thank you."

"May I offer you a suggestion?"

"Yes."

"Perhaps you shouldn't use the crystal ball again. It appears to have a negative effect upon your body."

Looking at the clear ball laying on the floor, Iris stated, "I guess you're right. I'll put it away in a little while. Right now, if you don't mind, I think I'd like to get some sleep."

EIGHTY-EIGHT

Michael put down his guitar and listened. Something abnormal stirred. He strummed several notes and waited. As before, the musician detected an unusual sound.

After adjusting his amplifier, he shrugged his shoulders and resumed his playing. Halfway through the next song, he turned off his electronics and searched for Franklyn. The scientist was sampling segments of rock when Michael arrived. Looking up from his microscope, he inquired, "What brings you around?"

"I got a question."

"What is it?"

"Well," Michael said, "it's really hard to explain."

Franklyn moved away from his makeshift examining bench and said, "Try me."

"I'm hearing something really strange."

"You'll have to be more descriptive."

"I hear an echo."

The scientist thought momentarily, "I'm not surprised. In a room of this size and architectural design, an echo is probably normal."

"No, this is different."

"How?"

Getting slightly frustrated, Michael said, "It's just different."

"Could you give me a few specifics?"

"I can't tell you exactly, but it's something I've never heard before."

"What type of echo was it? Did it follow a pattern?"

The musician shook his head, "I've played in a lot of different sized places and haven't ever heard anything like this before."

"I'm afraid I can't help you unless you give me more details."

"How about coming over and I'll show you?"

Looking at the pile of rocks on his table, Franklyn said, "Why not! This work can wait."

They walked across the room, Franklyn waited while Michael prepared his equipment. After strumming a few notes, the young musician stopped, "Did you heard it?"

"I'm not exactly sure what I'm supposed to hear."

"Listen to each note carefully." Once he completed several bars of music, the musician again inquired, "Well?"

"I think I hear something different, but I'm not sure."

After playing another note, Michael stated, "Well?"

"It sounds different."

"That's what I've been telling you. When I hit a B, an A echoes." Touching his pick to a string, he said, "Listen to this G."

"It's different!" exclaimed Franklyn.

"It's a C."

"Has it always been like this?"

"No. I just noticed it."

"It's very odd."

"That's why I called you, you're the scientist."

Franklyn examined the ceiling and nearby walls. "It's most unusual."

"What's the answer?"

"I haven't the faintest idea, but I'll see what I can find out."

Frustrated, Michael strummed several notes and said, "When you get the answer, let me know."

"I will," Franklyn said after hearing another series of changed sounds. "Most unusual!"

Upon returning to his workbench, the scientist was immediately greeted by Todd. "Franklyn, come with me." Without questioning, he followed the man to a nearby wall. The huge athlete raised his hand to the wooden structure and he struck it loudly.

He repeated the action several times then turned to the scientist. "What is it?"

"I don't know."

"How can that be? I hit it two times and I hear three sounds in return."

Franklyn duplicated the action and achieved similar results. He then gazed back at Michael's area and shook his head. "Something is not right."

They walked to another wall, but could not reproduce the action. "What are you going to do?" Todd asked.

"I'm going to take down the wall and see what's behind there."

"I'll help!"

"Thanks." Together, the two men worked hectically at tearing down the structure. Once the wooden barrier was removed, they discovered a solid rock base. Franklyn struck his hammer against the dense wall and listened carefully. It echoed twice, but remained unblemished. After several attempts, he shook his head. "We won't get through this wall and the increased duplication of sounds is beyond my current knowledge."

Staring at the rocky barrier, Todd slammed his hammer against the impending stone. "Damn this place!" he screamed. "It's—" His words were cut short by four piercing chimes from the great overhead clock. Looking upward, the athlete cursed, "I hate that thing!"

Franklyn nodded, "It can be annoying at times." The lights started to dim and the scientist gathered his tools. "I'll work on it tomorrow." As expected the wall was reconstructed during the darkness.

During the next meal, Franklyn spoke to Michael. "Hear any more strange notes?"

"Nope! Everything is back to normal."

"Are you sure?"

"Yeah. I listened real carefully, but my A is now an A."

"Good. That solves *one* problem." He walked to the wall and struck it firmly with his fist. Only one sound echoed in return. He repeated the experiment several times, only to achieve similar results. Shrugging his shoulders, he returned to his workbench and started to analyze the situation. Nothing made any scientific sense. Finally, he picked up a sampling of rock and began evaluating its composition.

EIGHTY-NINE

Alice and Tara were adjusting to their limited confines. Alice gazed at the sleeping form on the floor and asked, "Why do you insist on keeping him here?"

"I'm not exactly sure, but I really feel sorry for him."

"But he's obviously just a bum," Tara quickly responded.

"He's a human being like us and deserves a chance."

"I can't believe he's still alive after all this time."

"Neither can I, but he is."

"He seems much cleaner."

"That's because I clean him each day and have washed his clothes several times."

Giggling, Alice asked, "Is he well endowed?"

"How can you ask such a thing?"

"I just heard black men are bigger."

"I didn't look, if you must know the truth."

"Why not?"

Tara was getting embarrassed by her friend's questioning. "Please change the subject."

"You don't have to get upset; I was only kidding." The woman added, "I apologize."

"Accepted."

"Has he moaned any more since that one time?"

"No. He hasn't moved or uttered a sound since that day."

"Do you think it's odd he's here at all?"

"Not really. Why do you say that?"

"After all, we're all white and he's black."

"I hadn't given that much thought."

"Don't forget you're of a higher social class also."

"I didn't know social classes still exist."

"Don't be so naive! They do and they'll continue to exist forever."

"Maybe I'm from a low class too."

"Impossible." Alice stared at the man's black face and said, "You're white, not trash like him."

"I don't think that's very fair."

"Why don't you just drag him to the other side of the room and let him die."

"We are not bothering anyone. Just leave us alone."

Their conversation was interrupted by Father McShane's sudden appearance. "I hope I wasn't disturbing anything important."

"No," Alice stated. "We were just having a friendly conversation."

"Girl talk," Tara said. "Just plain girl talk."

"Anyway, I think this box belongs to our sleeping friend."

He held up a wrapped box and asked, "What shall I do with it?"

"Let's open it up," Alice suggested.

"No," Tara quickly responded. "It's his! We don't have the right to do that."

Father McShane placed the cartoon on the ground, "I'll leave it to the two of you."

After he left, Alice studied the attached card. "At least we now know his name."

"How?"

"It's written right here."

"What is it?"

"J.C. Smith."

Tara looked at the man's face and repeated the name. "J.C. Smith. At least, I can now match your face with a name."

"So let's open his box."

Tara grasped the package from her friend's hands and said sternly, "No, it's his!"

"You don't have to get so indignant about it." Alice sulked and said, "Besides, I was only kidding. I could give a damn about the box."

Tara placed the box at the man's side and whispered, "It's all yours and no one is going to touch it but you."

Alice looked down at the sleeping man. "It probably contains drugs."

Tara wiped moisture from the corners of the man's eyes. "Please don't say those sort of things around him."

"Don't worry, my dear, I wouldn't want to hurt old J.C. Smith's feelings. After all, old J.C. Smith is probably a very sensitive man."

Word spread quickly among the group and soon everyone was teasing Tara about J.C. Smith's name and status. Finally, after much ridicule, she exploded. "Leave me alone, all of you. I'm sick and tired of it."

Father McShane apologized for the group. "I'm sorry, we were only kidding."

"Yeah," Todd said. "I know a football player with the same name and he's one cool guy."

"Maybe our J.C. plays the sax," Michael quipped. "I've been looking for a good sax player for years."

"I think he's a doctor," Franklyn said. "His hands are certainly big enough."

"I don't find that funny," James answered. "I think he is a

scientist."

"Please!" Father McShane pleaded. "Let's try to be civil."

Sandra added, "We must try to control these outbursts, otherwise, they could have a negative effect upon our overall ability to function and subsist."

"I agree with Dr. Sandra," Todd jested. "I don't know what she said, but it really sounded good to me."

Sandra was about to verbally lambaste the huge athlete, but was interrupted by Tara's shout. "Stop it! You're all a bunch of sick people!" The young woman ran back to her sofa, leaving the rest of the group in silence.

Sandra was the first to speak. "I think we'd better stop teasing her about him. For some reason, she's developed a dependence on caring for his body."

"Probably a psychological dependency," James stated. "I've seen it many times before."

"What shall we do about it?" Joanne asked.

"Just humor her and hopefully, when the man dies, her mental health will improve. She'll probably require a great deal of professional assistance when we get out of here."

"Is her obsession curable?" Sandra inquired.

"Yes," James said. "But it could be contagious."

"Like group hysteria?" Father McShane asked.

"Precisely, Father, and that's why we must play along with her little game." After much discussion, the group decided James' strategy would be followed. None ridiculed the young woman about J.C. Smith's condition or his social status. Finally Tara mellowed and reluctantly resumed her previous relationships with the various members of the group.

N I N E T Y

An unexpected darkness filled the room. Though most of the group were within a short distance of their individual resting places at the time of the occurrence, several persons were forced to blindly grope and crawl to their specific sites. Banging his knee on a table, Todd cursed loudly before settling onto his sofa. Others laughed, but soon a great silence engulfed the area. All sounds, other than that of the great wall clock, seemed muted. Awakening later, each discovered that the darkness persisted. Tara was the first to respond to the unaccustomed situation. She shouted, "What's going on? Why is it still dark?"

"Because the lights are still out," Michael said trying to maintain calm.

"I do not find you funny," Sandra said.

Joanne added, "I'm frightened. The night has never lasted so long."

"I agree," Father McShane said from his site. "Something is wrong."

"Let's not get too excited," Franklyn commented. "I'm sure there's a logical explanation."

"Maybe we didn't pay our electric bill?" Michael joked.

Sandra shouted. "I'm sick and tired of your sarcasm and jokes."

"Up yours!" Michael responded.

"I'll second that!" Todd added. "That's telling her!"

"What about the lights?" Hugo interrupted. "Where are the lights?"

"Does anyone have a flashlight?" the priest asked.

"I left one in the stock room," Jeffery said.

"Great move!" Michael said.

"Please, Michael!" Father McShane pleaded. "Please behave!"

"What about the candles?" James suggested.

"I saw them on the kitchen shelf," Iris said.

"Can anyone make it over there?" James questioned.

"I can," Todd answered. "It's no big deal." Moments later, the huge athlete cursed out loud.

"What's wrong, Todd? Are you okay?" Father McShane asked.

"Goddamn it, I'm just great."

"What was all the noise?" James inquired.

"I just walked into a table."

"Are you hurt?" James questioned.

"I'm okay. I just don't know why it was there."

"Can you make it to the candles?" the physician asked.

"No sweat," Todd answered. Moments later, he yelled loudly.

"What's happening?" Sandra asked.

"I walked into another table. I just don't get it."

"Get what?" James asked.

"I walk this room every dark period and never bump into any furniture. Why now?"

"Just relax on your sofa and we'll see what's going on when the lights come back on," the priest suggested.

"Fine with me," Todd said turning back. "I don't want to break a leg over a stupid candle."

Tara spoke in a nervous tone, "What are we supposed to do?"

"Nothing, but sit and wait," Franklyn answered. "There's nothing else we can do. We are incapable of controlling our own destiny at this point."

"That's a very frightening observation," Sandra stated.

"I agree, but unfortunately quite true," Franklyn added.

"As for now, just relax and see what happens." Father McShane advised.

Michael picked up his guitar and attempted to strum a few chords. Having no success, he cursed.

"What's wrong?" Alice asked.

"No electricity. I can't even play my guitar."

Sandra laughed, "A miracle! It's a damn miracle."

"That's not funny," the rocker replied.

Before anyone could respond, the lights flickered once and then shone brightly. Alice's scream reverberated through the entire room. Everyone gazed upon their surroundings in shock. "How?" Father McShane mumbled quietly. "How could a whole room change overnight?"

The entire group walked silently toward the kitchen. Tara turned to Franklyn and inquired, "The kitchen was over there! How can it be here?"

The scientist shook his head and stammered, "I just don't know..."

"The doors have changed," Alice said.

Jeffery said, "Nothing, except for our sofas, is in the same location."

"I didn't hear anything last night," Tara said.

"Neither did I." Joanne added. "And I'm a very light sleeper."

"Look," Sandra said as she pointed upward. "The chandeliers and clock have also changed."

Hugo sat in a neighboring chair and gazed at the contents of the room. "The toilet is at least in a more private spot."

No one responded to the statement. For the next few hours, they broke into groups and explored the room in further detail. Finally during lunch, they decided to resume their normal activities and to simply accept the most recent phenomena without questioning its rationale or scientific foundation.

NINETY-ONE

James meticulously trimmed his newly grown beard in the mirror. He gently massaged his face and gazed affectionately at his own reflection. After completing his morning grooming, he exited the shower room and was immediately met by Iris. "Your beard is quite becoming, Doctor."

"Why thank you, Iris." Rubbing his hairy chin with vigor, he added, "It's beyond the itching stage and is feeling much more natural."

"It makes you look much more distinguished."

"And older?"

"Not at all." The woman added, "I'd say sexier and more prestigious."

"Perhaps I should keep it once we get out of here?"

"I think your patients would love it," Iris giggled and added, "And I bet the nurses would like it also."

"They already love me."

"Is that a fact?"

Smiling, James said, "No further comment."

"Would you like to explain that statement to me, Dr. Harrison?"

The physician walked back to his site. Once there, he completed his grooming and reminisced about the many nurses he had been sexually involved with during the past few years. His risqué thoughts were interrupted by Iris' presence. Turning he asked, "What do you want now?"

"I have a question for you."

"If it is regarding my sexual preference or personal lifestyle, then it's really none of your business."

"No," Iris stated. "It's a medical question."

"You know how I feel about providing medical advice."

"Dr. Harrison, I am not looking for a freebee. I have insurance that will pay your fee."

"Fine." James picked up a pen and pad and prepared himself for the consultation. "Ms. Lansing, what is your problem?"

"Do we have to be so formal?"

James replied impersonally, "You are seeing me as your physician and not as a fellow room member. Please tell me your problem."

"I have a lump on my breast."

"Have you seen anyone about it before this?"

"I saw my family doctor several weeks before waking up in this room."

"What did he say?"

"*She* wanted me to see a surgeon."

"Did you?"

"Not yet."

"What were you waiting for? You must always follow your physician's advice."

"I was scheduled to see someone but being in this damn room is preventing that from happening."

Placing his pad on the chair, he asked, "I'd like to examine your breast."

"Sure."

Upon checking the lump, he said, "It must be removed quickly."

"How can I do that? We're stuck in this damn room."

"You're right. You've got a real problem."

"Can't you do it here?"

"You've got to be kidding me! I'm only an orthopedist— not a breast surgeon."

"A doctor is a doctor and a surgeon is a surgeon."

Instead of arguing, James stated coldly, "I cannot and will not do any surgery of that type."

"But suppose it gets worse?"

"You must see a specialist as soon as possible."

Raising her voice slightly, Iris inquired, "Can you pull one out of a hat for me?"

"There's no reason to be sarcastic; I'll monitor it for you."

"What good will that do?"

"I'll be able to send a detailed report to your breast surgeon."

"I guess that makes sense."

"Of course it does! It's sound medical advice." Picking up his pad once again, the physician asked, "Please let me have your insurance information so that I can file the necessary forms when we get out of here."

"I have Medicaid."

James shouted, "Medicaid! I never accept Medicaid! Why didn't you tell me?"

"I told you I had insurance."

"That's not insurance! That's a handout to society's lower echelon."

"I find that insulting. In fact, I find it appalling."

"I intend it to be. None of my colleagues ever accept that kind of insurance." Shaking his head in disgust, James added, "We'd all go broke over their low fee schedules."

"But what about my lump? I need you to monitor it for me."

"I'm afraid my office has been temporarily closed for the remainder of my time in this room. You'll have to find another physician."

"No one else is a medical doctor except for you!"

"I guess then you're out of luck."

"It might get bigger!" she pleaded.

"It will!" Iris held her hands to her face and started to cry.

"Stop sniffling and face the facts. Breast tumors have a poor prognosis. Why don't you save the taxpayers some money and just forget the whole thing?"

Iris sobbed, "But my family doctor takes my Medicaid."

"She's a woman!"

"Her partner is male and he takes it!"

"They're either stupid, idealistic, or plain crooks."

Iris sat upright and verbally defended her doctors. "They are highly principled and never turn anyone away because they lack payment."

"They probably double bill Medicaid and the rest of the insurance companies."

"They would never do such a thing!"

"Every physician does it on a regular basis, including me. It's called getting the most out of a poorly run system."

"That's dishonest!"

"Taking public assistance is also fraud; especially when one holds a job."

"That's none of your business."

"It is when I, as a taxpayer, am paying for your medical expenses."

Iris commented, "I believe I've heard enough for one day."

"I'm not done, young lady! You're an outright thief and I'm going to contact the proper authorities to report your actions once we're free of this damn room."

"Please, James, I'll do anything! Just don't report me. I'll do anything you want and I mean anything. Just don't tell anyone."

Looking her straight in the eye, he stated icily, "I do not want anything from scum like you. Besides, who wants to make love to a woman with only one breast."

Iris ran back to her site. James sat on his sofa and laughed. *That dumb bitch. I can't believe her stupidity. All she has is a fatty non-malignant tumor; it's benign and doesn't need any surgery, it's just fine the way it is. That'll teach her to take my tax money!*

N I N E T Y - T W O

Todd waited until silence filled the darkened room before crawling to Phyllis' site. Having memorized the route, the huge athlete was easily able to avoid the furniture since the recent change. "Hi," he whispered.

"Hi yourself," the woman answered coolly.

"You don't sound so chipper; what's cooking?"

"Nothing."

As if not hearing her response, Todd began pawing her body. After he roughly tore at her blouse, he asked, "What gives? You're like a dead fish."

"I said nothing is wrong."

As he tried to kiss her, she turned her head, "I'm not in the mood."

"What do you mean you're not in the mood?"

"That's exactly what I said; I'm not in the mood."

"That's a twist; you're usually the one raping me."

"So," Phyllis countered. "That was then and this is now."

"Up yours!" He rigorously forced her onto her back and tore at her clothing.

The older woman scratched his face and said, "Leave me alone; I'm sick and tired of your crudeness and rough behavior."

Touching his bleeding skin, Todd stared at her and uttered, "You bitch, I'll show you who's boss." As he grabbed her, she raised her voice slightly and said, "Leave me alone or I'll—"

"You'll what? Call your husband?"

"You bastard!"

"That's exactly what I am and right now I'm in the mood for your body."

He forcibly wedged himself onto her smaller frame and smiled as she attempted to escape his grasp. "Leave me alone," she cried. "You're hurting me..."

"That's how I like my women," Todd whispered as he caressed her exposed flesh. "Full of fight and spunk."

Positioning herself, Phyllis vaulted her knee swiftly and forcibly to Todd's groin. The huge man fell backward clutching his genitals. He moaned loudly as she scampered to pull her clothes together. Collecting her thoughts, she mumbled, "I told you I didn't want to do it."

Finally Todd was able to speak. "You bitch. I'll get you for this."

Phyllis cocked her fist and stated, "You touch me again and I'll kill you."

"I think your husband will hear from me real soon."

"He'll hear from me first; I'll tell him how you raped and took advantage of me." Grinning, she continued, "I wouldn't be surprised if you went to jail for your crimes."

"Bitch," Todd said.

Feeling more confident and arrogant, Phyllis continued her verbal attack. "With his influence with certain judges, I'm sure your football days are numbered."

"You son-of-a-bitch!" Todd shouted.

Suddenly, a male voice from the darkness interrupted the conversation. "For God's sake, you two, cut the crap and let us get some sleep."

Another voice quickly followed, "Yeah! Every damn night it's the same thing; keep it down."

Todd stared into the blackness and then at Phyllis' silhouette. He grimaced as he held his injured groin and mumbled, "I'll get you for this, bitch."

Phyllis did not back off, "Fuck off and don't ever try to touch me again."

The athlete slowly hobbled back to his sofa. There he tried to ease his pain. He continued to curse Phyllis for her actions. *Bastard! I'll get you for this! And screw your husband too! And you'll get no more screwing from me again either!*

NINETY-THREE

To prevent further discord among the members, Father McShane and Sandra worked feverishly on developing a project that would promote harmony and unity. The number of discussion groups was increased and greater audience participation was encouraged. Though minor skirmishes did periodically occur, their highly organized plan seemed to be working nicely.

As the great wall clock struck four, Hugo, Jeffery, Todd, and Michael prepared for their daily poker game. As the deck was owned by Hugo, most of the games were held by his site.

Hugo dealt out the first hand of cards. Todd was the first to respond, "I open."

"I'm in," Michael said. "This hand is too good to be true."

"I'm out," Jeffery said as he tossed his cards down onto the table.

Hugo studied his cards for a moment and then said, "I'm out also."

"I can't believe it!" Michael stated. "The great Hugo is out for one hand."

"Shut up!" Todd responded. "Give me three cards."

307

Hugo dealt him the cards and waited for Michael. "I'm good."

All eyes turned to Todd who said, "I'll bet three hundred."

Michael looked at his cards and responded, "I'll see your three and raise you another five."

Todd squirmed, looked at his opponent, and tossed in his cards. Michael smiled and lay down his hand.

"Damn!" Jeffery shouted. "The kid didn't have anything!"

"He was bluffing!"

"Some balls!" Todd said with respect.

"So how do I stand?" Michael asked.

Jeffery added the results to the rocker's total. "I have you behind by fourteen thousand."

"Damn!" Michael said. "I'll be working for nothing unless I get some luck."

"You!" Todd replied. "I'm out over forty thousand since we started."

Jeffery completed his calculations. "So far, I have Hugo ahead by nearly one hundred thousand dollars."

"I can't believe your luck," Michael said as he picked up the cards. "Who's deal is it?"

"Mine," Jeffery answered. "Maybe I'll deal myself a good hand for a change."

"Give me one!" Todd added. "I'm running out of money."

"Up yours!" Michael said. "You've got more money than God. I'm the one who needs the luck."

Hugo remained quiet and watched each card with great interest. As with the previous hand, he dropped out quickly. "Maybe your luck has run out," Michael jested as he again won the hand.

Hugo smiled and replied, "Maybe you're right."

"I hope so!" Todd said. "I want some of my money back right now."

"Anyone object to raising the ante?" Jeffery asked.

Seizing his chance to increase his income, Hugo spoke, "I think that's a great idea; how about tripling it?"

"Tripling it?" Michael shouted. "I'll go broke."

"What are you, a nerd?" Todd accused. "I agree with Hugo. Let's make it more interesting. If you can't stand the heat, get away from the fire."

"I'll do it!" Michael said.

Jeffery responded, "Maybe the stakes will be too high for you. After all, you're still not making the big money as yet."

"That's my problem."

"No, that's my problem," Hugo said. "I want to make sure you'll pay up when we get out of here."

"I will."

"How do I know that?" Hugo commented.

"You have my word on it."

"That's a laugh!" Todd replied. "Where are you going to get the money from? A tree?"

"I have my ways."

"I'm sure. Rockers make a fortune playing in bars. Why don't you drop out and let us real men play?"

Turning to each player, Michael stated, "I'm in. I can get the money if I lose!"

"We have your word on it?" Hugo asked.

"Yes. Now deal."

By the time the great wall clock chimed five rings, Hugo had successfully won another fifty thousand dollars. Todd looked at the winner and said, "I can't believe you won again. You've got some luck."

"Yeah," Michael added. "How do you do it?"

"Skill and experience," Hugo said.

"My ass!" Jeffery responded. "I've been playing for years, and you are just running lucky."

After the three had left, Hugo picked up his cards and hid them safely in his box. *You guys are making me a lot of money. This is better than working for a living. I've got to get several more packs when*

I get out of here.

Later on that evening, Hugo was approached by Sandra. "Since all the decks of cards have disappeared several dark periods ago, I have a small favor to ask," she began.

"Certainly Sandra, what is it?"

"I was wondering if we could borrow your cards?"

"No!" he responded quickly.

"Oh," Sandra said, surprised.

"Why do you want them?"

"Several of the woman want to play cards."

"What game? Bridge?"

"No, they want to play poker."

"Who?"

"Joanne, Phyllis, and me."

"I'll do it if you follow my rules."

"What are they?"

"I always deal and we must play for money."

"Why?" Sandra asked.

"I don't want anyone ruining the cards, and without any monetary incentive, there's no reason to play."

"I'll speak to them later."

"By the way, ask them if they would rather play strip poker."

Sandra laughed, "Hugo, you're a character! I'll see you later."

After supper, the women agreed to his terms for the game. Hugo thought, *More suckers and more money. This room ain't so bad after all!*

NINETY-FOUR

Tara continued to care for the sleeping man. Daily she would wash and groom his motionless body. Much to her surprise, and that of everyone else, the man survived. Tara would sit at his side and read to him as if he were fully conscious.

"May we speak to you for a moment?"

Tara looked up and found Joanne and Phyllis. Standing quickly, she answered, "Yes."

Phyllis said, "We all think you should take him into a tunnel and let him die there."

"I will not!" Tara retorted loudly. "And who is we?"

Joanne spoke, "Most of us in the room."

"Why?"

"Because we don't want his kind around here," Phyllis said.

"What do you mean by that?"

The actress responded, "We do not want a vagrant in here."

"Why not? He's not hurting anyone!"

"We just feel very uncomfortable about his being here."

Tara pushed, "Why?"

"Maybe he's involved in drugs or a murder?" Phyllis suggested.

"Or maybe he's a common thief?" Joanne added.

"How can you prejudge anyone without actually knowing anything about him?"

"It's easy; just look at him!" Phyllis raised her voice.

"What are you really trying to say?" Tara asked.

"For God's sake, Tara, don't be so naive, he's nothing but black trash!"

"Phyllis! How can you say that?"

"It is easy," Phyllis said. "Those people are nothing but trouble."

"Yes," Joanne added. "Most crimes are committed by them."

"That's not fair, he hasn't done anything to anyone."

"How can you be so sure?" Joanne asked.

"I can just tell."

"He's nothing but a dirty nigger!" Phyllis shouted. "And they're scum of the earth!"

Tara grasped the man's hand and held it tight. "Stop it!" she shouted. "I don't want you to speak like that in front of him."

Joanne laughed, "He's half dead, do you really think he can hear us?"

Phyllis added, "He's probably so stupid he couldn't understand what we are saying."

"Anyhow," Joanne said, "we want to place him in Franklyn's next tunnel."

"I won't permit it!"

Placing her hand around Tara's waist, Phyllis said, "You're not thinking logically, my dear."

Joanne continued her verbal attack. "Why are you wasting your time anyway, do you think he'd do the same for you?"

Phyllis laughed. "He'd probably knife you in the back or steal your property. That's what all the blacks do where I come from."

Tearing herself away, Tara sobbed, "He didn't do anything to you!"

"That's true," Joanne said. "And we want to keep it that way."

"Let's just call it insurance," Phyllis chuckled.

Each woman grabbed an arm of the unconscious man. Tara searched the room for assistance. She spotted Father McShane in the kitchen area. "Father!" she cried, but he did not respond. Again she called his name, but as before he neither acknowledged her cry nor looked in her direction.

As the two women prepared to drag the sleeping body to a tunnel, Tara grabbed a heavy lamp from a nearby table. Swinging it overhead, she shouted, "Leave him alone or I'll whack you with this lamp."

Joanne tried to appease the younger woman. "Why would you do that? We're your friends!"

With perspiration flowing from her forehead, Tara shouted, "Just leave us alone!"

All eyes turned to James as he entered the conflict.

"What's going on here?" he asked.

Tara screamed, "They're going to kill him!"

"Is that so?" he asked.

"We're just going to put him into one of Franklyn's tunnels."

"Yes," Phyllis added. "We're not really killing him, we're just protecting ourselves in case he does wake up."

James looked at the unconscious man, "Why waste your time on him? He's practically dead now."

"Is that your professional opinion?" Joanne asked.

"Yes. His color is pale and his respiration is worse than before. With the jostling you just gave him, he'll be lucky if he lives a few more hours."

"If that's the case," Joanne concluded, "you can have him." The actress dropped the man's arm onto the floor.

"I agree!" Phyllis said. "But don't look for any help when you try to get rid of his body. I don't want anything to do with a dead nigger's body!"

Tara watched as the two women walked away before speaking to James. "Thank you for your help."

"What help?" he stated. "I simply told you the truth. He looks much worse than before."

Kneeling by the man's face, Tara stroked it tenderly. "Isn't there anything you can do to help him?"

James turned, "No, and don't ever ask me again!"

Tara waited for him to leave before she whispered in the unconscious man's ear. "We'll show them. Don't listen to any of them. Just get better for me."

NINETY-FIVE

"Have another drink," Hugo slurred as he passed the bottle to Jeffery.

"Don't mind if I do."

The two men sat with their backs to the wall, and continued to relish the taste of a newly discovered bottle of rye.

"God, how I hate this room," Jeffery moaned.

"I know what you mean," Hugo added, "and the people, they're all so boring."

After another mouthful, Jeffery inquired, "Tell me about your life."

Hugo responded, "I already told you guys about my past."

"No, I mean about the good stuff."

Hugo roared, "You mean the real life of Hugo Winters!"

"Yeah. What's it like to be at the top of one's profession in your country?"

"And to have all that money?"

Jeffery added, "I bet we've got a lot in common."

"It's the very best. I have everything a man could want."

"Power, money, and beautiful women?"

"Precisely."

Jeffery whispered, "How many millions do you have?"

"I don't mind bragging a little," Hugo stated. "I'm worth in the neighborhood of one hundred million dollars."

"That's what I calculated."

"Speaking of worth," Hugo asked, "what's yours?"

"About seven hundred million." Giggling, Jeffery added, "Give or take a hundred million either way."

"What are you invested in right now?"

Jeffery looked at his friend and said, "I'm heavy into drugs."

"Yes. I invest in pharmaceuticals also."

"No, you idiot," Jeffery said. "I'm invested in several South American drug deals."

"That's illegal."

"I'll triple my investment within two months. Can you beat that?"

Hugo thought momentarily and answered, "No."

"That's why I did it. The return was too good to turn down."

"How do you know you can trust them?" Hugo asked.

"I've done business with them many, many times before. In fact, I made over thirty million dollars on a gun import business last year alone. If they cross me, they'll never live to do another deal."

"I'm not sure I understand what you are saying…"

"Nobody screws me and lives to tell about it. That's what I am saying. Everyone I do business with knows the rules."

Hugo stared at his friend. "I don't ever want to ever get on the wrong side of you."

"Then don't ever try to fuck with me."

Hugo inquired, "Do you get many good deals?"

"All the time. In fact, I was working on something really big before getting stuck in this room."

"What was it?"

Jeffery looked him in the eye and said, "It's none of your business."

"But I thought I might want to invest in some of them."

"You can't! These people only do business with people they fully trust."

"But I can be trusted. Ask anyone who does business with me."

"You're a nice guy and I like you. When we get out of here, maybe I'll cut you in for a small share of it."

"That's great. How much would it cost and what would be my return?"

"You'll probably have to come up with ten, and will double your money within three months."

"Twenty thousand. That's a great deal."

Jeffery laughed. "No, you idiot. I'm talking ten million."

"Ten million cash? How do I get that much in cash?" Hugo asked.

"That's your problem, but for a small fee I can have it arranged."

Hugo asked, "Are you sure it's a good deal?"

"I give you my personal guarantee. I'm putting fifty million into it myself."

"I thought *I* was big."

Jeffery stated, "Hugo, you're a small fish in a big pond. Stick with me and I'll make you very, very rich."

Hugo filled his friend's glass. "Let's drink to a long, successful relationship."

"With your money and my contacts, you'll be among the world's wealthiest men."

"How will I get paid?"

"In cash."

"I never saw so much cash at any one time. What's it like?"

Jeffery smiled and said, "Like heaven. It's one of the greatest sensations in the world."

"I can't believe this is for real."

"It is, Hugo, and welcome to the big leagues."

"Don't you ever feel guilty?"

"Do you feel guilty when you advertise inferior products to the public or when you lie about things in your ads?"

"No. That's part of the business."

"Investing in projects is my business. I deal only with people and money; I'm not interested in causes or morality."

"Sounds good to me," Hugo agreed.

"I'm going to offer one million dollars to anyone finding a way out of this room," Jeffery said. "and I suggest you add another million also." Without hesitation, Hugo agreed.

"Can you get away for a week or so?" Jeffery inquired.

"It's difficult. Why do you ask?"

"After we conclude this deal, I know of a tiny island resort where the women are trained to pamper us men."

"I think it can be arranged."

"Good." Jeffery took another mouthful and asked, "Ever have a virgin?"

"Not in a very, very long time."

"Good. I'll make all the arrangements. You're going to have the time of your life."

"I can't wait. By the way, are there still any virgins left in this world?"

"A few," Jeffery laughed. "We'll make sure you get to break one in on your vacation."

"How do they find them?"

"They're bought on the black market and shipped to the island."

"Kidnapped?"

"Yes. In fact, that's one of my better investments."

"How could you invest in such a thing?"

"It's simple. I made fifty million dollars up front and work on a percentage of the gross."

"Amazing," Hugo responded.

"Stop thinking so American! It's a whole other world out there and you'll soon be an active player in the game."

"I don't know how to thank you."

"Just get us out of here and don't ever try to screw your friends."

"You have my word on it."

"Good. Now let's have another drink. My mouth is getting dry from talking so much."

Hugo poured the remainder of the bottle into Jeffery's glass. He then toasted their friendship.

NINETY-SIX

"What's the matter, Father? You look so depressed."

The priest looked up and saw Iris. "It's nothing, I guess I'm just a little homesick."

She placed her hand on his. "Care to talk to someone about it?"

Chuckling, he said, "That's a twist. I'm usually the one offering to listen."

"You are human, aren't you?"

"Yes, I'm afraid I am."

"So what's wrong, Father?"

"I loathe being cooped up in this room and I miss my church."

"We are all feeling the same way. I can't wait until I see the sunlight again and feel its warmth against my pale skin."

He sighed heavily and continued speaking, "I miss my Sunday walks after Mass and feeding the pigeons in the park."

Trying to cheer up her friend, Iris sought to change the subject. "Tell me, Father, what does a priest do during the weekdays?"

Father McShane answered, "I'm usually so busy I don't have a single minute for myself. Except for my golf, my time is spent doing church-related activities."

"You're certainly a dedicated person."

"To become a priest, one must prepare for many personal sacrifices."

"I'm really shocked; I never thought you worked so hard."

"Most people don't realize the scope of my job. The responsibilities are endless and the demands by my congregation are incessant."

"Do people really call you for things?"

"All the time, my phone rings all the time."

Iris asked, "What do they call you for?"

"I received a call several days before I came here from a woman who lost her dog. She wanted me to say a prayer for its safe return."

"Did you?"

"You've got to be kidding. I'm too busy for such bull." Father McShane continued, "I told her I'd do it and asked her to say a few prayers at home."

"Did it work?"

"They found the dog dead the next day."

"The poor thing."

"Don't feel too bad; I talked her into giving a donation in the dog's honor to our church. So Fido's death was a financial blessing to me and my flock."

"I hope they're all not that bad."

"Some are even worse."

"In what way?" Iris inquired.

"Some idiots want me to bless their boats, their homes, and their beds."

"Their beds?" Iris giggled loudly. "You're putting me on!"

"Not at all," the priest continued. "During my first year as a priest, a young woman asked me to say a prayer over a bed."

"Why?"

"She was spending her wedding night there and desired to lose her virginity in the presence of God's blessings."

"So what did you do?"

"I blessed the bed, her sheets, and even her see-through night-gown."

"Her nightgown?"

"Yes. I pressed my cross against the groin area and uttered a few words of Latin."

"What prayer did you say?"

"None. I just made something up. Her family was pleased and within nine months, she had her first child."

"I guess you must have said the right thing." Iris then asked, "Tell me more."

Father McShane responded, "I once nabbed a murderer."

"Wow! That's exciting! How did you do it?"

"It was no big deal. He came to confession and told me about the murder. I recognized his voice and called the police. They caught him the next day."

"Did he ever know it was you?"

"Not at all! I called anonymously." The priest added, "I do it all the time. Whenever someone confesses to a crime, I simply call the police and report them."

"I thought things said in the confession booth were held in the strictest of confidence."

"Only in the movies. I turn them all in."

"And you never got caught?"

"Never."

"What do you do with kids?"

"I shock the pants off their little bodies. I tell them about being tortured and having their eyes plucked from their little heads."

"It sounds gruesome!"

"It is, but it works every time."

"And you miss all of that?"

"Every bit of it! That's why I'm so upset; I miss the fun and humor of my job."

"Why don't you hold confession here?"

"Who's going to come?"

"I'll come for fun. I'll make up a bunch of stuff," Iris joked. "That'll keep you from getting rusty."

"Maybe I'll take you up on it if we don't get out of here soon."

"I'm sure we will, just keep the faith!"

NINETY-SEVEN

Michael strummed several bars of music and then quickly repeated the sequence. Once satisfied, the musician inscribed the notes onto a piece of paper. James, observing the proceedings, sat down nearby. The younger man asked, "Am I bothering you again?"

"No. I just wanted to see how you do it."

"Why?" Michael asked defensively.

"I've always had a strange fascination for music; however, my medical training and practice have afforded me little time for such enjoyment."

"That's too bad, man. You've got to let your hair down once in while."

Instead of arguing with the youth, James chose to change the direction of the conversation. "Tell me about your career."

"Like what?

"How long does it take to write a song?"

"It depends."

"On what?"

"Lots of things."

"Such as?"

"Why are you so interested?" Michael asked suspiciously.

"I just am."

"Okay. You'll get no hassle from me." Picking up his guitar, Michael picked several notes. "Whatever you say."

"What things does it say?"

Losing his temper, the musician asked, "Are you trying to get me upset on purpose?"

"Not at all," James stated. "I wanted the information."

"Why?"

"I want to write a song and have it published."

Handing James the guitar, Michael said, "Go to it!"

"I can't."

"Why not? You told me you wanted to write a song."

"I can't play it."

"Can you write out the notes?"

"No."

Michael was again becoming impatient, "What do you want from me?"

"I want to write a song with your help."

"I don't get it."

James said, "I'll give you the words and you work on the music."

"And you'll call it your song?"

"Yes."

"Why should I waste my time on you? I can write the words myself."

"Because it's something I've always wanted to do and as long as I've got plenty of free time, I thought it might be a goal."

Michael laughed, "I don't have any free time. My music keeps me busy."

"Oh. I thought we might work together each day on the project."

"Give me a break, Doctor! I'm a professional musician, not a teacher."

"I'll gladly pay you for your services and time."

"Now, you're talking, Doc."

"What are your fees for the project?"

Michael thought for a moment and then responded, "I'll do the entire deal for five thousand dollars."

"That's outrageous!" James shouted.

"What do you get for cutting up bones for an hour?"

"I'm a professional who has been training for years."

"And so am I!" the musician countered.

James asked, "That includes everything?"

"You'll get all the music."

"In my name?"

"Doc! It'll be all yours."

"What about making it into a record?"

"Now we're talking bigger bucks."

"How much more?"

Michael scratched several figures onto his pad. "It'll cost you another five thousand for the studio, my band, and one master recording."

"Ten thousand dollars! Isn't that a lot of money?"

"It's too damn cheap! My band usually gets four thousand for one 3-hour show and we'll have to spend nearly eight hours in the studio."

"I didn't realize the expense."

"So how about it?" Michael asked impatiently.

"Let's do it."

"Fine. Come back tomorrow and we'll start."

"How about today?"

"Too busy," Michael said. "Take two aspirins and call me tomorrow."

"Do you think we could write a platinum record?"

"It depends on your words; our music will be great."

"What about getting someone really big to sing it?"

"No problem. We've got contacts all over the industry."

"This is getting very exciting. I can't wait to see my friends' faces when I win an award for my song."

"Let me get back to my work and I'll be ready to help you tomorrow." James walked away enthusiastic about his prospect.

Michael picked up his instrument and thought to himself, *You stupid ass! You're such an egotistical bastard. It'll be a pleasure to take your money. I think I'll give you some of Blondie Kessler's music; nobody's heard it for quite awhile.*

NINETY-EIGHT

Tension filled the room. During lunch, most of the group curtailed their conversation. Finally, Father McShane addressed the assemblage. "I realize the past few discussion groups have been rather boring; however, I've prepared a fascinating topic for today's meeting. How many of you plan on attending?" Finding not one positive response, the priest turned to Tara and asked, "Aren't you coming?"

"No, Father, I'm too busy."

Todd snickered and mumbled, "She's taking care of her little nigger friend."

"You're a racist!" Tara complained.

"I agree," Sandra stated. "We must learn to coexist more harmoniously."

"Sandra's right," Hugo added. "We must stop our bickering and act like civilized adults."

"Why thank you," Sandra said. "I could not have been more articulate myself."

Father McShane intervened, "As long as we're confined in this room together, each of us must make a concerted effort to reduce any friction and resolve disagreements and that includes any sarcastic remarks or caustic statements that might hurt any other person in this room."

Hugo immediately added, "I agree with Father McShane. Each of us must try harder. Not only for ourselves, but for the group as a whole."

"Does everyone agree?" the priest asked.

"Could you please be more specific?" Phyllis inquired.

"Precisely what I stated," Sandra elaborated,. "All of you must treat the other members of this group with respect, honor, and dignity."

"Treat someone as you would expect to be treated by them," the priest said.

"Does this mean they'll stop picking on the sleeping one?" Tara asked.

"That's exactly what it means!" Sandra said. "As long as he's alive, he still deserves our respect."

"I ain't never respecting him!" Todd blurted.

Phyllis cheered him on. "You're right, big guy, we aren't respecting a sleeping nigger."

Father McShane called for attention: "In a world of mixed feelings, we cannot force any values upon your individual thinking; however, all we're asking for is a little social control while we're still in this room."

"Yes," Sandra said. "Once we're out, I do not care what your sentiments are, but we must have some social control here."

Hugo then spoke. "I don't usually associate with the sleeping one's kind; however, while I'm in this room, I will tolerate his presence and accept his being."

"That's all we're asking," Sandra said. "Let's try to get along with one another until we get out of here."

Father McShane asked, "Does everyone agree?"

All heads nodded. "Good," Sandra stated. "From now on, we're all going to attempt to reduce friction among ourselves."

"Now what about my discussion group?"

"I'll come," Iris answered.

"Me too," Alice stated.

Turning to Tara, the priest asked, "How about you? Are you coming?"

Tara said. "I will after I attend to several personal things."

Sandra added, "Our very survival depends upon our relationship with one another. Please try to remember this fact and think twice before you tease or fight with another person in this room." Turning to Hugo, she asked, "Do you have anything else to say?"

"No. You've expressed my sentiments perfectly."

NINETY-NINE

Things seemed more relaxed as the group made an earnest attempt to follow the trio's recommendations. Tara continued to be extremely protective of the sleeping male; however, everyone either ignored his presence or never inquired about his status.

Following a large dinner, Hugo volunteered to help Sandra with the dishes. Once everyone departed, Sandra gave Hugo a quick kiss on his cheek. Chuckling, he inquired, "What's that for?"

"For your support the other day."

"I did it because both of you were correct in your thinking."

"I'm glad we were able to convince the others."

"Remember," he jested, "we must have social control."

"Don't get me started!" Sandra giggled. "At least, I haven't heard any fighting lately."

"That's true and even Michael has reduced the volume of his music."

"I noticed that myself. That in itself is a near victory."

"If you're happy, then I'm pleased."

Sandra turned to Hugo and asked, "I'm sensing something, but I am not exactly sure what it is. Why don't you just come out and say what you mean?"

Hugo said, "Sometimes sentiments are difficult to express."

"Try me."

After a slight pause, Hugo stated, "I find you extremely attractive."

"Why thank you! But is that all?"

"No. Not exactly, there's more."

"So."

"I want—"

"For God's sake, Hugo, we're both adults. Are you trying to ask me to make love to you?"

"Yes."

"Why didn't you just say it in the first place and stop wasting both of our time."

"I'm not sure what that means."

"Exactly how I said it. I'm willing to make love to you as long as it's done discreetly."

"I can't believe this."

"Why not? We're both consenting adults."

Touching her hand, he said, "I've always been attracted to you—since first awakening."

"May I offer a suggestion?"

"Yes."

"Cut the bull! We both know what each other needs."

"I couldn't agree more."

"Good." Sandra thought momentarily, then said, "I'll meet you in the storage room tonight, we can do it there."

"I agree. This room lacks the privacy we deserve."

"By the way, Hugo, are you impotent?"

He answered, "I guess you'll have to wait and find out for yourself."

"I do not want to waste my time if you are. Forget your ego, if you can't get an erection, then don't bother even showing up. I'm too old to be your mother!"

Hugo kissed her lightly on the cheek and whispered, "Get plenty of rest this afternoon because you're certainly going to need all your energy tonight."

Sandra watched him walk away. Recalling her past sexual exploits, the professor whispered to herself, *You'd better give me more than you give the other women in this room or you'll die of a heart attack. I didn't earn the title Champion of The Nymphomaniacs for nothing!*

ONE HUNDRED

Todd continued to exercise daily in hopes of maintaining his over-all physique and high level of strength and endurance. Challenged by limited space and lack of formalized equipment, the athlete managed to improvise a makeshift gymnasium and jogging course. Though most of the group was disturbed by his programs, no one complained or protested during his workouts.

Completing a rather grueling run, Todd stopped near Franklyn's latest construction site and rested. After catching his breath, he questioned the scientist, "What do you do for fun?"

Looking up from his microscope, Franklyn answered, "My work is all I need."

"You mean you don't have any hobbies?"

"None."

"That's awfully dull."

"I happen to love my work."

"You don't play tennis or golf?"

"No. I work seven days a week and don't have time for such frivolous behavior."

"What about women?"

"What about them?"

"Are you married?"

"No."

"Date?"

"Rarely."

Todd asked, "What's wrong with you?"

Franklyn responded, "I'm dedicated to science; she's my mistress and my only true love."

Todd shook his head. "Where did you go to college?"

"Why do you ask?"

"Just curious."

"I did my undergraduate and graduate work at Cornell."

"No shit! Did you know anyone by the name of Susan Leah?"

"I can't seem to recall the name."

"What about Nan Suytham?"

"Doesn't ring a bell either."

"Are you sure you went to Cornell?"

"Why do you keep asking?"

"No reason! By the way, was Coach Tom Costabile still there when you went to school?"

"I believe he was."

"His football teams were the greatest! Did you see them win the National Championship?"

Franklyn recalled it, "Yes, I remember it quite well."

"I never saw such a close game in my entire life; it was the best."

"I agree. It was a wonderful game."

"Are you sure you don't remember someone by the name of Susan Leah?"

"I don't!" Picking up several nearby tools, the scientist said, "I must excuse myself, I've got some work to do before the lights go out."

"Did you take classes in the Lake side or Midtown campus?"

"The Midtown campus."

"That's on Redbank Street, isn't it?"

"Yes." Frankyn turned to walk away. "I really must be going."

Todd grabbed the man's hand. "Did you ever hear of a football player named Kevin Whellin?"

"No." Growing more impatient, the scientist walked away.

"Franklyn!" Todd shouted.

"What is it now?"

"You're a goddamn fraud!"

Turning back around and facing the huge athlete, Franklyn stated, "I have no idea what you are talking about."

"Did you really go to Cornell?"

"I already told you. I received my B.S, M.S., and Ph.D. from the University."

"You're full of shit!" Todd continued to shout. "You're a fraud."

Instead of responding, Franklyn ignored Todd and again the athlete yelled, "You're nothing but a fraud and you didn't go to Cornell! You probably got your degree in the mail!"

Hearing the commotion, Father McShane came running. Panting, he inquired, "What's all the noise? Did Franklyn find a way out?"

"He couldn't find nothing, he's a goddamn fraud!"

"How can you say that?" the priest asked.

"I can tell, Father. He's full of shit!"

"I'm afraid I don't understand what you are saying."

"He didn't even know the name of the school's president and founding father!" Todd continued. "He didn't even know the name of the streets of the campus!"

"Maybe he just forgot."

"No way! He's a fraud!"

"Perhaps it's the stress of being in this room."

"Believe what you want! That man is a total fake."

Touching the athlete's shoulder, Father McShane spoke. "Does it really matter at this point in time?"

"How can he do all that research? Didn't anyone check on his background?"

"Please, Todd, try to forget the whole thing! Let's not upset everyone at this point."

Nodding his head, the large man said, "Okay, but when we get out of here, I'm going to report this to the government."

"In the meantime, how about teaching me some exercises for my stomach."

"Fine." Shaking his head, Todd added, "I just made up names and he said he had heard of them! That man is one hell of a quack."

"My stomach exercises?"

"Come on, Father, at least you'll get something from a man who is not a liar."

"Please—"

Todd interrupted the priest, "I won't say another word, but just wait until we get out of here. That faker is dead meat!"

ONE HUNDRED ONE

"Come on, it'll be a lot of fun!" Alice assured Tara.

"I don't want any part of it," Tara responded.

"Why?"

"I-I just don't!"

"Are you afraid?"

"Yes."

"It's only going to be a party."

"I don't consider a seance fun. In fact I think it's dangerous."

"Why don't you learn to loosen up? Even Father McShane is coming."

"Why would he come to such a thing?"

Alice responded, "Because it's really just a party!"

Tara shrugged her shoulders and looked down at the sleeping man. "No thank you, I'll stay right here."

Alice gave up and said coolly, "It's your choice. I just wanted to be friendly."

"I really appreciate it, but I'm scared of those sorts of things."

"Tara! You're so childish at times."

"Perhaps, you are correct, but..."

"You'll be the only one not there."

"Maybe I'll come. I'll let you know."

Once Alice left, Tara began her daily ritual of grooming the sleeping man. *I really don't want to go, those things can be dangerous. I'll stay here and take care of you. They can have their old party.*

Iris sat at the head of the long table and asked for attention. "Please be quiet!" Todd shouted, "When's the food coming?"

Michael laughed and added, "I'm starving! Bring on the cakes."

Father McShane pleased, "Please keep quiet for a moment."

Once everyone was silenced, he continued, "Let Iris do her seance and then we can eat."

"Forget the seance and bring on the food!" Todd again said loudly. "I'm starving."

"Please keep quiet for God's sake!" Alice yelled, then turned to Iris and said, "Whenever you're ready."

Iris spoke in an authoritative tone. "No one is to break the circle or speak." Looking at Todd and Michael, she sternly added, "Do you understand?" She closed her eyes. Each person held their neighbor's hand tightly and watched as Iris slowly slipped into a self-induced trance. Moments later, she rocked forward in her seat and opened her eyes. A sheen of sweat formed on exposed skin as she began to moan softly.

Sandra nervously whispered to the Father, "I am going to leave; I do not want to be here."

The priest answered softly, "Relax, it's probably just a show. Let her continue."

Iris moaned loudly as her body shook at a more intense rate. "Show us who you are!" she shouted suddenly. "Do not conceal yourself any longer."

The great wall clock rang one loud chime as the overhead lights simultaneously dimmed. Across the room, Tara grasped the sleeping man's hand and whispered, "Don't be afraid. I'm here!"

This time the great wall clock rang twice, sending its piercing resonance through the confinement of the room. Iris shouted once more, "Show yourself!"

James clasped Alice's hand and gazed in her direction. As the lights grew dimmer, he asked, "Who's controlling the lights?" Before she could respond, the table's single candle provided the only illumination.

"Father," Sandra asked in a frightened voice. "I want to go."

"Relax," the priest said. "Let's see what comes next."

Iris suddenly sat bolt upright. A strong rush of air caused her hair to flutter wildly as her lips slowly moved. An eerie voice spoke. "I am your last chance!"

"I think I've had enough of this," Sandra stated. "I'm getting nervous."

Holding her hand tightly, Father McShane said, "Stay where you are and don't break the circle."

"Who are you?" Todd shouted.

"I am your last chance," the voice repeated. A creaking sound filled the air as Iris' lips again moved, "You have been warned...."

Michael interrupted the voice, "Hey, man, cut the crap. How do you do it?"

"Yes," Sandra added, "I've had enough, Iris, please stop it at once."

A noise overhead caused everyone to shudder. Franklyn attempted to objectively analyze the situation. Before he could concluded anything, Hugo shouted, "The table's moving!"

"Man, this is cool! How do you do it?" Michael asked.

After vibrating slightly, the entire wooden table slowly levitated. Sandra turned to the Father and cried, "I've had enough, tell her to stop!"

Watching the table, Father McShane yelled, "Iris! Please stop it."

With a blank stare, Iris' head turned in his direction and responded, "This is your last chance, Father Donald McShane."

The great wall clock chimed ten loud rings as the table lowered itself to the floor and just as suddenly, remained stationary. "Great trick!" Joanne said. "We should take it to Hollywood."

An overhead light emitted a solitary beam onto Iris' rigid body. Her head turned spasmodically as the strange voice again spoke, "There are no more chances. This was your last."

Todd shouted, "Get us out of here, you dumb shit! Just cut the crap and let us go."

"Yes!" cried Phyllis. "I'll pay you any amount, just let us go."

"I'll second that," Hugo added. "I'll pay your fee, just open the door."

The candle flickered as a strong breeze blew through. "I have spoken!" the voice said as it faded in intensity. "This is your last chance!"

Iris abruptly slumped forward onto the table causing the candle's flame to be extinguished. "Turn on the lights!" Sandra screamed.

"Someone's touching my head!" Phyllis shouted. "Please help me."

"Father! Help us!" Alice pleaded.

Before he could respond, the overhead lights suddenly turned on. With their hands still clasped, everyone remained silent. Iris moaned and sat upright. "Are you okay?" Alice asked.

"I-I'm not sure."

"Great act!" Joanne said.

"Yeah. It was the best!" Michael concurred.

"I don't remember a thing."

Alice touched her shoulder and said, "I'll tell you later, but you must tell me how you controlled the lights." Before she could respond, Iris collapsed.

"Help her, James," the priest pleaded. "She looks awful."

Standing, James refused, "I will not! Besides, this is probably just part of her act! She'll be just fine."

"Let's eat!" Todd said loudly. "This spook business made me even hungrier."

"Me too!" Michael added. "I want some of that apple pie with ice cream."

Alice and Father McShane assisted Iris back to her sofa while the others prepared the food for another meal. The priest knelt by the resting woman and asked, "Tell me, Iris, how do you do it?"

"Father, I didn't do anything."

"Do you remember what happened?" Alice inquired.

"Nothing."

The priest glanced at Alice, "We'll discuss it at another time. Right now, just rest."

Iris mumbled before she slept, "Didn't do anything."

Before Alice could ask another question, the woman was fast asleep. Father McShane turned to Alice. "What do you think?" he asked.

She shook her head and whispered, "Probably an act of some type."

"I agree," the priest said. "Iris is a professional and can probably fool the best of us. It's all fancy tricks of some sort or other."

Alice said, "That was some voice she had, if I didn't know any better, I'd be quite frightened."

"Let her sleep and I'll try to get the truth from her tomorrow. In the meantime, let's eat, I'm starving."

ONE HUNDRED TWO

Alice approached Father McShane, "Father, do you have a few minutes?"

Laughing, the priest responded, "That's all I do have lately, plenty of time."

"There's something I'd like to speak to you about."

"Have a seat."

After sitting, Alice said, "I trust this conversation will be confidential."

"By all means! I'm a man of the cloth."

"Good." She asked, "How would you like to be the head priest in my country?"

"Me? Are you serious?"

"Quite. For years, my friends and I have been searching for a new person. I think you'd be the perfect man for the job."

"Why me? I'm not Mexican nor do I speak the language."

"Totally unimportant. The job is a token position. All the work is performed by the church's peons."

"I've never heard of such a thing."

"Father, in my country, we run everything, including the

343

church."

"What about the Pope?"

Alice answered knowingly, "He'll do what we want."

The priest thought momentarily and then said, "Why should I leave my current church? I'm happy there."

"Two reasons: money and power."

"What about the priest who's there now?"

"He will be leaving soon."

"Is he retiring?"

"It is best not to ask, Father. He's simply being replaced."

"May I ask why he is retiring?"

"Certainly. He's been getting too influential for his own good of late."

"In what way?"

"He crossed the line between the church and the government."

"Oh."

"That's why he will be gone when I get out of here."

"Will the people accept me?"

"They'll accept whoever we tell them to accept."

"That doesn't sound very democratic to me."

"It isn't, but who really cares? Our system works best in our country."

The priest then inquired, "How much money?"

"More than you could ever spend. We also will provide you with a huge home, chauffeured limousine, an extremely large salary, and line of credit from our national bank."

"It sounds too good to be true."

"You will also be provided with a full staff to serve all your wants and needs."

"All of them?"

"They will perform any task requested and of course, confidentiality is assured."

"Do you have a golf course?"

"Membership is included with the job."

"How can I say no to such a job?"

"Just say yes and I'll make all the arrangements."

"What about my church and congregation?"

"Would they really care if you went or not? Within a short time, you'll be replaced by a younger, more energetic man."

Father McShane pondered and then responded, "It sounds very tempting, but the move is extremely difficult."

"How can you go wrong? Say yes and your world will change dramatically."

"Can I have a contract?"

"No."

"What security do I have?"

"As long as you obey our rules and orders, the job will be yours for eternity. Cross us and you'll be replaced."

"When do you want an answer?"

"By yesterday; however, you can have until we leave this room."

"It sounds too good to be real, but I'll take the job."

"Excellent choice! I'll make all the arrangements when we get out of here."

"I must also give adequate notice to the bishop and cardinal."

"Once our man is removed, the job will be yours."

"How do I ever thank you?"

"Just do as I say and you'll be the happiest and richest priest on the face of this earth."

"That's true!" Father McShane added, "And I won't have to do those damn confessions any longer."

"Father, you can do whatever you want, whenever you want. Other than to my friends and me, you'll answer to no one else."

"Alice," the priest said as he touched her knee. "Some day, I'll thank you the correct way."

"How's that, Father?"

"You'll find out in time, but for now, please don't tell anyone about my decision."

"I already forgot it! Until then, mum is the word."

After she left, Father McShane thought about the offer. Smiling, he said to himself, *All that money and free time! Finally, my Holy God looked out for my interest and took care of me!*

ONE HUNDRED THREE

During their next community meal, Phyllis spoke, "Can I have everyone's attention? I have an announcement."

"Don't tell me you're starting a rock band?" Michael quipped.

"Cut the crap and let her talk," Todd responded.

"This morning during my visit to the stock room, I found this device."

She held up a miniature control box. Sandra asked, "What is it?"

"I was afraid to push any of the buttons."

"Give me that thing." Michael responded. "I'll do it."

"Perhaps it's a bomb or something really bad!" Joanne cautioned.

"What do we have to lose?" Father McShane pointed out. "We've been locked in this room for a very long time."

"Yeah!" Michael stated. "I'll do it."

Phyllis raised the controls overhead, grimaced once, and pushed one of the three buttons. Instantly the room was flooded with jazz music. Joanne immediately shouted, "That stuff is awful!" Phyllis pressed the controls again and hard rock sounded loudly overhead.

"Great!" Father McShane said. "Now we can control the music."

Phyllis pressed another switch and the volume decreased. She grinned and declared, "It looks like I can now control what we hear."

"What do you mean by *you* controlling the music?" Michael questioned.

"I found the controller, therefore, it belongs to *me*."

"No way, babyface!" the rocker said, "I want to hear *my* kind of music."

"Me too!" Joanne stated. "I loathe jazz."

Looking to the priest, Phyllis asked, "Help me, Father. Tell them it belongs to me."

Father McShane considered then said, "I don't think one person should have the power to control the music."

"But it's mine! I found it!"

"I want to hear classical music!" James shouted.

"No way!" Todd shouted. "I'm sick of that stuff. Give me the mellow stuff—or maybe we can get a football game on it."

"It's mine!" Phyllis yelled.

"Tell her, Father. It belongs to all of us," Sandra demanded.

Father McShane held out his hand, "Give it to me, I'll hold it for the group."

"No way! It's mine."

As the priest walked towards Phyllis, she threatened, "Don't come any closer or I'll..."

"You'll what?" James asked.

"Yeah, Phyllis, what are you going to do? Tell your husband on us?" Michael teased.

Raising the control high overhead, she yelled, "Come any closer and I'll..."

Jeffery walked quickly in her direction and screamed, "Give me that goddamn thing!"

Phyllis panicked and threw the apparatus to the floor. It shattered into many pieces. "You stupid bitch!" Alice shouted.

"She broke it!" Michael whined. "Maybe that last button would have opened the door!"

Picking up the many pieces, Franklyn examined the parts. "It's too late to tell now! Even I can't repair it."

"I told you not to come any closer!" Phyllis cried.

"Dumb bitch!" Michael shouted, "What a stupid jerk!"

Little more could be said. Father McShane asked softly, "Anyone want to lead our meeting today?" Finding no volunteers, he canceled the meeting for lack of interest.

ONE HUNDRED FOUR

Closing his eyes, Franklyn escaped the present. Using meditation, the scientist permitted his mind to wander and his body to relax. Sighing he recalled his lab and his classified projects. Working closely with the government's secret agencies, he had worked himself into a successful and unique position. Franklyn was able to procure unlimited funding without restriction or question as to its purpose. He was able to dabble, germicide and poisonous gases being his specialty. Remembering his deal with Jeffery, the scientist began calculating his profits from the sale of certain classified information. Though Franklyn was able to purchase any material goods via special secretive sales to foreign agents, Jeffery's proposal was the most lucrative. He mumbled, "I could retire nicely on that baby."

Smiling he recalled many of his other pet projects. Though none benefited humanity, each was still in great demand by the government's military and information agencies. With the success of his discoveries, thousands upon thousands of lives had been destroyed or crippled. Finally, he allowed himself to awaken and again face reality.

Looking up, he observed Joanne walking in his direction. Shaking his head to clear it, he said to himself, *Dumb bitch...no brains but nice buns.*

The actress inquired, "Are you sleeping?"

Yawning, he replied, "No."

"Good. I've got a favor to ask."

"Fire away! What is it?"

Without hesitation, she asked, "Could you teach me some math?"

"I'm not a teacher."

"You're the smartest one here and I'd like to learn some of that stuff."

"Why math?"

Whispering, she said, "Because I want to sound intelligent for my friends and the studio."

"But I'm a researcher."

"It doesn't matter to me. You're the smartest one here."

"Thanks, but I don't think I have the time or the skill."

Grasping his hand, she commented, "I'll make it worth your while."

"I don't need any money. My government paycheck is more than adequate and my pension is wonderful."

Giggling at his innocence, she stated, "I wasn't thinking of money."

Thinking for a moment, he said, "I don't follow..." He suddenly grinned and blushed.

"You got it now?" Joanne inquired

"Yes. It's just..."

"When do our lessons begin?"

"Classes start tomorrow."

She quickly interjected, "And your classes begin tomorrow night."

"I don't know what to say or how to respond."

"Just say yes and you'll never regret your decision."

Speaking eagerly, he said, "Yes."

"Good, teacher, let's hope we each benefit from this relationship." She turned and walked away.

Franklyn thought for a moment and grinned. *Stupid bitch, I'll just keep feeding you worthless information and I'll get... Wait till my friends hear about this, I'll be the envy of everyone in the lab.*

ONE HUNDRED FIVE

James turned the last page of the novel and read quickly. Upon completing the book, he placed it on the table and thought about the author's concepts and story line. Satisfied he had grasped the substance and gist of Alpert's *The Swan Song Pentad*, he walked over to the library portion of the room and replaced the book on the shelf. James slowly surveyed the many volumes for his next choice. His attention was broken by Sandra. "So many books," she mused as she approached.

"Yes, there are."

"May I recommend one to you?"

"Surely. Though I'm a book aficionado, I am always open to the advice of a fellow intellectual."

Sandra gazed at the shelf and then spoke, "How about *Of Mice and Men*?"

James answered instantaneously, "I read it years ago."

"How about *War and Peace*?"

"Read it several times."

The professor laughed, "I wish my students were as conscientious as you."

"My dear, I am a legitimate intellectual." James paused, "I pride myself on my cerebral prowess."

Gazing at the shelf, Sandra pointed to a particular volume. "Have you read this one?"

"Several times."

"You're not making my task any easier."

James responded, "I take great pleasure in my selection of reading materials. Why don't you just leave it up to me?"

"I was only trying to be helpful."

"I understand and appreciate your assistance." His eyes settled at last upon a particular volume. He removed it from the shelf. Grasping it tightly in his hand, he turned to Sandra and asked, "Have you ever read *The Prelude?*"

"No, but I saw the movie."

"May I suggest reading it?"

"Certainly," Sandra responded. She took the book from him and opened the cover. "Thank you for the recommendation."

Once she left, James examined another book. "*The Exit,*" he said as he gazed upon the dusty binding. "I never heard of this one," he said as he opened the cover. Suddenly, a metal object fell to the floor. He picked up a key. "What the heck?" he said. "Where did this come from?"

Going back to his seat, he studied the book and then the key. Suddenly, as if inspired, he shouted. "It's the key!" Staring at the bold print embossed on the crude leather binding and then to the metal object, he grinned. "I found the way out!"

"What way out?" Todd inquired

Looking up at Todd, James stammered. "I-I was just talking to myself."

"You were saying something about the way out."

Nervously, the physician responded, "I was just talking about this book." Holding it upright, he added, "The name is *The Exit.* See?"

"Oh," Todd said, "I thought you found the way out of here."

"If I did, don't you think I'd share it with the rest of you?"

"I suppose so."

"Of course I would. We're all friends, in this together."

"You're right. I'm sorry to bother you." Once Todd had jogged away, James removed the key from his pocket. *You big jerk! Do you think I'd share anything with any of you?*

The great wall clock chimed six rings. James placed the key in his pocket and walked to the kitchen area. He waited impatiently for the others. During the meal, Father McShane turned and asked him, "James, what's the matter?"

"Nothing. Why do you ask?"

"You're not eating anything."

"I'm a bit under the weather."

Michael chuckled, "Why don't you see a doctor?"

Instead of responding, James thought to himself *I have and I think I'll be fine soon.*

"James!"

"Yes, Iris, what is it?"

"Would you pick out a book for me to read?"

"Certainly, it'll be my pleasure," he answered in a laid-back tone.

"What about making James our chief librarian?" Sandra suggested.

"I concur," Hugo said. "The man is the wizard of the page. He's selected many great books for me to read."

"Are we going to get library cards?" Michael wondered.

"No," Sandra laughed. "He'll simply be our expert advisor...if he agrees to the position?" All eyes turned to James.

He looked at the far door and then answered. "I guess I'll take the position, but I'd like to start tomorrow."

Forcing a cough, he said, "I'm not feeling all that good."

Father McShane patted the physician on the shoulder and spoke. "Perhaps we should delegate other responsibilities to each of us..."

"Not a bad idea, Father," Todd stated. "I'll be in charge of our athletic teams."

"Can we get a game against Notre Dame?" the priest asked.

"I'll try."

While the others conversed, James excused himself and walked to his location. Reclining on the sofa, he studied the key. *Yes*, he said as he rubbed the small metallic object, *Soon, this room will be a thing of the past.* The physician waited until everyone was busy before he walked to the door. Reaching into his pocket, he withdrew the key and placed it into the cylinder. The fit was perfect. As he was about to unlock the door, his actions were interrupted by Hugo's presence. Turning his back to the door, he waited.

"What are you doing?" Hugo echoed.

"I-I was just walking."

"It seemed to me you were trying to unlock that door with a key," Hugo accused.

"No way! I was just examining the lock." Stammering, he added, "I don't have a key."

"Then move away and let me see for myself."

"Are you accusing me of being a liar?" James responded.

"No. I just asked you to move aside and let me see the door for myself."

"What if I refuse?"

"Then I'll call the others over here."

Realizing the consequences of Hugo's action, the physician stepped aside. "Here."

Hugo stared at the door and locking mechanism and then added, "I'm sorry, I must have been mistaken."

James quickly turned and stared. The key was missing. He stuttered, "I-I told you I had no key."

"I guess my wishful thinking just got the best of me." Hugo surveyed the door again. "Please forgive my accusations, it was wrong to me to think so little of you."

"No sweat. Your apology is accepted."

As soon as Hugo walked away, James dropped to his knees in search of the key. For the next few hours, he combed the immediate area, but the key could not be located. Finally, as the great wall clock struck three blaring rings and the lights dimmed, the physician walked dejectedly back to his sofa.

ONE HUNDRED SIX

The blackness was filled with an unfamiliar sensation. Though no one acknowledged the feeling, everyone sensed its presence. By the time the lights illuminated the area, everyone was relieved to see everything was still status quo.

During breakfast, no one mentioned the subject; all chose to ignore it. "Anyone want to read a really great book?" Phyllis asked. Getting no response to her question, she consumed her portion of food and quickly left. Soon the others dispersed. Father McShane and Sandra lingered behind and washed the dishes.

"How did you sleep last night, Father?"

Unable to look her directly in the face, the priest answered, "Just fine. How about you?"

"Excellent," she lied.

"Why do you ask?"

"No reason. I was just curious."

Changing the subject, Father spoke, "I'm sensing another negative period."

"I was just about to tell you the same thing. Unless we're found soon, I don't know what's going to happen."

"We've tried everything. What else is left?"

Shaking her head, Sandra moaned. "Everyone's spirits are pretty low. We need a central or common cause to unite the group."

"When you discover one, please let me know."

"I will, Father."

Wiping the last dish, the priest asked, "Are you coming to my discussion class today?"

"I don't think so, Father. I'm kind of tired."

"I think I'll cancel it. I'm also beat and could use the additional time to rest." Across the room, Tara was grooming the sleeping man. She neatly trimmed his long, bushy beard, and then combed his hair. Satisfied she sat back on the sofa, gazed downward, and said softly, "I'm glad you're still alive!"

The lights suddenly blackened, leaving everyone unexpectedly in total darkness. Before anyone could utter a sound, the great wall clock sounded fourteen ear-piercing rings. As the final sound reverberated, the lights abruptly again illuminated. Tara adjusted her vision. She was speechless for several seconds before she shrieked. Everyone ran to her location.

"My God," Father McShane uttered.

"I can't believe it," Sandra said.

"When did it happen?" Iris inquired.

"When the lights came back on, he was sitting up," reported Tara.

"Has he said anything?" the priest asked.

"Not yet."

James looked at J. C. Smith and shook his head. "I can't believe he's conscious. He defies all laws of nature."

Tara placed her hand upon the man's shoulder. "I told you he'd make it."

"You did, indeed," Sandra said. "I guess you know a lot more than any of us."

The priest knelt and looked more closely. The man's eyes were no longer glassy and he seemed to be assessing each member of the group. "James, is he aware of his surroundings?"

"I told you before, Father, I'm not going to provide any professional services to this man."

"For God's sake," Sandra shouted. "Get off your high horse and give us an opinion."

"Come on, Doc," Michael pushed. "Give us a freebee."

Buckling under from their pressure, James examined the man's vital signs. Shaking his head, he stated, "He's healthy as a horse."

"How can that be?" Sandra inquired.

"He hasn't eaten or drank during this entire period."

"I haven't the faintest idea; however, his pulse is that of a twenty-year-old."

"Perhaps a miracle," Tara suggested.

"I agree," Father McShane added.

"Let's not push it too far," James countered.

"Do you have a better answer?"

"Not yet, Father, but I'll try to get you one,"

"Do you think he hears what we're saying?" Phyllis asked.

"I'm sure." James answered. "But his eyes are definitely following us."

"It's really weird," Michael observed. "He gives me the willies."

"Yeah," Todd agreed. "Now what are we supposed to do?"

"Just wait," Father McShane suggested.

"I ain't waiting for him to do nothing," Todd said. "I've got plenty to do without his kind."

"Please stop talking like that in front of him," Tara pleaded. "Suppose he can hear you."

"I really don't give a damn!" Todd replied. "I was here first."

"Why don't we all go back to our normal activities?" Sandra suggested. "And if anything new happens, Tara will let us know."

Nodding, Tara responded, "Yes, I will."

Father McShane was the last to depart. Before he left, he whispered, "If you need me, just call."

Touching his hand, Tara smiled, "Thank you for everything, but

I'll be just fine." Once the priest walked away, she turned to the man and stated, "I'm very glad you're alive."

Before she could say another word, the man suddenly stood, "My God!" she cried, "you're awake."

With an indifferent stare he said, "Yes."

"Could you hear what was said?"

As before, he tersely answered, "Yes."

"I'm very sorry. They didn't know you could hear."

"It does not matter."

"How did you manage to stay alive all this time?"

"It is none of your concern."

"But—"

"I said it is none of your business."

She softly said, "My name is Tara. What's yours?"

"It's already known."

He stood erect and lifted his arms high overhead. Concerned, Tara asked, "Are you hungry? I'll be glad to make you something to eat."

Instead of looking at her, he surveyed the far corner of the room and then said, "No."

"Do you want a tour of the room?"

"It is not necessary."

Trying not to seem upset over his cool reception, she asked, "What can I do for you?"

"Nothing." The man glanced down at her trembling body and added, "I'm going over there."

"Why there?" she asked. "You can stay here with me."

He walked to the far corner of the room and sat on the floor.

ONE HUNDRED SEVEN

"Can you believe it?" Joanne said.

"What do you expect from a nigger?" Phyllis stated. "They're all the same."

"But Tara did everything for him."

"I'm not shocked."

"She kept him alive all this time and now he sits across the room and has nothing to do with her or any of us."

Phyllis said, "I expected nothing more from his kind."

"Maybe James was correct. Bums are simply bums."

"James was indeed correct and black bums are the worst."

Gazing at Tara, Joanne asked, "Shall we try to cheer her up?"

"Don't waste your time. Let her suffer a little for her sins," Phyllis said.

"Don't you think you're being somewhat harsh?" Joanne accused.

Phyllis replied, "You think about how she defended that nigger and then you'll agree with my logic."

"You're right," Joanne laughed. "She really was dumb."

"Can you imagine crying over a bum?"

"Not me! I wouldn't cry for any man, especially a black shiftless derelict." Phyllis giggled. "I nearly died last night when Todd and Michael suggested we hang him from the chandelier."

"It was pretty funny, wasn't it?"

"I thought it was an excellent idea, but there's no long rope around here."

Joanne inquired, "Do you think they'd really do it?"

"Probably not, but they'd give him one heck of a scare."

The actress turned to Phyllis and asked, "How about a shower?"

"Sure. Why not?" Smiling, Joanne added, "If you're a really good girl, I'll even wash your back."

"Sounds good to me. Speaking of showers, maybe we should suggest that the bum take one. He must be filthy after all this time."

"If that smelly son of a—"

Phyllis laughed, "I was only kidding. Besides, his kind do not take showers. They're just allergic to water."

Joanne gathered her towel and soap. "I'll see you in the water and don't keep me waiting."

ONE HUNDRED EIGHT

Father McShane approached J.C. Smith and asked, "May I have a word with you?"

The man answered frigidly, "Yes."

The priest placed the medium-sized box at the man's feet and squatted, "This is for you."

Without acknowledging the neatly wrapped gift, he said, "I wondered when you would bring it."

"You can open it after I leave."

"It won't be necessary."

Trying to break the ice, the priest inquired, "What name do you want to be called?"

"Whatever! A name is simply a name."

"Do you recall anything about your past?"

"I remember everything."

"Where are you from?"

"Just a place."

Pushing harder, Father McShane asked, "Do you know where we are?

"Yes."

"Please let me know."

Staring into the priest's eyes, the man answered flatly, "No."

"Why not?" pleaded Father McShane.

"Because."

"Because why?"

"Just because!"

Not wanting to antagonize the man any further, Father McShane stood. "I'd better be going. Would you care to join us for dinner?"

Without looking up, the man responded, "No."

Father McShane described the conversation to Sandra and James. The physician asked, "Do you think he really knows where we are?"

Shaking his head, the priest responded, "Not at all. I believe he can't remember anything."

"You're probably correct," James agreed. "Otherwise his answers would be more helpful."

"Let's just try to tolerate the poor man," Sandra suggested.

"I agree," the priest added. "After all, what can we do about it anyway?"

"Do what you want, but I don't trust his kind at all," James stated. "In fact, I think we'd better keep a close eye on him at all times. There's something about him that scares me to death."

Neither Sandra nor Father McShane commented on the last statement. Instead they stared across the room as the man picked up his box and moved behind a large sofa. Within seconds, he disappeared from sight.

ONE HUNDRED NINE

Iris stroked her friend's hand and softly said, "Come, you've got to eat."

Tara looked up and shook her head no. "Please leave me alone."

"Why are you doing this to yourself?"

The young woman turned her head and wept. "I have my reasons."

"No man is worth it, especially that one."

"Please leave me alone."

"You've been like this for days; please try to eat something."

Tara cried out as her small frame quivered, "I can't eat; I just want to die."

"I'd better speak to Father McShane; he'll know what to do."

Instead of going to Tara's location, the priest walked to where the derelict was last seen. Finding him resting on the floor, he asked, "May I speak to you for a moment?"

The man answered abruptly, "What do you want?"

"I'm worried about Tara; she hasn't been eating lately."

"That is not any of my concern."

"It should be!" Father McShane responded. "She's not eating

because of you."

"That's her decision, not mine."

"I can't believe your disregard for humanity. She was responsible for saving your life."

"I didn't ask for anyone's assistance."

"That's true, but she gave it anyway."

"That was her choice and I have made mine."

"How can you be so callous?"

The man stated, "She's not my problem."

"But she is going to die."

"We all are going to die eventually."

"But..." the priest stammered. "How can—"

The man interrupted, "Tell your Dr. James Harrison to rescue her; isn't he a doctor?"

Shaking his head, Father McShane spoke in a low tone. "I've already asked him, he won't help either."

"Then why should I? She means nothing to me."

"But—"

"Father," the man stated. "Why don't you just leave me alone?"

Instead of arguing, the priest walked away. He summarized his conversation to Sandra, who shook her head in disbelief. "How could anyone be like that?"

Father McShane agreed. "I'm simply at a loss."

"What can we do about her?"

"I've spoken to her several times, but she's not listening to anything I've said or suggested," the priest reported.

Sandra added, "I'm having the same results."

"We cannot, however, just allow her to die."

"I'll try talking to her again, maybe she'll listen."

The priest nodded and said, "I sure hope you succeed; I'd hate to see such a young thing die over a worthless bum like that."

ONE HUNDRED TEN

Tara's screams brought everyone running except for J.C. Smith. She rocked frantically and cried. Todd was the first to reach her side and held her firmly. Alice gazed at the trembling young woman and asked, "What happened to her?"

"Probably a nightmare," Sandra stated.

"Will she be okay?" Hugo asked.

"She seems to be okay," Father McShane noted.

James looked at her, "She's fine, just leave her alone."

"Are you sure?" Iris asked.

Looking at the woman, he responded, "I am a fully licensed physician. How dare you challenge my diagnosis!"

Tara shouted again and was restrained by Todd's huge body. "Now what?" the athlete yelled.

"Leave her alone!" James ordered. "She'll be just fine."

Noticing no one was heeding his advice, the stout doctor left. Michael said in jest, "I guess he doesn't do house calls."

Tara suddenly demanded, "Please leave me alone."

"But you were screaming for help," Sandra informed her.

"I was having a nightmare." Sitting up, she repeated, "I'd like

368

to be alone."

"No sweat," Michael joked. "I've got plenty of work to do before the night comes."

"Glad I could help," Todd said sarcastically.

"Me too," Alice added.

"I just love being appreciated," Phyllis chuckled.

One by one everyone left. Father McShane assisted Tara to her sofa and turned to leave.

"Father!"

"Yes, Tara. What is it?"

"Can you do confessions?"

"Certainly. Why do you ask?"

"I'd like to do one."

"Why now?'"

"For some reason, I can now remember my past." She hesitated then said, "There are things that must be confessed."

"I'll be right back." Minutes later, he returned in his robes. Nodding, he prompted, "I'm ready whenever you are."

Making sure no one could hear their conversation, she began. "Forgive me, Father, for I have sinned..."

Holding his rosaries tightly, the priest said, "Please begin, my child."

Crying, Tara said, "Oh Father, I don't know how to start."

"When is the last time you did a confession?"

"Many, many years ago." Tara paused to think and then said, "Probably when I was ten or eleven."

"That's a very long time."

"I know, Father. My life has been a mess."

"In what way, my child?"

Looking once more to make sure they were alone, she whispered, "I've been living on the streets since that time."

"What have you done?"

"Father," Tara wailed, "I've done it all."

"Be more specific."

"Must I?" the young woman asked.

"To seek forgiveness from God and Jesus, one must honestly account for their sins."

Sighing, she answered, "I've taken drugs."

"Drugs! Are you an addict?"

Nodding, she sighed. "I have a habit."

"What else?"

"I have sold."

Shaking his head, the priest inquired, "Sold what?"

"I sold drugs."

"Why would you do such a thing?"

"I needed the money to live."

"Why didn't your parents help you out?"

"They both died."

"Oh," Father responded. "Don't you have any other relatives?"

"No."

"What about public assistance?"

"Have you ever seen a welfare hotel, Father?"

"No."

"If you did, then you'd see why I turned to the streets."

The priest thought for a moment and then asked, "Anything else?"

"I was forced to steal to survive."

"Stealing also?"

Tara sobbed, "Yes, Father, I had to."

Touching her arm, he stated, "God is forgiving, I'm sure He'll understand your dilemma."

"Oh, thank you, Father. That means so very much to me."

"You see, Tara, confessions aren't really so bad."

"There's more, Father."

"More?"

"Yes." The young girl hung her head and added, "I was a street-walker."

"A streetwalker?"

"A prostitute."

Shocked, Father McShane confirmed, "You are a prostitute?"

"Yes, Father." Crying loudly, she confessed, "I'm so ashamed."

"My God, how could you do such a thing?"

"I had no other choice."

Father McShane clutched his cross to his chest. "I think we'd better work on this."

"Please make God forgive me." Grabbing his arm, she pleaded, "Father, ask Jesus for compassion."

Kneeling beside the young woman, the priest began to silently pray. Tara cried, "Please ask Him to forgive me. I had to..."

For the next two hours, the two continued to pray. Finally, the priest pushed her gently away. "I'd like to see you again. We have a lot of soul cleansing to do."

"I'll do anything you want, Father." Tara broke down completely.

Shaking his head, the holy man said, "So many evils for someone so young."

Tara looked up into his eyes and wept. "Please, Father, I'm such a worthless person."

"We'll meet again tomorrow." Sighing, the priest added, "Repentance requires a great deal of time and prayer."

Touching his hand, she sobbed, "Thank you Father for listening. You're such a great person."

Father McShane neatly folded his robe, and thought to himself, *Why did you ever send a tramp like that to this room?*

ONE HUNDRED
ELEVEN

Hugo impatiently struck his fork against the tabletop. "May I please have everyone's attention for a moment?"

"What gives?" Michael responded. "Are you planning on selling advertising space on the back wall?"

Joanne howled with laughter, "The rocker's got a sense of humor. Maybe you should give up your musical career for comedy."

Todd quickly joined in the fantasy, "I think I'll forget football and join the act."

"I'm sure it'll be a success," Iris chimed in.

"A real knee-slapper," Jeffery mumbled under his breath.

Hugo slammed his fist against the tabletop and yelled, "I want everyone's attention."

"What's the big deal?" Todd replied.

Hugo said, "I think we should consider an organizational structuring of our group."

Michael questioned, "A what?"

Instead of responding to the musician's skepticism, Hugo continued, "We need to establish a chain of command and ruling party for our group."

"Why?" Iris asked. "We're doing okay the way we are."

"Besides," Phyllis added, "why go to all the trouble? Hopefully, we'll get out of here soon."

"Until that time occurs," Hugo went on, "I believe we are too disorganized. We have yet to develop any mode of operation or authority."

"I agree," Father McShane said. "Our morale is declining daily and we lack a true sense of purpose."

"My purpose is to get out of here!" Michael shouted.

Joanne said, "Until we locate an exit or are found, I believe Hugo is correct. We should set up our own government."

Sandra was the next to speak. "How shall we set up this temporary government and what configuration shall it follow?"

"I believe we, as a group, should decide those elements."

"Like a democracy!" Iris said. "Let's vote."

"I disagree," Alice commented. "I prefer a totalitarian or autocratic form of government."

"A what?" Todd asked.

"She wants a dictatorship," Hugo clarified.

"Not a bad idea if I'm the boss," Todd laughed. "I want to be called King Todd."

"Please!" Hugo pleaded. "This should not be taken lightly."

Father McShane agreed. "For us to survive as a group, we must form an organizational plan."

Alice called for attention, "Democracies don't work."

Hugo said defensively, "Ours does and I think we should have one here."

"I agree," Phyllis added. "Unless I'm the boss, I want a democracy."

Michael interjected, "I vote for J.C. Smith as my leader."

"Yeah," Todd laughed. "I second the motion."

"That's not funny," Tara defended.

"If he joined the group and didn't stay to himself, maybe he'd be better accepted," Joanne pointed out.

"That's his choice," Tara responded.

"Why are you sticking up for him?" Todd inquired. "He still doesn't talk to you either."

"Please!" Father McShane interrupted. "Let's stay with the subject at hand. I think we should first vote for the type of government we want, and then decide what to do."

Alice said. "Why go to all the trouble? It won't work until an experienced government official actually runs the organization."

"Who?" Iris asked.

"Me!" Alice stated boldly. "I'm the best qualified."

"I disagree," Jeffery said. "I'd be a better ruler. After all, I'm experienced in dealing with governments on an international basis."

"Why does government experience have to count?" Joanne asked.

"I think the best person should rule."

"I agree with her," Sandra added. "Any of us is used to dealing with people."

Hugo interjected, "Why don't we think about it for a while and then vote on it after our next meal."

"Does that mean we're going to have a democracy?" Alice inquired.

"Not at all!" Hugo answered.

Because of Alice's strong objections, they decided to wait for two more meals before making the final decision. Before adjourning, Hugo asked, "During that meeting, can we also select three men to run our government?"

"I believe we should have some sort of campaign period for those of us interested in the position. We should be free to formulate our platforms," Sandra stated quickly.

"Why go to all that trouble?" Michael said. "I want to be the boss and shall campaign vigorously for the job."

Hugo then announced, "Anyone considering the job should seek the support of the others."

Father McShane added, "Let the race begin and may the best

man win."

Hugo again asked, "Are we all in agreement?" Finding no opposition to the proposal, he reminded, "Please take this seriously. The people you elect will ultimately make decisions that will influence your life."

ONE HUNDRED TWELVE

Tara carried the small tray of food over and placed it at his feet. Meekly, she said, "I brought you something to eat."

Without looking up, the vagrant responded, "Just leave it."

"May I stay for a few minutes?"

"Do as you wish." Gathering her strength, she asked, "Why are you doing this to me?"

Sampling the food, he answered, "I have done nothing."

Tara remained composed, "There is going to be a vote on our leadership. I thought you'd like to be at the next meeting."

He said flatly, "No."

"But they can tell you what to do," the young woman pleaded.

"I have no concern for them. They've had their chance."

"I don't understand what you are saying."

Picking up his fork, the vagrant began to eat. With a mouthful of food, he said, "Leave me alone."

"Mr. Smith?"

"What now?" he responded in an impatient tone, "Can't you just leave me alone!"

Sobbing, Tara whispered, "I'm sorry if I did anything wrong."

ONE HUNDRED THIRTEEN

"Let's get started!" Todd shouted.

Hugo called again for order, "Please, let's get on with the elections."

"Just call me King Michael."

Once each person was seated and quiet, Hugo began. "The first order of business is to reach an agreement over our ultimate decision. Does everyone here fully agree to abide by the outcome of this election?"

"What about those absent?" Phyllis inquired.

"They must also live by the laws and rules of the majority."

"I concur with Hugo," Sandra added. "We must have regulations and laws."

Hugo continued, "What type of government are we going to have?"

"I propose totalitarianism," Alice announced.

"I have Alice's motion on the floor. Do I have a second?"

Finding no response, he said, "We cannot vote on it because there is no second."

Alice leaped to her feet and shouted, "That's stupid. I demand a vote."

"There is no second for the motion—"

"Hugo!" Alice responded, "that is a stupid rule! We don't have such things in my country; I charge that we take a vote."

Instead of arguing, Hugo asked, "All those in favor of having a dictatorship, please raise your hand." Laughing, he stated loudly, "The motion is defeated by the count of twelve to one."

Alice looked at each person and said, "I'll accept your decision, but you are making a grave mistake. A democracy will not work in this environment."

"Let's get on with business!" Todd prompted.

Within a short time, the group voted to have a democratic government. Smiling, Hugo spoke, "I believe we should elect three to our governing board."

"Why only three?" Iris asked.

"That's not very many."

"It's a good working number," Hugo responded. "Having too many elected officials can decrease their efficiency and cause too much red tape."

Sandra agreed, "For the size of our population, three is a realistic number."

The vote was taken and quickly passed. Alice abstained from the discussion. Hugo then announced, "Now for the most critical vote. We must decide who will govern our group."

Everyone shouted at once. Finally, the advertising executive called for order. "Please! We must have some order."

Alice said, "I told you a democracy won't work."

Instead of responding to her comment, Hugo asked, "Is there anyone not interested in running for office?"

"I'm not interested." All eyes turned to Tara.

Sandra then asked, "Are you positive?"

"Yes."

"That eliminates two," Hugo stated.

"Who's the other?" Father McShane inquired.

"Smith!" Hugo said. "His absence from this meeting automatically disqualifies him from running."

"I don't think that's fair," Tara stated.

"Vote on it!" Todd shouted.

"I don't want anything to do with him," Phyllis whispered to Joanne, "Can you imagine a nigger telling us what to do!"

"Not on your life," the actress giggled. "They're good for working in factories and shining shoes."

The motion passed with only Tara's negative vote being registered.

Hugo said, "I believe I would make an outstanding leader."

Michael cheered him on, "Tell us why, Mr. President."

"I possess a great deal of experience in the administrative process and am extremely intelligent. I have no doubt I am best suited for the challenge."

"I agree," Sandra stated. "Hugo is leadership material."

"I think Father McShane should be one of the three," Tara added. "He was the first to wake up and has kept us spiritually together."

Everyone readily agreed with this choice. The priest stood and spoke, "Though I have been raised with the concept of a distinct separation between church and state, I will serve, if elected. I do so with the desire to create the best and most humane government possible."

The election was unanimous. Hugo then announced his next choice. "I feel that Dr. James Harrison should be our third and final government official. He's a proven warrior under pressure and by the sheer nature of his profession, a humanitarian."

James instantly stood and shouted. "I accept the position."

Hugo demanded. "I'd like a vote right now. All in favor, please raise your hand."

Sandra shouted, "I object!"

The advertising executive stopped. "What do you object to?"

"I object to the whole thing."

"The whole thing?" Hugo continued. "I'm afraid I do not understand your logic."

"It's very simple. We're being railroaded!"

"That's one heck of an accusation. What makes you say such a thing?" Hugo countered. "After all, you did vote in a positive manner thus far."

"That's true, but I don't believe James is the best person for the third position."

James was indignant. "And why not?"

"Because you have no experience in such matters."

"I've handled multiple hospital staffs. This is small potatoes compared to my previous experience."

Iris said briskly, "I agree with Sandra!"

"Who would you like to see in my place?" James asked.

Sandra stared him in the eye and stated boldly, "Me."

"You?" Hugo laughed. "You must be kidding."

"I am serious."

"It can't be," James said.

"And why not?" Sandra inquired. "My experience equals or surpasses yours."

"You can't do it because you're a woman," James replied.

Alice shrieked, "What did you say?"

James remained adamant, "It's a man's job."

"I won't lower myself to debate that issue," Sandra stated. "It's below my dignity."

"I believe I called for a vote," Hugo interjected.

Joanne yelled, "Screw your vote. I agree with Sandra; she gets my vote."

Laughing, James added, "It won't do you any good. The men outnumber the women."

Sandra turned to Michael and Todd and asked, "How are you guys voting?"

The rocker quickly answered, "I'm for the Doc."

Todd chortled, "You girls are great, but it's a man's job to rule."

"I can't believe any of you," Joanne said.

"I called for the vote!" Hugo again shouted.

"I'm not voting," Sandra stated.

"Neither am I," Iris added.

"It makes no difference to me."

The advertising executive called the vote. "All in favor of Dr. James Harrison as our third official, please raise your hand."

Counting the responses, Hugo proclaimed, "The vote passes seven to six."

"I want no part of any of this," Sandra stated.

"I'm afraid it's already been passed and agreed to by all of us," Hugo said smugly.

"Hugo!" Alice shouted, "You can take your election and stick it up your—"

Father McShane interrupted, "I agree with Hugo; we each agreed to abide by the outcome of the elections."

Joanne stated, "I consider this entire session a mockery of justice and will not abide by anything you say."

"I told you democracy doesn't work," Alice pointed out.

Hugo attempted to calm the group. "You're just overreacting. Once we get started, you'll see the three of us are the best choice."

"It's not going to happen," Sandra remarked.

"I'm afraid it already has." Hugo turned to Todd, "If anyone shouts again in this meeting, please forcibly remove them."

"What?" Phyllis shouted. "You lay one hand on me and I'll sue your tail right off."

Sandra stood her ground and glared at the three leaders.

Taking a deep breath, she proclaimed, "I am seceding from this government. Should you wish to speak to my newly formed government, I'll be on the other side of the room."

"I'm with you!" Alice shouted.

"Wait for me," Joanne joined in.

Within minutes, every woman moved her belongings to the other side of the room. Upset by the rebellion, Father McShane turned to Hugo and asked, "What shall we do now?"

"Nothing, Father. They'll eventually give in and join our ranks."

"I agree," James gloated. "They're just headstrong and rigid. Give them time and they'll come crawling back to us on their hands and knees."

Todd inquired, "Do you want Michael and me to use force?"

Hugo smiled, "I don't think it will be necessary at this time, but if they don't return in the near future, we will reevaluate our government's position."

ONE HUNDRED
FOURTEEN

The two groups were deadlocked. As each faction prepared for a long conflict, every member became more incensed by the opposing side. Schedules were issued and rigidly enforced so all publicly shared sites were kept neutral and not occupied at the same time by members of the opposite party. Communication was usually written and minimal. Father McShane approached Hugo and asked, "How long do you think it will be before the women give in?"

"Any day, I'm sure."

"I hope you're correct because the strain is beginning to get to me."

"Father, I miss the women as much as anyone else, but they have to learn who rules the room," Hugo said.

"So what can we do?"

"Just sit and wait. Hopefully, they will come to their senses."

Across the room, Sandra, Iris, and Tara sat in conversation. "Must you continue to visit Smith?" Sandra asked.

Tara responded, "Yes. What harm is it?"

"He's a man!" Iris replied.

"Yes," Tara answered, "but he's neutral."

"I don't care, he's still a man."

Sandra spoke, "I agree with Iris. All men have a tendency to unite and take us women for granted."

"He's not like that at all," Tara revealed.

"Have you told him about the fighting?" Iris asked.

"Yes."

"What did he say?" Sandra questioned.

"Nothing really. He prefers to remain isolated from the conflict."

"Is he now speaking to you?" Sandra asked.

Tara considered the question, then lied, "Yes. He's very interested in all of us and is concerned about our safety."

"I still don't trust him," Iris abruptly stated.

"Until he does something wrong, I see no reason why Tara cannot see him," Sandra offered.

"Must I have your permission?" Tara asked in a sarcastic tone.

"Of course," Iris answered. "You're part of this group, aren't you?"

"I suppose so."

"Then you must get our permission for anything that involves an interaction with the men," Sandra informed her.

"Including Mr. Smith?"

Iris nodded, "Yes."

"That doesn't seem fair," Tara objected.

Sandra was quick to respond. "That is the rule; if you don't like it, leave!"

Tara mumbled, "It doesn't seem very fair, but I'll go along with your rule."

"It's for your own good," Sandra said. "All those men are up to no good."

"Right on!" Iris agreed. "Who needs them anyhow? We're doing perfectly fine without them."

ONE HUNDRED FIFTEEN

The great wall clock chimed eight loud rings. Moments later, the lights suddenly illuminated. Joanne was the first to shout, "There's a door missing!" Within seconds, everyone except for Smith, was at her side.

"How can that be?" Iris asked.

Michael touched the wall, "How can a door just disappear?"

Franklyn reminded them, "My openings disappear each night."

"That's true," James said. "But this was a fixed structure and not one newly opened."

Sandra said, "What does this mean?"

"I'm not sure," Hugo replied. "But I don't like it one bit."

Looking at her adversary, Sandra said, "Perhaps all of us should consider reuniting into a single entity."

"I couldn't agree with you more; there's strength in numbers," Hugo responded.

"Does that mean us men are the bosses?" Todd ventured.

"If it does, then we'll go our separate ways once again," Iris insisted.

Hugo thought for a moment, "I suggest Sandra and I share the responsibility for leadership."

"That sounds good to me," Joanne conceded.

"What about Father McShane and me?" James inquired.

Hugo responded, "The new organization will have only two directors and nobody else."

"Too many cooks can spoil the broth," Alice quoted.

"That's precisely the point," Sandra said. "This way both sexes are equally represented."

"I'd like to vote on this as quickly as possible," Hugo stated. "All in favor, please raise your hand." The motion passed without any opposition.

"Now that *that's* settled, what are we going to do about the missing door?" Phyllis asked.

"We can't do anything," Hugo stated. "It's beyond our capabilities to prevent or act upon."

"Out of bad comes good," Father McShane noted.

"I don't get it, Father," Michael questioned.

"The door to a small empty storage room disappears, but on the other hand, we're once again united."

"Father is right," Sandra said.

"Who removed the door and why?" Phyllis pondered.

"How do they work so quietly?" Iris asked.

"I'm a light sleeper and never hear a thing," Franklyn said. "I stayed awake one entire night by one of my openings and when the lights came on, it was sealed and reconstructed."

"And you never heard *anything*?" Father McShane asked.

"Not a sound."

"Look!" Phyllis said.

"What is it?" Sandra asked.

Raising her voice nervously Phyllis continued. "The pictures are all missing." Everyone examined the many walls and quickly discovered Phyllis' observation was correct.

"How?" Alice inquired.

Hugo shrugged his shoulders, "It seems as if someone is toying with us."

"I concur!" Sandra said.

"If I ever get my hands on him, I'll break his ass!" Todd angrily yelled.

Looking at the bare walls, Phyllis sobbed, "All those beautiful works!"

Trying to change the general negative atmosphere, Hugo suggested they eat breakfast. Todd bellowed, "Great idea!" Turning to Iris, he asked, "Would you mind cooking this morning? I miss your scrambled eggs and bacon."

"Sure!" Laughing, she grabbed his arm and pulled him towards the kitchen area. "Come on, big guy, I'm glad to be missed for something."

After the meal, Tara walked to Smith's site. He looked in her direction, but remained silent. Finally, she said. "Did you see it?"

Maintaining a cold attitude, he answered, "See what?"

"One of the doors is gone and all the pictures are missing."

"So."

"What kind of an answer is that?" she said. "Aren't you at all concerned?"

"No."

"Why?" Tara asked. "Our very lives could be at risk!"

Without looking up, he said, "What is destined to be, will be."

"What exactly do you mean by that?"

He looked into her eyes and said, "Leave me alone and don't come back."

Tara started to cry. She pleaded, "I'm sorry if I upset you, please don't..."

Turning his back on the young woman, he stated, "I said get out of here and never come back!"

"Why do you continue to hurt me? I never harmed you!"

He picked up a book and started to read. Tara stared at him for several minutes and then painfully replied, "I will not be back! Thanks for the gratitude!"

ONE HUNDRED
SIXTEEN

Hugo sought James by the bookcase. He said, "I need a favor."

"Sure! What do you need?"

"I need your professional opinion."

"You know that I don't give any advice—"

Hugo interrupted in a raised voice, "You'll examine me or I'll have Todd break your neck."

"You wouldn't dare!"

"Don't tempt me; just let me know what you think I have."

"Fine, but remember I will deny everything once we get out of here."

"I'm not looking for a lawsuit; I just want your opinion."

James led Hugo behind one of the couches and loosened his pants. Pointing to his genitals, he asked, "What is it?"

The physician examined the area for several minutes and then grinned. "Hugo, my boy, you've got yourself a case of syphilis."

"Syphilis! Are you sure?"

"Positive. I saw a lot of it when I was stationed overseas."

"How could I have gotten it?" Hugo mumbled.

James laughed. "We all hear you at night with your many

women. You probably picked it up from one of them."

Hugo stared out into the room, "Which one?"

"It doesn't matter at this point, you probably have spread it to all of them."

"What can I do about it?"

Sounding professional, James answered, "Seek medical help as soon as we get out of here."

Sounding nervous, Hugo inquired, "What should I do until then?"

"There's nothing you can do; however I certainly would refrain from any more sexual activities until you're treated for the disease."

"And the women?"

"I suggest you alert them about the possibility of contracting the disease."

"I will, like heck! One of them gave it to me, let the rest of them suffer also."

James shrugged his shoulders and said, "Do as you wish, but I suggest it be treated quickly. It looks like a bad case."

Pulling his pants up, Hugo mumbled, "Thanks, Doc, for the advice and help."

O N E   H U N D R E D
S E V E N T E E N

Days later, during lunch, James addressed the group, "Has any-one been taking books from the library and not returning them?"

"Probably Todd!" Michael quipped. "We all know how the brain loves to read." The athlete did not rebut the comment.

Joanne spoke, "I have two books."

"I have a copy of *Hamlet*," Sandra confessed.

"I'm reading *Alice's Adventures in Wonderland*," Father McShane added.

James then inquired, "Has anyone removed any books in bulk from the library?"

Sandra asked, "Is there a problem?"

"You're goddamn right, there is!" Raising his voice slightly, the physician said, "Half the books are missing."

"Half?" Hugo responded, shocked.

"That's right! Half the books are missing."

Hugo stated, "It seems our capturers are still playing with us."

"How can that be?" Iris questioned. "One of us should have heard something during the night."

"I agree," Franklyn added, "but like the door, it defies logic."

Suddenly, the lights flickered, turned themselves off, and then relit. "Stand where you are and don't panic!" Hugo shouted.

Phyllis grabbed Joanne and quivered, "I'm frightened!"

"So am I!" the actress responded. "I'll be glad to get out of here."

For the next few hours, the group remained in the kitchen area. Finally, the lighting remained constant.

"Do you think it's safe to move?" Tara asked.

"What else could happen?" Alice responded.

Once the group dispersed, James attracted everyone's attention, "*All* the books are now missing!"

Standing by the empty shelves, Sandra asked, "How can they do it?"

"There were at least a thousand books when we started and they are all gone," James stated as he shook his head in disbelief. "How?"

The book I was reading is missing from my sofa," Father McShane said. "Did any of you take it?"

"*Hamlet* is also gone," Sandra reported.

"And the two novels I had are missing," Joanne remarked.

Instead of trying to solve the mystery, everyone stared at the empty shelves and then returned to their individual sites. Tara quietly walked toward Smith's sofa. Peering over the top of the furniture, she noticed he was reading. *How can he still have his books and we don't?* she wondered to herself. Afraid to confront the man, she kept the discovery a secret. Since no one else ventured near Smith's area, she realized there was little chance of anyone else exposing the truth.

ONE HUNDRED EIGHTEEN

"I'm sick and tired of classical music," Iris said. "I wish we could hear some country and western."

"I miss my jazz collection," Alice continued. "I'd often listen for hours." Suddenly the overhead music stopped. Everyone in the room stared upward and waited. The great wall clock chimed three shrill rings.

"What happened to the music?" Joanne asked.

After a while, jazz filled the air. Alice grinned, "A gift from the gods!" Soon, however, the music ceased and silence again filled the room. Before anyone could speak, country and western music suddenly played. Shortly thereafter, the melodic noise abruptly stopped as quietude prevailed.

"Now what? Swiss army music?" Alice asked.

Iris conjectured, "I guess we'll just have to wait and see."

Nothing stirred for a long time. As Michael plugged in his guitar and prepared to play, radio static filled the room. "God!" he shouted. "That's awful!"

Holding her ears from the deafening sound, Joanne said. "What can we do to stop it?"

"Nothing," Franklyn yelled above the din. "I have no idea where the controls are."

"I cannot stand it!" the actress cried.

Across the room, members were sitting on their sofas with pillows held to the sides of their heads. Finally, Todd picked up his football and threw it upward to the ceiling. He struck a chandelier, causing the huge fixture to swing erratically overhead. Then it came crashing downward. Glass shattered and flew in all directions; luckily no one was injured.

The great wall clock rang two ear-piercing rings. Almost simultaneously, the static ceased and silence once again was present. Nobody spoke, they simply waited for the next audio assault.

Hours later, after the shattered chandelier was removed and the floor cleaned, Hugo suggested that everyone eat. Though emotionally drained, each person walked slowly to the table. Sandra and Alice served a quick lunch. In the middle of the meal, Phyllis broke down and cried. "What are we going to do? I can't take it any longer."

Touching her shoulders, Iris softly spoke, "Everything will be fine...."

"Fine, my ass!" Todd shouted. "Someone's trying to break us down."

"Let's not get over-dramatic," Hugo replied.

"Hugo's correct," Sandra added. "Mechanical things often break, the radio is no exception."

"Bull!" Todd screamed. "Someone's trying to get us."

Father McShane said, "We have nothing in common. Who would do such a thing and for what purpose?"

"Why don't we try to prepare something really special for tonight's meal?" Sandra suggested.

"A wonderful idea," Father McShane seconded.

"I'll cook my favorite soup recipe," Iris said.

Phyllis sobbed, saying, "I have a good way of cooking a steak."

"Excellent," Hugo said. "That settles it, tonight's going to be a special occasion."

"What is it?" Michael asked.

After thinking momentarily, the advertising executive declared, "Tonight will be an anniversary of our awakening."

Though it made no sense at all, everyone eagerly awaited the meal. Sandra leaned over to Hugo and whispered, "Good job."

Nodding, he responded, "No, it was a *great* job."

ONE HUNDRED NINETEEN

Throughout the rest of the day, everyone prepared for the celebration. Michael, Todd, and James decorated the kitchen with festive accouterments. Spirits were high as Tara, Joanne, and Alice neatly set the table in a holiday fashion. Sandra, along with Phyllis and Iris prepared the gourmet meal. Hugo, Franklyn, and Jeffery cleaned the area and then assisted the rest of the men decorating the kitchen. Father McShane, with his superb gift of gab, moved from group to group, offering his support and assistance.

Upon completing their individual tasks, each person walked back to their sites and groomed themselves for the special celebration.

As the clock sounded six rings, everyone went to the kitchen. Once all were seated, Hugo raised his glass and proposed a toast, "To all of us."

Sandra added, "And may we be rescued soon." Everyone gulped down the glass of champagne.

"Why didn't someone invite Smith to the celebration?" Todd jested.

"Yeah. He's part of the group, isn't he?" Michael chimed in.

To maintain the original harmony and theme of the meal, Hugo said, "Mr. Smith was personally invited by me, but he is not feeling too well and has decided to stay at his location, rather than ruining our evening."

"I don't trust that nigger," Phyllis whispered softly to Joanne.

Before the actress could respond, Hugo asked, "When do we eat? I'm starving!"

"Me too!" Todd bellowed. "I could eat a horse."

"Wait until you taste my soup," Iris said as she started to stand. Suddenly every light turned off, leaving the room black. "Damn!" she cried, "Not right now."

Hugo said, "It's probably just a short blackout like we've had before. Let's just sit it out and then enjoy our meal."

For nearly an hour, they sat in complete darkness. Smelling the air, Jeffrey shouted, "I think I smell something burning."

"I smell it too," Joanne said.

"I hope it's not my steak," Phyllis said. "I spent so much time preparing..." Her words were cut short by the sudden illumination of the room.

Michael screamed, "The stove's on fire."

Smoke filled the air as everyone scurried about. Jeffery and Franklyn attempted to smother the fire by throwing blankets onto the stove, but they quickly caught on fire. As the heat intensified, the surrounding kitchen burst into flames. As the decorations burned, everyone worked feverishly at minimizing the damage. Using water from the shower room and the sinks, they were finally able to extinguish the fire.

Surveying the damaged kitchen, Sandra spoke. "The whole thing is gone."

"What about the refrigerator?" Iris asked.

"Gone."

"The stove?" Tara asked.

"Likewise. There's nothing left."

"How are we going to cook from now on?" Phyllis inquired.

"We'll have to use the small sterno stoves in the storage room," Sandra answered.

"How will we preserve our food?" Alice questioned.

"We can't," Sandra said.

"Is there a chance anything can be fixed?" Tara asked.

"No," Sandra responded sternly, "Everything is beyond repair."

"What are we going to do?" Phyllis sobbed.

"We're going to survive until someone either lets us out of this room or we are finally rescued," Hugo announced.

"That's easier said than done," Phyllis responded.

"If you have a better idea, I'm open to your suggestion," Hugo replied, "Until that time, we'll continue to work in a united fashion to endure whatever hardships or barriers are placed in our way."

ONE HUNDRED TWENTY

Todd stormed to the center of the room. The huge athlete screamed, "Who did it?"

"For God's sake," Hugo said mildly. "What are you talking about?"

"My football!" he shouted. "Who punctured my football?"

Everyone remained silent. Sandra said finally, "It appears none of us did it."

"Don't give me that crap! I know one of you did it."

Alice inquired, "How can you be so sure?"

"I know none of you like my playing in here and..."

"I think you are overreacting," Father McShane said. "Perhaps it was punctured when it struck the chandelier."

"No way, Father. I've used it since then."

"Maybe the same person or persons who took our door also deflated your football." Phyllis conjectured.

"No way!" Todd answered. "One of you did it and when I find out who it was, I'll make them pay dearly."

"Please, my son, try to remain calm."

"Father!" Todd snorted. "Up yours!" The big man jogged

away.

"Man, is that brute pissed," Michael observed.

"I suggest we all stay away from him for the time being," Hugo proposed.

"I agree!" Sandra added. "He's liable to strike before thinking."

"As long as we're talking, I was wondering if anyone has noticed anything unusual during the past few days," Franklyn inquired.

Everyone shook their heads. "Why do you ask?" Hugo said.

"I was just curious."

"Stop beating around the bush and tell us what you are thinking," Sandra stated. "Since the fire, everything appears to be running correctly."

"Except for the chandelier and radio!" Michael noted.

"Those can be explained by natural causes," Franklyn said. "And that's precisely my point: nothing is happening."

"Maybe it's all stopping," Alice suggested.

"Maybe help is close at hand," Phyllis added.

"Perhaps both of you are correct," Franklyn stated. "All I know is it's been very, very quiet."

"The calm before the storm?" Sandra said.

"I hope not! I tend to agree with Phyllis. I think help is close at hand."

"Do you have any concrete evidence?" Hugo asked.

"None. Just my intuition."

Michael refused to comment. Returning to his sofa, he discovered his guitar's strings had all been cut. Slumping onto the floor, he clutched the instrument to his chest and cried. Mumbling, he sobbed, "That jackass!" Looking in Todd's direction, he continued thinking *I didn't touch your damn football. You didn't have to do this!* After the longest time, he carefully placed the damaged guitar into its case. He clutched his fist and swore, *I'll get you for this! You picked the wrong guy to mess with! You're dead meat, you oversized baboon!*

Across the room, Sandra approached Franklyn as he worked at his bench. Looking up, the scientist smiled, "How's everything going?"

"Other than Todd's outbreak and a few other minor problems, things seem quite tranquil."

"That's what I was saying before. I hope my premonition about being discovered is also correct."

"I'll keep my fingers crossed. Can anything be done about the kitchen sink?"

"Nope."

"You mean we have to listen to that constant dripping?"

"I'm afraid so. Without the proper tools and fittings, I can't repair it."

"Can't it be improvised in some way? I can't sleep at night with that noise."

"Just get used to it. There's nothing I can do."

Sandra shrugged her shoulders and moaned, "I tried!"

"By the way, tell everyone not to touch it."

"Why?"

"The drops of water are extremely hot."

"I'd better put a sign up to warn everyone."

Franklyn nodded, "That's a good idea, I'd hate to see someone get burned."

"Is it that hot?"

"Nearly 100 degrees centigrade."

Sandra admitted her ignorance concerning scientific measurements. "It sounds quite warm."

"It could nearly boil."

"I'd better get that sign up fast." Before she left, she asked, "Do you really think someone will find us soon?"

Noticing they were alone, he whispered, "No."

"Then why did you say those things about being discovered?"

"I thought it would be good for the group's morale."

"I see your point and believe it helped decrease everyone's anxiety."

"Then I accomplished my goal."

"Just let Hugo and me in on your motives next time."

Looking down at his workbench, the scientist went back to his research.

O N E H U N D R E D
T W E N T Y - O N E

Alice gasped, "Father, please hurry." Grabbing the priest by his arm, she tugged impatiently.

"What's wrong?" he inquired, shocked at her insistence.

"No time," she panted. "Just come."

"I—" Before he could say another word, Alice was pulling the priest across the room. As they approached the bookcases, Father McShane stared. "What's going on?" he asked.

She answered, "I don't know. He's been like this for over two hours."

"Two hours!"

"Yes. I woke up early and saw him standing up there on the table. At first I thought it was some sort of joke, but..." Alice suddenly started to sob. "Oh Father, what's happening?"

He touched her arm gently and then proceeded slowly toward Jeffery. Nearing him he stopped and surveyed the man's face. Noting his eyes were closed, the priest moved slightly closer and then spoke. "Jeffery, can you hear me?"

Alice whispered, "Is he awake?"

"I don't know." Staring at Jeffery, he again asked, "Jeffery, can you hear me?"

"What should we do?" asked Alice.

"I don't know," Father McShane stated.

"Shall I get the others?" she inquired.

"Wait one more minute and see what happens." Looking at Jeffery as he stood atop the large table, the priest moved closer and tugged at the man's arm. "Jeffery!"

"Father, he opened his eyes!" Alice reported.

Nodding, Father McShane inquired, "Jeffery, can you hear me?" The priest turned to Alice and whispered, "You'd better get the others."

Within a few minutes, everyone was standing by the table. Hugo was the first to speak, "What's he doing up there?"

"I have no idea; I woke up and found him standing on the table," Alice said.

Father McShane added, "He hasn't moved an inch since."

Sandra looked at Jeffery and turned to James. "Doctor," she asked, "what's your diagnosis?"

"You know I don't offer my services…"

Before he could complete his sentence, Todd grabbed him harshly by the arm and said, "Cut the crap and just tell us what's wrong."

James reached forward and grasped Jeffery's wrist. Locating the pulse, he said, "His pulse is regular, but extremely slow. He appears to be in some sort of catatonic state."

"Like sleep walking?" Hugo inquired.

"Possibly."

"What should we do with him?" Sandra asked.

The physician surveyed the situation and suggested, "I think he'd be safer off the table." Several of the men carefully lifted Jeffery's form from the table and lay it gently on the floor. James examined the man's reflexes and vital signs. "He's physically stable; however, I've never seen anything like this before."

"How do we treat him?" Alice questioned.

"I'd try to wake him as soon as possible."

"Any methods?" Hugo asked.

"I'm an orthopedist, not a sleep expert." Todd moved closer to the physician, causing James to quickly add, "Let's try putting him in the shower."

With a united effort, the group carefully carried Jeffery across the room and placed him on the tiled shower floor. Satisfied, Father McShane turned on the cold water and watched as it tumbled upon the sleeping body. Moments later, Jeffery coughed and abruptly sat upright. He surveyed his surroundings and asked, "What's going on?"

Sandra informed him. "You must have been sleepwalking and we had to wake you up."

Shaking his head, Jeffery responded, "I never did that in my entire life. That's impossible."

Todd helped him into a nearby chair. James touched his wrist and after a few moments, the physician said, "His pulse is normal."

"How are you feeling?" Sandra asked.

"Fine, but I don't understand what happened."

"Can you recall anything?" Hugo inquired.

Jeffery rubbed his head and mumbled, "Only that I had some sort of nightmare."

"Can you remember any specifics?" Father McShane questioned.

"No."

Todd studied Jeffery and turned to James. "What are you going to do now?"

"What do you want me to do?" he answered. "Do you suggest an MRI or a workup by a neurologist?"

"You don't have to be sarcastic," Michael said. "He was only concerned."

"Great!" James responded. "Try practicing medicine without any equipment; it's a real blast."

Todd announced, "I'm taking him back to his sofa, but I expect a follow-up examination." Staring James directly in the eye, he stated sternly, "Do I make myself perfectly clear?" James nodded and walked away.

Michael helped Todd while Sandra and Hugo remained behind. "What do you think?" the advertising executive asked.

"I have no idea, but it frightens me," Sandra replied.

"Why? Many people sleepwalk."

Sandra answered, "Just a woman's intuition, something is not right."

"I don't agree."

"Fine, but how can you explain Jeffery's sudden siege of sleep-walking and how did he get onto the table?"

"He climbed up," Hugo answered.

"With no chairs around the table and still asleep, he climbed up and elected to remain stationary?"

"Yes."

"And his nightmares? They really scare me!" Sandra said.

Touching her hand, Hugo answered, "I think you're overreacting."

"Perhaps, but I'm still uneasy about the whole thing."

Whispering into her ear, Hugo asked, "Are you in the mood?"

Shaking her head, Sandra responded, "Maybe some other time, I'm too shaken."

"No problem, and remember, you're a very special lady."

She kissed him on the cheek and softly said, "Thanks, I'll make it up to you on another occasion."

As she walked away, Hugo stared at the other women. Smiling, he said to himself, *Damn am I horny; I wonder who's in the mood.*

ONE HUNDRED TWENTY-TWO

A pattern quickly developed. Each succeeding night, another member of the group was discovered standing on the same table in a catatonic state. None had a history of such a condition and each was equally shocked to awaken. As the men carried Sandra's limp body to the shower, Michael asked, "Why did this happen to everyone but Smith?"

"I don't know," Father McShane answered.

"Why don't you ask him yourself?" James stated.

"You must be kidding," Michael joked. "I ain't talking to that nigger. He's antisocial!"

Todd laughed, "Maybe he can teach you about rhythm. His kind are really good at dancing and prancing."

Michael stated, "And they're really great at sports also."

"Bull," Todd responded. "They're all a bunch of chicken-shit bastards. Hit them real hard once and they'll avoid you like the plague."

As they reached the shower room door, Hugo turned the knob and opened the door. Everyone stared; they carefully lowered Sandra's body to the floor to examine their latest discovery.

"Why?" Father McShane said in a dejected tone.

Hugo ran his hand along the fresh masonry wall just inside the door. "Who would do such a thing?"

Franklyn retrieved several of his handmade tools and began probing, poking, and striking the newly built barrier. Getting nowhere, he dropped his hammer and cursed. "The damn thing is solid."

"Let me try," Todd responded, but after several powerful blows, he lay down the hammer and quit. "It won't budge."

"We must have use of that room," James stated. "We'll just have to break down the wall somehow."

Instead of his usual joking, Michael nodded, "We've got to have water."

Dazed, Sandra stared at the wall and then at the men. "What..."

"Remain still; I'll explain later." Father McShane told her. The priest turned to Michael and whispered, "Go to the kitchen and get her a glass of water." Minutes later, the rocker returned empty-handed. Father McShane asked, "Where is it?"

Shaking his head, Michael began to sob. "It's gone."

"For God's sake!" Hugo shouted, "what's gone?"

Michael moaned, "The water cooler is missing."

No one spoke. Weeping, the musician asked, "How are we going to get water?"

Franklyn responded to the question. "The only water available is the dripping faucet and the bathroom sink."

"Thank God!" Father McShane stated.

"But the water from the faucet is burning hot," Todd said.

"We'll have to collect it in containers and allow it to cool," Franklyn responded. Todd assisted Sandra to her feet and walked her back to her sofa.

Michael asked, "How are we going to make it without show-ers?"

Hugo answered, "Because we're strong. We may stink a little more, but we still have plenty of water to drink."

Though each member was distraught, Hugo and Sandra were able to organize a water salvaging policy. Working without a break, the group quickly assembled an adequate inventory of fresh drinking and cooking water. Looking up at the ceiling, Todd clenched his fist and shouted, "You haven't defeated us yet!"

ONE HUNDRED TWENTY-THREE

For the next few days, things seemed to settle. Though demoralized, everyone tried their best to adjust to the more primitive conditions. Father McShane's classes were discontinued because of poor attendance; community meals were quickly becoming a thing of the past. Hugo and Sandra met daily, but little of any importance was ever decided.

Blackouts continued to be commonplace, making sleep and daily activities difficult to plan. Tara, though drawn by an overwhelming urge, elected not to visit the vagrant. Despair steadily engulfed everyone present.

O N E H U N D R E D
T W E N T Y - F O U R

Franklyn, Phyllis, and Tara slowly consumed their lunch. Lacking motivation, the three sipped cans of cold vegetable soup. None spoke; they silently directed their full attention to providing their bodies with sustenance. The lights dimmed slightly and then shone brightly. After several repetitions, the room suddenly remained dark.

Phyllis began to cry. "I can't take it any longer..."

Tara tried to console her friend. Finding Phyllis' arm, the young woman tenderly stroked and whispered, "Just stay calm. Everything will be fine."

The music switched from classical to hard rock. Franklyn pounded the table with his fist and shouted, "Turn it off! I can't stand the racket." As quickly as the words left his mouth, jazz filled the airways. With no pattern, the music again changed without warning.

Phyllis shook wildly as clamorous sounds continued to fill the room. Tara hugged the woman and attempted to comfort her. Meanwhile, Franklyn held his hands to his ears to block out the various songs and sounds.

Without warning, the great wall clock began to chime. Each ring flooded the room with additional sound and added further to the reverberation. Sandra held tightly to Hugo and shouted, "What's happening?"

Equally troubled by the most recent auditory invasion, Hugo responded, "I don't know, but I hope it ends soon."

Minutes later, all sound ceased and the chandeliers exhibited a brilliant light that flooded the room. Not knowing what to expect next, everyone waited. Finally after almost an hour of silence and light, life returned to routine.

"Can we prepare for any of it?" Father McShane inquired.

"How?" Hugo answered. "Everything's so unpredictable."

"Perhaps each person should keep some food and water by their site," the priest suggested.

The co-leader agreed and relayed the suggestion to everyone.

Returning from the storage room with a handful of supplies, Jeffery pulled Hugo aside. Making sure no one was listening, he whispered, "We have a problem."

"Now what?" the executive questioned.

"Rats!"

"What are you talking about?"

"I just saw several large rats in the storage room."

"Are you sure?"

Holding out his hand, the scientist revealed several samples of droppings. "They're all over the place."

Shaking his head, Hugo stated, "How can we kill them?"

"We can't! We don't have any traps or poisons."

"Just great!" Hugo thought for a moment and then asked, "What about our food?"

"It's in danger. From the number of droppings I observed, it's evident there are a great many rodents."

"How about bringing most of the food in this room?"

Franklyn thought and then said, "The rats will probably follow." The lights flickered and then dimmed. The scientist stated,

411

"At least it's—" Before he could complete his sentence, the wall clock chimed. After seventeen earsplitting rings, static filled the room.

Hugo shook his head and shouted above the noise, "I'll speak to you when it stops!"

ONE HUNDRED TWENTY-FIVE

Sandra stared in wonder at her surroundings. Michael ran up and asked, "How did it happen? I was up all night and didn't hear a thing." Shaking his head, he added, "It's impossible."

Picking up several pieces of a broken table, Sandra sighed, "It may be impossible, but it's real."

Everyone congregated by the center of the room. Alice said, "Is *everything* destroyed?"

"Accept for our sofas, every piece of furniture has been destroyed," Hugo reported.

"Everything?" Phyllis questioned in a dejected tone.

"Yes," Father McShane responded, "even the bookcases have been torn apart."

Jeffery added, "Most of the wallpaper is mutilated around the entire room."

"Who would do such a thing?" Joanne asked softly.

"Who?" Todd shouted. "Whoever they are, I'll kill the sons-of-bitches!"

"I'll second that idea," James concurred. "I'd like to do unto them as they have done unto me."

Father McShane said, "The ceiling is severely damaged."

"And so is the molding," Franklyn added. "It's been torn apart and splintered."

"I don't get it," Michael stated.

Hugo said somberly, "That's the question of the year. Someone or some group is either sadistic or is holding out for a great deal of money."

Phyllis cried loudly, "My husband should have paid them by now; why don't they let us go?"

"Maybe he didn't pay them," Michael stated.

Taking the defensive, Phyllis lashed out, "Of course he paid, I'm his wife!"

"Let's try to remain calm," Hugo pleaded.

Sandra suggested, "Let's resume stockpiling food and water."

"Fun for the feeble-minded," Michael jeered.

"It might be for you, but it's a matter of survival for the rest of us," James countered.

"Don't get your bones bent all out of shape, Doc. I was only kidding."

"Some joke," James responded. "Maybe you should begin to take things more seriously."

"Up yours!" Michael retorted.

The physician controlled his temper. Looking at the ripped and strained carpeting, he asked, "Can anything be done to salvage the rug?"

Iris answered, "It's beyond help."

Trying to perk up everyone's spirits, Father McShane suggested a community meal.

"What are we going to sit on?" Todd inquired. "Our asses?"

"Yes," responded the priest. "Unless you have a better suggestion."

Instead of saying another word, Todd joined the others for breakfast. After the meal, everyone began transporting cartons of food from the storage room to the kitchen.

Once the day's work was terminated, Tara walked toward Smith's site. Knowing that he refused to speak with her did not deter her humanistic emotions. She approached his area quietly and carefully looked to see where he was. Immediately she noticed all of his furniture was still intact. Before she could move closer, he appeared and stared menacingly in her direction. Frightened, she returned quickly to the safety of her sofa.

ONE HUNDRED
TWENTY-SIX

Jeffery examined the can closely and complained to Franklyn, "I didn't get a full can. It's only partially filled."

Overhearing the conversation, Iris said, "I've had the same problem for the past few days. The food in my cans has been less than in the past."

The scientist looked at his own can and quickly realized his ration was also significantly reduced. "What's going on?" Jeffery asked.

"I'm not sure. Perhaps it's another little game by our secret captors."

Iris complained, "There's not enough to fill my stomach."

"Thank goodness, we have additional supplies in the storage room," Jeffery reminded. "Otherwise, I'd probably starve to death."

"You wouldn't starve; however, your nutritional input would be greatly reduced," Franklyn corrected.

Iris chuckled, "Can you imagine Todd's reaction if he had to reduce the amount of food he eats."

"He'd go crazy. He's a madman about his health and diet anyway!" Jeffery said.

Looking at the cases of food Iris added, "I still don't see the reason for bringing all this food here. What's wrong with keeping it in the storage room?"

"Personally," Franklyn said, "I believe it was something Hugo and Sandra simply made up to fill our time."

Jeffery instantly commented, "Like a psychological ploy?"

"Precisely! And I think it was a very good idea."

Iris thought for a moment, "Do you really think we needed one?"

Franklyn answered, "Absolutely. Without an organized strategy, idiots like Todd and Michael would turn this place into chaos."

"Isn't it already?" Iris asked.

"It could be much worse," Jeffery answered. "That's why I went along with the moving of the food and why I'll go along with any other plan they contrive."

"It sounds awfully childish," Iris responded.

"It certainly does, but remember, everyone is not as smart as the three of us," Franklyn stated.

Looking at her partially filled can of food, Iris said "At least I won't starve."

"I—" Jeffery was interrupted by a shriek from the storage room. Another scream quickly followed the first. Todd, Michael, and Hugo rushed to the source. Minutes later, additional threatening sounds could be heard.

"What's going on?" Iris asked.

"No idea," Franklyn responded.

The three men returned from the storage room carrying a bloody body. Todd slammed the door and then assisted the others in transporting the unconscious man to the middle of the room.

"What happened?" Father McShane shouted as he neared the area.

Todd shouted, "Rats!"

"Rats?" Alice questioned.

"Yeah," Michael stated. "There are thousands of them in the storage room." Phyllis looked at the door to the hallway and inquired, "Can they get in here?"

"I'm not sure, but that room is definitely off limits," Hugo said as he tried to catch his breath.

Watching Sandra and Tara apply emergency aid to James, Iris inquired, "What happened?"

"He was probably picking up his day's ration of food and was attacked," Hugo speculated.

"Attacked?" Father McShane asked.

"Are you sure?" Phyllis questioned.

"You're goddamn right we're sure! We had to tear them off his body," Todd said.

Michael added, "They were eating him alive."

"My God," Father McShane sighed as he crossed himself.

"What are we going to do?" Phyllis sobbed. "I don't want to be eaten by them."

Noticing James' wounds had finally stopped bleeding and were mostly bandaged, Hugo turned to Sandra, "How's he doing?"

"Not very good."

"Will he live?" Franklyn asked.

"I believe so, but they chewed his hands up pretty badly," Sandra answered.

"He's still breathing," Joanne reported.

"I think he's in shock," Tara said.

"But what else can we do for him?" asked Franklyn.

Hugo responded, "Probably just keep the bleeding from starting again and make him as comfortable as possible."

"I'll say a prayer for him," the priest added.

Hugo looked at each person and said, "No one should go into that room again."

"But what about our food supplies?" Sandra asked.

"We'll have to live off what we have in this room," Hugo said then added, "We must board up that door as quickly as possible."

"Can't they get to us anyway?" Jeffery asked.

"Perhaps they'll be content in the room; there's more than enough food in there to fill their stomachs," Hugo answered.

"I suggest we begin some form of food rationing," Sandra said.

"No way!" Todd shouted. "I need all the protein and carbs I can get."

Hugo intervened. "I think we should discuss this matter later on. Right now, our priorities should be securing the door and ensuring James' survival."

Michael joked, "In which order?"

"It could have been you there instead of him," Joanne pointed out.

"But it wasn't," Michael countered.

"Besides, would Dr. Harrison help me if the tables were reversed?"

Looking at the blood-soaked physician, Sandra responded, "I believe he would."

Todd laughed, "If the price was right, he'd do anything."

Hugo turned to Franklyn and said, "Get your tools and meet us over by the door."

Once everyone had departed, Tara knelt by James' body and whispered, "You'll be just fine."

Sandra rewrapped several of the bandages and with Tara, maintained a steady vigil of their wounded comrade. Days later, James regained consciousness. Upon learning about his injuries and the circumstances, the physician withdrew into a deep depression. Gazing at his missing finger and badly damaged hands, he wailed, "I'm a surgeon. My life is over."

Tara, Sandra, and Father McShane continued to assist the weakened man. Despite all their attempts, James ate and drank meagerly and refused to converse with anyone.

O N E   H U N D R E D   T W E N T Y - S E V E N

Joanne whispered to Phyllis, "Are you asleep?"

"I haven't slept since James was attacked," Phyllis confessed.

"Try to get some rest, you look terrible."

Phyllis sobbed, "I just want to go home."

"We all do, but by not sleeping, you're only hurting your body."

Phyllis sniffled, "I don't think we are ever going to leave this room. For some reason, these bad people are torturing me."

Joanne moved to her friend's side and stroked her hair. "We'll get out of here, you have my word on it."

"Do you really think so?"

"Yes."

Phyllis asked, "What about the rats? What if they come in here and attack us?"

"Stop worrying about such things. We'll be long gone before they get in this room."

Closing her eyes, Phyllis said, "I'm very tired. Thank you for your kind words." Joanne remained at her friend's side until the woman was fast asleep. Looking upward at the ceiling, she heard faint noises overhead. *Damn rats*, she said to herself. Laying down next to Phyllis' warm body, the actress tried to fall asleep. "Hopefully," she muttered, "I won't get those nightmares again."

ONE HUNDRED
TWENTY-EIGHT

Joanne, Alice, Phyllis, and Iris congregated around the broken kitchen table.

"Without a shower or bath, I'm afraid my body is beginning to smell," Joanne conceded.

Phyllis laughed, "I often took two baths a day; this is very difficult for me to handle."

Alice added, "In my country, where it's extremely hot, I often take two or more showers a day."

Iris looked at the three women and then at her torn clothing. "Does anyone have any clothes they could lend me?"

"Forget it!" Joanne answered. "This is my last dress. All the others are ruined or filthy."

Phyllis added, "I'm even short on undergarments. All I have left is what I'm wearing."

"I'm in the same boat. And I don't know how much longer I can wear them before I have to peel them off my body."

"I know how you feel," Iris said. "I feel disgusting."

"Maybe we can use some water to bathe," Phyllis wondered.

"Forget it!" Alice stated flatly. "The men will not allow that to happen. Besides, we need it for drinking."

"I wonder how the men are coping with dirty clothes," Phyllis pondered.

"They're all a bunch of filthy pigs anyhow, so they must feel right at home," Joanne responded bitterly.

"God," Alice whispered, "Todd smells like a gymnasium."

"All jocks smell the same," Phyllis added.

"Why does he continue to work out? Doesn't he know how badly he stinks?" Iris questioned.

"His ego wouldn't understand what you're saying," Joanne commented. "Just walk away when he comes close; maybe he'll get a hint that way."

"Even Hugo's beginning to smell," Iris whispered.

"He always did, my dear," Joanne said. "In fact, his breath smells like onions and garlic all the time."

"Thank God we're so perfect," Phyllis joked.

Touching her knee, Joanne stated, "You're so very right and don't ever forget it."

"Meanwhile, what can we do about the situation?" Iris asked.

Joanne answered, "Nothing. Just sit and smell like the rest."

ONE HUNDRED TWENTY-NINE

"Man, I'm blistering," Michael said.

Father McShane wiped his forehead. "I agree, it does feel warmer to me too."

"Warm? I'm toasting," Michael said as he proceeded to take off his outer shirt.

Hugo looked around the room, "It's hotter than usual." Turning to Franklyn he asked, "What do you think?"

The scientist studied his thermometer and shook his head.

"What's wrong?" Jeffery inquired.

"My instruments must be defective. They're recording a twenty degree increase in room temperature."

"Are you sure they're broken?" Hugo asked. "It's really hot in here."

Re-reading the thermometer, Franklyn answered, "The average daily temperature for this room has been 72 degrees Fahrenheit. Right now, it's reading 92 degrees Fahrenheit."

"It certainly feels like 92 degrees," Michael responded.

"How do you know the average temperature is 72 degrees?" Hugo inquired.

"As part of my routine, I record temperature and other objective findings."

"Perhaps the 92 degrees is correct," Father McShane suggested.

"Why the sudden change in temperature? It's never been this hot before," the scientist wondered.

"You're the man of science! You should have all the answers," Michael said callously.

"I don't need any of your crap, young man," Franklyn retorted. "If you're so damn smart, figure it out yourself."

"Cool it," the rocker responded. "I ain't no scientist."

Franklyn readjusted his instruments and recorded the data. Finally he said, "Assuming my instrumentation is functioning properly, I'd say we have a problem."

"What temperature is it now?" Hugo asked.

Without changing his facial expression, Franklyn answered, "It's 93 degrees Fahrenheit."

"That's one degree higher!" Jeffery said with alarm.

With sweat pouring from his face, the scientist walked the perimeter of the room. Upon his return, Hugo asked, "Find anything?"

"The room is uniformly hot. Regardless of what section I stood in, the thermometer always read the same.

"So the whole room is recording 93 degrees?" Jeffery asked.

"That's not true," replied Franklyn.

Hugo was beginning to lose his temper. He raised his voice slightly and said, "You just told us the room was uniform in temperature. Am I correct?"

"Yes, I did."

"So then it's 93 degrees all over," Michael clarified.

"No."

"Stop the crap!" Todd said, "I'm very hot and I don't need any of your double-talk. What gives?"

The scientist calmly replied, "The temperature throughout the entire room is not 93 degrees, it's 95."

Father McShane uttered, "The temperature is going up awfully fast."

"Too fast!" Hugo added.

"What can you do about it?" Jeffery inquired.

Shaking his head, Franklyn answered, "Nothing. I've never seen a thermostat or other temperature controls in here."

Wiping the perspiration from his forehead, Michael moaned, "This heat is killing me. I'm going to get some water to cool off."

Hugo raised his voice, "You can't! It should be used for drinking only."

The rocker looked at Hugo, "If I want water, I'll take it."

Hugo gestured to Todd and ordered, "If he or anyone else uses our water for any purpose other than drinking, you are ordered to stop them by any means necessary."

"What gives you the right to stop me?" Michael objected.

"You and the others did, when I was elected your leader."

"I'll speak to Sandra about this," Michael challenged.

"Sandra does as I say!" Hugo boldly added, "She will not countermand any of my orders."

"And what if I take the water anyway?"

Todd closed his fists tightly. The huge man snarled, "I'll break your arms and legs."

Father McShane interceded. "The heat's getting to all of us. Why don't we just go back to our areas and rest?"

Following his suggestion, everyone dispersed. Several hours later, the women met at Sandra's site. They discussed the unbearable heat and its implications. Finally, Joanne relented, "I can't take it anymore." She began to unbutton her blouse.

"What are you doing?" Phyllis asked.

"I'm taking my clothes off. It's too damn hot."

Tara responded, "How can you do such a thing? The men will see you!"

"Wearing my underwear is no different than wearing a bathing suit, in fact, my bathing suits show much more skin."

"I think it's a marvelous idea," Phyllis said. "I think I'll join you."

Tara watched as the rest of the women stripped off their outer clothing. "But—"

"Don't be such a prude," Alice chastened.

"Look," Sandra said as she pointed across the room. "All the men are also in their underwear."

"Father McShane too?" Tara inquired.

"Yes," Iris added. "He just took off his pants."

"It's disgusting." Phyllis looked at the younger woman and said, "You can keep that hot clothing on all day. As for me, I'm feeling somewhat better already."

Instead of arguing, Tara sat with her clothing still intact and watched as the two groups mingled. Despite their near-nudity status, the extreme heat forced illicit behavior or comments to a minimum. Everyone tolerated the unbearable change in temperature as best they could.

During the night and the next day, the room's temperature reached 101 degrees Fahrenheit. Throughout this period, Sandra and Hugo were successful in rationing the group's limited inventory of food and water.

ONE HUNDRED THIRTY

"Do you notice anything unusual?" Jeffery questioned.

Hugo looked around and answered, "I'm not exactly sure what you're getting at?"

"Listen very carefully."

The executive shook his head. "I don't hear anything."

"That's precisely what I'm driving at! It's too quiet."

"We've had periods where the music stopped before."

Jeffery continued, "It's more than that. It's as if someone or something is waiting. It's just too silent."

"I think you're just getting paranoid. Maybe this damn heat is getting to you," Hugo suggested.

"Perhaps you're right, but I still don't like it."

The two men walked over to James. The physician remained mute. Hugo finally asked, "How are you feeling?"

James looked at his healing wounds and said sarcastically, "Just great."

"Any more pain?" Jeffery inquired.

Nodding his head, the physician responded weakly, "Some."

"Can we do anything for you?" Hugo asked.

"No."

"Can we bring you something to eat?" Jeffery asked.

"No."

"You must eat something," Hugo stated. "Otherwise you won't heal."

James sneered, "Why don't you just leave me alone?"

"But—"

Interrupting Jeffery, the physician stated, "My life is over." Holding up his crudely bandaged arms, he shouted, "Leave me alone! Go take care of the other lowlifes in this room. I don't want any pity or help from any of you."

Hugo turned to Jeffery and whispered, "We'd better go." The executive then said, "Feel better!"

James responded, "Give me back my hands and arms!" Sobbing, he moaned, "That's how you can help!"

ONE HUNDRED THIRTY-ONE

"What's wrong?" Michael inquired.

"The humidity is rising," Franklyn stated as he reread the barometer.

"I don't need any scientific instrument to tell me that; just look at my skin."

"This—"

The scientist cut his sentence short and stared at his workbench.

"What now?"

"Shut up for one minute! I thought I saw something." Moments later, he pointed to the barometer, "Watch that for a minute."

Michael watched and waited. Finally rubbing his eyes he said, "It moved on the table."

"That's what I saw."

"Things just don't move by themselves," Michael stated.

"Tell that to the barometer," Franklyn responded. Placing his hands lightly on the table, he quickly discovered the reason. "The table's vibrating."

The rocker put his hand alongside Franklyn and waited. He

smiled, "The goddamn thing is really shaking."

"But why?" Franklyn asked. "An object will only react when a force is applied to that object."

Michael shrugged his shoulders, "Whatever you say Franklyn, but why is the table shaking?"

"I'm not sure, but I'm afraid that's only part of a larger picture." Putting his hands on several items, Franklyn found everything was vibrating. "I think something might be happening and—" Before another word could exit his mouth, the entire room began to vibrate. Dishes crashed to the floor, chandeliers swung wildly over-head, and the remaining furniture rocked.

"What's happening?" Michael shouted.

"Earthquake!"

"An earthquake?" the rocker questioned. "I thought those things only happened in California."

Franklyn held onto his workbench and watched as huge cracks inched their way down one wall of the room. Abruptly, everything stopped. Dust filled the air and the room's structure creaked as members of the group began to assess the damage.

Hugo walked to Franklyn and asked, "Is it over?"

"I'm not sure," the scientist continued, "It's too bad I don't have a seismograph here; I'd be able to tell you much more about the quake."

Hugo looked around the room and stated, "It looks like we were hit pretty hard."

Franklyn corrected him, "On the contrary, this was just a small one. A major quake on the Richter scale would have crushed this room into tiny fragments."

The rest of the group gathered at Franklyn's site. He briefed them on his analysis and warned them of possible further tremors.

"Why is this happening to me?" Phyllis sobbed. "I can't take much more!"

Joanne consoled her friend while Todd spoke. "I was in an earthquake several years ago and it was horrendous. This was just a

431

little baby quake."

As they were about to disperse, the room once again began to vibrate. Instinctively, individuals clung to each other. A large chandelier came crashing to the floor. More violent than the previous tremor, a high-pitched sound emitted from the center of the room. As it approached unbearable intensity, furniture flew upward, and a deluge of steam flooded the room. As the trapdoor erupted from its hinges, fragments of rock and wood flung in every direction.

The assault lasted only a few minutes; however, the effect was devastating. The outpouring of scorching steam only further raised the room's humidity to an intolerable level. Hugo and Franklyn walked to the opening in the floor and peered downward into the steamy void.

The executive meekly inquired, "Do you think it's over now?"

"I certainly hope so." Franklyn pointed to several quake-produced damage sites and said, "I don't think this room will hold up to any more tremors."

Hugo responded, "Let's hope it's over; otherwise, we may all leave this room in body bags."

ONE HUNDRED THIRTY-TWO

As a matter of routine, Phyllis' first action when the lights came on was to open her box and inspect her possessions. Reaching under her sofa, she fumbled for the box. Not able to feel it, she dropped to her knees and peered underneath. Finding nothing, she screamed, "Who stole my money?"

Todd came running over and lifted the hysterical woman to her feet. "What's going on?" he asked.

Flailing wildly, she shouted, "Let me go! I've got to find my money." She crawled onto the floor and frantically inspected her area. Sobbing she said, "It's got to be here! It's got to be here!"

Alice joined Todd and asked, "What's going on with her?"

The athlete responded, "I have no idea. Something about money."

"Money?" Alice questioned. "Who's got money?"

"Evidently, she has."

Phyllis cried, "It's gone! Who could do such a thing to me?"

Across the room Franklyn rose and headed for his workbench. He stared in disbelief at the empty counter. "What the heck!" he said. "Where's my stuff?" After a thorough search, he walked to

Father McShane's site. He found the elderly man on his hands and knees. "Father," he asked. "Have you seen my instruments?"

"No," the priest responded. "Are they missing?"

"Yes," Franklyn answered tersely. "Everything's gone!"

"I'm sorry to hear that," the priest touched the scientist's arm. "Perhaps Michael is playing one of his jokes on you."

"He'd better not have broken anything or I'll—"

"Let's not jump to any conclusions! Remember, we're only speculating." Father McShane then questioned, "By the way, have you seen my Bible anywhere?"

"No. Why do you ask?"

"Because I can't seem to find it."

"That son of a bitch!" Franklyn cursed. "He's pulling his crap on everyone, I bet!"

"There's only one way to find out; let's go over and have a word with our young prankster."

As they approached Michael's sofa, they found the young rocker extremely disturbed. Father McShane asked, "What's wrong, Michael?"

"What's wrong?" the rocker shouted. "Everything is wrong!"

"In what way?" Franklyn asked, trying diplomacy.

"Not only did someone break my goddamn guitar strings, but now it's been stolen!"

"When did you see it last?" the scientist inquired.

"Last night!" Michael shouted. "It was right here, by my bed, when I went to sleep."

"This is much worse than I expected," Franklyn whispered. "I think we'd better organize a meeting."

The group met. Hugo and Sandra attempted to maintain control, but everyone was enraged. "Who stole my money?" Phyllis accused.

"Screw your money!" Michael shouted. "Who took my guitar?"

"Please!" Hugo screamed as he slammed his fist on the table's surface. "We must have order." Once conversation subsided, the executive again began, "I'd like to hear from each of you about your losses." Pausing momentarily, he said, "Why don't you begin Father?"

"My Bible is missing."

"Man, that's pretty low!" Michael responded. "Whoever stole that sucker must be a real bastard."

"Please," Sandra asked. "Let's not comment until everyone has spoken."

"I'm missing my crystal ball," Iris said.

"My football is gone," Todd said sadly.

"All my research instruments have been stolen," Franklyn said.

"Many of my books are gone. Have any of you taken them?" Jeffery inquired.

"My copy of *The Modern Day Atheist* is gone," Sandra reported. "All the rest, however, are still in the box."

Joanne spoke irately, "My Oscar is lost."

"I can't locate my journals anywhere," Alice added.

"My playing cards are missing," Hugo said.

Tara commented, "I didn't look in my box, but I did notice the top was open. That means something was probably taken from me too."

Everyone waited for James' answer. The physician stared at his scarred hands and remained silent. Finally Sandra asked, "James, what are you missing?"

Weakly, he answered, "It doesn't matter."

Hugo responded immediately, "It does matter. What is missing?"

James said softly, "My entire box was taken; there's nothing left."

Tara touched his shoulder and whispered, "I'm so sorry for you."

The physician did not respond, but instead looked at his damaged hands. Finally he sighed, "It is not important any longer; my life is over."

"There's so much to live for," Tara interjected. "For a great doctor and—" Before she could finish, James stood up and walked away.

Michael said, "Touchy old man, isn't he?"

Instead of reprimanding the rocker, Hugo spoke to the group, "I suggest that everyone bring the remainder of their belongings to one location and we'll guard them throughout the night."

Alice asked, "Who will guard them?"

"I'll delegate some of the men to that duty," Hugo answered.

Sandra responded immediately to his strategy, "I think women should also be used for the task."

"What can *they* guard?" Todd laughed.

Iris glared at him and said, "I think we should use both men and women together."

"Why two at a time?" Michael asked.

"How do we know one of us isn't the thief?" Iris stated.

"One of *us*! That's absurd!" Franklyn countered.

"I think two is an excellent suggestion," Sandra said.

"Before this room, we were all perfect strangers. Perhaps one of us is a pathologic liar."

"By having two people at a time on guard duty, they can secure our valuables from others as well as from the other guard," Iris said.

"I believe Sandra and I should take the first watch," Hugo declared. "Then we'll each take a turn with another person."

"What about James?" Tara asked.

"Forget him," Sandra answered, "he has too many other problems at this point." Once they adjourned, each person brought their personal goods to the designated location. Upon securing the goods, Sandra and Hugo waited for the darkness. As the wall clock rang thirteen loud rings, a thick cloud billowed out the open hole and filled the room with a dense fog. The lights suddenly switched off. Unable to see, Hugo spoke, "Use your ears and listen very carefully."

Throughout the night, various pairs guarded the valued possessions. Gentle tremors vibrated the ground, but no major quake ensued. Occasional sweltering breezes filled the room as the group members steadfastly protected the belongings. Hours passed slowly and the fog thickened, but the changing of the guard continued. As the cloud finally lifted and the lights emitted brilliant rays, Alice's eyes adjusted and then she screamed, "Where are the goods? I didn't hear a single sound during our shift."

As others arrived, each was aghast that everything had been pilfered. Hugo cross-examined every sentinel, but no further clues could be ascertained. Finally after a lengthy investigation, the executive stomped away in utter frustration and impotency.

"Now what do we do?" Phyllis cried.

"Have faith. Trust in the Lord and have faith," Father McShane advised.

Sandra stated coldly, "I have faith in myself and that's it."

Todd agreed. Making a fist, he said "As long as I have my strength, I'm ready to fight anyone."

"There must be something we can do as a group," Alice suggested. "Any effort is better than none. Let's meet again later and attempt to come up with a unified program."

"What about Hugo?" Jeffery asked.

"If he does not go along with our plan, then we will request his resignation," Sandra stated.

"I think you're right," Iris added. "Nothing positive has been accomplished since he's taken over."

The members dispersed to their individual sites. Minutes later, the wall clock chimed three loud rings, classical music returned to the airways, and the residue of the fog disappeared.

ONE HUNDRED THIRTY-THREE

"I feel so sorry for Joanne. What's she going to do?" Iris said to Sandra.

"She mentioned to me that she'll visit her plastic surgeon as soon as we're released."

"Can he do anything for her face?"

"I'm sure! Modern medicine is just marvelous."

Iris said, "I can't believe how it happened."

"Thank goodness *I* wasn't standing under that chandelier."

"I agree. The glass really cut up her face," Sandra continued.

"I'm glad we were able to stop the bleeding so fast."

"I've never seen so much blood in my life."

"Neither have I—and I never want to see that much again."

The women were joined by Tara. "In my dreams I still see that chandelier falling," the young woman stated.

Sandra added, "I think we all do, it was just unlucky that Joanne was standing directly under its path."

"What about Michael?" Iris continued. "His hands were also pretty cut up."

"I know," Tara said. "He's worried about playing the guitar."

Sandra added, "It wouldn't have been so bad if they had had their clothes on."

Iris changed the subject. "Do you think we can go into the storage room yet?"

"No," Sandra stated. "Hugo and Father McShane opened the door slightly the other day and were immediately attacked by a swarm of rats."

Tara shuttered, "That's frightening."

Iris said, "Have any of you noticed a change in Todd?"

Sandra responded, "Absolutely. He's not exercising anymore and seems to be losing a great deal of muscle mass."

Tara said, "He told me he's in the worst shape of his life; he's afraid if he doesn't get more food soon, his career in football might be over."

Iris giggled, "That's too bad. I guess Mr. Macho might be just one of the little guys soon."

"How's James doing?" Sandra inquired.

"Poorly," Tara answered. "All he wants to do is die."

"Let him," Iris said bitterly. "It's too bad he wasn't under that chandelier instead of Joanne and Michael."

Tara interjected, "Let's not get too petty. After all, it could have been one of us."

"I was only kidding," Iris said. "Don't get so uptight."

"Speaking of uptight," Sandra stated, "Franklyn is a wreck."

"I don't blame him!" Tara said defensively.

"How would you feel if you were in his situation?" Iris added.

"I agree. That wound on his hand is terrible and without any antibiotics, it could get much worse."

"Maybe we can ask James to look at it." Sandra suggested.

"The man's wrapped up in his own problems, he couldn't care less about anyone else," Iris replied.

"That was certainly a freak incident, wasn't it?" Tara said.

"I never heard of anyone getting such a big cut from a can opener. That cut was really deep," Sandra added.

"At least some of us are healthy," Tara stated.

With sweat pouring from her brow, Iris nodded. She turned to Tara and asked, "Have you seen Smith lately?"

The young woman's words were interrupted by a break in the static.

Everyone looked upward to the ceiling as a voice was heard. "I can't believe it!" Sandra whispered.

Everyone listened as the announcer began to speak, "And now for today's news. Still missing are the twelve persons who disappeared without warning. If anyone can assist the authorities, please contact this station immediately. For our listeners who are not aware of the names, the missing individuals are Joanne Hauser, actress; James Harrison, doctor; Hugo S. Winters, advertising executive; Sandra Golden, professor; Jeffery Graff, politician; Alice Serrano, judge; Franklyn Vincent, scientist; Michael Schwanz, musician; Phyllis Taylor, wife of a famous industrialist; Todd Warren, professional football player; Donald McShane, Roman Catholic priest, and Iris Lansing, world famous faith healer.

"The F.B.I. and Interpol are working together to solve this unique and exceptional case. We will keep you, our listeners, apprised should any news of their whereabouts be uncovered. And now for our local news, the..."

"Can you believe that?" Iris shouted enthusiastically. "They're still looking for us."

"Amazing!" Sandra responded. "There's still hope after all." Turning to Tara, she asked, "Why look so sad? They haven't given up yet."

"That's nice," Tara said blandly.

Iris said, "What's wrong Tara?"

The young woman sobbed softly, "They didn't even mention my name! They don't even know I'm missing."

Sandra replied quickly, "I'm sure it was just an oversight. Besides, it really doesn't matter; when they discover us, you'll also be found."

"I guess you're right, but it doesn't make me feel any better."

"I agree with Sandra," Iris added. "I'm sure it was the radio station's error."

The announcer spoke again, "The F.B.I. just announced they are currently working on a very hot tip and expect to make a formal statement within the next few days. In an exclusive interview with Doug Siddenburg, spokesman for the agency, he stated that—" Static filled the room once more.

Everyone stared at the ceiling and then at one another. "I can't believe it's happening!" Iris said.

"Who cares?" Sandra giggled. "It looks like our days are numbered in this room."

"Thank goodness," Tara said softly.

Sandra said eagerly, "I'm going to see Hugo. I think we'd better call another meeting."

"Why?" Tara inquired.

"Just in case we're discovered soon, I think we'd better prepare some sort of statement."

"Good idea," Iris said. "And I hope they get our kidnappers."

"Without a doubt," Sandra replied. "I want to see them put away for a long time."

ONE HUNDRED THIRTY-FOUR

Exultation raced through the group. Even James managed a positive reaction to the broadcast. Adding to the festive atmosphere was the discovery of a large, gift-wrapped present. Father McShane was the first to discover the gift and guessed as to its contents. "I think it's a cake to celebrate." The group crowded around the package.

"No way!" Michael impatiently joked. "I think it's a case of sardines."

"It's a new Rolls," Jeffery laughed.

"I think we're getting a year's supply of chocolates," Alice chimed in.

James looked at the box, "Maybe I'm getting a pair of new hands?"

"Why do we have to play such stupid games?" Phyllis said. "Let's just open the damn box."

"I agree!" Sandra shouted.

Franklyn and Father McShane unwrapped the brightly colored paper and then opened the top. The priest carefully withdrew the gift. "I can't believe it," he stated as he placed it on the floor.

"Great!" Todd shouted. "A television."

"Hold on! There's more," the Father said and withdrew another object.

"A VCR," Franklyn said.

Looking into the box, Father added, "And it looks like we also got several movies."

"Wonderful!" Phyllis said. "What ones?"

Reading the labels, Franklyn responded, "*In Search of The Panda's Crest, Passion's Lust, Thomas and Bonnie, Carol's Way*, and the last one is *Deena Takes A Vacation*."

"They're all my movies," Joanne said, exhilarated.

"I can't wait to see them," Father McShane eagerly said.

"That's really a nice gift," Hugo said as he examined the presents.

"There's one small problem," Franklyn stated flatly.

"What's that?" Sandra inquired.

"There are no outlets in the entire room."

"Is that right?" Hugo asked.

In a disappointed tone, Joanne moaned, "I knew it was too good to be true. Of all the luck, I wanted everyone to see me at my best."

During the next hour, everyone searched for an outlet, but all soon realized that the scientist's statement was valid. Once everybody had dispersed, Sandra asked Hugo, "Now what?"

"Keep the gifts in a safe place and after we're found, we'll draw to see who gets to keep them." Hugo added, "And I hope it's you."

Sandra smiled, "If I did not know any better, I would say you are fishing for something."

"Maybe I am!" the executive stated. "After all, it's been quite a long time."

Turning more serious, Sandra stated, "And it will stay that way until you have those sores on your penis checked out."

"I'm sure it's nothing to worry about," Hugo lied. "I had James look at them and he said they were nothing."

"Are you telling me the truth?"

"Would I lie to you?"

"I hope not and certainly not about something as serious as this."

Looking her straight in the eye, he pleaded, "So?"

Grinning, she answered, "Why not? I sort of miss your body anyway."

The executive gently touched her hand and whispered, "See you in the darkness."

Across the room, Franklyn and Jeffery conversed. Suddenly the ground began to vibrate. Noticing a neighboring chair fall onto the floor, Jeffery cursed loudly. "It's an earthquake!"

Overhead another chandelier swung and a light cloud was forming over the trapdoor's location. Franklyn was about to shout a warning, when a bulb from the overhead light dropped by his feet. As he was picking it up, it exploded in his hand. Bleeding slightly, he swore and sought refuge by Jeffery's side.

Looking at the scientist's hand, Jeffery asked, "How could the bulb fall from way up there without breaking?"

Holding onto a neighboring table for support, Franklyn responded, "Don't know." Clutching his hand, he added, "But just my luck! The goddamn thing nearly took my hand off."

"It seems to defy all logic."

As the dense cloud spread through the room, Franklyn said, "Nothing is logical in this room, so why should the bulb be any different?" Holding on for his very life, he said, "It looks like it's going to be a bad one."

One Hundred Thirty-Five

Hours later, after the last of the cloud had settled, and the ground stabilized, everyone cautiously walked to the center of the room. Michael asked for everyone's attention, "I'd like to say something."

"What now?" Hugo asked in a bored tone.

"Are you going to provide us with another of your Brahmin comments?" Sandra jested.

"No," Franklyn chided. "The young man has finally discovered an ingenious method of conversing with other humans of a similar genus and species."

"When you are all done, I've got a few things to say."

"Go to it, Einstein, and make them good," Alice teased.

Michael waited for silence, "I think Smith is behind the whole thing." Everyone listened as he continued, "The man is evil."

Finally Phyllis laughed, "Are you smoking those little funny cigarettes again?"

Looking at the woman, Michael stated boldly, "I'm serious, that man is behind everything."

Father McShane asked, "What facts do you have to substantiate this?"

The rocker answered, "I've never seen him eat anything and he never talks to anyone."

"That's *it?*" Sandra inquired. "I think—"

Alice interrupted. "Maybe Michael is correct. After all, I never see the man consume any food."

"How is he still alive without food?" Michael contended.

"Every living thing requires some form of nourishment to survive," Sandra concurred.

"So?" the rocker countered.

"Maybe he has some stockpiled," Father McShane suggested.

"Where?" Alice inquired. "In a secret vault under the floor?"

"Why does he hide all the time? What is he concealing?" Iris chimed in.

"Maybe Michael's right," Phyllis concurred. "You can't trust those kind of people."

"What do you mean by that?" Jeffery asked.

Phyllis instantly responded, "All niggers are the same."

"And you can't trust none of them," Todd added.

"I never saw him even get water to drink," Iris said.

"I never saw him take a shower either," Alice commented.

"They all smell anyhow and I think they're all allergic to water," Phyllis chuckled.

"Let's try to be objective," Hugo chastened.

"I am!" Phyllis countered, "They all stink."

Hugo said, "Why does he stay isolated from the rest of us? That's not a normal reaction to such a crisis."

"Perhaps we're overreacting," the priest said.

"Then why doesn't he ever sweat?" Iris replied. "In this heat, all of us sweat like heck. Why is he always so dry and cool looking?"

"And his box is still unopened," Phyllis reminded.

"Are you sure?" Hugo inquired.

"Positive! I saw it the other day behind his sofa."

"It is all very strange," Sandra responded. "Perhaps we should go over and speak to him."

"Forget *talking* to him!" Michael screamed. "Let's kill the bastard! It's obvious he's a spy."

"I think he's right," Iris added. "Things just don't make any sense."

Joanne said quietly, "Maybe he's a serial killer."

"I think we should go over and have a talk with Mr. Smith," Hugo stated.

"If we don't get the right answers, let's kill him!" Todd yelled.

Before anyone could react to the statement, Tara spoke, "You're all wrong about him."

"How can you be so sure?" Phyllis asked. "After all, he doesn't talk to you either."

"That's not entirely true." Tara gathered her composure and then continued, "We speak on a regular basis."

"You're lying!" Iris shouted.

"I am not!"

Tara shook as she pleaded, "He's a very good man."

"Then why doesn't he talk to anyone other than you?" Phyllis asked.

"He's very self-conscious."

"Give me a break!" Michael laughed.

"He has a speech problem and is extremely shy."

"What about eating?" Todd asked.

"I bring him food every day."

"And water too?" Sandra inquired.

"Yes."

"That eliminates most of my doubt," Father McShane conceded.

"Why does he still have his box?" Jeffery probed.

"It's empty," Tara replied. "He lost everything when we did."

"I guess we'd better find ourselves another scapegoat," Hugo said, admonishing himself and the group. "It appears Mr. Smith is no different than any of us."

"Oh yes he is!" Phyllis shouted. "He's a nigger."

Turning to the young woman, Sandra asked, "Are you telling us the truth, Tara?"

"Yes," Tara stated with precise enunciation.

Hugo terminated the meeting. Soon after, Tara walked to Smith's site. Upon her arrival, the black man coldly asked, "What do you want?"

"I need to talk to you."

"I don't want to talk to you. Just leave me alone."

Standing her ground, the young woman said, "I just lied to protect your skin. I think I deserve a few minutes of your valuable time."

"I didn't ask you for anything. Whatever you did was not done at my request, and therefore I owe you nothing."

"But—"

"Get out of here."

Losing her temper, Tara cried out, "You're a bastard! Can't you even give me a few seconds?"

"No!"

Turning, she replied, "I should have let them kill you. You're not a nice person at all."

"If you don't like it, go tell them the truth. In the meantime, leave me alone!"

By the time she got back to her sofa, Tara was able to regain her composure. There she was met by Hugo who asked, "What did he say?"

"About what?"

"Don't play dumb with me!" the executive continued. "I'm sure you told him about the group's conversation."

"He was very upset and said he would eventually mingle more with the rest of us."

"Good. That will reduce the tension."

Sighing Tara said, "I'm very tired. Will you please excuse me."

Watching her rest on the sofa, he said to himself, *You're a real freak! How can anyone care so much about a nigger like that?*

ONE HUNDRED THIRTY-SIX

Father McShane, Todd, and Joanne waited for the last of the tremors to subside. "This room is really getting on my nerves," the actress said.

Todd examined his atrophied biceps and uttered, "This place is killing me. I must have lost fifty pounds of muscle already."

"You," Joanne moaned, "My career is over unless I can get to my plastic surgeon soon."

Father McShane listened as the two continued to complain. Finally, he interrupted and said, "I believe it's time for a little Irish therapy."

"Irish therapy?" Joanne asked. "What kind of therapy is that?"

Reaching under his sofa and into his box, the priest replied. "Just have some patience, and you will soon see." Grasping the whiskey bottle, he placed it on the floor and joked, "Here it is, the best form of therapy I know."

"Why Father? I didn't know you drank," the actress jested.

"I really only take a sip or two for medicinal purposes; it calms my nerves."

Todd looked at the bottle and added, "It looks like you don't

449

drink very much, Father. The bottle is still three-quarters full."

"That's true, my son. I only take a small nip once in a while."

Joanne retrieved three glasses and watched as the priest filled them to the brim. "Father!" she laughed, "you're giving me too much."

"It's very mild. We'll have just this one glass."

Todd raised his glass and said, "A toast."

"Yes," Joanne agreed, "Let's have a toast."

Father McShane said, "To a speedy rescue."

"I'll drink to that," Joanne replied. "The sooner the better."

All three drank quickly. The priest immediately refilled the glasses, and stated, "That's what I call good."

"It really hit the spot," Todd agreed. Looking at the second glass, the athlete proposed another toast. "To our kidnappers! May they spend the rest of their lives in jail." Quickly the glasses were emptied.

Feeling less tense, Joanne watched as the priest again filled her glass and said, "That stuff is really good tasting."

"That's why I saved it for us."

"Perhaps I shouldn't drink so much," the actress slurred.

Pointing to the bottle, Father McShane responded, "We haven't drank very much at all; the bottle is still three-quarters full."

Rubbing his eyes, Todd muttered, "I thought we had a few drinks."

The priest shook his head and raised his glass. "To...To happiness and our freedom." All three swallowed the liquor.

After several more glassfuls, Joanne asked, giggling, "Do you want to hear a secret?"

Todd laughed loudly, "Sure! Why not?"

Unable to control her emotions, the actress whispered loudly, "I'm frigid."

"No kidding," Todd snickered "You could have fooled me."

Turning to Father McShane, Joanne stammered, "Another drink, bartender." Gazing at the three-quarter filled bottle, the priest carefully refilled each glass.

Todd raised the glass, swallowed quickly, and slurred, "I'm frightened."

Joanne touched his thigh and replied, "So am I. Let's have another drink."

The rapid consumption of liquor continued for the next few hours. All three became intoxicated and more talkative. Slouched on the floor, Todd chuckled, "I really don't like Hugo. He's...he's arrogant."

Joanne slurred, "He's an ass."

Father McShane downed another glassful and stammered, "Sandra is the most arrogant." The three roared.

"Alice is also a cold fish," Todd stated.

"You just have to get to know her," Joanne chuckled. "For a wetback, she's okay."

The Father looked with glazed eyes and said, "Sandra is...."

Todd laughed and whispered, "He can't hold his liquor."

"What do you think of Smith?" Joanne asked.

"Just a dumb blackie," Todd moaned, "I hate all of them."

"I don't see many in the movies."

"You're lucky," Todd replied. "I'm stuck with them in football. God, do they stink."

Father McShane chortled at the statement and sipped another glass of liquor. Joanne asked, "What about Tara?"

Todd responded, "A very strange duck."

"She really is," the actress added, "I never saw anyone like her."

"The way she takes care of that nigger."

Joanne nodded, sipped another mouthful, and giggled, "Maybe she likes black men."

"That girl doesn't like men at all," Todd stated.

"And how would you know?" the actress asked.

"Every man has tried to make her, but she always says no."

"Maybe she's gay?" suggested Sandra.

Todd responded, "I never thought of that; she's probably a god-

451

damn lesbian."

"Or totally frigid," Joanne offered.

Father McShane burst out laughing. "What's so funny?" Todd asked.

"You guys are all wet."

"All wet about what?" Joanne inquired.

"About Tara."

"In what way?" Todd asked.

The priest slurred, "I can't tell you; it's a secret."

"Since when do we have any secrets," the actress stated. "Come on Father, what's the big secret?"

Todd filled the priest's glass and watched as the man quickly downed it. "What's the big deal, Father, we're all friends here."

The priest gazed at the two and said, "It's about Tara."

"What about her?" Joanne questioned.

"You called her frigid."

"I know that already," Todd replied. "What's the big deal?"

Lowering his voice, the priest said, "She's not frigid."

"How do you know?" the athlete probed.

"I just know."

"Did you go to bed with her?" Joanne giggled.

"No."

"Then how can you be so sure?" Todd said. "I think she's nothing but a cold virgin."

Father McShane chuckled, "She's no virgin; that's for sure."

"How do you know?" Joanne inquired.

"I think you're making this up." Todd said suspiciously.

"No, I'm not."

Todd joked, "She's probably an ex-nun."

The Father giggled, "God forbid! She wasn't a nun."

"I bet she was," Joanne pushed. "In fact, she was probably a lesbian nun."

Getting slightly angry, Father McShane countered, "She was not! She was a..."

"A what?" Todd asked.

"Nothing."

Joanne pressed the priest for an answer, "I bet you're wrong. I still think she was a frustrated young nun."

"No," Father said. He took a mouthful of liquor and said, "You're both wrong, she was a..."

"For God's sake, Father, say it already. Was she a lesbian nun or what?" the actress stated. "It's not a disgrace, many nuns are lesbians."

Pushed to the limit, Father McShane stated, "She's not a nun, she's a prostitute."

"A prostitute!" Todd said, suprised.

"That sweet little thing is a hooker?" Joanne laughed, "Are you sure?"

The priest was lying on his back with his eyes glazed. Todd nudged him and said to Joanne, "He's passed out."

Joanne turned to the athlete and asked, "Do you think he was telling the truth?"

"I don't know."

"What are you going to do now?"

Todd smirked, "Right now, I'm going to have another drink and then go to sleep. My head is starting to pound."

Joanne stared at the empty bottle and giggled, "It looks like we finished off his Irish therapy; I hope he has another bottle hiding somewhere."

O N E   H U N D R E D
T H I R T Y - S E V E N

During the next communal meal, Todd sat next to Tara. Before anyone could say a word, the radio blared out another message: "The F.B.I. has announced today that it has had a significant breakthrough in the mass kidnapping case of six months ago. A possible suspect has been charged with the crime and is expected to cooperate fully with Federal authorities. Though the identity of the suspect is unknown, our sources have indicated that they were extremely close to one of the victims, possibly even a relative.

"A spokesman for the agency expects another announcement within a few hours. Again, our sources feel release of the hostages will be forthcoming."

As the last word echoed through the room, the radio suddenly went dead and static filled the air. Father McShane was the first to speak, "I told you to have faith. We're practically out already."

"I'm going to get myself one big hot dog," Michael joked, "and it's going to be smothered in relish, chili, mustard, and kraut!"

Todd added, "I'm getting myself one thick steak and then sitting in my hot tub for a few hours."

Turning to Tara, he placed his hand on her thigh and asked,

"What about you?" She quickly removed his hand and stated, "I—I'm not sure what I'll do."

While Hugo was talking about their release, the athlete smiled and re-placed his hand higher on Tara's thigh. The young woman became startled, "Take your hand off me!"

Everyone looked as he again rubbed her leg and said, "I was only having a little fun."

Michael taunted, "Let him have a feel, Tara. God only knows, he's as horny as a water buffalo."

Tara attempted to release herself from his grasp, but her struggles were in vain. As he slid his hand higher, she shouted for help, "Please let go of me!"

Hugo spoke authoritatively, "Let her go immediately."

"I'm just having a little fun."

"Take your hand off me!" Tara screamed. "What kind of girl do you think I am?"

Todd moved his hand higher and countered, "I know what kind of girl you are."

"What do you mean by that statement?" Sandra asked.

"She's a goddamn whore!"

"A whore?" Phyllis replied.

"How do you know that?" Alice asked.

Todd replied, "Father McShane told me."

Everyone, especially Tara, stared at the priest.

Hugo asked, "Is it true?"

The Father uttered, "I..."

"Goddamn it, Father," Michael screamed, "Is she a hooker or not?"

Tara glared at the priest, "Tell them, Father. Tell them I'm not that kind of woman."

The priest looked at his clutched hands and softly said, "I..."

Hugo grasped Father McShane by his arm and shook him violently. "Is she a damn whore or not?"

Shocked, the priest looked at the sobbing woman, at the irate crowd, and meekly answered, "Yes."

"She's a prostitute!" Alice shouted.

"A slut!" Sandra yelled.

"And I trusted her?" Jeffery added. "She's nothing but a tramp."

Todd snatched her body and held it. "Please," she cried. "Please let me go."

Pounding his fist on the table, Michael chanted, "Give the hooker what she deserves."

Alice shouted loudly, "Go, Todd, Go!"

Todd was joined by Franklyn, Michael, Hugo, and James. "Please!" Tara screamed. Not listening to her pleas, the men shoved her onto the floor and held her firmly in place. The rest of the group, including Father McShane, got caught up in the fervor. Each pounded their fists on the floor and shouted in unison, "Take her! Take her! Take her!" Their words echoed through the room as the huge man tore wildly at her tattered clothing.

As her breast became exposed, hands grasped at her naked skin. While the others held her tightly, Todd stood and shouted, "I'll screw you, bitch! I'll screw you and then they can have what's left."

Tara's attempts to escape were futile; she was held firmly by a multitude of hands and bodies. "Take her! Take her!" they chanted as Todd prepared to assault his young victim. When she sobbed loudly for help, Tara was struck by an unknown assailant. "Please," she finally pleaded, "Please..."

Another strike muted her cries. As the last article of clothing was stripped from her body, the radio began playing. With the finale of Tckaikovsky's 1812 overture further instigating the group, they shouted for Todd to consummate his quest. "Take her! Take her! Take her!"

Raising his arms high overhead and then striking his hairy chest, Todd lowered his body downward. Sneering, he shrieked, "Get ready, bitch! Here I come!"

Just as he was about to make contact with her naked skin, a gunshot exploded through the room. The music abruptly stopped and another shot immediately followed. Todd quickly stood up. A lone figure walked in their direction. With a gun pointed ahead, J.C. Smith weaved his way among the various pieces of broken furniture until he stood within fifteen feet. He looked at the naked woman and then aimed the muzzle directly at Todd's chest.

Hugo was the first to speak. "Drop the gun!" he ordered, but J.C. remained motionless.

Tara quickly wrapped herself in her tattered garments and stood. She looked at each person with hatred, then walked to the man's side. He did not say a single word, but instead gently touched her cheek.

Todd's anger was mounting as he stood naked among his peers. Attempting to control his rage, the flabby athlete stated, "Where are you going to hide?"

The man still did not verbally respond, but merely stared at each individual in turn with piercing eyes. Hugo again spoke, "Please put down the gun. We were just having a little fun."

"Yeah!" Michael added. "We were just joking around."

Phyllis sarcastically commented, "Maybe the nigger's deaf."

Tara trembled but remained at the man's side. "Smith," Sandra pleaded. "Let's talk this over. You really don't want to shoot anyone, do you?"

With unblinking eyes, the man took Tara's elbow and slowly led her back across the room. Todd turned to Hugo and laughed, "We *got* the black bastard. He ain't going anywhere."

"Yeah," Michael added. "We'll cut his eyes out and..."

"He can't have too many bullets left," Franklyn noted. "Let's see what happens if..." He faked a lunge and instantly Smith fired his pistol into the air.

Todd leered, "That's your third shot, nigger. A few more and you're all mine."

The entire group followed the twosome. "Where's he going?"

Father McShane asked.

"Nowhere," Michael laughed. "He's going nowhere."

"It looks like he's heading for the door!" Alice said, confused.

"So what?" Joanne laughed. "It won't open."

"Don't tell him that," Phyllis giggled.

Nearing the doorway, the pair stopped as the group moved nearer behind them. Smith held up his gun and fired another two shots into the air. Instinctively, they withdrew momentarily and then returned.

"Two more shots, nigger. You're dead meat!" Todd sneered.

Hugo suddenly shouted, "Spread out!" the dozen people formed a semicircle that further forced Smith and Tara to the wall. Raising his gun towards Hugo's chest, J.C. Smith smiled and reached into his pocket. Removing a shiny object, he held it up for all to see.

"What is it?" Phyllis asked.

"I can't tell," Alice stated.

Before anyone else could speak, Smith inserted the object into the door's locking mechanism and then turned the knob. Instantly, the door swung open. Everyone stood transfixed as the black man gently guided Tara through the doorway and out of sight. Laughing robustly, he faced the group from the doorway. Pointing the gun at Todd's chest, he pulled the trigger. Instead of a shot, only a clicking sound could be heard.

"The nigger's out of bullets! Get the bastard!" Hugo screamed.

"I'll kill you—" Todd's voice said, still quivering. Smith dropped the gun and shut the door behind himself.

Franklyn was the first to reach it and to turn the knob. Nothing happened. He cursed and watched as each other member met with the same results. Finally Todd picked up the gun, aimed it directly at the mechanism, and angrily pulled the trigger. The shot reverberated as the bullet struck the lock broadside. Hugo raced to the door and attempted to turn the knob, but as before, it remained unmovable.

For the longest time, everyone stared at the doorway. Suddenly, the great wall clock chimed three loud rings and the lights grew dimmer. As silence filled the room and gloom invaded, everyone returned to their individual sites. There, amid the blackness, each pondered the day's events and their future.

ONE HUNDRED THIRTY-EIGHT

A general frustration and negativism dominated everyone's outlook. Todd and Hugo attempted to open the door again, but it remained impregnable. Father McShane and James sat nearby and watched as the two men labored. The priest turned to the physician and whispered, "I don't think that door is going to budge."

James stared straight ahead, "I think you're correct."

"I can't wait until we're rescued. I'm sick and tired of this room."

"At least you're leaving with hands and your profession. My life is ruined."

A sudden blast of scorching air swept through. Wiping his brow, the Father moaned, "The temperature feels higher. I'm burning up."

"It's been rising steadily throughout the night."

"This is the worst it's ever been."

James nodded and said, "You're right."

Hugo joined them and stated, "It's too goddamn hot to work."

The priest watched perspiration flow from his exposed thighs and uttered, "I don't know how much more I can take."

Hugo agreed and said, "How about getting something to drink?"

The three men walked to the other end of the room only to find Sandra crying loudly. Hugo placed his hand on her sweaty shoulder and inquired, "What's wrong?"

She pointed to the sink and toilet and sobbed, "They're not working."

Frantically, the executive rushed to the commode and turned the faucets. Finding no water, he inspected the pipes beneath the stand. Shaking his head, he then examined the toilet. Like the sink, it was not working. Father McShane tried to comfort the hysterical woman, but she sobbed loudly, "What are we going to do now?"

Hugo appeared extremely concerned as he approached his comrades. James inquired, "What's wrong with them?"

"Nothing," Hugo responded. "Everything appears to be in good working order except...someone turned off our water supply."

Father McShane asked, "What about the water in the kitchen?"

The group instantly hurried to the burnt out area and inspected the faucet. Smiling, Hugo stared at the small stream of hot water that exited the broken pipe. "At least we still have this water supply."

"What if they turn this one off too?" Sandra asked.

Thinking quickly, the executive stated, "We'd better fill all available containers as soon as possible."

As the great wall clock chimed fourteen loud rings, the group worked at filling every vessel with the precious fluid. Gazing at the toilet, Alice inquired, "How do you go to the bathroom?"

Franklyn answered, "We can use some of this water to flush; however, we must ration everything frugally."

"Won't it stink?" Phyllis asked.

"Probably," the scientist answered, "But we'll all have to endure until we're rescued."

"What else could happen?" Iris moaned loudly.

"Not much," Sandra cried as she gazed at the room.

"I suggest that everyone exert as little effort as possible,"

Franklyn suggested. "Temperatures of this magnitude can easily cause heat exhaustion or stroke."

James concurred, "He's correct. Save your energy and conserve your body's fluids."

Days passed without change. High temperatures persisted, creating increased havoc. With food and water supplies diminished, activities were confined to the bare essentials of life. As Sandra reached into her food storage bin, she suddenly became aware that something was missing. After frantically searching, she began to shout for help. Hearing her distress, Jeffery, Joanne, and Iris came over.

Lacking enthusiasm, Iris inquired, "What's wrong now?"

"Some of my food is missing."

"Are you sure it was there in the first place?" Jeffery asked.

Trying to control her temper, Sandra replied simply, "Yes."

Joanne said, "Some of my water was missing yesterday."

"What's happening?" Sandra asked.

"It's obvious," Jeffery answered, "Someone is stealing our supplies."

"Stealing!" Sandra responded. "Who would do such a thing?"

"Probably Todd," Joanne said. "He spends more time in the kitchen area than anyone else."

Sandra then asked, "What can we do about it?"

Iris looked at the others, "We can't do anything unless we catch him in the act."

"I agree," Jeffery added. "I hate to wrongly accuse him if it was someone else."

"Maybe it was Michael," Iris stated. "He's been looking more fit lately."

"I think I'll speak to Hugo," Sandra stated. "He'll have an answer to this problem."

"I wouldn't talk to him just yet," Jeffery warned.

"Why not?"

Whispering, he said, "I caught him taking water from Father McShane's bottle yesterday."

"What did he say?" Iris asked.

"He told me he was getting it for the Father."

"Perhaps he was telling the truth," Sandra stated.

"I later asked Father McShane if Hugo had given him any water during the day and he said no."

"Just great," Joanne replied, "Who can you trust?"

"It appears very few of us are truly honest," Sandra stated.

"I take exception to that," Iris said defensively.

Sandra said, "From now on, I'm going to keep my food and water supplies with me at all times."

"That's a sad commentary about your fellow man," Jeffery stated.

Sandra looked at him and the others and replied, "I lost all my faith when someone stole my food."

"I guess I'm going to keep mine with me also," Joanne agreed. "It's all I have." Jeffery started to speak, but was interrupted by the emergence of words from the radio.

"The F.B.I. announced today that it has had a significant breakthrough in the mass kidnapping case of six months ago. A possible suspect has been charged with the crime and is expected to cooperate fully with Federal authorities. Though the identity of the suspect is unknown, our sources have indicated that they were extremely close to one of the victims, possibly even a relative.

"A spokesman for the agency expects another announcement within a few hours. Again, our sources feel that release of the hostages will be forthcoming."

As the message started to play for the second time, Iris turned to Joanne and began to cry. Ignoring her friend, the actress dropped to her knees and shook her head. "I can't believe it. The whole thing was a tape."

While the women sobbed, Jeffery wiped a tear from his eye and walked to his sofa. Minutes later, he dropped to the floor and wept.

"What should I do about Phyllis?" Franklyn asked.

"Nothing," James stated. "Just let her be."

"But she's been crying for hours."

"She'll get over it."

The scientist looked at the pathetic woman as she cowered in front of the locked door. Occasionally, she would gently stroke the panel with her hand and then sob uncontrollably. "We must help her..."

The physician looked at Franklyn and shouted, "Go hold her hand if you want, but leave me alone!" Gazing at his damaged hands, he added, "I've got my own problems."

Moments later, music suddenly filled the room. While Saint-Saens' *La Danse Macabre* reverberated, the overhead lights slowly dimmed. No one budged as an eerie blackness settled. The floor and walls trembled as a blistering cloud of hot air saturated the room. Chimes from the wall clock rang erratically, adding to the amalgamation of dissonant sounds.

One wall began to beam until its rays caused everyone to cover their eyes. One by one, each person walked toward the shining beacon in hopes of discovering a means of escape.

Father McShane was the first. The priest wiped his eyes and stared at the wall. After reading the words etched into the torn wallpaper he screamed, dropped to the floor, and began to spasm. After looking at his fallen colleague, Hugo read the writing:

DONALD MCSHANE	FRANKLYN VINCENT
JAMES HARRISON	MICHAEL SCHWANZ
HUGO WINTERS	PHYLLIS TAYLOR
SANDRA GOLDEN	TODD WARREN
JEFFERY GRAFF	IRIS LANSING
ALICE SERRANO	JOANNE HAUSER
ACCIPITE AD INFERNA	

Alice was the last person to arrive and read the message. She asked, "What does the last line mean?" She knelt down and lifted the priest's head. "Father," she asked, "can you hear me?" Father McShane's body continued to convulse. Alice shook the priest lightly and shouted, "Father! Wake up!" Father McShane opened his eyes and wailed.

Iris asked, "What happened?" Father McShane suddenly began to mouth each word of the sign.

"What's wrong with him?" Sandra asked.

James responded, "I never saw anything like it."

Hugo grabbed the priest's arm and pulled roughly, "Damn it, Father. Tell us what it means!"

The Father gazed at the wall once more and shouted hysterically, "Accipite Ad Inferna! Accipite Ad Inferna! Accipite Ad Inferna!"

Hugo seized Father McShane's throat and yelled, "For God's sake! Say it in English!"

With glazed eyes and a trembling voice Father McShane uttered, "It means WELCOME TO HELL."

Other books by Stanley L. Alpert

GERTRUDE AND THE PRINTED PAGE

MOHOP MOGANDE

THE SWAN SONG PENTAD

Available from

Alpert's Bookery, Inc.
POB 215
Nanuet, NY 10954

STANLEY L. ALPERT

E. M. Berger

ABOUT THE AUTHOR

Stanley L. Alpert is the author of *Gertrude and the Printed Page, The Swan Song Pentad,* and *Mohop Mogande.* He has two goals: to contribute to humankind through writing about controversial and ethical challenges; and to write 100 books by his 100th birthday. Mr. Alpert lives with his wife and daughter in the state of New York.